BLINDSIDED

A SPORTS ROMANCE NOVEL

AMY DAWS

Published by: Amy Daws, LLC
ISBN 13: 978-1-944565-28-2
ISBN 10: 1-944565-28-0

Edited by: Jenny at Editing 4 Indies, Nancy at Evident Ink, and Stephanie Rose
Formatted by: Champagne Book Design
Cover Design: Amy Daws

BLINDSIDED

CHAPTER 1

Freya

"**C**RIKEY, I WANT A PONY," I BLUBBER AND BLOW MY NOSE loudly into a tissue while staring wistfully at the telly as the ending credits of *Heartland* fill the screen. "Even after watching Jack Bartlett put his beloved horse, Paint, to eternal sleep, I *still* want a pony. Who knew a wholesome family drama that centres around the highs and lows of life on a ranch would change the core of my soul so deeply? I considered myself a proper city girl before watching this show. Yes, I grew up in a small village outside of Cornwall, but as soon as I was old enough to leave, it was big city life for me full stop. And London is arguably the greatest city in the world. I mean, there is nowhere else you can go to buy a cake and pet a kitten at the exact same time. But after falling in love with this Canadian program, I dream about having a simple life on a ranch with a pony and a grandfather who has a caterpillar mustache and bends his eyes in a way that makes me feel like every moment with him is a life lesson." I exhale heavily, realising I forgot to breathe during that last bit, and a light-headedness overwhelms me.

"You know I'm still here, right?" a deep Scottish voice asks from beside me.

I turn my gaze from the television and shake my head to focus on Maclay Logan—a professional footballer for Bethnal Green F.C. and, against all odds, my friend. I scrunch my nose and swipe away my lingering tears. "Of course I know you're still here."

A knowing smile lifts his face. "Well, you just went on a bit of a monologue there with a variety of run-on sentences without leaving any room for me to reply, so I figured you either forgot I was here or you were having another one of your outbursts."

My eyes narrow when he finger quotes the word "outbursts". "What are you talking about? I don't have *outbursts*." I repeat the word back in his rough and permanently sore-throated-sounding Scottish accent, rolling the *R* the way he does.

Mac's lips twitch with barely concealed amusement that makes me want to thump him. He always looks like he's laughing about something. It's maddening, really. I mean, what kind of human is constantly happy? It's just not right.

I should be the one having a laugh at the sight of him—a grinning, goofy giant sitting on doll furniture in my tiny one-bedroom East London flat. His large, muscular body is stretched out on my purple velvet sofa while his thick, tattoo-covered arms are wrapped tightly around one of my furry white throw pillows. It's like he's strangling a baby polar bear.

Mac glares at me while maintaining his smile. "Just last week, you had an entire conversation with your salad about how if you could take a pill that made the lettuce taste like crisps, the two of you could actually be mates."

"That was a conversation between me and the romaine," I quip, hating the way he mimicked my Cornish accent. No matter how hard I try to ditch it, that West Country twang slips out. "And you shouldn't have been earwigging."

"You invited me over for dinner!" he bellows, the motion

of his body causing his wavy red bangs to flop over his forehead. "Typically when one invites a guest over for a meal, the hostess is expected to provide conversation with someone other than the lettuce."

"You're just being dramatic now," I state, rolling my eyes and reaching out to sweep his strawberry blond hair back off his forehead. His hair curls at the ends and never seems to stay put. "Besides, I have a special connection with food, just like I do with ponies…and caterpillar-mustached grandfathers."

Mac remains silent as he smiles at me like I'm his nan with Alzheimer's and it's better to go with my narrative than to try to correct me.

"You seriously need to cut your hair again," I state when I can't get it to stay where it belongs.

"I thought you said it looks better shaggy," he replies, replacing my hand with his and forcing his locks back. "You said it makes me look more husky than Labrador, and huskies are more exotic."

"Indeed, but now we're venturing into the Old English sheep-dog category."

Mac huffs out a laugh. "Does that mean you'll give me a treat if I do a trick?"

With a smirk, I reach toward the sofa table for my package of wine gums. Without pause, I toss one in the air, and he catches it in his mouth with the deft ease of the seasoned athlete he is.

"Good dog."

He smiles proudly while he chews, and I can't help but shake my head at the view of him. Even with shaggy-dog hair, Mac's red locks are ten times nicer than mine. My shade of red is more in the Ronald McDonald family. And when I don't style it in my signature smooth, wavy curls, I look like those Chinese crested dogs that are always getting meme'd on the internet with something cruel. Poor dears.

I turn back towards the telly and grab the remote to queue up the next episode. Lately, Mac and I watch at least three episodes of *Heartland* when he comes over. And the fact that him coming over has become the norm in my life has completely blindsided me.

If someone had told me a year ago that I'd be plopped on a sofa eating wine gums and watching telly with a famous footballer, I'd have told them they were higher than a kitten that overdosed on catnip. But my job as a clothing tailor for a popular fashion boutique in East London brings all sorts of interesting people into my life, including Mac. The big ox walked into the shop with his PR rep and happened to catch an obscure television reference I made under my breath.

As a seamstress, I'm used to being invisible to ninety-nine percent of our clients, but I wasn't to darling Mac here. We argued over our favourite Netflix programs and became fast friends. Then I introduced him to *Heartland,* and he latched onto me like a stray puppy that found its new home. Thank goodness this puppy is potty-trained.

That's a Scot for you. They're overbearing, loud-mouthed, no boundary-having, spirited animals who are sweet, cosy cuddlers one minute and beating the fuck out of someone who looks at them sideways the next. Or perhaps that's just Mac?

"You are aware that some people may think what we do together is called Netflix and chill, right?" Mac asks, a knowing tone in his voice that I don't altogether like.

My brows pinch as I look over at him. "So? What of it?"

Mac hits me with a sardonic stare. "Don't you know what Netflix and chill means, woman?"

"Of course I know! It means watching telly and relaxing on the sofa."

Mac bites his lip to stop himself from laughing. It makes me want to strangle him. And hug him. How does he make me love him and hate him every minute of the day?

Mac clears his throat and angles toward me. His green eyes sparkle with mischief. "You got the Netflix part right, but the chill part is where you're wrong. The youngsters have a secret meaning for the word."

"Youngsters? What are you going on about? I'm young!" I pop another sweet into my mouth.

"You're turning thirty in a few months! You're not considered a young lass anymore, Cookie."

My eyes roll at the annoying nickname he pegged me with almost as soon as we met. My surname is Cook, and since Mac loves addressing people by their last names, he charmingly came up with Cookie. What a treat for me. The chubby girl gets a food nickname. How novel!

That's another thing about Scots. They're overly familiar. They meet someone in a pub who has similar interests, and you'd swear they'd just met their soulmate, never mind the fact that they've only spoken a dozen words to each other.

Beyond the nickname, the comment Mac made about my age niggles in the pit of my belly. I've been fretting over my upcoming birthday for the past few weeks because I'm not exactly where I thought I'd be at the age of twenty-nine. Don't get me wrong, I love my life. I have a great flat, my cat, Hercules, finally let me put him in a baby carrier that straps over my boobs, and I work in a clothing boutique with two of the coolest female designers in all of the land.

Seriously, Sloan and Leslie are the type of females anyone would look up to. They are mothers and wives and badarse businesswomen. And our marketing director, Allie Harris, is equally as ambitious. She and I have become extremely close over the past year. I'm actually going to be the maid of honour in her wedding in a few weeks. She's marrying Mac's roommate, Roan. Never mind that I still haven't secured a date for the occasion.

My point is, I live a good life, and I'm truly lucky to work with such wonderfully successful women, but seeing them interact with their partners often reminds me I've ignored a significant part of my life for quite some time: matters of the heart. The stuff I positively swoon over on Netflix. And despite telling myself I don't care about not being in a relationship with someone special, I do care.

I thought moving from Manchester to London a few years ago would be the kick in the arse I needed to try dating again. Instead, I'm still just a seamstress who's living alone and doing a lot of Netflix and *chilling*—or whatever Mac calls it—with a man who wouldn't dream of dating me in a gatrillion years.

"I'm not thirty yet," I mumble, flopping back against the sofa and grabbing my own polar bear pillow to strangle.

Mac scoffs. "Why do you get all twitchy about your age, Cookie? Own it. I'm thirty-four, and you don't see me moaning because I'm not young and braw anymore."

"Well, apparently you are young and cool because you're over there telling me I don't know what Netflix and chill means. So, why don't you tell me, Mr Cool?" I grab yet another sweet. I'm pouting, but bleddy hell, his comment about my age has put me in a mood. "What does *chill* mean?"

I turn just in time to see Mac's brows lift as he replies, "It means shagging."

I nearly choke on the food in my mouth. "What do you mean?" I sputter and clear the congealed sugar out of my esophagus.

"Netflix and chill means Netflix and sex," Mac explains.

"We don't do *The Sex!*" I exclaim and shift myself over so the sides of our thighs are no longer touching. He stated that word so easily. So matter-of-factly. My ears feel like they're on fire with discomfort. Did it suddenly get hot in this room, or is it just me? "You and I are just mates!"

"Well, obviously," Mac retorts, tossing his furry pillow on the floor and leaning forward to prop his elbows on his knees the way he does when he's on the sidelines at one of his matches. "I just meant that's what people might think we're doing if we tell them we watch Netflix together all the time."

"We aren't telling people!" I drop the remote in a huff and turn to face him. "I told you when you first started coming around that I wanted to be a secret friend. Not one that everyone knows about."

"Being my secret friend is fucking balls now," he replies, his brows furrowed in a serious scowl. "I went along with it in the beginning because you were worried about being photographed in the papers, but it's becoming ridiculous. We've been pals for over a year, Cookie. I think it's time you stop hiding. My teammates are always up my arse, asking nosy questions about what I do in my free time."

"So make something up!" I nearly scream. "Tell them you're drawing your next tattoo."

Mac's eyes narrow. "I don't like lying, Freya. And I'm tired of avoiding the questions, which is why I think you should come with me to a party I was invited to on Friday night. Loads of my teammates and their WAGS, or wives and girlfriends I mean, will be there. I think it'll be a nice laugh."

"Are you deaf, Mac?" I shout louder than I intended, making us both jump. "I said I don't want your mates to know about me. How could you think that going to a party with you is something I'd want to do?"

"I said I'm done hiding our friendship, and I meant it," he states firmly, casually spreading his arm out on the back of the sofa as if he's simply talking about the weather. "I'm going to tell them that we Netflix and hang whether you're with me or not."

"We don't *hang*. We Netflix and bicker at best!" I sputter and stand up, tossing my homemade raggy quilt on top of him while murmuring about how the word chill has been ruined for me forever. I pick up our Chinese takeaway containers from the sofa table and look down at him.

"What is your problem, woman?" Mac booms as he rises to his full height and stops me from scurrying away into the kitchen. His face is twisted up in confusion like he's trying to calculate the square root of pi as he looms over me, practically vibrating with annoyance. "You have no problem hanging out with me in front of the Harrises."

"The Harrises are different. They're like family," I state in a rush and then take a moment to calm my nerves, which are heightened from his statuesque stance. I really hate when he does this standing over me thing because it always gives my heart a little jolt. He's so big. Well over six feet tall, which means the top of my head barely reaches his chin when he's barefoot. When he's wearing all of his football gear, he looks like a demigod standing amongst children.

I shake off the dizziness his large stature causes and shove my way past him, through my dining area, and into my tiny galley kitchen. "People like me are secret friends, Mac. Trust me on this."

He storms in behind me, his close proximity sucking up all the oxygen in my flat. I toss the takeaway containers in the bin and then fix my eyes on the wooden countertop. I can feel him staring down at me when he says, "Explain yourself, Freya. Now."

"Explain what?" I reply weakly, feigning ignorance that I know he won't buy.

"What you meant by that last comment," he says, scowling down at me like I'm a naughty child. "People like you?"

I exhale heavily and turn on my heels to face him with my hands on my hips. "Mac, you're a big, fit Scottish footballer who's famous. The whole city of London adores you, and you have women who would shag you with a snap of your fingers."

His face brightens as he crosses his inked arms over his chest and shoots me a cocky smirk. "Careful now. That sounded dangerously close to a compliment, Cookie."

"Shut up, you cow," I scold and wave off his response. I point at his sizeable body. "My point is, you look like that." Then I gesture to myself. "And I look like this."

"I still don't have a clue what you're going on about." Mac continues to gape at me with a thick look that I want to claw right off his face.

What is it with fit people pretending like they don't see what's in front of them? If they have eyes, they know how I look. The game is up!

I level him with a stare and angrily state, "I am a short, round

Cornish seamstress with a West Country accent that only gets thicker when I'm flustered. I'm obsessed with cats, and my freckles look like the Milky Way galaxy on a clear night."

"I love your freckles!" he barks, splaying one hand out on the counter and using his other hand to bop my nose. "They make me want to play connect the dots on your wee face."

"That's not a compliment!" I screech, doing everything I can to not bash this adorable idiot's face in.

"And you're not round," he barks again, ignoring my reply with his haughty tone. He looks down at my body. "You're healthy. You actually eat! There's nothing wrong with that."

"I eat too much," I correct and turn to open the fridge for my chardonnay. If I have to deal with him pretending he doesn't see what's plainly in front of him, I need a drink.

I grab one of my kitty coffee mugs off a hook beneath my cabinet and pour myself a fortifying drink. "It's not news that I have never been a willowy waif, and I know that I'll never change because I've tried every bleddy diet in the universe and nothing sticks."

"You don't need to change, Cook," Mac states seriously, drawing my gaze to his green eyes that are soft around the edges in a way that makes my tummy do the flippys again. He wraps his arm around my shoulders and crushes me to his chest. "You're bonnie, and you're my best mate. You should never feel the need to hide."

The wind beneath my sails has ceased, and my huffy, defensive attitude from moments ago has been completely washed away by this sweet ginger giant standing in my kitchen. I set my mug on the counter and pull out of his embrace to gaze up at him curiously. "Did you say 'best mate'?"

He shrugs. "Aye, you have been nearly since the second we met, which is why I want my teammates to know you. You're my wee treasure, and I'm right proud of you."

A tender smile lifts my cheeks. Mac and I don't talk about our friendship often. Honestly, we're usually too busy bickering to be sweet to each other, so hearing him call me his wee treasure makes my heart practically explode inside of my chest. Who would have put the two of us together as mates in any type of situation? Certainly not me. That's why the closer we became, the more secluded I wanted our friendship to be. I can only imagine what the headlines would say if we ended up photographed in one of those online blogs you always see footballers tagged in.

Scottish footballer has found himself a stalker who looks like a plus-sized Anne of Green Gables.

Wankers!

At least my fashion sense is a touch better than Anne of Green Gables, who honestly could have been a lot more progressive with the Victorian Era. My stint in design school certainly helped with that, so, well done me.

Sadly, there's not much that can be done for my sizeable curves or my *Little Mermaid* red hair that I've tried to dye countless times to no avail. And my freckles are so defined, I quit wearing concealer full stop because all it did was make me look like I was covering up leprosy. Is leprosy still a thing? Could that be a headline?

Stay focused, Freya.

The point is, Mac is an attractive athlete who can eat an entire Big Mac and burn it off in one quick run. Bleddy hell, even his ankles are fit. I didn't know ankles could be fit until I saw his very large bare feet propped up on my sofa table for the first time. The veins that run up his calves are immense!

Then there is me. I'm someone who mindfully chooses to eat wine gums instead of celery stalks even though I know it'll take me days to burn them off. Not only do I like wine gums, but there's just something about the word "stalk" that makes me think it doesn't belong in my mouth.

All this means is that Mac and I are very different people, so the thought of him parading me in front of his team is terrifying, especially since I'm crap with men.

I grew up as a freckled, chubby redhead with an obsessive affection for knitting furry pink jumpers with kitten faces on them—an act that *really* didn't bring all the boys to the yard. And because of my horrible experiences with the select boys I did try to date, I can barely string together a declarative sentence around a bloke whom I think I may have a chance with. I really don't want Mac to know that side of me.

"Hellooo, Freya…Earth to Freya." Mac's voice snaps me back to reality, and I realise my mind was having one of those outbursts Mac mentioned.

"What?" I ask and blink to regain my focus on him.

"Did you hear me? I said I think it'd be good for you to come with me to the party on Friday night. You're not old enough to be cooped up like a wee old lady."

His words are a punch in the gut, even if he didn't mean them to be cruel. I have secluded myself quite a bit this past year. All my friends are married or are about to be married, so my social life has taken a nosedive. If it weren't for Mac, I'd be well on my way to becoming a proper spinster.

"What kind of party is it exactly?" I ask as I turn to heft myself up onto the kitchen counter, fretting over the idea of making a complete fool of myself in front of my apparent best mate.

Mac's face lights up as he hoists himself up beside me. God, he made that look so easy while I looked like a child trying to crawl into Papa Bear's chair. He nudges me with his shoulder. "It's called a No Bloody Kids Do at Tanner and Belle Harris' flat. The entire Harris family got sitters, so they'll all be there. Plus Roan and Allie, of course, and some other of my teammates."

All couples, I think to myself as I bite my lip nervously. *Just like it will be at Allie and Roan's wedding.* At least I'm somewhat familiar with this crowd. Allie is a cousin to the Harris family, and my colleague Sloan is married to the eldest Harris Brother, so I'll certainly be amongst friends. And in the back of my mind, I've known that

I need to find a date for the wedding or I'll be the sad bridesmaid wearing a puffy pink dress and sitting at a table drinking champagne alone while all the other couples are dancing.

Mac hits me with a dazzling smile like he knows I'm faltering. "Come for me, Cookie. Please?"

I exhale heavily because he is seriously impossible to say no to when he smiles like that. He gives me the same look when he begs for Chinese takeaway instead of Indian, and we always end up getting Chinese.

I suppose the fact that I didn't even know what Netflix and chill meant is proof that I need to get out more. "You are a proper pain in my arse, Mac. Do you know that?"

He beams happily. "It's a good thing you have a great arse then."

CHAPTER 2

Mac

"I'M COMING INTO THE HOUSE! I HOPE NO ONE IS WEARING their birthday suits inside!"

"Ag, shut up, you idiot!" my roommate, Roan, shouts down the steps in his thick South African accent. "We're decent."

With a wry grin, I take the steps two at a time up to the main level of the Georgian townhouse I live in with my teammate and best mate, Roan DeWalt. I find him sacked out on the sofa with his fiancée, Allie. She's lying on his lap, her blond hair spread out over his legs as he toys with her strands like they're woven from pure gold.

They have been engaged for over a year and still can't keep their hands off each other. It wouldn't bother me if it didn't take place inside my flat all the damn time, but I know they don't have any other choice. Allie still lives with her cousin, Camden Harris, and his wife, Indie, who is our team doctor. They have a wee bairn who's just turned one, so I'm sure Allie wants to stay out of their way until after the wedding, when she and Roan plan to move into

13

a flat of their own. Regardless, their infatuation with each other is why I find myself at Freya's more often than not.

Just to be clear, I am happy for them. Their love could make a lad jealous if that's what a lad wanted. Thankfully, I do not, so their googly eyes and lovesick murmurs have no effect on me. Life is too full of adventure to get tied down at my age. I know I'm over thirty now, and my mum is always asking when I'm going to bring a lass back to Dundonald. But I have no interest in being committed to a woman because I have no clue where my career will end up. My contract with Bethnal Green F.C. ends next year, and my agent and I will begin talks soon about getting it renewed, God willing. I like the club and training staff, not to mention my teammates, but the truth is, I'm getting older. My sore knees can attest to that. And I know I can't play football forever, so I have to give it my all while I still have my all to give.

"What are you two lovebirds up to?" I ask, propping myself on the armrest of the sofa and glancing at the telly.

"Just Netflix and chilling," Roan says with a smirk, his white teeth practically glowing against his dark skin.

I shake my head knowingly. "I just came from Freya's, and she didn't have a clue what that phrase meant."

Allie's eyes widen as she sits up off Roan's lap and pins me with a hopeful expression. "Did you talk to her about the party Friday night?" she asks in her American accent.

I nod. "Aye, she's coming."

"Yes!" Allie squeals. "I knew if you asked her, she couldn't say no."

I purse my lips because it sounds deceitful when she says it like that. "Just don't tell her you asked me to ask her. I don't want her thinking it wasn't my idea."

Allie mock zips her lips. "I would never, Mac. I'm just excited for her to come out with us. I've been so tied up with wedding planning and work at the boutique that I haven't taken her out for drinks in ages."

I nod knowingly. Allie used to be our PR rep for the team, but she was sacked after some pretty intense drama between her and Roan. It seems like it all worked out for the best, though, because she was offered a job in marketing at the Kindred Spirits Boutique where Freya works. The two of them became best mates almost instantly.

"Drinks would be good." I grip the back of my neck, rubbing at a knot that's been there since my run this morning. "I think her upcoming thirtieth birthday is getting her all twisted up in her mind."

Allie nods in agreement. "That's why she needs to get out of her flat and live a little. Maybe she'll meet a hot footballer at the party and make some bad decisions."

She giggles at the prospect, and my brow furrows reflexively because I know damn well there are some lads on my team who do a fine job of making bad decisions with women. I'm no saint myself, but I definitely don't fit the typical stereotype for footballers who whore their way around London. Roan's much the same. We both have sisters, and we were both raised by strong, fearsome mothers who didn't let us treat women like they are disposable. As a result, we never got the bad reputations many of our teammates acquired throughout their careers. And if any of those arseholes try to mess about with Freya, I'm not going to be okay with it.

The knot in my neck twitches again, so I reach up to squeeze the ache.

"What's the matter, Mac?" Allie asks, her eyes narrowing on me speculatively.

"Nothing. My neck is stiff, that's all. I have a massage with the team therapist booked for tomorrow."

Allie cocks her head. "You're not tense because the idea of Freya with one of your teammates bothers you, right?"

I scoff because she's clearly reaching. "No, Allie. Cookie and I are just pals. I've told you that a million times."

"You're pals with adorable pet names for each other who bicker like an old married couple," she retorts, and I see Roan squeeze her shoulder in silent warning.

I roll my eyes. "Since when does bickering make for a solid love connection?"

Allie's eyes flicker knowingly. "Bickering means there's passion."

I plug my ears like a wee child. "This topic is not up for discussion. Freya is a mate and nothing more. I'm picking her up for the party Friday night, and that's all, okay?"

"Okay, okay," Allie adds with a smirk and lies back down on Roan's lap. She smiles up at him happily and nestles in, giving me my cue to leave.

I stand up from the armrest. "I'll let you two get back to your Netflix and *chilling*."

Roan tips his head in thanks, and I retreat to my bedroom to give them space. Is it too soon to go back to Freya's?

CHAPTER 3

Freya

T HE HUM OF THE SEWING MACHINE IS MUSIC TO MY EARS AS I work on taking in the inseam of a pair of trousers that Sloan designed for some famous political figure in London.

I'm currently tucked up in the loft area that overlooks Kindred Spirits Boutique. The shop is a red brick building located on iconic Redchurch Street in Shoreditch—a really lovely nook in London away from the tourists. Our clients range from normal everyday people to famous athletes and affluent residents. Last month, we had a pretty popular movie star stop in and tweet about the shop, so business has exploded even more than usual.

Kindred Spirits carries both menswear and womenswear, custom and one-of-a-kind pieces from up-and-coming designers. Sloan heads up the menswear department, and her business partner, Leslie Clarke, designs for women.

I met Sloan back in Manchester when she hired me away from a bridal shop where I was working crazy hours. It was the job I accepted right after design school, and I kind of got stuck there, so I was happy to work for a new American stylist who was developing quite a reputation for herself.

Then, when Sloan's personal life imploded and she divorced her husband, I ended up moving in with her and her daughter, Sophia. Sloan had a rough go of it for a long while until she met our seriously famous client, a Man U footballer named Gareth Harris. After a few bumps in the road, it was a fast track to happily ever after for both her and her daughter.

When Gareth retired from Man U and they started talking about moving to London, Sloan decided it was the perfect opportunity to open her own boutique with Leslie. They are both fashion design transports from America and felt kindred when they met, hence the name Kindred Spirits Boutique.

I was thrilled when they begged me to come on board to help, because they are lovely to work with. The boutique itself has transformed into a melting pot for all sorts of clothing, art, and accessories. All it's missing is furry pink jumpers for my cat, and it'd be perfect!

"Freya! Do you have that Naomi Sharp gown finished yet?" Sloan's voice calls up the staircase, and I lift the pedal on my sewing machine to hear the last bit of her request.

"It's on the form up here!" I call down, glancing over the railing to see her standing at the bottom of the steps.

"Thank God!" Sloan says as she hustles up the stairs and into my giant loft office that is covered in items at various stages of the process. Sloan's brown hair is piled on top of her head in a frenzied mess as she exhales the weight of her stress. "You would think chasing after a teenager and a toddler would have me in better shape."

"I'd think being married to a seriously sexy footballer would have you in better shape." I waggle my eyebrows suggestively and rev my sewing machine.

Sloan laughs as she moves towards the mannequin holding the

gown. "Speaking of footballers, I hear you're coming to Tanner and Belle's party tomorrow night? Looking for a footballer for yourself, perhaps?" She shoots me a lascivious smirk, and I can't help but roll my eyes.

"How do you even know I'm going to the party? I just agreed to it last night."

She levels me with a flat look. "You forget your dear friend Allie is a Harris. There are never secrets in the Harris family."

"It's a good thing Allie's at a meeting or she'd be the subject of my withering stare right now." I shake my head and pop up the heel of my sewing machine to twist the trousers around. "Mac thinks I should get out a bit more, and he's a whiny toddler if he doesn't get his way."

Sloan gets a strange look on her face. "Well, do you know what you're going to wear?"

My eyes lift to her. "No...why?"

Sloan squeals with delight and yells over the railing, "Leslie, Freya doesn't have her outfit picked out yet!"

I hear a squeak of giddiness before rapid footsteps are running up the stairs. Leslie's auburn hair comes into view first. Then I see a lush black dress in her hands. "I have been saving this for you!"

"What is it?" I ask as she places what looks to be a gorgeous wrap dress on my workspace.

"A dress. A perfect dress that I made with you in mind."

I level her with a serious look. "Why on earth did you make a dress with my body in mind?"

Leslie waggles her brows and glances down at my chest. "'Cause I love your shape, and I had this really fun idea for a bustline with a wrap bodice that would only work on a full-chested woman. And well—"

My brows lift. "I certainly fit that description."

Leslie presses her hands on my desk. "Try it on, please? Give us a fashion show. We've all been working like dogs today."

"Yes!" Sloan adds with equal exuberance. "Fashion show!"

I lift my hands defensively. "If you two are going to make me try on clothing, I need coffee first."

I step out of the shop and into the humid, warm summer air in London. Weather is so hit or miss here in the summers. The last week of May can feel like winter or bring a crazy heatwave. You never truly know what you're going to get. Growing up in Cornwall was always mild to cool weather since it's so close to the sea. This sweating in the middle of the day thing is not something I'm keen on.

I make my way around the corner towards Allpress Espresso—a coffee shop located less than fifty metres away. Squaring my shoulders, I push the door open to stride into the tiny coffee shop that always smells divine. It has a secondary school canteen vibe about it that somehow manages to be hipster at the same time.

"Freya!" A deep voice booms my name loudly as I walk up to the counter. "Bienvenida!"

I do my best to quell the flurry of emotions that niggle in my belly every time I see Javier—the Spanish barista who works here all the time. His accent is dreamy, and his dark eyes are always so welcoming, but I'm sure he's like that with all of his regular customers.

I prop my hands on the coffee counter and admire Javier's beard. It's dark and scraggly and looking extra beardy today, which is something I apparently fancy. My gaze drops to his white T-shirt that's stained with coffee. You'd think a barista would wear an apron to stop from ruining his clothes, or at least wear dark colours to hide it. But Javier's obviously very committed to his coffee craft, and I admire that for some reason.

"Good to see you again, Freya," Javier says, his Spanish accent like a warm blanket I want to nuzzle.

My mind skips over his words as I imagine what I'd like to hear him say. *"I love how your face shines in the morning sun."*

"Hot day outside, isn't it?" he adds with a pained look towards the window.

Imaginary translation: *He worries about my well-being.*

"I like the colour of your dress today."

He notices the little things.

"Did you pop in yesterday for coffee? I didn't see you."

He misses me when I'm not here.

"Having the usual? Iced coffee with extra milk?"

Our wedding photos would be magnificent.

I shake my head to silence the voice in my mind that's as fanciful as a telenovela and stutter out, "It's good to see you as in the also, Javier." My lips form a thin line, and I die a little inside over how stupid I just sounded. To try to cover up my awkwardness, I point behind me at the shop that's filled with people. "Busy…here… around this general region."

Shut up, Freya! Shut up! Why did you say region? Are you trying to ruin your life?

Javier's face scrunches up as if I'm the foreigner, and he's attempting to interpret my words. I don't know why I can't speak around this man. It's like the moment I see him and his dimples buried inside his beard, my brain cells start to deteriorate on the spot.

"Would you like the usual for your friends as well?" he asks as he types in the order on his point of purchase device.

"Yes, please," I mumble. It's better if I limit my words in front of him because I've been popping in here for weeks, and I still can't string a normal sentence together in his presence.

I pay with the company card and quickly back away from the counter, kicking myself for being so pathetic. There have been roughly three men in my life who were responsible for turning me into this horrid, mumbling idiot in front of blokes.

The first was a boy who sat in front of me in year five. He used hair gel to style his locks into spikey weapons that I always felt an uncontrollable urge to touch, so much so that I actually did reach out and prick my finger on a strand once. The entire class witnessed my lapse in judgment, and I became known as Fingerling Freya for years after. I couldn't walk to class without the boys in school dashing away from me and covering their heads protectively.

The second boy was my boyfriend in year eleven. I thought that relationship lasted for almost a year until I realised he'd broken up with me, and I somehow missed the notice. I discovered it when I asked him what colour tie he was wearing for the formal, and he said it was the same colour as his girlfriend, Mandy's, dress.

Okaaay then.

The third was a boy I met in design school. We were partners for the fall fashion show and began dating shortly thereafter. Things moved oddly slow between us, but I thought it was because he was Mormon. During one late night of studying and far too much tequila, the truth came out. The memories of that night still haunt me to this day.

It took me quite a few years to get over those traumas only to discover the new trauma of online dating. The first man I met at a pub called me "Piggy" before walking out on me. When I tried with another guy, he confessed over dinner that he was still sleeping with his ex-wife. And when I finally let my friends in Manchester set me up on a blind date, my stomach was in such horrible knots from the memories of how bad my other experiences had been, I couldn't even string together human-sounding sentences! It was like an alien invaded my body and was speaking in its tribal tongue through the chubby cheeks of a Cornish redhead.

I was so broken, I gave up on men altogether.

Honestly, Barista Javier is the first man whom I've allowed myself to be attracted to in ages. A Spanish barista with a dad bod is apparently what gets my ears burning. Who knew? Perhaps if I could figure out how to actually speak to him, he'd be a suitable prospect for a date to Allie and Roan's wedding.

Javier loads the coffees onto a tray, and he quickly sticks the receipt on the side of one of the cups as I approach. With a crooked smile, he hands them over to me. "It was nice to see you again, Freya. Say hello to your friends for me."

I tug on my burning ear. "It's nice you see me, too," I state while reaching out to grab the coffee.

I barrel my way out of the shop and find a bench to sit down on to catch my breath before heading back to the boutique. The last thing I need is Allie, Sloan, and Leslie finding out that I fancy Javier. They'd never let me hear the end of it. I grab my iced coffee to take a fortifying drink and notice some extra writing on the receipt that's stuck to the cup.

Call me. Xoxo Jav

I blink back my shock and stare at the phone number scrawled beneath.

Javier gave me his number?

Bleddy hell!

CHAPTER 4

Freya

WALKING UP TO TANNER AND BELLE HARRIS' FLAT FOR THE party feels a bit like walking into a member of the royal family's flat. Don't get me wrong, I know they're not truly royal. And since Sloan is married to Gareth, and Allie is a cousin of theirs, I'm aware they're normal blokes with families. But the Harris family story as a whole is extraordinary and reads like it's straight out of a movie.

There are four painfully attractive brothers who all play professional football for England, and a sister who's literally one of the coolest women I've ever met. They were all raised by their father after their mother passed away when they were very young. Their family is so packed full of talent. The four brothers even won the World Cup for England a couple of years ago.

Now everyone is married and having photographs published in the papers with stunning toddlers on their shoulders and smiling at their brilliant wives like they're all in a bleddy Hallmark film. It's properly mental! You don't even have to like football to consider their family more interesting than the royals. Even their cousin, Allie, who moved here from America last year, found herself a footballer to marry. Talk about a family that has all the luck!

And somehow, someway, little old Fingerling Freya has found herself entrenched in this world of power couples. It's no wonder Mac and I became mates. We're the only single people left!

"Have I told you how nice you look tonight, Cookie?" Mac asks, stepping aside to let me climb the stairs to the building entrance first.

"Don't call me Cookie in front of these people," I hiss as the noise of the party increases the closer we get. "I doubt any of them has ever eaten a cookie in all their perfectly attractive, wildly successful lives."

Mac laughs at my remark, and replies, "Well, you're looking rather bonnie yourself tonight. I know you wear dresses a lot, but that one suits you differently."

"Thanks," I murmur half-heartedly and tug at the sweetheart neckline of the dress where I've stuffed Javier's number for some ridiculous reason. I swear I'll lose it if I put it down, so I've been gripping it in my hands for the past twenty-four hours like a lunatic.

Mac joins me on the top step and brushes back his red hair that's flopped over his forehead, to scan the call buttons on the panel. He looks quite fit himself tonight wearing faded jeans and a green T-shirt. It's so easy for men to look effortlessly handsome. Meanwhile, I have to scrutinise whether my cleavage is too much or not enough and if these shoes make my ankles look fat.

He finds the proper button and presses it before turning his charming boy-next-door smile at me. His eyes do a sweep of my body. "Are your wee ears on fire yet?"

He touches one, and the contact of his warm finger on my hot ear sends a wave of shivers down my body, so much so that I begin to totter in my strappy black heels.

I slap his hand away. "Don't do that!"

His head drops back as he laughs. "It's cute how your ears get hot whenever you're nervous."

"It's not *you* making my ears hot, I can promise you that."

"Believe me, I'm aware," Mac replies, a knowing set to his taut jaw. "I could say you're a beaut of a lass tonight, and I wonder what it would be like to shag you senseless, and it would have absolutely no effect on your ears."

I roll my eyes and steel myself to ignore his remark. The thought of Mac wanting to shag me is like a Great Dane having the hots for an overweight Shih Tzu. Just not going to happen.

And, objectively, I know I look nice tonight, so he's just stating a fact. Leslie was right—this black wrap dress was made for me. With the minor alterations I did, it hugs my figure perfectly as well.

I didn't always know how to dress for my body type. I grew up with large hips and bustier breasts than all my friends at school. My mother was always on the bigger side as well, and since plus-size fashion didn't exist in her days, she taught me how to sew at a young age. So I altered my clothes to help conceal my less-attractive bits. Full, flirty skirts, A-line seams, and sweetheart necklines were always flattering on me. When I went to textile design school in Manchester, I really embraced the 50s era for my own style. Now I've come to actually like my hourglass shape and double-*E* breasts, even if they venture well beyond Kardashian sizes.

Regardless of my larger size, I enjoy transforming clothing for any body type. I take great pleasure in the simple act of altering something to work with what the good Lord gave people. The world can often feel like a one-size-fits-all place, but applying a few alterations can make life a perfect fit.

That and Spanx.

God bless the creator of Spanx.

The buzzer goes off, indicating we can go through the door, and my ears swell with heat. "I feel like I could shit out three kittens right now."

Mac bursts out laughing. "What the hell does that mean?"

I turn an accusing glare at my friend. "I'm nervous, that's what it means. My ears are on fire because this isn't my scene. My scene is fuzzy pyjamas, a sewing machine, my cat, and Netflix. You are the cause of my gastrointestinal issues at the moment. Therefore, it's important for you to know that you and I are in a fight."

He shakes his head as he leads me up the single flight of stairs to the flat entrance. "That's the fourth fight we've been in this week. I must be trying to break my record."

The door opens to Tanner and Belle's two-story flat, and I glance around the crowd full of attractive Londoners packed inside. We step in, and as I hand my bag to the security man at the door, I see the party is already in full swing. Tanner is standing on a sofa table in the living room with his fist thrust in the air while his brothers and several other men cheer him on to, "Chug, chug, chug, chug!" The scene looks straight out of an American college party instead of a party full of adult couples having a laugh.

I spot the ladies huddled around a giant charcuterie spread in the kitchen and sigh with relief when I see that they seem to be acting normally for the most part. First, I see Belle and Indie chatting to each other. The two of them are brilliant surgeons and best friends who ended up marrying the twin Harris Brothers, Tanner and Camden. Then there's the blond bombshell Harris sister, Vi, who's the matriarch of the whole family. She's standing by her husband, Hayden, and they are busy talking with Sloan. Then there's my dear friend, Allie, who rushes over as soon as she spots Mac and me standing awkwardly in the entryway.

"Oh my freaking God, you look so hot!" she states, pushing past Leslie to get out of the kitchen. "Is this Leslie's design?"

"Damn right it is!" Leslie sings with her matching muddled American accent. Both Allie and Leslie have spent part of their lives in America, so their tones have a unique sound to them. Leslie eyes me up and down. "Good God almighty, you look even hotter than you did at the shop yesterday! I told you this dress would be perfect for you. Didn't I tell her, Sloan?"

Sloan smiles from the kitchen, and calls over, "You told her."

I blush under their praise and feel weird with Mac standing beside me to hear all of it. I make a joke to deflect. "Well, Leslie, you're the designer, so you're really complimenting yourself more than you are me."

"Damn right I am," Leslie replies with a smirk and takes a sip of her drink.

Allie nods appreciatively. "It's about time you let them play dress up with you, Freya."

Mac is still hovering near me like a protective watchdog, so I wave my hand at him. "I'm fine, Mac. Go on and play with your friends."

He shoots me a wink and then makes his way towards the boys in the living room.

Leslie slinks her arm around my waist. "I should design all your clothes."

"Like you have the time!" I retort with a huff. Leslie and Sloan are both so swamped with custom order requests that we've had to turn some away. "Who has Marisa tonight?" I ask, referring to Leslie's four-year-old daughter.

"She's with Theo's parents in Essex for the weekend. Theo and I haven't had a weekend off in ages, so this is cause for copious amounts of alcohol consumption. They have Vi and Hayden's daughter too, so the girls are running them ragged, I'm sure," she says with a laugh. As Theo and Hayden are brothers, their two daughters are cousins. This group is seriously an interconnected web of not quite related connections.

Suddenly, Leslie's eyes go wide. "Good grief! You don't have a drink in your hand. Tisn't right, tisn't fair, tisn't proper!"

Leslie scurries back towards the kitchen, and Allie gives me a rueful smile. "She's quoting Poldark to the Cornish girl. In case you didn't know she's tipsy, you do now."

I exhale happily as Sloan approaches and gives me a hug. "You look gorgeous, Freya. Like always."

"Thanks," I reply. "Mac was yelling at me the whole time I was getting ready because I was taking too long picking out my bag and shoes. I have way too many gorgeous options, I'm afraid. What can I say? Accessories always fit."

Sloan touches my soft red curls appreciatively. "You two really go at each other."

"That's what I keep saying," Allie chimes in with a sneaky smirk.

"Don't start," I reply with a huff. "We're just mates."

Sloan mock zips her lips. I can tell she wants to say more, but she won't. Sloan's good like that. She always just lets me be me. She's really the first friend I ever had whom I truly felt understood by. And I loved the little family I stumbled into with her and her daughter back in Manchester.

Leslie emerges with four red and orange mixed cocktails on a tray. She thrusts one into my hand, and I stare down at it dubiously. "I regret to inform you that hard alcohol and I do not mix."

Leslie waves me off. "They're tequila sunrises. It's the drink of all the Harris wives. You won't taste a drop of the alcohol, I swear."

We clink glasses, and I take a sip of what tastes like orange juice with cherry syrup. My eyes go wide. "These could be dangerous."

The rules of the game *Never Have I Ever* are simple. You sit in a large circle and take turns saying statements about things you have never done before. If anyone in the group has done it, they must take a drink. Sounds like a straightforward game. A bit strange for grown-ups to play, but the host of the evening is a big man-child, so I guess that's the excuse.

And because a man named Santino—who is apparently the Bethnal Green F.C. team lawyer—walked into Tanner and Belle's flat three hours ago and oddly attached himself to my side, I must use all of my strength not to vomit out words in nonsensical order. Perhaps if I focus on being really good at the game, I won't notice the fact that we're seated right next to each other and our legs keep touching, or the fact that his eyes keep glancing down at my cleavage.

One little problem, though.

Never Have I Ever is a game that is entirely about The Sex.

And considering I've never had The Sex, I realise with ominous regret that I am in very big trouble.

There are a number of reasons why I am a twenty-nine-year-old virgin. One of which is because my Nanna Dot used to call my virginity my "maiden tag", and she mentioned something biological about a skin flap and searing pain. The entire conversation horrified me so much, I never dreamt of opening my legs as a teen.

As I got older, I realised that my nanna may have embellished a bit, but my experiences with men were so bleddy awful, I never managed to get the job done. In fact, the one person I got the closest with was my design school boyfriend who waited until we were lying naked on his dorm room floor to tell me he was gay. It was so horrifying that I still cringe when I think back to my awkward response.

My exact words as I lay there, spread-eagle and waiting for him to enter me were, "Good on you."

Honestly, I should probably discuss that with a therapist at some point in my life.

But right now, I'm focusing on another problem: The very serious issue of me being gravely overserved this evening.

The bartender did way too good of a job keeping my fruity drink filled. And because somewhere in my genetic lineage there's a pleasantly plump ancestor who can't handle booze, I'm in serious trouble.

Why didn't I stick with wine? Wine and I are mates. I know what to expect from wine. Now the injustice of my heritage means that this room of seriously attractive people and one Italian-looking bloke who smells rather nice are about to get hot-eared Freya who's never had The Sex...Unplugged.

My ears have basically melted off at this point.

Also, why do I keep calling it The Sex? Even hearing the words in my mind is embarrassing.

My eyes narrow at the culprits who got me into this state. Firstly, Mac for bringing me to this horrid place. He's sitting straight across from me, laughing with his teammates like it's a typical Friday night, while I'm over here having a panic attack that I'm going to tell the Santino bloke about the time I licked battery acid off the grasscutter because it was blue, and I thought it might be candy floss.

The paramedics assured me that I was wrong.

Then there are the villainous ladies tonight—Allie, Sloan, Leslie, Belle, and Indie. They were culprits in mixing those delicious tequila sunrises all night. And the title of the drink is deceiving because I didn't taste a drop of tequila. Every sip tasted like delicious, refreshing OJ. It even gives the illusion of being healthy! But five drinks later, I've greatly exceeded my vitamin C intake for the day.

Time to initiate a backup plan.

I'm going to fake my way through the game. I was the Wicked Witch of the West in year ten, after all. The critic claimed I was the wickedest of all the wickeds they'd ever seen. Granted, that critic was my mum, but she doesn't pass out compliments for free, so you better believe I sewed that quote into my year twelve memory quilt.

Tonight, this room is getting a bit of theatre. Freya Cook is headlining to conceal her lovely maiden tag in front of all these adorable, sexually experienced couples.

Let's do this.

"Never have I ever…kissed a girl," Santino states beside me as he takes a drink, and his head swerves around the group of us huddled in the living room with drinks in hand.

A few of the girls roll their eyes and giggle while taking a drink, including Belle, Indie, and Leslie. They're all drinking! So what do I do? I giggle-snort and take a sip myself, like the sexually curious woman that I am.

Santino's eyes flare curiously at me and glance down at my chest again. From across the room, I hear Mac clear his throat loudly, and I turn to find him staring at me with a frown. I shrug like kissing girls is no big deal because it's obviously not. Then I take another drink because the drink is my acting juice at this point. The more I drink, the better my performance will be.

"Never have I ever done reverse cowgirl!" Belle states next, holding her glass up proudly.

The crowd cheers, and my eyes widen. Reverse cowgirl? Is that like a role-playing thing? Perhaps the girl dresses up like a cowboy and the boy dresses up like a cowgirl? Gender swapping? How modern! I take a big gulp of my drink because I used to play cowboy with the neighbour boy next door to me. But one day he tied me up and spanked me until his mother caught us, and she threw me out of their house.

I quickly take another drink because something about this cocktail is making me parched. When I finish, Santino hits me with a high five. Okay then! Drinking gets you high fives. I'm rocking at this *Never Have I Ever* game!

"Never have I ever…" the youngest Harris Brother, Booker, says, "…had sex in a car."

The eldest Harris brother, Gareth, tips his glass to Sloan before drinking along with Camden, Indie, Vi, and Hayden. This bunch must have a thing for cars. Bleddy hell, looks like I'm up again! I take a sip.

"Never have I ever pierced anything below my neck," Booker's wife, Poppy, says, fluffing her blond pixie hair coyly as she takes a sip. I take a sip too, wondering what on earth could sweet little Poppy have pierced?

I notice Allie watching me curiously, probably because she's one of the only people who knows about my virginal status. Well, she kind of knows. It's not something I've flat out admitted to her, but last year, I mentioned something to her about a twenty-plus-year dry spell, so I'm sure she got the picture. She's thankfully decent enough not to bring it up to me.

Out of the corner of my eye, I notice Mac looks rather moody for some odd reason. My brows furrow because, shit, is he judging me for being falsely promiscuous? He certainly better not be!

Allie's lips purse together like she sees Mac's displeasure, so I guzzle another drink. Mac tilts his head and tries to mouth something to me, but I'm distracted by Santino pulling me close to whisper in my ear.

"Did you get the car dirty?"

I bark out a really unattractive snort laugh. Then the laugh sort of develops a mind of its own and takes off on a noisy journey, which seems to amuse Santino because he laughs with me. At least if I'm laughing, I'm not talking. Drunken Freya talking is bad. Very, very bad.

I turn to see Mac is still watching me. With a frown, I shake my head and focus on my cocktail because if I make eye contact with him, he might see right through me.

"Never have I ever had sex in a public loo."

What the hell, sounds exciting! I take a drink.

"Never have I ever given road head."

I have no clue what that one is. Road. Head. Hmmm. I imagine it's something done on a road, but how does it involve your head?

Suddenly, Santino drapes his arm over the back of my chair, and I can smell the pungent scent of his cheap cologne all over me.

"Never have I ever had a threesome," someone says from somewhere.

I pause on this one and give it a proper think. At this point, I feel like I'm drinking, not for things I have done, obviously, but for things I'd like to do. Feels a bit more honest if I think about it that way. And since I actually know what a threesome is, perhaps I'd fancy one!

I take a drink.

"Never have I ever done anal."

Fuck me, I know what that one is. I drink.

"Never have I ever sixty-nined."

More drinking, yay!

"Never have I ever done it with a boss."

Drink.

"Never have I ever masturbated in public."

Drink, drink, drink.

I've lost track of how many drinks I've had. I know someone at some point put a refill in my hand, so now I have a fresh cocktail gleaming up at me. Suddenly, a chunk of ice pelts me in the chest and falls down the deep cavernous region between my breasts. I try to grab it, but it's too late. *Gone forever now.*

Santino leans towards my chest to inspect the damage as I look up to see that the ice thrower was Mac, who looks angry for some odd reason. What's his problem? He points his finger at me and then at the door. *Does he want to go? Now?*

A voice from somewhere far away says, "Never have I ever done a dirty Sanchez."

The room is a mixture of groaning and howling at this point. And I don't know why, but I feel my fist thrust into the air as I take another drink. This act elicits more cheers and prompts Santino to move so close to me, I think he might be sitting on my lap.

Who knew that being so sexually experienced would make me so popular? Pity I didn't have sex ages ago! And done anal and a dirty Sanchez…whatever that is.

I am just about to take another drink when the glass is suddenly whisked out of my hand and a large, firm grip wraps tightly around my wrist. I glance up to see an enormous Mac staring down at me with a scowl on his face. I don't know if I've ever seen Mac with a proper frown.

He yanks me up out of my chair, and barks, "We're leaving."

My jaw drops. "But I'm having fun."

"Not up for discussion, Cook."

At least he didn't call me Cookie, I think to myself just as Santino stands up beside me and begins to open his mouth. Mac turns his hard eyes on him, and I swear his chest inflates like a pectoral-shaped water balloon as he towers over the poor bloke. Without a word, Santino sits down, and Mac's hand grips my wrist and drags me behind him. I glance back at the party and see everyone watching us with complete fascination. I'm quite fascinated, too, to be honest. I've never seen Mac upset like this. What happened? What did I miss?

He's silent as we make our way outside to his grey Lexus SUV where he shoves me into the passenger seat and stomps his way around to the driver's side. When he folds his giant frame into the car and takes off down the road, a loud hiccup erupts from my mouth. I part my lips to speak, but another one goes off before I have a chance to stop it. But this time, a bit of acid bubbles up in the back of my throat.

I slap my hand over my mouth and brace myself on the doorframe. "Pull over! I'm going to be sick!"

Mac growls under his breath and turns down the first side street he can manage to find. He has barely stopped the car when I swing open the door and puke the contents of my stomach onto the curb.

Saints preserve me, why does it look like that?

"I'm vomiting blood!" I cry out to the gods up above.

"No, you're not," Mac replies flatly.

"I'm going to die!" I sob and feel snot dripping out of my nose.

"No, you're not." Mac exhales heavily. After a short pause, he reaches across the centre console and pats me reassuringly on the back. "You were drinking cherry grenadine, Cookie. That's why your vomit is red."

"Oh," I reply stupidly and sit up to wipe the tears off my face. "I didn't think of that."

"You clearly didn't think about a lot tonight," he grumbles through clenched teeth.

"What does that mean exactly?" I growl like a pirate and close the door. I turn to look at Mac, and his stony face is illuminated by the dashboard lights. "Why are you cross at me?"

Mac's nostrils flare. "What the hell were you doing back there, Cook?"

"Having a laugh," I reply with a shrug.

"Drinking like a fucking fish and saying you did all that stuff in that ridiculous game when I know damn well you haven't isn't having a laugh."

"How do you know I haven't done all that stuff?"

"Because I spend nearly every night with you. If you were out giving blow jobs in cars and masturbating in public, I think I'd notice."

I cringe at the last one, only vaguely remembering drinking to it. I brush off my reaction and square my shoulders to reply, "You don't know everything about me, Mac. I had a life before I met you."

How dare he act like he knows everything about me? We don't talk about our past relationships. Never have! It's a bizarre no-fly zone we've had for the past year. Mac doesn't ever mention his sex life around me even though I'm sure he's getting laid on a regular basis when he's travelling for football. So for him to assume I've never done any of those things gets right up my nose.

"There are several hours in a day when you don't see me, you cow. How do you know I'm not on dating apps, swiping right for lunch dates?" I quip, internally shuddering at the thought of those stupid apps and how horrible an experience I had the last time I used them.

"Well, are you?" Mac asks, pinning me with a look I can't altogether decipher, especially since I'm seeing two of him.

"It's none of your business!" I point at the road. "Just take me home. I don't want to be in your presence anymore. "

Mac eyes me harshly for a moment before he finally puts the car in drive and continues towards my flat. When we arrive, Mac gets out to walk me inside. I don't bother arguing because my tummy heaves like it wants to be sick again.

A strange urge to cry comes over me when I can't find my keys in my bag. As if reading my emotions, Mac gently moves me aside and unlocks the door with the spare set I gave him several months ago when he took care of Hercules for me.

"Took care" is a bit of a stretch, considering Hercules won't go near him. But Mac made sure Hercules had food, water, and a clean litter box, so perhaps I shouldn't be so hard on him right now.

Mac rides the lift up the five floors with me. Once we've arrived, he unlocks my flat door just in time to see orange-spotted Hercules bolt back into my bedroom.

"Even Hercules is cross at you," I state as I undo my heels and drop them on the ground with a loud thud.

"He's always cross at me," Mac replies flatly. "I forgot he was orange until just now."

"He's shy," I reply as I shuffle into the kitchen and grab a bottle of water out of the fridge. "Not everyone likes to be the centre of attention like you."

Mac follows in my wake, glaring at me with narrow, accusing eyes. "You definitely weren't shy tonight when you played that game and made a complete tit of yourself."

"Don't have a go at me! I was just playing along," I groan defensively as blips of the game come back to me. I cringe inwardly at how right he is. "And you don't know that I haven't done all of those things."

Mac exhales roughly out of his nose and crosses his inked arms over his chest. "You're right, but I know for a fact you didn't do at least one of them."

"How do you know?" I hiss.

He splays his hand out on the counter and lowers his eyes so they're level with mine. "Freya, do you even know what a dirty Sanchez is?"

My brows furrow, and I take a swig of water before replying, "Of course I do."

He stares at me expectantly. "I'm all ears."

I falter for a moment but then realise that Mac probably doesn't know either, so I just make something up. "It's when you have The Sex on a dirty tribal blanket."

Mac closes his eyes as if he's embarrassed. "Not even close. And for the record, people who say 'The Sex' generally don't have a lot of it."

"Then what is a dirty Sanchez, Mr Sex Haver? First, you educated me on Netflix and chill, and now this. I had no idea I was friends with a sexual savant!"

Mac ignores my jab, and replies, "A dirty Sanchez is when a lad sticks his finger up the bum of a lass, then wipes it across her upper lip."

"That's fucking disgusting!" I screech loudly.

"I know!" Mac roars, standing back up to his full height and puffing out his chest. "And you took a drink in front of all those people like you you've done it when I know damn well you wouldn't do that if your life depended on it."

"I wouldn't do it if Hercules's life depended on it!" I agree in earnest. "I love my cat, but if the choice was between me smelling my own arsehole or Hercules having to meet his maker, he'd have to go." I do a quick sweep of my flat, worried that Hercules might be listening.

Mac's heavy exhale turns my focus back to him. "Then please tell me, what in God's name you were doing tonight, Cookie? What was that performance all about? And don't blame the alcohol because I know it had nothing to do with you being a wee bit pissed."

I shrug helplessly and clutch the water against my chest like it's a shield that will protect me from Mac's scrutinising eyes. "I was just trying to fit in."

He scoffs with disbelief. "Since when are *you* desperate to fit in?"

Since I decided I didn't want to tell a room full of people that I'm a twenty-nine-year-old virgin and my sexual experiences are bleak at best!

"I didn't want everyone in the room to know," I murmur and press the cool plastic water bottle against my forehead in some vain attempt to gain strength.

"Know what?"

My eyes flare angrily as I jerk the bottle away from my face. "Isn't it obvious?"

"What?" Mac asks thickly.

I close my eyes as if in pain. If the big ox hasn't figured out by now that I still have my maiden tag, I'm certainly not about to tell him. "That I haven't had a proper date in years, never mind kissed a bloke. That no matter how hard I try, I can barely string together a comprehensible sentence around a man. I was hoping to find a date for Allie and Roan's wedding, but I'm hopeless! You should see me around blokes. I turn into a tongue-tied freak who says words backwards and out of order. It's like I'm reading a crossword puzzle aloud."

"You speak in front of me all the time," Mac argues, his brows furrowed in confusion. "You even use words I have to google the meaning of later."

"Well, you're not a proper bloke." I turn away from him to exhale so he doesn't smell the vomit on my breath.

He steps in close behind me, and his voice is husky when he replies, "Last I checked, my cocker and balls were upstanding citizens, though I do think they crawled up inside my body when you drank to dirty Sanchez earlier."

"Enough talk about dirty Sanchez. Do you want me to be sick again?" I twirl around to eye him angrily. "I just mean you're not a bloke that I fancy. I was trying to impress that Santino fellow, or at least not make a fool of myself in front of him."

"So you fancy the lawyer? He's a fucking creep. He used to make the Harrises take him out to clubs and stuck to them like glue in hopes of shagging their cast-offs."

"I don't fancy Santino!" I exclaim. "Are you thick?"

"Christ, I must be because I'm lost."

"I fancy Javier! The Spanish barista who works at the coffee shop by the boutique. He's bearded and wonderful, and he gave me his number yesterday. I've been in a state about it ever since."

Mac blinks at me stupidly. "So call him. What are you waiting for?"

Heaven help me so I don't bash this man's head into the refrigerator.

"Haven't you been listening, Mac? It's obviously not that easy for me, and I still have no idea *why* he gave me his number. He must have magically forgotten about the time I spilled an entire tray of coffees and was in such a tizzy, I marched behind the counter and grabbed a mop and bucket, which apparently isn't proper because the health inspector was there, and I wasn't using the mop correctly, and Javier almost got a violation because of it! He wasn't even cross at me for it!"

Mac smiles at me like I'm his nan with Alzheimer's again. "Probably because he fancies you."

"Fat lot of good that will do me if I can't even muster up the nerve to call him." I look up and eye Mac seriously. "In case you didn't realise tonight, I'm a little inexperienced with The Sex."

"You really have to stop calling it The Sex."

"I'm not taking lessons from you on the English vocabulary, okay?" I snap defensively as my chest heaves with anxiety because admitting these suppressed feelings I've had for Javier for months feels like I've shit out a giant elephant. Forget shitting kittens. This admission is shitting an elephant. Although, I still haven't told anyone that I'm an actual virgin, and that's probably where most of my anxiety comes from.

All of these thoughts cause my balance to sway. Mac notices, and in a split second, he wraps his arm around my shoulders and begins leading me towards my bedroom door. "Why don't you go to bed and we can talk more about all of this tomorrow?"

"I don't want to go to sleep," I pout. "I want to die from

embarrassment because that entire party thinks I've done a dirty Sanchez."

"Everyone was drunk. Don't even worry about it, Cookie."

"I need a cookie is what I need."

"I'll bring you cookies for breakfast tomorrow," Mac says, opening the door and standing at the threshold. He flips the light on and glances inside like my bedroom is a curious place he's never seen before.

Come to think of it, the loo down the hallway is probably the closest he's got.

"Promise you'll bring me cookies?" I ask pathetically while slumping against the doorframe.

"Promise," he replies with a grin and glances down at my dress. "Are you…okay to get out of that and put yourself to bed?"

My eyes go wide, and I quickly cover up my cleavage. "Yes! Crikey, I think I've embarrassed myself in front of you enough for one night. I don't need to scar you for life with the sight of all my wobbly bits as well." I shudder at the thought of Mac seeing me in my knickers.

Mac looks up at the ceiling and shakes his head. "Utter shite."

"It's not *shite*," I retort. "You don't want to be around when I take off my Spanx. I'll look like a cast member of Cirque du Soleil, or possibly a crime scene."

Mac's shoulders shake with laughter as he leans in and kisses me on the head. "I'll lock up."

I sigh heavily and watch his large, fit frame turn and walk down the hallway to my front door. If I had an ounce of Mac's sweet, boy-next-door charm, I would've totally had The Sex by now.

CHAPTER 5

Mac

SOMETHING TELLS ME I'M GOING TO REGRET THIS, I THINK TO myself as I turn down Freya's street with fresh cookies and coffees sitting in my passenger seat. It's not the treats I'm worried about. I still have seven weeks left in the off-season, so I'm going to enjoy the taste of freedom while I can.

I'm actually concerned about what I'm about to offer Freya because there's a chance it could change everything between us, and I don't relish that thought at all.

But my friendships are everything to me, and after seeing Freya so disappointed in her behaviour at the party, I realise I haven't been a good friend to her at all. I feel like shite because I clearly let her "secret friend" request go on for far too long. Because of that, I never realised how hard dating and being around men is for her. So, after some serious tossing and turning in bed all night, I know exactly how I can help my pal.

Selfishly, I enjoy having Freya all to myself, though. The woman makes me smile. Aye, sure we argue more often than not, but that's because she doesn't take any crap from me. She is so unapologetically herself that I always know right where I stand with her, and I like being around that kind of person.

As a footballer, I've been traded around to different teams in the UK a fair amount. I even played in Germany for a year. All that shuffling made finding genuine friends whom I actually got on with a bit difficult. And no matter what team I played for, the women I met were always trying way too hard to please me, or they were killing themselves to look the way they thought a footballer's WAG should look. Big, pushed-up tits, artificially plumped lips, and makeup that's caked on so thick, you have no clue what they look like underneath.

Now that I'm well into my thirties, I feel too old for all that fake shite, and I don't fancy wasting my time on women like that. I think that's why when I met Freya at Kindred Spirits and her freckles shone as bright and real as her personality, I instantly took a liking to her. Not in a sexual way, mind you. To be truthful, I think I was keen on being friends with her because I was able to enjoy the company of someone who didn't care about the world of football. For that reason, we became proper pals, and we've grown damn close over the past year.

Hunkering down in Freya's flat, we've been able to share a lot about ourselves. Surprisingly, we've never really spoken about her dating life, and that fact makes me feel awful. Though, in all fairness, she hasn't asked me about mine either. Not that there'd be much to report. Since my friends have all wifed-up in the past year, I'm in the middle of what one might call a dry spell, and my hand is practically calloused from the overtime.

Never mind me, though. It's Cookie who needs some help, and I'm keen on being there for her. Especially if it means I can keep her away from that worm Santino, who looks at every woman like a melting ice cream cone he wants to lick. A chill runs up my spine from the memory of him rubbing himself all over her last night. She was so oblivious to his leering, it took everything in me not to bolt across the room and wrap my hands around that absolute wank's throat. Santino and I have history. And it's a history I'd rather Freya not know about.

Hopefully, the barista she fancies is a better prospect that I can help her with. After her performance last night, I'm imagining Freya's dry spell has been even longer than mine. Maybe if she got laid again, she'd be a bit sweeter to me, too.

Probably not.

I smile at the thought.

I park outside her flat and use my key to get into the building. When I knock on her door, I hear the sound of Hercules's paws sprinting down the hall and a pained yelp from Freya. In a rush to check on her, I let myself in and find my friend bouncing on one foot in the hallway outside her loo, wearing nothing but a wee towel. She's gripping her other foot and cursing expletives up at the ceiling.

Even though this is my best mate whom I do not fancy, my eyes can't help but lower. The towel is covering all her naughty bits, but I do get a rare view of her creamy white legs and can't help but smile at the state of them.

"Christ, woman, if you have bonnie legs like that, why the hell are you always covering them up with long skirts and trousers?" I ask, closing the door behind me and setting the cookies and coffee on the dining room table.

Freya ignores my remark and scowls towards her bedroom where Hercules must be hiding. "Saints preserve me, Hercules, you truly are a psychotic little shit."

I move down the hall, laughing. "Last night, you were defending your precious cat. This morning, he's psychotic?"

"He just caught a whiff of your scent and bolted right over my little toe!" Freya nearly shouts, flipping her wet red hair away from her face and giving me a view of her freshly washed freckles. "The day Hercules doesn't go berserk at the mere scent of you will be the day that I'll start to believe you when you tell me I'm bonnie." She lowers her injured toe to the ground and pinches the bridge of her nose.

"Headache?" I ask knowingly.

She nods and slumps back against the wall. "Why did I let them give me booze last night?" I reach out for her neck, and she flinches. "What are you doing?"

I level her with a hard stare. "Would you hold still, woman? It's a wee bit early in the day for you to be so bristly. Turn your head and look forward."

She does as I say, and I sweep the wet strands over her shoulder to give myself access to the back of her neck. She smells like minty shampoo and a hint of lavender. It's a pleasant combination, but I focus on the task at hand. My fingers wrap around the base of her skull, right on the narrow part of her neck, and squeeze.

She closes her eyes and lets out a low moan. "Oh, ouch."

"This is a trick my mum taught me," I murmur softly. "Just ride out the pressure, and it'll be worth it."

"That's what she said," Freya says, and her shoulders shake with a breathy laugh.

"You're such a child," I reply, rubbing my thumb and forefinger over the tendons in her neck.

"You're rubbing off on me," she replies and then sinks into the pressure.

My eyes move from where my hand is on her neck to her shoulders, and eventually to her chest. There's a stirring that happens deep in my groin at the sight of her skin on display, and I quickly look up at the ceiling to stop that crap right in its tracks. After thirty seconds, I release her neck, and her eyes flutter open.

When she turns to look at me, her forest green eyes are ten times more relaxed than before.

"That's incredible. My headache is gone."

I nod. "I'd still take some aspirin if I were you. You drank enough for an entire football team last night."

She gives me a shove before turning to head into her bedroom. "I'll be right out."

I make myself at home in the living room, flicking on the telly to a sports channel and setting up our cookies and coffee. I'm taking my first sip when Freya comes out in a pair of black leggings and a white T-shirt.

I shake my head. "Covering those bonnie legs is a crime."

She rolls her eyes and flops down beside me, gesturing for her coffee, which I hand her. We nibble on the cookies silently for a few minutes before she croaks out, "So tell me, how awful was I last night?"

My brows lift. "Do you not remember?"

She shrugs. "I remember, but I'm wondering what the outsider perspective would be."

I sit back on the sofa and prop my feet on the table. "I think the people who didn't know you have no idea you were pissed. Sloan, Leslie, and Allie, on the other hand…I think they might suspect you were out of your mind a bit."

Freya groans. "Yeah, I've been texting with Allie this morning. I was so stupid. I knew I shouldn't have drank that tequila. I don't know what I said to that Santino bloke, but he texted me this morning, too. I don't even remember giving him my number."

I stiffen and level her with a glare. "What did he say?"

"Nothing. Just that he had fun." She shrugs. "I have absolutely no idea what to do with that, so I haven't responded."

"Good," I reply. "Don't."

Freya frowns at me. "Why not?"

I clear my throat and set my coffee down. "Santino isn't a guy you should be messing about with. Please just trust me on that one."

Freya huffs out a disbelieving laugh. "Who should I be messing about with?"

I exhale heavily. "Well, that's what I came here to talk to you about."

Freya's eyes widen. "Mac?"

"What?" I ask blankly.

"What are you about to say?"

I look from side to side in confusion. "Um, I don't know. What do you think I'm about to say?"

Freya's head tilts, and she nervously watches me while popping a bite of cookie into her mouth, and mumbles, "You're not about to tell me you have feelings for me, right?"

"What?" I bark out loudly with a laugh. "Christ, woman, no! What would make you think that?"

Freya's cheeks flame a bright red. "You're acting weird! I mean, first you ripped me out of the party last night. Then you just got twitchy over the mention of Santino and said you came here to talk to me about whom I should be messing about with! If this was an episode of *Heartland*, you'd be a cowboy about ready to drop down on one knee and propose!"

"For fuck's sake, get out of your Netflix fantasies. I'm here to talk to you about something real."

Freya flips her wet hair off of her shoulder. "Believe me, you proposing to me is sooo not in my fantasies."

"Good," I reply sharply.

"I couldn't even imagine," Freya adds.

"Good!" I snap again.

"I could laugh just thinking about it."

"All right!" I roar angrily and turn to face her. "Christ, woman, I'm trying to do something nice for you, and you're driving me so mental, I'm about to shove a pillow over your face to shut you up for a damn minute!"

Freya pulls her lips into her mouth and shrugs helplessly. "Speak then. I'll be quiet. Promise."

I exhale heavily. "I want to help you with that barista fellow you fancy near your work."

"Javier?"

I nod.

"How?"

I rub my hands down my thighs. "Well, you said you're shite at talking to men, and I think I can help you with that because, contrary to what you may think, I am, in fact, a man."

"How can you help me?"

"I can train you," I reply simply.

"So like, you want to be my love coach?" Freya bursts out laughing and nearly slops her coffee on her legs.

I clench my jaw in frustration. "Christ, I should have known you'd make me feel daft about this."

Her entire body shakes with her giggles. "Well, it sounds ridiculous!"

"I thought it might help. You're all bent out of shape about your upcoming birthday. Maybe going out on a proper date would help you lighten up a bit."

Freya's humour disappears. "You think I need to lighten up?"

"No," I respond and reach over to rest my hand on her leg reassuringly. "I think you're great. You know that, Cookie. But I also think you've been cooped up with me for the past year, and I hate to think I'm holding you back from something or someone you want to pursue."

Freya ponders my response, which makes me hope she's finally starting to take me seriously.

"What did you have in mind?" she finally asks.

I shrug. "Why don't you tell me a bit about him first?"

Freya pulls her legs up into a pretzel and turns to face me, her eyes lighting up like I've never seen them light up before. "His name is Javier. He's from Madrid, and he's magic."

I have to fight back the urge to roll my eyes. "Okay. So why exactly can't you talk to him?"

"I don't know." She begins waving her hands by her ears, trying to cool them down. "I suppose because the first time we had a proper conversation, he thought I didn't speak English."

I hit her with a disbelieving look. "Come again?"

"True story," she replies sadly. "After I'd been going to the shop for a few weeks, he casually asked me where I was from. After stuttering over my words, I finally puked out Cornwall because I apparently couldn't remember my village's name at the time, and he responded with, 'Oh, I thought you were Danish and just learning English.'"

My jaw drops. "He didn't say that."

"He did," she says with a wee wobble in her voice. "It was months before I could go back there for coffee."

"Christ, I'm impressed you returned after that type of awkwardness."

"I'm chubby. We're resilient when we need to be."

I shake my head. "Would you stop with the body shaming you do to yourself? That's your first problem."

Freya jerks away from me. "I don't consider it body shaming."

"What do you consider it then?"

"Calling it like it is. I'm not a stick figure, and I'm okay with that. But I don't like that we have to tiptoe around these labels society has put out there. If you have eyeballs, the game is up. I'm chubby."

"Well, do you think chubby is beautiful?" I ask, quite certain I already know her answer.

Freya opens her mouth to answer, but no words come out.

"See?" I reply knowingly and shake my head in disappointment. "You're body shaming yourself, even if you don't realise it. If you can't admit that chubby can easily be bonnie, then I think I've figured out your first lesson."

I stand up off the sofa.

"What are you doing?" Freya asks, staring up at me.

I hold out my hand. "Come on. We're going shopping."

Freya

"So what do you want me to do exactly?" I ask as I stand inside the dressing room area of Debenhams—a department store on Oxford Street that took us nearly thirty minutes to drive to.

Mac stretches out on the long, mauve-coloured duvet and gestures to the curtained-off changing area. "Put on the fancy dress the nice lady put in there and then come out and show me."

"Why?" I whine, seriously hating that Mac had an entire conversation with the saleswoman about what he wanted her to pull for me, and I wasn't allowed any input whatsoever. I went to design school for bleddy sake!

Mac hits me with a serious look. "Freya, don't question the teacher. I thought you said you were a good student when you were wee."

My brows furrow. "I was."

He waves me off with a patronising flick of the wrists. "Then off you go."

With a tiny growl of frustration, I turn and immerse myself in the quietness of the changing area and set about stripping off my clothes. I didn't even wear proper underwear for the type of dress he's chosen. The dress is a total Spanx-necessary garment. I can't believe I let Mac talk me into coming here with him. I must be rufazrats… or hungover…if I'm agreeing to let him be my love coach. What the hell have I got myself into?

And what's his plan for putting me in a short dress? I'm going to look ridiculous. I know how to dress my body, and tea-length dresses are my style. Tea-length dresses and flowy skirts with pinup model curls.

"Cookie," Mac calls from the other side of the curtain, and I freeze with the dress stuck over my head.

"What?" I mumble through the fabric.

"What size shoe do you wear?"

"Um, a six and a half?" I reply with a frown.

"Perfect," Mac says and shoves a shoebox under the curtain.

"Dear God, please don't let me kill this man today," I state out loud and continue to wrestle the dress down over my body.

I slide the fabric into place and cringe over how formfitting it is before I even have the zipper pulled up. It's a simple shimmery black dress, but it has stringy straps that crisscross over my chest, and the hem cuts well above my knees. It isn't my style at all, and I hate my friend for bringing me here.

"Do you have the shoes on yet?" Mac asks, and it's like he's in the damn room with me because his voice is so close. "You're taking ages."

"Have patience, you pushy ox!" I snap and angrily drop down on the bench to put the gorgeous booties on. I slide them on, and my purple painted toes peek out the front.

I'm just standing up when light bursts through the open curtain as my giant friend comes barrelling in. "Christ, woman, are you sewing the damn dress on your body?"

I hold the back of my dress together in a vain attempt at some modesty. "I'd like to see how fast you could get a dress and heels on, you big bully. I can't even zip this one, so you might as well send that sales assistant out to find me a bigger size with more bolts of fabric to cover my girth."

"Turn around," he demands and twirls his fingers to force me to face the mirror as he steps up behind me and struggles with the zipper.

"See? It's too tight," I whine, feeling slightly mortified.

"It's supposed to be tight," he murmurs, and his warm breath sends goosebumps down my bare arms.

I glance at the pair of us in the mirror. Even when I'm wearing heels, Mac towers over me, making me feel surprisingly petite. I've never dated a bloke who made me feel small. Perhaps I should start. My eyes move from him just as he gets the zipper all the way up, and the reflection staring back at me is surprising.

The dress is more fitted than a lot of the clothes I buy, and my legs actually don't look too bad when I'm wearing heels. I thought I knew how to dress my body type, but I honestly never would have picked this gown out on my own, and it doesn't look half bad.

"Well," Mac states, stepping back and eyeing me in the mirror. "What do you think?"

I shrug. "It's a beautiful dress."

"Aye, sure…" Mac says, silently encouraging me to continue.

"The fabric is very luxurious."

He nods in agreement.

"The bodice seams pull me in perfectly. The shoes are a nice touch."

He harrumphs under his breath, and I swivel to face him. "What? What am I saying that's so wrong? I'm telling you I like the dress and shoes. What more do you want?"

"I want you to remark about how *you* look in them," he snaps and shoves his hair back off his forehead. "Remark on your own body. Your own features. If you want to be able to form complete sentences with your coffee shop lad, you need to be able to form a complete sentence about yourself first."

Mac rushes into my space, grabs me by my shoulders, and turns me to face the mirror again. "See how nice your hair looks draped over your bare shoulders. Your skin, freckles included, is striking, aye?" His hands slide down my arms. "The creamy colour of your skin is attractive and lush. Sensual when exposed."

His hands slip around to cup my waist, and my ears burst into flames.

"Now, see how this dress shows off your shape? It doesn't hide your tits, which is good because you have some damn nice tits on you, Cookie. You'd do well to see them as a virtue rather than a fault."

"And your legs," he says, and my insides clench when his hands slide from my waist to my hips and then down the outsides of my thighs, causing a riot of goosebumps to erupt over my skin. "They're fucking bonnie, and any lad would be right lucky to have them wrapped around him."

His gaze lifts from my legs to my flabbergasted eyes, and his heated look makes my nipples tighten. "Your size and your shape are bonnie, and you don't need to trip over your words in front of a guy you fancy because you should never doubt how beautiful *you* are." He swallows a seemingly uncomfortable lump in his throat, and adds, "But even if I can't cure you of this warped view you have about your body, you need to remember you're funny, and smart, and talented, with loads of other qualities that make the fact that you're drop-dead gorgeous a really nice perk. Any man would be lucky to talk to you."

Mac finishes his rant and stares fiercely into my eyes without an ounce of humour in his expression. Both of our chests rise and fall with the intensity of this exchange, and I feel all the oxygen being sucked out of the small space. My eyes flick to Mac's lips for only a moment, but that one shift in attention breaks the spell we're both under, and he steps back, pulling the curtain open.

"Ring it all up," Mac says to the sales lady who's walking into the dressing area with a pile of clothes over her arm. "I'm buying."

Mac exits quickly, and I find myself gasping for air as everything he said sinks in. I then realise with great surprise that my best friend just took my breath away.

CHAPTER 6

Freya

GOING INTO WORK ON MONDAY IS NERVE-WRACKING BECAUSE I didn't see Mac again this weekend after our little shopping excursion. It's kind of strange because he usually comes over to watch Netflix on Sunday nights. But his texts seemed like he was busy with something, so I let it go.

I'm doing my best to stop thinking about our dressing room encounter when his voice nearly sends me through the ceiling.

"Hey, Cookie, it's field trip time."

"Saints preserve us!" I exclaim, lifting my hands from my sewing machine and placing them over my terrified ears. "I didn't even hear you come up the stairs!"

"You must have been too focused on your work," Mac says, glancing down at the mess I have in front of me. "Come on, it's time for a break."

I push back from my desk and stand up. "Where are we going?"

"You'll see," he replies and then glances down at my legs. "Trousers again? Did my lesson mean nothing to you?"

"It did. I'm…working," I reply stiffly. "That dress you bought for me isn't exactly work attire. In fact, I still don't know why you bought that dress for me, anyway."

"Every lass should have a sexy date-night dress," he says with a cheery lift of his brows as we make our way down the stairs.

"Where are you two off to?" Allie asks as she strides into the shop from whatever marketing meeting she was attending.

"I wish I knew," I reply as Mac grabs my hand and pulls me out the door, barely glancing at Allie.

When we step outside, I yank my hand out of his and stop in my tracks. "Seriously, Mac, where are we going?"

"To get coffee, of course." He shoots me a lopsided smile.

I shake my head. "No, Mac."

"Come on, Cookie," he says, grabbing my hand again to drag me along.

"No, no, no," I beg and pull backwards against his pressure, but it's no use. He's way stronger than me.

Mac laughs at my resistance. "I need to meet this coffee snob and make sure he's good enough for you."

"No, you don't," I plead, and my ears begin to boil. "You really don't. I'm not ready for this. We've only had one lesson!"

"You're ready," his voice is firm. "I'm going to help you, so no worries."

"Yes, worries. Lots and lots of worries!"

Mac practically shoves me through the coffee shop door, and I stumble to a halt before running into a patron who's holding a piping hot cup of coffee. I turn on my heels and glare at Mac accusingly. He rubs the back of his neck and offers me a rueful smile. I quickly glance over my shoulder and breathe a sigh of relief when I don't see Javier.

"He's not here, so we can go now," I state and make my way towards the exit.

Suddenly, a Spanish voice booms, "Freya!"

I freeze in my tracks, my eyes wide on Mac as my ears burst into flames. Mac has the cheek to look amused, and it takes all of my strength not to punch him right in that smug face of his.

I plaster a smile on my face and turn to face Javier. "Hiyaaa," I manage to croak out without screwing up the pronunciation too bad.

"Happy Monday. You look lovely today," Javier says and gestures to my yellow top.

"Greatest, thanks," I reply and then cringe while balling my hands up into fists.

I feel Mac's warm hand on my back as he slowly pushes me towards the counter. His breath is hot on my ear as he whispers, "You're smart, funny, and fucking bonnie. Imagine he's a Canadian cowboy from *Heartland* and go get him."

A small laugh bubbles up my throat at that last part.

When I finally reach the coffee counter, Javier eyes Mac curiously. "Who is your friend here, my Freya?"

Did he just say, 'my Freya'?

"Brother," Mac says crisply, reaching out to shake Javier's hand. "I'm her brother."

You'd have to be blind to miss Javier's confused look over Mac's Scottish accent as he replies, "Pleasure to meet you."

"We'll take a black coffee and a large iced coffee with extra milk, thanks," Mac says in a clipped tone and then turns to me. "You pay, sis. I'll go grab a table."

Mac winks a ridiculous wink at me and retreats towards a small counter by the window. I turn a stiff look back at Javier.

Come now, Freya, you're beautiful, smart, and clever. You can do this!

"How...was your weekend?" I ask and mentally pat myself on the back for stringing together a coherent sentence.

"It was excellent," Javier replies with a smile as he sets about pouring our two cups of coffee. "I made cheese."

My brows lift from his unexpected response. "You…made cheese?"

He purses his lips and nods. "Do you like the cheese?"

"Who doesn't like the cheese?" I bark out an unattractive laugh and then turn a mortified face to Mac, who gives me a way-too-eager thumbs up.

Javier snaps a lid on the first cup. "I could show you the cheese."

"Sorry?" I ask and begin nervously tugging on my ear.

"If you wanted to come to my cheese hut."

"You have a cheese hut?" I ask flatly, so confused by the bizarre topic of cheese and the thought of a human being actually having a facility to make his own cheese.

"Yes. Cheese and homemade wine. If you want to partake sometime."

He pushes the prepared cups of coffee towards me, and I open my mouth to reply, but I suddenly feel like all the spit has been sucked out of my mouth. What used to be saliva is now kitty litter. Dry kitty litter that makes it impossible for me to respond.

Out of nowhere, Mac appears beside me. "Just to be clear, are you asking my dear sister out on a date?"

Javier turns a confused look at Mac and nods nervously. "I am."

"She'd love to go," Mac rushes out and drops a tenner on the counter while grabbing the two cups of coffee. "How's tomorrow night?"

Javier smiles at me. "Tomorrow night is good for me if it is good for you."

"Great, she'll text you tonight," Mac replies and then shoulder pushes me away from the counter. "Let's go, sis."

I smile and wave uncomfortably at Javier. Then, before I can stop myself, I dip my head into a bow before turning and following Mac out the door.

When we're finally out of sight from the windows, I grab my ears in agony. "Oh, good God, I just bowed to Javier."

Mac's nose scrunches. "I saw that."

"Why the fuck did I bow? Why couldn't I have at least curtsied like a lady? Given an ounce of a sign that I'm a delicate female? But no, not Freya Cook. She decides to bow like a proper bloke. I'm doomed!" I run my hands through my hair and squeeze the roots in agony.

"You're not doomed," Mac replies, rolling his eyes.

"And you're my brother now?" I say with a cringe. "Where the bleddy hell did that come from?"

Mac shrugs. "What? We're both redheads. It's not that big of a stretch."

"The thought of you and I coming from the same gene pool is a very big stretch." I fan my ears as Mac eyes me harshly.

"We're both wee stunners, Cook."

I bark out a laugh because I've seen photos of his family back in Dundonald. His sister, Tilly, is super model beautiful. Tall and thin with silky strawberry blond hair. His dad is the mirror image of Mac sans tattoos. And his mum is so cute, she made me question my allegiance to my heterosexual identity. Honestly, his whole family looks like a successful genetic experiment in breeding handsome gingers.

Mac does not appreciate my laughter as he adds firmly, "We could be related."

"Stop saying we're related!" I exclaim and then reach out to take my coffee. "It's creepy."

Mac winces. "Yeah, it is a wee bit weird." He gestures back towards the coffee shop. "So, that's what does it for you?"

"Who? Javier? Yes, I think he's fit. Why, what do you mean?"

"Nothing, I'm just shocked is all," Mac says with a shrug of his shoulders as he pops the lid off his coffee and blows inside the cup. "I didn't know the Luigi brother look is what revs your engine."

My jaw drops. "He doesn't look like Luigi," I shriek. "He looks nice!"

"Aye, you're right," Mac says, flashing me that dimple he has

58

beneath his ginger-tinted, five o'clock shadow. "He's a wee lad, so he's Mario at best."

"Shut up, you cow!" I retort with annoyance. I reach out to wallop him on the shoulder, but he hops into the street to avoid my attack. "What happened to 'everyone is bonnie in their own way'?"

"I didn't say he's not bonnie. I was just surprised, that's all." Mac eyes me curiously for a moment and then falls back into step with me. "Is it the accent that does it for you?"

I scrunch my lips off to the side. "I don't know. It certainly doesn't hurt. He just looks like a real man, you know?"

"What the hell do I look like?" Mac asks, looking mildly offended.

I shrug. "Like a ginger version of a real man?"

He nods, seemingly pleased by my answer. "Well, whatever gets your knickers in a twist, Cookie."

"Please don't say knickers to me," I reply with a groan. "It's too weird."

Mac huffs out a small laugh, and we continue walking for a silent moment before I ask, "So how in the hell am I going to be ready for a date tomorrow night? I think the only reason I didn't make a complete fool of myself is because I was distracted by cheese. I love cheese."

Mac nods thoughtfully. "Don't worry. We're going to have a two-a-day workout, and I'll come up with a great training session for tonight."

"Oh, joy. I can't wait."

CHAPTER 7

Mac

THE CHEESE BAR.

Only Freya Cook could get me to set up her next lesson in a place like this. Though, I do love cheese. How can you not? However, going to a cheese bar with a burd is not something I ever would have seen myself doing. My history with women is of the fun and casual variety, usually involving minimal clothing, but I'd do just about anything for my Cookie.

I'm walking towards the restaurant that's north of Covent Garden where I told Freya to meet me when a group of young lads stops me outside for a selfie. I oblige, hoping their attention won't raise more attention, and then politely excuse myself.

Getting recognised isn't a new thing for me. Being a big, tattooed, ginger footballer doesn't exactly help me blend in with the crowd. But ever since Bethnal Green was bumped up to Premier League, our fame has definitely seen an increase. I don't play football for the fame, though. I'm in it for the honour of playing the greatest sport in the world. As a wee lad, my grandad all but beat into me what an important game it was and that he would disown me if I wasn't a Rangers fan. He's a wiry old git and probably my favourite human, even if he barely forgave me for never landing a contract with his beloved Scottish team.

I do have other aspirations outside of football, though. My mum always told me I couldn't fall back on athletics, so I went to university and got a degree in computer science. I do continuing education in the off-season just so I'm not completely out of the loop when I eventually retire.

The sun is beginning to set as I walk into Seven Dials Market, which is a high-end, indoor food court of sorts with two levels of places to eat and canteen-style seating in the centre. It's also home to this magical place called The Cheese Bar.

When I heard about the coffee guy's cheese hut, I thought it might be a good idea for Freya to brush up on her cheese knowledge. She always told me about what a good student she was in school, so I figured she can look at this like cramming for an exam. Along with cheese knowledge, I'm hoping we can cover some first date experiences. I might not take a lot of girls on formal dates, but my mum taught me how to treat a lady, so I know how it works.

I told Freya to doll herself up and meet me here like we were meeting for a proper date. She seemed terrified.

I love it.

To be truthful, I'm enjoying the new development in my friendship with Freya. She's normally so confident and sure of herself, and she's always having a go at me for something I do that's barbaric. Call me crazy, but it's nice to be better at something than she is for a change.

The Cheese Bar is a bright and cheery spot with a large square counter in the centre that features a conveyor belt of colourful plates of cheese with glass domes over the top. The place is nearly full, but I manage to grab us a couple of seats towards the end of the bar.

I picked up a few items for Freya, which I set down on the floor beneath my seat, and look towards the doorway to see Freya walk in right on time. I wave her over and can't help the devilish smile on my face as I watch her make her way to me. She looks nervous but nice in her fitted green and white-checked blouse with a pink jumper over top and a wee pair of black shorts. She still has her signature vintage style to her, but the outfit is different than her others.

I swivel my stool to face her full on as she approaches, and my gaze can't help but lower to her legs. "You follow directions quite well, Cookie."

She rolls her eyes and slips onto the open stool beside me, placing herself squarely between my legs. "I went shopping. Let's not make a thing out of it."

My smile grows. "Freya Cook, does this mean you're actually starting to listen to me?"

She shoots me a warning scowl, and I swear her greenish-brown eyes darken. "Maclay Logan, I just said let's not make a thing of it. Are you trying to get me to thump you?"

My shoulders shake with silent laughter, and I lean in to softly reply, "Aye, maybe that's my kink."

She elbows me square in the chest, and it only makes me laugh harder. Then I reach down to grab something. "Maybe this will make up for my cheekiness." I hold up a bouquet of pink carnations.

Freya's jaw drops. "What's this?"

I shrug. "We're on a date. Dates bring flowers."

"I was trying to forget about the date part," she murmurs, shooting me a nervous look as she takes the flowers from me.

"It's a practice date but still a date. Pretend you fancy me so we can work out all your kinks before your real one tomorrow."

"Can we stop using the word kink?" she asks as she brings the bouquet to her nose. The pink brightens the freckles on her face as a soft smile plays on the corners of her mouth. "Pink carnations are my favourite."

"Aye, I know," I reply, noting that her ears are turning a pink shade before my very eyes. I move to face forward on my stool. "I've heard your ramblings about Carrie Bradshaw enough times to take a hint. I'm very trainable, you know."

I feel Freya's eyes on me as I glance at the cheese passing by on the conveyor belt. "You actually listened to that?"

I shrug dismissively. "Not the point, Cookie. The point is, I'm a lad who brought you flowers. The correct response would be…"

"Thank you," she quickly spits out.

I nod, impressed. "Good. See? You're already better at dating than you think."

A server comes over to take our drink orders. Freya gets chardonnay, as I knew she would, and I request a pint for myself. When the guy returns with a glass of wine, I stop Freya before she takes a sip and reach down to grab the wee gift bag I brought.

"More gifts?" she asks in shock. "I highly doubt Javier will give me flowers and a present."

"If he's worth a shite, he will," I reply with a frown. "Just open it and don't question your coach."

She pulls out the tissue paper the gift shop was kind enough to provide and extracts a kitten coffee mug. On the side, there is a picture of a cat and thick black text that reads, "I work hard so my cat can have a better life."

She smiles at the saying. "I bleddy love this!"

"I knew you would." I reach out for her wine glass. "I washed the mug already, so I'll pour your drink in it because I know that's how you like to take your wine."

I dump her wine into the mug and hand it back to Freya who looks so touched, I think I see a shimmer of tears in her eyes.

She falters over her words as she cups the mug to her chest. "I don't know what to say."

I roll my eyes because she's getting soft on me. "I'm doing this because you need to learn how to handle some flattery. You're attractive and fun, Cookie. If your coffee guy is worth anything, he should say and do nice things for you. And I want to be sure you know how to respond appropriately when he does."

She nods thoughtfully and sets her mug down. "So what's appropriate?"

"Thank you is always a good start," I reply firmly, propping my elbows on the counter.

"Thank you."

I smile and wink at her. "You're welcome. Also, I hope this guy is someone who pays attention to you. You've been going to the coffee shop for months you said? Does he know how you take your coffee?"

"Yes, he does!" She practically squeals with delight. "Large iced coffee—"

"With extra milk," I finish and waggle my brows at her playfully.

She gets an uneasy look on her face for a few seconds but then quickly brushes it off. "Okay, be gracious and thankful for flattery. Got it. What's next?"

"A lesson in cheese," I reply and gesture towards the loads of plates passing us by. "Let's grab a few plates, do some sampling, and ask our server some questions. Consider this a cramming session for your big test tomorrow."

Freya's eyes light with excitement as we set about picking out various cheese samplings. I have no damn clue what most of the stuff is, but I'm keen to try anything. Even the smelly cheese that has weeds rubbed all over it. Freya snort laughs when I spit it out because it tastes fishy.

After the cheesemonger—an expert in selling cheese—gives us a lesson on everything we've tasted, I realise that I'm two pints in and actually having a nice time on this mock date.

We order one more round and have eaten our fill in cheese when Freya says, "Mac, can I ask why you consider yourself an expert in dating?"

I frown at her question. "What do you mean?"

"Well, I've given you all this power over my dating life, but we rarely ever speak about our dating experiences. How do I know you're not an even bigger disaster than me?"

I level Freya with a flat look. "What do you want to know?"

She shrugs her shoulders. "What was your last relationship like?"

A pang of unease hits me because what Freya is asking isn't exactly a short story. There's really no reason to hide it from my best mate, though, so I tell her what I can.

"I don't really do relationships, but I had this sort of casual situation with a woman I met when I first started playing football for Bethnal Green. It went on for a couple of years."

"A couple of years?" Freya barks out in shock, her eyes wide and disbelieving. "Who was she? Where did you meet her? When did it end? How have you never mentioned to me before that you had a two-year relationship with a woman?"

I roll my eyes at her last comment. "Her name is Cami, and she was the photographer they hired to shoot me and Roan when we signed on with the club. I didn't mention her because it ended around the time I met you, so I didn't really see the point."

Freya processes this information and then asks, "Why did it end?"

I shrug dismissively. "She met someone."

"Met someone?" She gapes at me. "So you two were together for two years, and you weren't exclusive?"

I cringe and rub my palms down my thighs. "Not exactly. We went out occasionally, but it was mostly physical."

"Oh, like a friends-with-benefits situation?" Freya pries.

"I guess you could call it that." I shift uncomfortably in my seat because this isn't a subject I like to discuss. "I wasn't surprised when she ended it, though, because she was always going on about wanting to settle down with someone serious. The guy she met is a lawyer, so I guess that's what she was looking for at the time."

"So, she was with you for two years and didn't think you were long-term material?" Freya asks. Her brows pinch together in the middle, and I think I see an edge of protectiveness in her posture.

I shrug. "You know what my life is like. I travel a lot, which doesn't exactly make me good boyfriend material. None of it really mattered anyway because I didn't want anything serious either. My focus is one hundred percent on football."

Freya ponders my response for a while, and then asks, "So were you in love with her?"

"Christ, no," I bark out defensively. "Cami was just sex."

Freya wilts and gets a sad sort of expression on her face. "You slept with her for two years, and you never fell in love?"

I eye her seriously. "Love isn't a requirement for sex, you know."

Freya swallows, and her face blanches. "Sure."

I watch her carefully. "You do know that, right?"

"Of course I do!" she snaps and then takes a drink of wine from her kitten mug.

"Cookie," I state and wait until she looks at me. "Are the only guys you've slept with ones you were in love with?"

"We're not talking about me!" Freya retorts. "I wanted to hear about your last dating experience, and I have, so thank you for sharing."

I stare back at her and can read her like a bloody open book. Freya thinks she needs love in order to have sex. Maybe that's been her problem all along. If she thinks she needs to be in love with every man she is sexually attracted to before they can roll around in the sack, she's putting a lot of bloody pressure on herself. Maybe casual sex is actually what Freya needs more than dating advice.

I may have to draw up a new lesson plan for her.

CHAPTER 8

Mac

"I'M COMING OVER," FREYA BARKS INTO THE PHONE LINE before I even have a chance to say hello. Her voice sounds shaky, making my entire body tense.

"Freya, what's going on?" I ask, my voice low and steady. "What happened?"

"It was awful. Awful!" she cries into the line.

"Did he do something to you?"

"I'll tell you when I get there," she answers with a sob.

"Freya Cook, tell me right now. Are you okay? Are you hurt?" I ask, anger coursing through me at the thought of that bawbag hurting my Freya.

"My pride is in shambles," she cries, and my body relaxes instantly. "I'm in your neighbourhood, and I'm coming over."

"Aye, sure, I'll see you soon."

A few minutes later, the bell to my flat rings. I step out of my bedroom located just off the kitchen and yell up to Roan, "It's for me." He and Allie are shut off in his bedroom on the second level, so it's not like he would have come out to answer the door anyway.

I jog downstairs and unlock the door to find my friend standing on the threshold, looking like a beautiful wee mess. She's wearing a tight skirt that hits just above her knees with a leopard-print blouse and a black belt that nips her in at the waist. Her red hair is curled and swept over one of her shoulders, and her black eyeliner is smudged around her eyes.

In a breath, she throws herself against my chest and groans loudly. "It was awful, Mac. Your lessons were no help."

"What happened?" I ask, wrapping my arms around her and hugging her close.

She sniffs and looks up, swiping at her damp eyes. "I just experienced the absolute worst kiss of my life."

For some reason, my jaw clenches at the mention of the barista kissing her. Then I remember that Allie and Roan can probably hear everything Freya's saying, so I grab her hand and pull her inside. I lead her up the stairs, bypassing the living room, and head right to my bedroom.

"Sit down and tell me everything that happened," I state, gesturing to the rumpled, plaid duvet on my unmade bed.

She perches herself on the edge. "Well, the date was going fine. We were in his cheese hut in some remote place in North London where I thought I might get stabbed."

"Christ," I mumble under my breath.

"It really was going okay. I didn't wear my hot first date dress because I didn't think it was cheese hut chic, you know? Anyways, I still felt good about myself, and I was actually forming complete sentences, and we sampled some of the cheeses." She runs her palms over thighs nervously, her face wincing like what she's about to say is going to be bad. "Well, there was this parmesan he had me try that made my mouth particularly dry. And I'd only had one glass of his homemade wine, which tasted curiously like cat piss, so I was dying of thirst. As we continued talking, I could feel the corners of my mouth caked in dried spit. It was not sexy. Not at all."

She exhales heavily, and adds, "I was about to excuse myself to go to the loo so I could suck down some tap water when he had the nerve to go in for a kiss!"

I run a hand through my hair and grip the back of my neck. "That doesn't sound good."

"It wasn't good. It was bad. Very, very bad." She scrubs her hands over her face and smudges a bit more of her makeup. "But I figured, in for a penny, in for a pound, right? So I returned the kiss and sort of tried to press my tongue into his mouth, not realising his teeth were closed. He gasped and jerked away, bumping into this mighty cheese shelf where he has some precious three-year-aged cheddar he got from his nan's farm in Spain and smuggled into the country. The shelf toppled over, and the cheese fell apart all over the dirt floor. It was horrifying. Javier dropped onto his knees, and I think I actually heard him weeping."

"Weeping?" I ask disbelievingly.

"Yes, weeping!" she replies, throwing her arms up. "I was so mortified that I got the hell out of there! I jumped in my car, stopped at a corner shop, drank a gallon of water, and came here."

"Christ," I murmur under my breath.

"I know. It was horrible," she says with defeat and then glares at me. "You didn't go over kissing with me at all, so I blame you entirely."

"You didn't tell me you don't know how to kiss!" I reply defensively. "I thought you just had trouble talking to lads."

"Well, considering I can count on one hand the number of men I've locked lips with, I think it's safe to say I don't know what the bleddy hell I'm doing."

With a heavy sigh, I drop down on the bed beside her, shaking my head and staring at the floor. "The kiss couldn't have been that bad."

"It was," she mumbles defeatedly.

"There's no way," I argue, glancing at her lips. "You have nice lips. Perfect for kissing."

"It doesn't matter," she replies, her lower lip quivering slightly. "I am incapable of using them. I'm a wanker."

"You're not a wanker."

"I'm a lip wanker."

"How do you know he's not the lip wanker?" I ask with a gruff reply. "Maybe you just didn't have the right partner. Any man with a cheese hut doesn't sound like he's kissing a lot of burds."

She turns a flat look at me. "I promise you, Mac. Even if I had the right partner, I would be crap."

Now I'm getting angry. "Prove it."

Her brows pinch together. "I'm not about to kiss my hand or something stupid like that just so you can take photos of me and use them for blackmail the next time you're cross at me."

"Aye, not your hand," I reply, taking a deep breath before adding, "Practice with me."

"Me," she repeats with a huff. "Me, who?"

"Kiss me and I'll show you that it wasn't you. It was him."

"I'm not going to kiss you!" Freya shrieks, her voice rising to a high pitch at the end. "You're mental!"

"I'm not mental. I'm your best mate, and I'm telling you to kiss me so I can show you how it's done properly."

"It would be too weird," Freya says with a nervous laugh as she shuffles to the corner of the bed, putting space between us even though there is a glimmer of intrigue in her eyes.

"It wouldn't be weird." I scoot over to her. "I'm a lad. You're a lass. Kissing is natural."

She swallows nervously and glances down at my lips. "You better not be taking the piss."

"I'm not taking the piss," I reply, my voice dropping lower as I shift closer to her so our legs are touching. She smells faintly of cheese. Curiously, my heartbeat increases.

Freya goes very still. "Are you sure about this, Mac?"

I take a minute to glance down at her lips. They are a nice rosy hue from the lipstick she had on earlier and rest in a perfect pout. How did I never notice how kissable they are until right this second? There's no way she's bad at kissing with lips like hers.

"Live a wee bit, Cook," I state softly and lick my lips in preparation. I lean in, and her eyes whirl with worry but also something resembling anticipation. I have to fight back my smile.

I run my fingers along her cheek before combing them through her hair and pulling her face to mine. With one last breath, I touch my lips to hers, and she lets out a surprised squeak that makes me smile.

Despite my grin, I move my lips against hers, trying to get a feel for the softness and warmth. Her lips feel just as good as I expected, so I bring my other hand up to her face in hopes of coaxing her to relax into this. She's being a cautious kisser. I hate cautious kissers. Kissing shouldn't be safe. It's an animalistic act. It's connecting on a fundamental level that humans should embrace with their base instincts, not their minds. I know she had a bad experience earlier tonight, but I'm her best mate. She doesn't need to worry with me.

Without warning, I plunge my tongue into her mouth, and she lets out another sound that isn't quite a squeak. A moan, maybe? She grips my forearms as I cradle her face in my hands and continue to explore her technique. I'm doing everything I can to give her something to respond to, and I almost growl with pride when her tongue slips out and gently moves against mine. *That's it, Cookie. Let go. Let your gut take over and just give in.*

With a shuddered breath, I tilt my head and deepen the kiss. She responds in kind, her lips sliding over mine as my tongue draws hers out to play. Truly play. Our tongues stroke each other in a perfect rhythm that's ramping up to something resembling indecency. When her hand falls from my forearm onto my lap, and her fingers brush over my groin, I realise it's not just our kiss that's become indecent.

I pull back with a grunt, tearing my eyes from her lips and doing everything I can to ignore the damn near painful throbbing inside my shorts. I hunch over my lap, propping my elbows on my knees to hide my state.

"Christ, woman," I croak and clear my throat, shifting away to give myself some space before my cock decides to spring through my jersey shorts.

"Was that bad?" she asks, her large breasts rising and falling with each heavy breath she takes.

I turn my back to her, willing my body to calm the fuck down before I come off looking more inexperienced than her. "Not bad. Good."

"Good?" she asks excitedly as she shuffles over next to me.

I leap off the bed and run my hand through my hair. *Old lady in a garden. Picture an old lady all sweaty in a garden, Maclay.*

"Your coffee shop guy is a wank," I bark out of nowhere. "You're a great kisser. End of lesson."

I chance looking over my shoulder at Freya, who looks confused.

"Okaaay." She chews her lower lip. "So what do I do about it then?"

I exhale heavily and purse my lips in annoyance. "If he's not an idiot, he'll call you tomorrow and apologise. If he is an idiot, you're better off without him."

She nods, absorbing my advice, and then glances at the clock on my dresser. "It's late. I suppose I should go."

I nod, thinking a bit of space from her is probably a good idea. When she stands, I conceal myself enough to walk her out of my bedroom without too much embarrassment. I see her safely to her car and reassure her one more time that she's not a bad kisser. Then she drives away.

My mind is whirling as I lie on my bed thinking about how Freya is not a bad kisser. In fact, she's quite good. Too good apparently because my hand is inside my shorts and I'm stroking myself while picturing my best mate's lips wrapped around my cock instead of that idiot's fucking shite cheese.

Fuck me, what have I done?

CHAPTER 9

Freya

I T'S DARK WHEN I FEEL THE GENTLE BRUSH OF FINGERTIPS ALONG my shoulder. The sensation is delicious, and it causes my body to roll into the mattress with need as goosebumps erupt all over me. When I finally come to, I turn onto my back to see Mac standing in my bedroom.

Shirtless.

My mind swims with confusion over why Mac would be in my bedroom in the middle of the night, wearing nothing but a pair of shorts. What is he doing here? And why is he looking at me like that?

As if answering me, he slowly reaches out and peels back the duvet to reveal my body. My apparently very naked body.

What the bleddy hell happened to my pyjamas?

I sit up to cover myself, but Mac shakes his head and presses his hand against my shoulder to lay me back down. His eyes break away from mine and rake hungrily over every square inch of my flesh.

My chest heaves, but I am surprisingly not embarrassed. I'm aroused.

"Don't ever cover yourself up in front of me, Freya," Mac says, his voice low and dripping with wickedness. "Your body deserves to be appreciated." The bed dips as he kneels beside me.

"Is this another lesson?" I ask, my voice a mere whisper.

"Aye," Mac replies in his husky Scottish accent as he drags the backs of his fingers from my shoulder, down my side, and up my belly. "I want to kiss more than those lips of yours. I want to taste all of you."

"Taste me?" I belt out unattractively, but Mac doesn't seem to care. His rough hand cups the weight of my breast before he dips his mouth and captures my nipple between his lips.

"Oh, my sweet heavens!" I exclaim as his assault on the sensitive nub causes a sharp stirring between my legs. A stirring that feels more intense than I expected. "Mac, this is wrong. We're friends."

"It's because we're friends that I can do this to you," Mac growls and bites down on my breast, eliciting a harsh shriek from my lips. As soon as the burn from his bite stops, he sucks harshly while reaching out to cup my other breast.

Manhandling them.

Like a couple of hunks of meat.

It's brilliant.

He shifts his head over and gives the other nipple equal treatment, and my body curls into his touch for more.

When he bites me again, I combust between my legs.

Like eruption combustion explosion.

"Was that a…a…?"

"It's called an orgasm, Freya, and I intend to give you another."

"You do?" I croak, shocked that orgasming from nipple stimulation is even possible.

"Aye," he replies and moves himself over top of me to look into my eyes. "Do you want to taste my cheese?" he asks seriously.

My face falls. "What?"

He tilts his head. "I asked if you want to taste my cheese."

"Why are you talking about cheese? Go back to the tasting me thing."

"You can taste his cheese but not mine?"

Bleep, bleep, bleep, bleep, bleep.

I shoot straight up out of bed, my chest heaving with anxiety as I struggle to catch my breath. I slam my hand on top of my mobile to get my alarm to stop chirping. When I've finally silenced the monstrous device, I look around my room and see absolutely no sign of Mac. My brow pinches as I glance down at my chest and see one of my many long, kitty-themed night shirts right where I left it, covering all my wobbly bits.

"It was a dream," I say with a strange breathy noise. But the pulsing sensation I feel between my legs is most certainly a reality.

"And that is why I can never go get our coffee ever again," I groan to Allie from my upstairs sewing room at Kindred Spirits after unloading my entire sob story.

It's been days since my horrible date with Javier. I tried to keep the details of my embarrassment all to myself, but I've been going absolutely mental over it. Perhaps if Mac wasn't avoiding me, I wouldn't have felt so desperate to share. But he's been MIA ever since our kiss three nights ago, and I'm too much of a chicken-shit to ask him why.

Because I know why.

My kiss was shit, and he thinks I'm hopeless and doesn't know how to tell me without ruining our friendship.

So now I'm dragging Allie into my dating mess to try to make myself feel better. Of course I'm not telling her about the Mac kissing me part because she would have a field day with that. And I will take the dirty dream I had about him to my grave. *Saints preserve me!*

Allie's legs swing beneath her as she sits on top of my cutting table in an adorable trouser suit and processes everything I shared. "I can't believe you never told me you had a thing for Javier! Why wouldn't you mention that to me?"

I shrug helplessly. "I never talk about my dating life."

"Why not?" she asks, pinning me with a serious look.

I drop my head into my hands. "Because that's not really the narrative I put out there about myself."

"What the hell does that mean?" Allie asks, clearly not getting the picture.

I exhale heavily and sit back in my sewing chair to think about how I can put this into words that don't make me look completely mental. "I prefer being the plucky best friend whom everyone needs for comedic relief. I'm the Sookie to your Lorelai, you know? And I have a great shoulder to cry on when my friends need it. Like when Sloan was going through her divorce. That's what this body was built for," I state, gesturing grandly to my sizeable chest like it's a fluffy pillow for her to fall on. "My love life is nonexistent, and I prefer not to speak about it so I can avoid the sympathetic looks, like the one you're giving me right now."

"It isn't sympathy!" Allie exclaims, her head jerking back defensively. "It's confusion. You're my maid of honour, Freya! I love you. I want to know everything about your life. Not just a pretence you're trying to show me."

I wince at her interpretation. "It's not a pretence. The fact is, I don't crave male attention the way some women do. Sure I get flustered by hot, incestual naked scenes on *Game of Thrones* just as much as the next gal. I mean, I'm not sure why it has to be incest that does it for me. But hey, it's artistically well-shot, so I can appreciate it!"

Allie bursts out laughing and shakes her head. "Freya, what are you talking about?"

"Oh, don't act like that didn't stir your loins," I scoff and continue. "And apart from the very rare crushes I have on Spanish baristas, I don't really fuss over my love life, and I'm happier for it. I love my job. I love my friends. I love my agoraphobic cat. It's plenty for me."

Allie nods thoughtfully. "Of course it is. Let's forget Javier ever existed. We can find a new coffee shop and burn his to the ground."

"Steady on," I chortle, my head pulling back because Allie has a startlingly serious look on her face. "No need to become an arsonist on account of one bad date. Plus, I really want a date for your wedding so I'm not sitting by myself as the sad, single lady all night."

"But you'll have Mac," she says, touching my hand.

"I won't have Mac," I reply with a laugh and pull my hand away. *Especially if he's still not talking to me by then.* "We'll walk down the aisle together as maid of honour and best man. Then he'll be charming the knickers off of some sweet, unsuspecting female while I'll be sitting in the corner like a sad, lonely troll."

"You could never be a troll," Allie states firmly, her brows furrowing angrily. "Why don't you let me set you up with someone?"

"I don't need to be set up," I answer quickly. My friends in Manchester used to try to do the exact same thing, and it's horribly humiliating. "I have another prospect."

"Oh?" Allie asks, a curious glint in her eyes. "Who?"

I wince and mumble under my breath, "Santino."

"The team lawyer?" she barks in surprise.

"He's been texting me since that party, and I think he'd be a nice enough date. He basically knows everybody, so I suspect he'd fit in well. Mac doesn't care for him for some odd reason, though, so I'm not going to tell him unless our date goes well."

Allie frowns. "I thought Mac liked everybody?"

I shrug. "Not him, apparently."

"So when is this date?"

"Tomorrow night," I reply, and a swirl of nerves takes flight in my belly at the reminder. I'm hoping that since Mac trained me to date Javier, the same rules will apply to Santino. Although, the two men are a night and day different, so we'll see how it goes. "We're having tapas at some posh place called Radio Rooftop? I guess reservations are impossible to get, but Santino *knows a guy*. His words, not mine."

Allie cringes slightly, and I can't say I blame her. "Well, do you want me to come over to help you get ready or anything?"

"God, no. I'll be fine," I answer, already thinking about wearing the dress Mac bought for me the day we went shopping. "Just…if you happen to see Mac, don't tell him? I don't want him to know about the date in case it turns out to be a bust."

Allie nods thoughtfully and then slips off the table. "Well, text me and let me know how it goes, okay?"

"Can do!" I beam.

She retreats to her office while I get back to working on the bust of a shift dress—something I'm much more successful at navigating my way around than my dating life.

CHAPTER 10

Mac

"**Y**OU STILL HAVEN'T TOLD ME WHAT YOU WANT TO DO FOR your stag party in a couple of weeks," I grunt as I heave the barbell up towards Roan, who's currently spotting me on the bench press.

"I could workshop some ideas for you if you'd like," Tanner Harris states as he spots his brother Booker beside us.

The four of us are in the Tower Park weight training facility where we meet with our physiotherapist three times a week during the off-season. We've been lifting for nearly an hour, and my muscles are shattered.

"Don't let Tanner plan anything," Booker huffs, dropping the bar in the rack and sitting up. He wipes the sweat from his brow and hooks his thumb towards his brother. "He hired a stripper for my stag night and a bloke showed up."

"What do you mean a bloke?" Roan asks with a laugh. "Like, to strip?"

Booker nods. "And he wasn't like one of those Chippendale

strippers. He looked like our uncle Charles." I turn my head just in time to see Booker shudder with disgust.

Tanner hoots with laughter. "The hilarious part is you think I screwed up! I selected that guy specifically for you. Your wife had just had twins, and I knew you didn't need to get your willy excited when there was no chance of you getting any action at home."

Booker's face falls. "Why on earth are you thinking about my willy at all?"

Tanner shrugs. "I think about everybody's willies. That's what family is for."

Booker winces. "No. No it's not, Tanner."

Roan laughs and shakes his head while helping me set my bar into the placeholder. "I told Mac no strippers. I don't want a wild night out. I want something quiet and remote, you know?"

I sit up and grab my water bottle, taking a long drink before throwing out, "What would you say to a bed and breakfast in Scotland?"

Roan's brows lift. "What do you have in mind?"

I wipe the sweat trailing down my temple and reply, "The Dundonald Highland Games is in two weeks, and my grandad has a big estate that's sitting empty right now. It was a bed and breakfast he ran with my gran, but she died a few years ago and he's finally got around to selling it. The new owner takes over in a month. We could all stay there, drink our weight in whisky, and see if you have what it takes to compete alongside a true Scot."

Roan smiles. "As long as you have what it takes to compete alongside a true South African."

"Your mum is British, you wank," I say with a laugh and give him a playful shove.

Roan nods. "It sounds perfect. Let's do it."

"And I assume the cousins of the bride are invited." Tanner interrupts Roan's and my conversation. "You can't have a proper stag night without the Harris Brothers."

I look at Tanner standing there, gripping his long beard with a wee bit of desperation on his face that makes me laugh. "Don't you all have children to worry about?"

"That's what nannies are for," Tanner scoffs.

"More like grandads," Booker adds with a smirk. "Dad loves taking the kids."

I nod at the two of them. "Very well then. There's plenty of room, so I'll prepare for the Harris Brothers to be there as well. Anybody else you fancy inviting to this stag weekend you've invited yourself to, Tanner?"

"You should invite Santino," Tanner states and props his foot on the bench. "After what he did for me a couple of years ago, I basically owe him my life."

I instantly stiffen. "Not Santino."

Roan's voice chimes in next. "What is your problem with him anyway? You've always hated him, and you've never told me why."

"Don't worry about it," I answer and stand up, my muscles tensing from this very annoying subject matter. "It's irrelevant."

"I am worried about it." Roan steps towards me with an uncomfortable look on his face. "Especially because he's out with your friend Freya tonight."

"What?" I snap, my jaw dropped. "What are you talking about?"

Roan shrugs. "I wasn't supposed to tell you, but you should consider telling your friend not to date him if he's a bad guy."

"What are you saying, DeWalt?" I snap again, my eyes laser focused on him. "You're not making any fucking sense to me right now. Freya wouldn't go out with *Santino.*"

"She told Allie they are going to some posh rooftop tonight," he says, tossing his towel over his shoulder. "I wouldn't lie to you, man. Not about this."

I clench my jaw so hard, I swear I feel my teeth crack. Without another word, I turn on my heels and all but sprint to the showers. This will not fucking do.

"Where is she?" I growl into the phone when Allie picks up my call.

"Mac?"

"Is she with him now?" I ask, all pleasantries leaving my voice.

"Roan wasn't supposed to tell you!" Allie retorts, clearly anxious. "Why did he tell you?"

"Allie, just tell me where she is, and I'll handle it."

"Handle it? What are you going to do, Mac? Throw her over your shoulder and drag her out of their date because you don't like him?"

"If I have to."

Allie harrumphs into the line. "It's no use. She's determined to have a date for the wedding, and I don't think you should interfere. This is good for her. She should be putting herself out there."

"This isn't up for discussion right now, Allie," I state, trying my best to remain calm because I know Allie cares for Freya, but at this moment, I care more.

Allie huffs. "If I didn't know any better, I'd say you're acting like a jealous boyfriend, Mac."

"If I didn't know any better, I'd say you're acting like a shite friend because you wouldn't want your mate out with the likes of Santino if you knew what I know about him. Now, tell me where she is."

Minutes later, I'm pulling up to Radio Rooftop, and I can feel the blood pulsing through my veins from my rage.

Fucking Cookie.

I know I've been avoiding her for the past few days, but it was just so I could get control of myself. I didn't know what our kiss meant, and I definitely didn't understand what I did afterwards. None of it made any fucking sense, so I needed some space to get my head on straight.

Regardless, she should have fucking told me about her plans tonight. I'm her fucking love coach or whatever she called me. And she knows how I feel about Santino, so the fact that she's out with him feels like a complete betrayal of our friendship. I'm keen on telling her right fucking now.

I take the lift up to the rooftop restaurant where Allie said I could find them. The second the doors open, I know this is not a jeans and trainers sort of place, but I don't give two flying fucks. The host eyes me up and down as I approach, his lips curling upward in judgment as he takes in the state of me.

"Sorry, sir, we have a strict dress code." He looks down at his notebook full of utter shite.

"I'm just here to pick up a friend. I'll be in and out."

"I can't let you go in there, sir," he says with an awkward laugh as he eyes my ink-covered arms. "We have a reputation to uphold."

My jaw cracks as I state through clenched teeth, "Your reputation will be destroyed if I send one tweet out to my 200,000 followers."

"Your what?" he asks in disbelief.

"James!" a female voice squeals from beside us. "We can certainly find a table for Mr Maclay Logan, midfielder for Bethnal Green."

I turn my gaze to the woman who's now moved to stand beside Mr Twat Waffle, who is in serious need of a shaking. The woman eyes me hungrily, and the look irritates me further.

"I don't need a seat. I just need to get in and grab my friend."

I point towards the rooftop full of couples who are bathed in warm, romantic lighting, all enjoying the twinkling views of the London night skyline. My eyes do a cursory sweep, and I nearly keel over dead when I see Freya. *My fucking Freya* walking past the tables with ease, like she's Moses parting the Red Sea. She's wearing the fucking stunner of a dress that *I* bought for her. Even the damn shoes that came out of my fucking credit card are on her feet, mocking me. Her red hair is glossy and loose down her back, curled to perfection. I swear to Christ, every man in the room is turning to watch her walk by.

Cracking my neck, I make my way past the daft gatekeepers and towards my best mate, knocking into chairs like a bull in a china shop the entire way. Freya must hear the commotion because she turns her head, and her mouth opens as soon as she sees me barrelling towards her.

"Mac," she says with an awkward laugh when I'm an arm's length away. "What are you doing here?"

"I'm taking you home." I grab her arm, but she quickly yanks it out of my grip.

"What do you mean, taking me home? I'm on a date." She looks around nervously at all the eyes focusing on us.

I cringe slightly when I see the attention I'm drawing, but it doesn't stop me from replying. "I've heard all about your *date* with Santino."

She falters for a few seconds, her long-lashed eyes casting downward in shame as she attempts to find her words. "I would have told you, but—"

"Aye, it's because of him that I'm taking you home."

I reach for her hand again, but she evades my grasp. "Mac, you're embarrassing me."

My eyes fly wide, and I drop my head to level her with a serious scowl. "You should already be embarrassed for being seen in public with the likes of that wank stain."

"Lower your voice," Freya hisses, her jaw taut with aggravation. Her eyes dart to the right, and I follow her gaze to see the absolute sleekit, no-good bawbag in question.

Santino rises from his seat and eyes me with an arrogant look that I want to knock right off his smug face. He has an uncanny ability to look around the world as if it's his. Like he's done a lot of work to get here and he gets to enjoy it. I fucking hate it.

I stride towards him, ignoring Freya's quiet pleas behind me. "I didn't expect to see you here, Maclay," Santino drones, his voice like a wet fucking blanket full of premature ejaculation stains. "Are you joining us?"

"Fuck no," I reply flatly, my pulse quickening. "And neither is Freya."

Santino cracks an awkward smile, but it doesn't reach his eyes. "Is there a problem here?"

I exhale heavily through my nose and place my hands on my hips. "Of all the women you have at your disposal, you really needed to seek out *my* best mate?"

"Best mate?" Santino repeats the words like it's the first he's ever heard them. "Freya said she hasn't spoken to you in days."

His words feel like a punch in my gut, and I turn my hurt expression towards my friend.

Freya chews her lower lip. "I didn't say it like that. He asked about you, and I said I hadn't spoken to you. That's all."

She nervously wrings her hands in front of her, and I hate it. I hate this entire scene. And I especially hate that Santino thinks he has the right to voice my fucking name to my fucking friend.

I redirect my lethal stare back to him. "You don't need to worry a thing about my friendship with Freya, all right? You just need to know that she's mine, okay, pal?"

"Yours?" he scoffs. "I didn't force her to come here tonight, Maclay."

My knuckles crack in fists at my side as I turn to eye Freya. "Tell him you're leaving with me, Freya. Now."

"Leaving with you?" she asks, her wide eyes whirling with confusion. "What on earth are you talking about, Mac? I'm on a date."

I shake my head slowly. "I need you to trust me when I tell you that we need to leave."

"Mac," Freya states, her chin trembling. "Why are you doing this?"

"Who do you trust? Him? Or me?" My voice is increasing in volume, but I can't help it. Every time I'm around Santino, I lose my fucking temper.

Freya sniffles as she glances at Santino. With a resounding sigh, she leans over and picks up her clutch off the table. "I'm so sorry, Santino," she says, her voice shaky and on the verge of crying.

Fuck it. I don't care. This is what best mates are for. I reach out to grab her hand, but she yanks it away from me like I burnt her and storms off towards the exit. I give Santino one last withering stare and turn to follow her out the door.

Freya

Mac and I are both completely silent as he drives in the direction of my flat. Part of me wants to reach across the console and punch him square in the nose. Another part of me wants to scream at him that he has some bleddy nerve sabotaging my date and humiliating me.

A larger part of me is scared to do anything because I've never seen him like this. So angry. So demanding. So unapologetic. This isn't the Mac whom I've grown to know on my sofa, eating take-away, and catching wine gums in his mouth. This is a different beast altogether. I need to tread carefully.

What on earth is his history with Santino that turns him into such a raving lunatic? I want to ask, but I'm afraid to.

I honestly don't want to give a toss. What he did to me back at the restaurant was completely uncalled for and unacceptable. I'm a grown-arse woman. I should be able to make my own decisions about whom I will date. The only reason I agreed to leave with Mac is because everyone was staring at us in the restaurant, and I was horrified by the thought of someone taking a photo.

Mac pulls up to my flat, and without a word, I get out of the car and storm towards my door. I hear him approaching behind me, so I turn on my heels and nearly thrust my chest into him as I exclaim, "Don't think for one second you're coming inside!"

He has the nerve to look shocked. "Why the hell not?"

My eyes go wide, and my jaw drops. "Because you and I are in a very, very big fight. Do I seriously have to tell you that?"

Mac scoffs and aggressively shoves his hand through his hair. "What I did back there was for your own good, Cookie."

"Don't you Cookie me," I growl, stepping forward and jabbing a finger into his chest. He doesn't budge. *God, he is maddening.* "You don't get to ignore me for days, then show up at my date and act like an overprotective father who's caught his daughter having The Sex in a car or something!"

"Would you stop saying 'The Sex'? You sound ridiculous," he growls, his angry eyes fierce on mine.

"Thanks to you, any chance I had of having The Sex tonight has been completely shattered."

Mac's eyes flare with rage. "I'd rather die than see you have sex with that fucking wank," he seethes and actually spits on the ground beside us. "He's slept with half the population of London, Freya, and only because the other half are all men."

"Who cares?" I scream and grip the sides of my head because I feel like the entire world is spinning. "Maybe I'm looking for an easy shag!"

"The fuck you are," Mac replies harshly. "You're not the casual sex type, especially since the only people you have shagged are the ones you've been in love with."

"You don't know me as well as you think you do, you arrogant, conceited animal!"

"What the fuck are you going on about? I'm around you all the time. I know you, Freya. I know you better than most people. I—"

"I'm a virgin, you big, stupid ox!" My voice is loud and echoes down the nearby alley as I shut him up for good at last.

There's a strange suspension of reality that happens around us for a few seconds, where it feels like the earth has stopped rotating and all that exists is my anger and Mac's anger, sizzling between us like an electric current.

When I finally realise what I just shouted for all of London to hear, my legs suddenly feel like pudding. With a shaky exhale, I turn away from Mac's stupefied expression to go sit down on the front step of my building before I proceed to die of mortification. If I don't die of mortification, then I will murder myself in the name of mortification. Whichever comes first.

My eyes are wide and shooting back and forth in horror. This is all my fault. This entire night, this entire week, this entire situation is something I put myself through by allowing Mac to be my stupid love coach. How ridiculous! All I wanted to do was find a nice date for Allie's wedding, and, oh yeah, perhaps lose my virginity in the process before my thirtieth birthday. Was that really too much to ask the universe? What a fool I am!

I look up to find Mac blinking back his shock. His mouth is hanging wide open like a fly trap, and he still hasn't moved a muscle since my humiliating confession.

"Don't just stand there like an idiot," I hiss, ready to strangle him for his reaction because it's only adding fire to the flames of my embarrassment.

Finally, Mac shakes his head and turns to look at me, his eyes narrowing. "You're fucking with me, right?"

I gape at him. "Why would I fuck with you about something so pathetic?" I pin him with a furious glower. "I'm serious, Mac. I'm an almost thirty-year-old virgin. I've never had The Sex, and I'm sadly inexperienced."

Mac's mouth opens in shock again as he moves to sit beside me, stretching his long legs out in front of him. The corner of his mouth tips up as he softly laughs. "You're not a virgin. You would have told me."

"Oh, just like you would have told me why you hate Santino?" I retort, bringing him up short.

All humour vanishes from his face as he turns to look at me, his brows furrowed sharply together. "But when I started coaching you, you said you were just having a dry spell. To have a dry spell means you would've had to have been wet at one point."

I shake my head. "You took it that way, and I didn't bother to correct you. But honestly, Mac, think about it. You know me. Do you think I really would have agreed to let you be my love coach if I was just having a dry spell?"

"Christ, woman," he snaps, his eyes dropping down my body like he's seeing me in a new light. "You're a fucking virgin, and you never told me? I'm your best mate! Why wouldn't you share that information with me?"

"We don't talk about The Sex!" I exclaim defensively.

"I know, but this seems like something you should have mentioned to me at some point." He stands up and begins pacing in front of me, shaking his head like he's just been told the world is round for the first time and he can't fully wrap his mind around it. "Christ, a virgin?"

"Would you stop saying it like it's that big of a deal?" I snap, my entire body folding in on itself with embarrassment.

"It is a big deal," he replies, stopping his pacing to glower down at me with his hands on his hips.

"It's not a big deal to me!" I exclaim and stand up to meet him eye to eye. Well, more like eye to chest. "I'm not saving myself or something. It's not some religious thing, and it's not for lack of trying. I've put myself out there in the past, in all my awkward glory, and it just never happened for some reason," I huff, angry that I have to explain how romantically unlucky I've been. "Then I just got tired of trying so hard, so I took a break and focused on my career. A long break, I suppose. But I'm done with all that now. I'm eager to get shot of my maiden tag as soon as possible, which is why I thought going out on a date with Santino would be a good idea. Especially if he's experienced like you say."

Mac's face contorts. "What the actual fuck is a maiden tag?"

I flush, not realising I said that bit out loud. Shrugging, I reply, "It's what my gran called my virginity." I cross my arms over my chest, suddenly feeling very exposed under the London night sky.

Mac visibly tremors. "You're not giving your *maiden tag* to that fucking arsehole," he seethes, finally realising what my last comment meant.

"Well, not now obviously," I reply with agitation. "You basically ruined that chance for me."

"Good," he retorts.

"Not good for me!" I snap and jut my chin up at him. "I don't know what your problem is with Santino, but you are my friend, so I'll trust you and stay away from him. But you have to understand that you can't protect me from everything, even if you do fancy yourself my love coach. I'm going to lose my virginity to someone at some point, and he's probably not going to be perfect."

"I can't believe I didn't know you're a virgin," Mac replies, staring down at me, his eyes softening around the edges. "I'm a shite love coach."

I laugh at his candid response and then reach up to brush his hair off his forehead. Thank God, he sounds like Mac again—the guy who has the decency not to laugh when I cry during emotional scenes on *Heartland*.

He closes his eyes, and his entire body relaxes into my caress. When he opens them, his green eyes hold something in them that I've never seen before. Tenderness, perhaps?

"I'm sorry, Cookie," he croaks, his voice low as he wraps his inked arms around my shoulders and crushes me to his hard body. "I shouldn't have barged in like that. I just see red when it comes to that guy."

I exhale against his chest and breathe in his familiar scent of soap and detergent. "Someday you're going to have to tell me why."

I feel his head nod as it rests on top of mine. "Someday maybe I will."

I pull back and smile softly up at him. "I'm going to bed. Having my friend cause a scene on a rooftop in London has a surprisingly exhausting effect on me."

He shoots me a rueful smile as he grips the back of his neck. "Sorry about that."

I shrug. "There wasn't a love connection with Santino anyway. I'll find some other sorry bloke to hand my maiden tag off to." Mac grimaces, and I reach up to playfully chuck his chin. "Come on, love coach. Talking about my virginity label shouldn't make you so uncomfortable."

He laughs awkwardly, and then I give him a quick squeeze before waving goodbye and heading inside.

I've just stepped inside the lift when Mac suddenly slips in through the door before it closes on him. "Most people lose their virginity at sixteen," he says, seemingly out of breath for some odd reason.

I frown at his very random statement. "Yeah, I know, Mac. I'm not like most people." I reach past him to press the number five on the panel, and the lift takes off. "Thanks for reminding me of that sad fact."

Mac shakes his head and turns me to face him. "No, I just mean most people are young, so they forget how bad it is. You're not young, Cookie."

"Fuck off," I snap, yanking my arms out of his grasp. I turn forward to scowl at the lift doors, willing the ride to go faster before I punch my best friend in his annoyingly square jaw.

"I'm trying to tell you that you're not just a kid giving it away in the back of a car." Mac moves to stand in front of me, demanding my full attention. His expression is earnest when he adds, "Your... maiden tag is special. Your first time should mean something. It should be with someone you care about. Someone you trust."

I exhale heavily, his words causing a pang of uneasiness inside my chest. "Look, Mac, you know I'm crap at dating. I can't even find a date for Roan and Allie's wedding, let alone find a man whom I trust enough to have sex with. If I keep waiting for a boyfriend to have sex with, I might never lose it."

"I'm not talking about a boyfriend," Mac replies, his voice getting weirdly husky.

"What are you talking about then?" I nearly whine because this entire conversation is seriously my worst nightmare.

He swallows and looks down, an uncomfortable stiffness to his shoulders that I rarely ever see on him. "I'm talking about me," he murmurs to the ground.

The lift doors open, and I stare at my best friend, mouth agape, eyes blinking in complete and utter shock. "If this is you taking the piss..."

"It's not, Freya," he says, grabbing my arm to lead me out into the hallway. His expression is fierce when he adds, "I was blindsided when you first told me, but then it dawned on me. It makes perfect sense to me. I'm your best mate. You trust me. Maybe if I help you with this, you won't be so crap at dating anymore. I suspect walking around as a thirty-year-old virgin is part of the issue you have when speaking to men. Maybe if you were more experienced, you wouldn't get so tongue-tied."

I burst out laughing, my entire body shaking with hysteria because he has to be having a go with me. "Mac, I don't believe what you're saying right now."

His face is stony serious when he replies, "Freya, I wouldn't joke about this."

My humour begins to die. "You kissed me, then I didn't hear from you for days. If we have sex, surely I will lose my best friend forever!"

Mac winces at my very pointed jab, but I don't care. If he thinks he can have sex with me and act normal, he's seriously delusional.

"That was me being daft. I'm sorry about that."

"You're sorry," I repeat, turning my shoulder on him and digging into my handbag for my keys. I unlock my flat door, and Mac follows me inside. I turn on my heels and hold my hand up to stop him in the foyer. "You and I haven't gone a day without texting in over a year. Then after one stupid kiss, you ghosted me for days. Why would I risk losing you for sex, Mac?"

"You won't lose me," he says softly, his eyes wide on mine as he reaches out and tries to touch my cheek.

I pull away from his grasp and walk into my dining area to drop my handbag on the table. "How do you know?" I ask, making my way into the kitchen for some water.

He falters for a moment before answering, "Well, I'm still mates with Cami, and we had sex for over two years."

I freeze with my hand on the refrigerator handle and slowly turn around to look at him standing in my dining room. "You still speak to her?"

Mac nods, his jaw tense. "We have lunch nearly every week when I'm in town."

"You have lunch with her every week?" I exclaim, opening the fridge and grabbing a bottle of water. I close it and turn to face him again. "Why have you never told me that?"

Mac shrugs. "I think you and I are finding we still don't know a lot about each other."

"And you think adding sex is a good idea?" I ask with a laugh, walking past him and into my living room.

He follows me. "Sex with me is always a good idea, Cookie."

I turn to see his comedic face, and I can't help but laugh at him trying to give me sexy bedroom eyes. "You can't be serious."

"I'm dead serious." He shoots me a cheeky smile and shrugs. "You know what they say, 'A beard that rocks the red is a beard that rocks in bed.'"

I burst out laughing. "Who says this? I've never heard this said. Who is the *they* you're referring to?"

Mac's smile falters. "*They* are clearly dead brilliant, that's all I know."

"Answer me then, who are *they*?" I repeat, my eyes wide and curious.

"Stop asking me that," he snaps, his face turning red. "I don't know, but *they* clearly know what they are talking about because I have it on good authority that I'm great in the sack."

My brows lift. "If you don't know who *they* are, then you can't possibly know that."

"Stop talking circles around me, woman. You know I can't keep up with the spinning of that fucking gerbil wheel you call a brain!"

I smile sweetly. "For a love coach, you really should be better under pressure." I offer him my water bottle and drop down on the sofa.

He takes a fortifying sip and sits down beside me. "I just don't want your first time to be with some arsehole who doesn't take his time. Doesn't make sure you're ready. Or worse yet, some polite, shy lad who has a good job and pleated trousers. Who holds doors open and picks up the cheque before asking, 'Ma'am, may I come inside you, please?'"

I blanch at his filthy words. "What's wrong with asking to come? Perhaps it's his polite way of asking if I've come!"

Mac eyes me knowingly. "If I'm balls deep in a lass, I know exactly when she comes, Cookie."

"Oh, shut up. You can't know everything."

"I'd absolutely know when you come, Freya."

"How?"

"Because I imagine you'd get a look on your face similar to when you're watching a gut-wrenching scene on *Heartland*."

He turns his green eyes to me, and the way he's looking at me starts a stirring in my lower belly. "That is a very bizarre assumption," I state, embarrassed at the sudden shift in my voice.

His brows lift as he realises I'm actually considering his offer. "Aye, Freya. Only because deep down, you know it's probably true."

I inhale sharply at the wicked promise in his velvety eyes and feel myself reach out and grab my water bottle from him. Our fingers brush, and it feels like our touch is electrified. When did Mac and I start having sexual tension? Has it always been there, and I've just ignored it? It makes no bleddy sense. He's him, and I'm…me.

I take a long sip of my water, avoiding his gaze because I can feel him staring at me, and I hate that it's making my thighs clench together.

"Don't you at least have to be attracted to someone to have sex with them?" I ask, staring straight ahead and feeling the blood inside my ears begin to simmer.

Mac says nothing so I chance a glance at him and feel my lips part when I see his eyes are laser focused on my exposed legs in the short dress he picked out for me. "I've never once said I wasn't attracted to you, Cookie."

A coughing spasm rips itself up my throat, and I quickly down the rest of my water in an attempt to splash out the fire burning inside of me.

His voice is deep and husky when he asks, "Are you not at all attracted to me?"

Deep breaths, Freya. Nice, deep, calm breaths. "What a stupid question," I retort and squeeze my plastic water bottle tightly in my sweaty hands.

"Have you ever thought about me sexually?" Mac asks, shifting closer to me on the sofa. I can feel the warmth of his breath on my shoulder when he adds, "Because I have thought about you."

"You have?" I bark out, feeling like cameras are going to come out of the shadows at any minute because I'm most certainly being Punk'd.

But Mac has zero humour on his face when he replies, "Aye, you're a bonnie lass. I'd have to be into blokes not to fancy the idea of shagging you."

My eyes slam shut, feeling horribly overwhelmed by everything he's saying. I begin rubbing my painfully warm ears, certain I look like a complete idiot but not sure how to stop myself. "I can't believe this is happening."

Mac clears his throat, and replies, "But if you're not attracted to me like that, then there's no sense in us—"

"I think you're fit!" My eyes pop open at my embarrassing chirp of a response, and I turn to face his adorably bemused face.

Mac's eyes drop to my cleavage, and he extends his arm around the back of the sofa. "Are you sure about that?"

I roll my eyes and try to ignore his delicious scent being wafted all over me like a sexy skunk spray. *Are sexy skunk sprays a thing?*

"I mean, you're fit in that obvious athletic footballer sort of way. It's basically a true or false question, though. Asking if a big, tattooed, handsome footballer is attractive is what one would call an objective inquiry. There's no subjectivism involved."

"You're having another one of your outbursts, Freya," he states seriously, reaching out and tucking a lock of my hair behind my ear, then pausing to grip my earlobe between his forefinger and thumb. "And your ears are objectively on fire right now."

"Shut up, you cow," I whisper, feeling a prickling sensation erupt all over my skin at his tender touch.

Mac shakes with laughter, and I feel it squarely between my legs. "But subjectively or objectively, I think you're beautiful, and it would be my pleasure to make your first time special."

"Just as friends?" I ask, turning to eye him with nervous curiosity.

"Best friends," he replies, his eyes becoming more serious and less sexy. "But you should give it some time and think about it."

He stands up from his seat, and I stare up at him, my mouth agape. "What?"

He shrugs, completely breaking the heated moment I thought we were sharing. "It's a big decision. You've held onto your virginity this long, so you should be sure that you're ready."

"Um, I'm damn near thirty. I think that makes me overly ready."

Mac offers me a lopsided smile. "Sleep on it. We'll talk tomorrow." He leans down and presses a kiss to my head and then pauses for a second, his hand moving to my chin and raising my face to his. He brushes his lips with mine, and says, "Night, Cookie."

"Good night?" I breathe out on a sigh, and all I hear is Mac's infuriating laughter as he lets himself out of my flat.

What a fucking cow.

CHAPTER 11

Mac

"I NEED TO TALK TO YOU ABOUT SOMETHING, BUT YOU HAVE TO promise not to breathe a word of it to anybody. Not even Allie." I eye my roommate seriously the next morning as we find ourselves face to face in the kitchen. I've caught Roan in a rare moment when his fiancée is nowhere in sight, and I'm going to take full advantage of it.

"Okay," Roan replies curiously. He's got a bowl of oatmeal in his hand and his spoon is frozen midair. "Should I sit down for this?"

"Don't be daft," I scoff and lean back against the kitchen counter and cross my arms over my chest. "But you can't do that thing couples do where they think they don't have to keep secrets from each other because they're in love and they share the same mind. I genuinely don't want you to tell Allie about this. Can you promise me that?"

Roan puts the spoonful of oatmeal into his mouth and moves to set his bowl down on the counter to give me his full attention. He crosses his arms over his chest to match my pose. "What the hell is going on, Mac?" he says around a full mouth.

I exhale heavily. "I offered to take Freya's virginity last night."

Roan begins choking on his oatmeal. "You're lying."

"I'm not lying," I state seriously. "I didn't even know I was going to do it until all of a sudden, I was in her lift offering to take her maiden tag."

"Her what?" Roan exclaims, beating his chest to get the last bits of food down his throat.

I shrug. "It's what she calls her virginity. It doesn't matter. Do you think I'm a fool? Do you think I've ruined everything?"

Roan barks out a laugh and hoists himself up onto the counter opposite me, trying to shake off the obvious shock he has over this recent development. "That's a loaded question, man."

"I know," I reply and grip the back of my neck. "What do you think, though?"

Roan grabs his glass of water and takes a sip before saying, "I think it depends."

"On what?"

"On whether you love her."

"Love her? What do you mean?" I snap, annoyed that he's going in this direction with his advice. "This isn't about love, Roan. This is about my friend thinking it's wise to just go out there and have sex with some stranger like Santino because she doesn't want to be a thirty-year-old virgin with no date for your bloody wedding."

"Oh, I see," Roan says knowingly. "So you're planning to take her virginity as a charity project."

"Fuck off...that's my friend you're talking about."

Roan's brows lift knowingly. "Mac, if you're trying to tell me that you taking Freya's virginity is some selfless act that you're doing just to be a good mate, I'm going to have to call you a liar. You wouldn't have offered to have sex with her if you didn't have feelings for her."

This brings me pause. "I don't have feelings for her...not like that at least. I mean, aye sure, I've always thought she's bonnie and recently, there's a new sort of attraction between us that's been growing."

"An attraction?" Roan lowers his chin and eyes me with curiosity.

"A spark or something," I state, having flashbacks to Freya's lips on mine in my bedroom and how that seriously awakened the beast inside me. "It wasn't there before. Not as much, at least."

Roan frowns, clearly not believing me.

"But the minute she started talking about dating other blokes, I started seeing her in a new light."

"A sexual light," Roan offers helpfully.

"Aye, sure, whatever you want to call it. I know we won't end up together. I don't want to settle down, and even if I did, I drive her bloody nuts. We'd never make it as a couple. But maybe…maybe if we…give in to these urges…we can get back to the way we used to be…before."

"Before you saw her in a sexual light?"

"It sounds daft when you put it like that," I growl, wondering why the fuck I agreed to be this arsehole's best man. "I shouldn't have said anything."

I move to head into my bedroom, and Roan reaches out and presses his hand to my shoulder. "I'm sorry for teasing you, man. I just want you to be careful."

"Careful?" I ask with a frown.

"You remember what it was like when Cami ended things with you."

I inhale sharply at his mention of her name. "The problem with Cami was that it went on for too damn long. I became dependent on her, and when she ended it, I was fucked in the head. That was my problem, not hers."

I cringe when I think back to some of the worst games of my career last season after we split. Coach threatened to bench me on more than one occasion. I can't say I blame him. All I could think about while I was out on that pitch was the advice my grandad gave me as a wee child about staying far away from women or they'll mess up my game.

He was right.

It wasn't until I started seeing Cami again, truly as just friends, that my game began to improve again. It was a serious mindfuck.

"I wouldn't do this long-term with Freya," I state by way of explanation. "She's different than Cami."

Roan nods, clearly believing my words. "Then I think it can be okay. As long as you're both clear on what it is exactly."

"Just sex," I confirm. "Just the one time."

"Right." He shrugs and shoots me a weird smile. "You'll be all right."

My brows furrow because he has a strange sort of look on his face that could be interpreted differently. But I don't want to interpret it differently. I want this to work. I need this to work. I ignored Freya for days after our kiss because I wasn't sure I could stand not to kiss her again if I saw her. Us having sex together, doing this, it'll help scratch that itch and get us back on track.

Fuck me, I hope she says yes.

I make my way into my bedroom, and my phone pings, indicating a text message has come through. I flop down onto my bed and pull it out of my pocket to see it's a text from Freya.

Cookie: Are you wanting to back out?

Me: Is this some kinky sex position you're propositioning? Cookie, I really think your first time shouldn't involve the back door.

Cookie: Shut up, you cow. I just mean...do you want to back out on your offer of The Sex.

I don't even try to fight my smile.

Me: Christ, seeing it in text is even worse than when you say it out loud. Promise me after I shag you, you'll stop calling it THE Sex.

Cookie: So this means you're not backing out?

Me: Cookie, I wouldn't have offered something I'm not fully committed to providing. I'm a doer.

Cookie: That's what she said.

Me: That's what you'll say.

Cookie: Oh! I should tell you that I don't take birth control pills, so do I need to buy condoms or something? Don't I need to know your size? Do you have one of those flexible craft tape measurers? If not, I can come over and measure you.

Me: …

Cookie: Mac?

Me: …

Cookie: Mac? Are you measuring right now?

Me: …

Me: Freya, I've never in my life had a woman ask me to measure my cock, and I'm not sure I'm okay.

Cookie: What? Is that weird? I thought it seemed responsible.

Me: For starters, men should buy the condoms. It's literally the least we can do. Secondly, if I don't know the size of my cock by now, I'm not doing this bloke thing right. And thirdly, if you ever come at my dick with something that has the word "craft" in it, I'll never have a hard-on again.

Cookie: Fine, no need be dramatic about it.

Me: When it comes to my cock, there's no messing about. Got it?

Cookie: Got it. So when are we doing this?

Me: I'll pick you up at 5 tomorrow.

Cookie: Tomorrow? Why don't you just come over here tonight and get it over with?

Me: Cookie, I'm taking your maiden tag to make it special, not to just get it over with. I need time to give you an epic, craft -free memory. Just trust me, all right?

Cookie: Okay…What should I wear? That dress you bought me?

Me: If Santino touched it, burn it. Just…surprise me.

Cookie: Okay…see you tomorrow. Xx

Me: xx

CHAPTER 12

Freya

I**S THIS THE RIGHT OUTFIT TO WEAR ON THE NIGHT YOU'RE GOING** *to lose your virginity*? I wonder to myself as I stare at my reflection in the full-length mirror propped inside my bedroom. I purchased an obscene number of potential options for tonight, but the black velvet mermaid-shaped dress I found in a vintage shop refuses to be ignored.

It hits me mid-calf like all the other things I love to wear, but it's formfitting, so I'm hoping Mac will approve. He's still technically my love coach, right? So I guess this means I want to please him. Plus, the gorgeous crisscross halter bustline certainly accentuates *all* my more favourable assets.

I even splurged on some new black lace knickers for the evening because the thought of Mac seeing me remove my Spanx is a humiliation I'd like to avoid for the rest of my life if at all possible. Black Mary Jane heels finish off the chic look along with my red sweeping curls that I've gathered around onto one shoulder. I feel good. I feel ready and prepared to pass my maiden tag off to my good friend, Mac.

Now if only I knew what we were doing tonight.

Part of me wishes Mac would just show up and do me right away. Get it over with so I can stop fretting. But then part of me thinks it might be fun to pretend this is a real date with a real man who might actually fancy me as more than a friend.

There I go with my *Heartland* fantasies again. Mac is no Canadian cowboy, and I'm not riding down the aisle on a pony to marry him at the end of all this. This is a realistic means to an end. Nothing more.

A knock on the door sends Hercules sprinting for my bedroom, and I get an overwhelming sense of wrestling kittens niggling in my belly. I quickly slick on my matte red lipstick, ignoring the kittens and grabbing my green handbag off the counter. When I open the door, my heart skips a beat because it's not just my friend standing on the threshold in his normal casual wear.

It's my friend standing there looking really sexy. He's wearing freshly pressed black trousers and a white dress shirt cuffed at the sleeves showing hints of his tattooed arms. It's sophisticated with a touch of edge. A heady combination.

He's had his hair cut too, leaving a good amount of his ginger length intact, but it's lost the shapeless flop it had before. I finally look him in the eyes and am flabbergasted when I realise Mac isn't looking at my face. He's looking at my body.

And the way his dark gaze sweeps every square inch of my curves is positively *indecent*.

I clear my throat and touch the smooth velvet of my skirt. "I know it's not showing off my legs but—"

"You're perfect," Mac interrupts, his voice husky, and breathy, and wicked all at the same time. He haphazardly hands over a giant bouquet of pink carnations, and adds, "You're the bonniest lass I've ever laid eyes on."

I bring the flowers to my nose and level him with a

disbelieving look. "Look, Mac, I know you said you wanted tonight to be special for me, but seriously, you can save the cheesy inflated compliments for another girl. It would be a shame for me to vomit all over my nice new dress."

"Dammit, woman," Mac growls, his face turning from heated to angry in the blink of an eye. "Could you just take a compliment without a self-deprecating reply for once in your life?"

My shield of humour vanishes as I look up at Mac with my lips parted. "I'm sorry," I reply on reflex because I didn't realise poking at myself would get him so wound up. "I didn't mean anything by it. Humour is sort of my default."

Mac's face instantly softens, but his eyes remain fierce on mine. "Aye, I know, Freya. But I meant what I said. It wasn't a polite remark. You look beautiful."

"Thank you," I manage to reply without sounding too disbelieving. I glance down at my bouquet. "And thank you for the flowers."

"You're welcome," he states firmly. He exhales a heavy breath as though he's holding the weight of the world on his shoulders, then offers up his arm. "Now, can I take you on this date that I spent nearly the entire day organizing? I'm dying to see your reaction."

There are those kittens in my belly again.

With a soft smile, I set the flowers down on the inside table and slip my arm in his. I have no clue what to expect tonight, but if Mac spent the whole day on it, I'm sure it's going to be unforgettable.

Mac

The car ride is quiet as I drive Freya to our first stop of the evening. The sun is just beginning to set, and the golden rays shining through her red hair are agonizingly distracting.

Christ, she's beautiful tonight.

From her seriously ridiculous curves in that sexy dress to the wee freckles that give her sexy look the perfect touch of innocence, my entire fucking body suddenly feels like a live wire waiting to be tripped.

I can't tell if she's actually more beautiful tonight than she has been all the other times I've seen her, or if it's the fact that I know I'm going to be inside her in a matter of hours, and that fact has escalated her beauty into the stratosphere of obscenely gorgeous.

Fuck me, this is going to be a long night.

I shouldn't have snapped at her like that earlier, though. That was a bad start to the night.

I've just got it in my head that I want this to be special for her, and I let my emotions get the best of me. I hate how she's constantly acting like I'm doing her some sort of favour, and everything I say is for show. None of this is for show. This arrangement was my idea, and I wouldn't have volunteered to take her virginity if I didn't want to fuck her.

Bloody hell, do I want to fuck her.

My cocker thumps inside my trousers, and I grip the wheel

tightly, trying to shut down my wandering thoughts because we have plans tonight that go well beyond getting naked and rolling around the sack. This date cost me a pretty penny, but it was worth it because I'll do just about anything to make this night extraordinary for my best mate.

We pull up in front of a nice family home in Essex and there's a van parked on the side of the road across the street. The driver waves animatedly to me, and Freya waves back, frowning curiously.

"Do you know who that is?" she asks, offering the man a polite smile even though her brows are pinched together.

"Aye," I reply, my palms sweating with nerves because, fuck me, maybe this is all too extreme, and Freya is going to think I'm a nutter.

"Are you going to tell me who he is?" she asks, turning her big round eyes to me.

With a nervous smirk, I hop out of the car and jog over to her door, fiddling with the sleeves of my shirt for a moment before opening her door and offering my hand like the gentleman my mum taught me to be. "Promise you won't give me shite about this, all right?" I state with a heavy sigh. "Forget that you know me better than most people and try to imagine I'm capable of just doing something nice."

"You? Nice?" she says as she stands and stares up at me with barely contained humour. "The man who once referred to his dick as the Loch Ness monster is suddenly doing something nice?"

I can't help but smirk down at her. "Aye, lucky for you, tonight you'll find out if the legends are true."

She giggles at that. "Already calling it a legend? I really hope this is a self-fulfilling prophecy."

My eyes narrow on her, and I have an overwhelming urge to snog her senseless right here on the street. "Let's keep those charming smart-arse remarks to yourself for a few moments, all right?"

Freya grins and gazes up at me through her long, thick lashes.

"If my remarks are charming, then why on earth should I hide them from the world?"

I growl and give her side a cheeky squeeze while directing her across the street. The tall, slender man hops out of the van with a big smile on his face. "Hiya, Mr Logan. Nice to see you again."

"Roger, I told you to call me Mac." I reach out to shake his hand. "This is Freya."

"Hiya, Freya."

"Hiya, Roger."

"Are you ready for this?" Roger asks, his eyes wide and excited as he makes his way to the back of the van.

Freya looks at me, tugging her ear nervously as she follows him. "If this is the part where I'm taken somewhere to sell my virginity off to the highest bidder, I'm afraid you boys could be disappointed at the price I bring in."

My eyes narrow in silent warning, and she shrugs like she just can't help herself.

Roger's happy smile falls instantly. "I'm sure your virginity would bring in a smashing rate, ma'am." Freya and I both freeze, staring back at Roger with dumbfounded expressions.

"Thanks for that, Roger," Freya finally replies, turning to me with an amused look on her face.

"He just called you ma'am." I chuckle and wince when Freya's elbow connects with my ribs.

Roger opens the van door, and our attention shifts to the three pet carriers with wee cats inside.

"Oh my God!" Freya squeals and rushes over, nearly knocking Roger on his arse in hot pursuit. He looks a wee bit frightened as Freya exclaims, "Look at these beautiful creatures! I must have them all!"

Roger laughs awkwardly and turns to me with wide eyes. "I'm afraid that won't be possible."

"Why? What do you mean?" Freya asks, not even looking back

at him as she fingers the cages and lets the wee animals lick her through the metal barricades.

Roger clears his throat and does his best to sound professional. "These cats have already found loving homes, and today you're going to help me deliver them to their new families."

"Are you serious?" Freya asks, turning her gaze to me for more explanation.

I step forward, gripping the back of my neck nervously. "Roger works for a nonprofit organization I heard about from one of my teammates called Best Birthday Ever, and their job is to deliver rehabilitated pets as gifts. All the pets that are adopted through them have been rescued from kill shelters and rehabbed until they're ready for proper homes. Basically, we get to help deliver three of them today and see the reaction of the receivers."

"Shut the fuck up," Freya says inelegantly, and her voice cracks at the end with barely contained emotion.

Roger and I both laugh.

"This is our date tonight? To give the gift of a pet?" Freya asks, tears filling her eyes before she turns to look at the wee kittens again. Her voice hitches to the octave of a wee babe as she coos into their cages, "How completely utterly, stupidly, wonderfully perfect of that big ox of a Scotsman. He's not as scary as he looks. In fact, he's a big cuddly teddy bear, isn't he, you precious babies?"

Roger elbows me and gives me an enthusiastic thumbs up. I awkwardly give one back to him before he steps in and opens the first cage. He pulls out a black and white cat that looks a bit like a kitten still. He cradles it to his chest, and says, "This little fella is going to a girl name Shantay. It's her tenth birthday, and it's from her mum and dad."

Roger thrusts the kitty into Freya's eager hands and her eyes go wide. "We're delivering the kitten now?"

He nods and points at the house behind us. "She's right in there."

"Stop," Freya says, turning wide eyes to the house. "What do I say exactly? This is a huge moment, and I don't want to screw it up for her."

Roger smiles and reaches out to pet the cat. "Just say Happy Birthday from your mum and dad."

"Oh my God, I'm so nervous!" Freya squeals, turning to me with obvious excitement all over her face.

"I'll go with you," I say, stepping up and wrapping my arm around her shoulders.

She looks up at me and nods her agreement, and we make our way to the front door.

"Oh, also!" Roger calls out as we finish crossing the street. "Make sure it's the right girl before you give the cat away. I screwed that up once, and I still have nightmares about that awful day."

The haunted look in Roger's eye is unmistakable, but Freya is too focused on the cat to notice as she turns back towards the house. She scratches the side of his cheek and presses her lips to his furry head. "How did you come up with this idea, Mac?"

I shrug. "I just googled things to do in London with cats."

Her shoulders shake with laughter. "And you found a place that lets just anybody deliver cats as presents?"

"Not exactly," I reply and grip the back of my neck.

She looks up at me in confusion.

I shrug. "I donated some money, and you getting to do this was one of my conditions."

Her jaw drops, and she adjusts the cat in her arms. "How much money?"

"It doesn't matter," I scoff and usher her up the front steps. "It's a great cause, and I love seeing you like this."

Freya stops in front of the door and turns to face me. "I love you, Maclay Logan. You truly are my best friend."

Her words hit me hard in the chest, but before I have a chance to respond, she turns and rings the doorbell. Within seconds, a girl with long black braids opens the door and gazes up at us curiously.

"Um, hi?" she says, glancing down at the kitten with a forlorn look on her face.

"Are you Shantay?" Freya asks, her voice garbled and full of emotion that makes a knot form in my throat.

Her parents emerge behind her with knowing smiles. "This is Shantay," her father says, placing his hands on her shoulders with a big, proud smile.

Freya inhales deeply, hugs the kitten to her chest once more, dropping a soft kiss to its ear, and then says, "Happy Birthday from your parents."

She passes the kitten into the unsuspecting girl's hands. Shantay's expression morphs from confusion to an almost angry look of shock. She turns to her mum and dad, and barks, "Is this for real? Is this a joke?"

"It's real, honey," her mum says, squatting down so she's eye level with her daughter. She pets the kitten, and says, "Dad and I are so proud of how hard you've been working at school."

"You got me a kitty?" she screams, and then her face contorts into full-on crying as she drops to her knees and sobs into the poor kitten's fur. The cat clearly has no idea what's happening as she lies limp in the arms of the girl who's now gasping for breath. "You got me a kitty? Oh my God. Thank you, Mummy. Thank you, Daddy."

The parents look up at us with grateful smiles, but their expressions fall when their eyes land on Freya. I step forward to see Freya is bawling just as hard as the girl. Maybe harder. I wrap my arm around her and wave to the parents, ushering my blubbering friend away from the seriously emotional scene.

"Are you okay? I thought you'd love this," I say, squeezing her in tight to my side and rubbing my hand up and down her bare arm.

"I do love this, you idiot!" Freya croaks, sniffing loudly and wiping away her tears. "Crikey, I'm going to remember that little girl's precious face for as long as I live!"

She clears her throat, and without warning, she launches

herself into my arms, locking me in a seriously strong hug. "Thank you, Mac. Thank you so much."

"Aye, sure," I reply with a laugh, dropping a kiss onto her shoulder. "We still have two more to go. Are you sure you're up for it?"

"Oh, I'm up for it," she says, jerking away from me and barrelling back towards Roger, who looks a wee bit terrified again.

I wish I could say the next two deliveries are less emotional, but they aren't. Freya is a snotty, happy, smiling-through-her-tears mess. And with the last delivery, the wee kitten had a ring box attached to his collar, which meant Freya and I had front row seats to a man proposing to his girlfriend with the gift of a kitten. By the time we finish, even I'm bawling like a wee babe. Who knew delivering pets as birthday presents would be such an emotionally taxing job?

After we're done, we end up in a dark restaurant tucked away in a cul-de-sac between Kensington High Street and Kensington Church Street called Maggie Jones's. It has a cosy, rustic ambience that's dark and romantic with melted taper candles propped in wine bottles and lighting so dim you can't read the menu.

We split a bottle of red wine with pies and mash, and laugh out loud way too much for such a quiet, romantic setting. But recounting our evening thus far is just too much fun. I'm sure Roger had no idea what he was in for with the two of us going door to door, but I think we managed to make every pet delivery a special one.

Freya's eyes haven't stopped twinkling since we sat down, and I can tell this evening is already unforgettable for her. And I have to say, I actually manage to stop thinking about our plans for later because I'm completely enchanted watching Freya gush over the wee kittens.

"How did you get Hercules?" I ask, sipping my wine and admiring her red hair as it glows in the candlelight. "You've never told me the story. You didn't have him in Manchester, did you?"

Freya's brows lift. "No, he was a stray outside my London flat, actually. The neighbour said she thought he was living on the roof, and she was going to call animal control to come deal with him. I couldn't bear the thought of that, so I left out a trail of tuna fish leading through my open fire escape window. He came in like he owned the place, and I quickly closed the window and then had a minor panic because I realised that I just locked a very possibly feral cat inside my flat with no real plan for what to do next."

My body moves with silent laughter. "What did you do next?"

She shrugs. "I did what any normal hard-working girl from Cornwall would do. I gave him a scone, some jam, and clotted cream, and we've been best mates ever since."

This brings a genuine smile to my face. "And why did you name him Hercules?"

The corner of her mouth quirks up. "He's a strong little bugger. I had to wrestle him into a cat carrier to take him to see the vet for the first time, and I nearly broke out in a sweat from all the effort. He's quite fit, even if he is a good twenty pounds overweight. He's what I call 'buff fat.'"

I stare back at Freya, who's giggling to herself as she sips her wine. I don't know why the hell her giggling about her cat causes my cock to stir in my trousers, but it bloody well does. My eyes instinctively lower to her breasts, and I do my best to envision what they're going to look like naked.

"What are you thinking about?" she asks, her voice quiet and charged with something…electric.

My gaze lifts. "I'm thinking about what your breasts are going to look like naked."

She begins to choke on her wine. "And what conclusion did you come to?"

I lean across the table and trail my fingers along her forearm. "I'm quite certain they're going to look fan-fucking-tastic."

"God, you're such a pig," she replies with a scoff and pulls back to mindlessly tug at her ear. "Is this how you're making tonight special? By talking about my taters at the dinner table?"

My brow quirks. "Did you just call your breasts taters?"

She shrugs and wrinkles her nose. "It's what my mother called them growing up." Her voice hitches as she mimics her mother's deep south accent, "Don't let your taters hang out of your blouse, Freya, or you're look like a proper harlot."

My shoulders shake with laughter. "Your mother sounds like a delight."

"Oh, trust me, she is. She's a Catholic, wholesome, southern woman whose best friends were nuns. It's amazing she didn't end up in the convent herself."

I shake my head knowingly. "If she ever meets my grandad, she'll probably die of a stroke."

Freya tilts her head curiously. "Is he a proper Scottish rogue?"

"Something like that," I reply and take a sip of my wine. "But he's not much of a lover. Granted, he loved my gran enough to run a bed and breakfast with her in Dundonald for years, but I wasn't even sixteen before he told me all women were the devil."

"The devil?" A fond smile spreads across Freya's face. "What a thing to say to a young, impressionable boy."

"Aye, he said women distract men with their beauty, and we lose sight of what's important in life."

Freya's head jerks back. "And what, pray tell, did he think was important in life?"

"Football, football, and football," I reply with a laugh. "My grandad is such a football fan that he literally weeps like a babe when his precious Rangers lose a match."

"Oh my God, how sweet!" Freya coos.

"Sweet and overly passionate. He was heartbroken when my

father never showed any interest in playing football beyond his teenage years. My dad got my mum pregnant with me when they were only eighteen and that basically settled that."

"Couldn't your dad pursue football and a family?" Freya asks, propping her chin on her hand and eyeing me seriously. "The Harris Brothers make it look quite easy."

"Aye, sure. But the fact of the matter is, my dad didn't want to be a footballer. He was happy to find a steady job and be home for dinner every night."

"What's so wrong with that?" Freya asks innocently.

"Everything, according to my grandad," I reply with a laugh. "Which means he directed all his hopes and dreams onto me. I don't have a single memory of my grandad that doesn't involve a football."

Freya's eyes twinkle with pride. "Well he must be quite chuffed now that your club is in the premier league."

"He'd be a bit prouder if I was playing for Rangers instead." I wink back at her so she knows that even though what I'm saying is true, I still love the shite out of my grandad. "My favourite memory with him was when I was only seven years old and he took me to a sold-out match at Ibrox Stadium. I thought we were just going to look at the people milling about, but I was wrong. He grabbed a piece of cardboard out of the back seat of his truck, and with a felt pen, he wrote: NEED ONE TICKET.

"We stood on Copland Road for ages, and I thought there would be no way we'd get in—the place was swarming! But sure enough, a guy came over, nudged us, and for a tenner, we were in the stadium with me seated squarely between my grandad's legs. That was the moment I knew I'd do just about anything to make him look at me the way he looked at that pitch."

"That's rather sweet," Freya says, her lips curling up into a smile.

"Aye, he's always been my biggest football supporter. He would take me to trainings when both my parents had to work. He even sold one of his antique tractors to get me into a camp so I could train with his beloved Rangers."

"He sounds incredible," Freya says with a soft smile. "I hope to get to meet him someday."

"If you ever do, don't take his surly disposition personally," I reply with a laugh. "He hates any girls I bring around him. He sees them all as potential saboteurs."

Freya giggles at that. "Is that why I've never heard you talk about any past girlfriends?"

I shrug. "I've never really done the girlfriend thing because football has always been my priority. And since I never know how long a team is going to keep me, the idea of settling down with someone, only to end up with a different team, makes relationships seem pretty pointless."

"I suppose that makes sense," Freya says, getting a curious look in her eyes. "But friendships are okay?"

"Friendships are sturdier," I state simply. "There aren't the emotional ties that come with a relationship. You and I can do what we're going to do tonight and go right back to just being mates the next day because we've created a foundation for it."

Freya nods thoughtfully. "I suppose that's why you appreciated your arrangement with Cami. You got to have your cake and eat it too."

"Aye," I reply with an uncomfortable smile because what Cami and I had is a night and day difference to what I'm doing here with Freya. And I'm not sure what that means exactly. I shake my head and stop that train of thought in its tracks. "I just know it's simpler all around when feelings aren't involved. It's just about sex."

"It's just about The Sex."

My shoulders shake with my laughter. God, it is going to be fun tonight to see Freya experience all this for the first time. I let my eyes lower to her body. "And make no mistake, Cookie. It might just be sex tonight, but I'm still going to do my damnedest to rock your world."

She swallows a knot in her throat and reaches up to fan her ears. "We should, erm…get the check. I feel like it's really hot in this restaurant all of a sudden."

It's only going to get hotter.

CHAPTER 13

Freya

"**D**OES IT HURT FOR MEN WHEN THEY DO IT THE FIRST TIME?" I hear my stupid, ridiculous voice ask out loud as Mac and I stand across from each other in my bedroom.

The corners of Mac's mouth twitch in the dim nightstand light.

"You swore you wouldn't laugh at me!" I exclaim and reach out to smack him.

He catches my hand against his firm chest and holds it there. "Firstly no, it doesn't hurt. It feels fucking fantastic. And Cookie, we're not Mac and Freya if we're not having a wee bit of a laugh at each other through all this." He steps closer to me and places his other hand on my hip, the warmth of his touch sending shivers through my body. "Besides, laughter is a good way to defuse tension."

"It is?" I chirp, my voice sounding weird and high-pitched.

"Aye, do you want me to call my cocker the Loch Ness monster again so you can make fun of me?" He waggles his eyebrows playfully.

"I just don't understand how you think calling your penis a

monster is even remotely attractive in the bedroom. You should call it something sweet and cuddly like…Chip."

"Chip?" Mac repeats the name, and his chest shakes with laughter beneath my hand.

"Why not?" I shrug.

He pins me with a panty-melting smile. "If I call my cocker Chip, will that make you happy?"

I glance down at his trousers and nod. "Yeah, Chip sounds nice. Gentle."

He releases my hand from his chest and crooks his fingers under my chin to force me to look up at him. "I'm going to be gentle, Cookie."

"Please, no Cookie in the bedroom," I groan and chew my lower lip nervously. "It makes me feel like your mate, and I don't want to feel like your mate. I want to feel like a woman you desire."

"You *are* a woman I desire, Freya," he replies and moves his hand to my neck to trace the line of my jaw with his thumb. A riot of goosebumps erupt down my neck and over my breasts, causing my nipples to pebble beneath the black cropped bustier I bought for this occasion.

"Let me prove it to you," Mac says, his voice rougher than before as his strong hand threads deliciously through my hair, angling my neck so I'm looking into his eyes.

He smiles ever so slightly just before leaning in and connecting his lips with mine. Our noses brush against each other as he moves his lips against mine in soft, gentle strokes—just the way a Canadian cowboy would kiss his future bride on the steps of her grandfather's home.

Kindly. Gentlemanly. Respectfully.

Suddenly, he deepens the kiss and his tongue delves into my mouth with greedy firmness. Our bodies are flush together, and the whiskers of his chin tickle my lips as he plays with me, teases me, tastes me. *Fucks me…with his mouth.*

His tongue plunges in and out as one hand glides down my back and palms my arse, pulling me into his groin so I can feel the level of his arousal.

From just a kiss? Great heavens.

This is certainly no longer a gentle Canadian cowboy kiss. This is the kiss of a true, unbridled, untamed, unbroken bronco of a Scotsman, and I had no idea it was everything I was missing in life!

His other hand moves to pop the strap behind my neck open, and the top of my dress spills down, revealing my very sizeable breasts, which are now practically pouring out of my bra. *Jesus, did my breasts grow? Do breasts get bigger when you're aroused?*

He breaks our kiss, and I gasp for breath as his face lowers to my cleavage to devour me, pressing warm open-mouthed kisses to my flesh. I rub my cheek against the top of his head, holding on for dear life as his teeth bite the edge of my bra and yank it down with one firm tug. My breast tumbles out on one side, and I can't help but cry out with excitement because the flurry of arousal coursing through my veins is overpowering all my senses.

"Fucking stunning, just as I imagined," he growls, and without warning, he yanks the other one free.

I glance down and thank God for underwire because even *I* think my breasts look nice like this. Having double Es means you need support, so the scrunched down bra holding them up like this actually makes my breasts my new favourite wobbly bits.

Mac palms them both roughly as he wraps his lips around one of my nipples and sucks. Hard. The pressure causes a burning sensation in my vaginal region, and my legs nearly buckle on the spot.

God, Freya. Vaginal region? If you said that out loud, Mac wouldn't be able to stop laughing long enough to take your maiden tag.

He presses his teeth onto my other nipple, and I'm suddenly feeling very cheated by this entire exchange. When his lips move up to find mine, I press my hands flat on his chest and push him away. My fingers hurriedly reach out for his shirt and fumble with the buttons, but they're trembling so much I can't get his stupid shirt off. With a tiny growl of frustration, I grab the opening at the top and rip his shirt down the front, hearing the soft patter of plastic buttons hitting the hardwood floor. I glance up, and he's looking at me like I just scored a goal for the World Cup.

"I know a good seamstress," I croak, and my hands reach out and claw at Mac's very large, very sculpted chest.

I've fitted Mac for clothes before, so I know how beautiful his body is. But being able to drag my fingertips down his flesh, knowing that he's all mine for the night is a heady, overpowering feeling.

I push him backwards to my bed, and he drops down with ease, his eyes dark with arousal as I work towards shimmying out of my dress. Too many clothes. Too much pressure. We just need to do this so I can get a handle on the sweltering yearning coursing through me at rapid speed. It's so strong I feel like my entire body could take flight at any moment.

When I finally ditch the dress and move to take off my bra, Mac stops me. "Don't be taking my job, lass." He reaches behind me and unclasps my bra with deft ease.

When it drops to the floor, I realise belatedly that I'm standing in front of professional footballer Maclay Logan in nothing but a pair of tiny lace knickers. I know he's my best friend, but he's experienced. He's probably seen hundreds of gorgeous model types naked. And not plus-size models, either. Tiny, rail thin models that have enormous thigh gaps and visible ribs. How did I think I was going to be able to shag him without him seeing me naked?

He's going to notice that my tummy isn't flat. Not even close. It's soft and has a little pouch that jiggles when I move. He's seeing my Spanx-free belly! And my breasts without underwire aren't the perky porn star tits that I trick myself into thinking I have when I'm home alone. My breasts sag and droop and lay against my ribs. And don't even get me started on my thighs. The dimples there are not inherited through genetics. They are earned from a lifetime of wine gums, takeaway, and questionable life choices.

God, I'm such a fool!

I quickly reach over and click off the nightstand lamp, returning to Mac and hoping he didn't see the sheer panic on my face. I grab his cheeks and lean down to kiss him, but he pulls away.

"What are you doing?"

"Isn't it obvious?" I croak and try to kiss him again.

He grabs my wrists to stop me. "Why did you shut the damn light off?"

"More…romantic," I murmur and free my hands to begin fumbling with the belt on his trousers.

"Darkness is not romantic," Mac retorts, removing my hands from his groin. "Not seeing your body is the exact opposite of romantic."

I stand up and pinch the bridge of my nose, grateful that Mac can't see the pained look I know is on my face. "Trust me, it is better this way."

Mac rises to stand in front of me, his tall form like a giant shadow in the darkness, making me feel small and silly. "Trust me, it's not," he states through clenched teeth.

He swaps places with me and reaches over to click the light back on. I close my eyes so I don't have to see his reaction because I'm certain I can't bear it.

"Freya, look at me," he says seriously, his voice gruff and more Scottish than I've ever heard before.

My eyes flutter open.

"Your body is *everything* I fucking want." He leans down and presses a soft kiss to my lips. "Your curves." Kiss to my shoulder. "Your dimples." Kiss to my neck. "Your softness." Kiss to my breasts, and my belly, and my…*oh my fucking God, he's on his knees.*

"Your heat," he murmurs against my legs before hooking his fingers into the waistband of my knickers.

He drags them down slowly, and I'm suddenly hugely grateful that I splurged on a full Brazilian wax yesterday. He presses me down onto the bed and slowly spreads my legs and hitches them up onto his shoulders.

Good God, he's really getting in there!

I might be inclined to be self-conscious under normal circumstances, but the smoldering look on his face makes me feel like the hottest woman in the world right now.

When his lips touch my sex, my thoughts go to a very strange place. You know that feeling when your mind is stuck in a dream but your body is trying to wake you up? It's a delicious place that you don't want to leave, but since your body is fighting it, you're basically stuck in that strange space?

That's what Mac going down on me feels like. Somewhere between a dream and reality, and I'm not sure which one I should commit to, considering this is the first time in my entire life I've ever had a man's mouth down there.

Mac's movement is a gentle, slow-motion kiss. He licks and teases and sucks and…is he making out with my vagina? This is *so* not Canadian cowboy of him.

He pulls back and slowly presses a finger inside me. I glance down to see him looking up at me. "Are you okay?"

My body tremors. "Okay?"

"Yeah, you doing good?" he asks, his lips slick with my arousal as he slowly pumps his finger in and out.

"I think so?" I say stupidly. "You tell me."

He bites his lip, failing to hide his amused smile. "I think you're doing fucking fantastic." He gets a wicked look in his eyes and then inserts another finger, causing a really loud noise to come from somewhere deep inside of me.

"It's too much," I state, feeling this intense fullness building inside of me.

"It's not too much," Mac says, crooking his finger and stroking my G-spot, which I really only know about from hearing my girl-friends talk about their sex lives. I'm not a sex toy owner. I could barely look at my naked body in the mirror, let alone pleasure my-self. He quickens his pace, and my shoulders lift up off the bed.

"Oh my God!" I cry out, and he bites his lip, a look of pure fucking sex in his eyes before he descends on me again. He sucks my clit into his mouth while stroking that tender spot, and without warning, a sharp, overwhelming release goes off inside of me. It's so intense, my thighs begin to shake compulsively, causing a horri-ble sense of embarrassment to wash over me. Groaning, I cover my face with my arms, horrified by my body's ridiculous reaction.

"Freya, look at me," Mac's voice rasps, sounding deeper than I've ever heard it.

"No, I'm a freak. My body is betraying me."

"Cookie, you're not a freak," Mac states, gently extracting his fingers while standing up on his feet. He pulls my arms off my face to force me to look at him. "You just had an orgasm. A fucking nice one if I do say so myself."

"I was out of control," I say, frowning up at him.

Mac frowns back at me. "Have you never had an orgasm, Freya?"

I sniff in confusion. "I thought I had, but they felt nothing like that."

The corner of his mouth tilts up. "I'll take that as a compli-ment." He leans down and kisses me on the lips, the act doing a proper job of washing away my embarrassment. I kiss him back, my hands raking over his strong back.

"I think you're ready," he says against my lips, lowering his mouth to the hollow of my ear. "Your ears are telling me they're ready."

"Shut up, you cow," I reply and then bite my lip nervously.

Through foggy eyes, I can see his massive erection pressing outward, and with no fanfare, he grabs a condom out of his wallet and shucks off his trousers. He uses his teeth to rip open the foil packet.

"Done that a lot, I take it?" I ask stupidly because apparently, my idiotic body needs to fill all dead silence with ridiculous drivel.

"Enough." He winks before rolling the condom over his tip with exact precision. "Never with my best mate, though." He stands beside the bed and looks at me expectantly.

"So we're doing this now, then?" I ask, my body tensing up nervously as I move to the top of the bed. Pulling the blankets down, I wince against the cool sheets. "So soon, after…"

"Now is better," he states confidently. "You're soaked and relaxed. It will hurt less if we do it now."

"Okay, then."

The bed dips as Mac crawls over top of me, our flesh slick with desire and anticipation. He's hot and heavy, and I imagine what an excellent way it would be to die beneath the delicious weight of him as our smooth naked skin rubs together, igniting every single one of my nerve endings.

A stirring begins inside me again. How has my body recovered so soon? How am I still this turned on after all we've done so far? "Do I just lay here like this then?" I ask nervously, watching the tip of his wrapped erection glide up my thigh.

His breath is warm on my shoulder with a soft laugh. "I'd prefer it if you participated."

"Participation. Got it," I state, nodding and trying to clear my mind of the earlier moments to focus on the task at hand.

"Freya," Mac says, his heavy weight sinking down over top of me. "Stop thinking so much."

His lips crash with mine, and it's a glorious, desperate kiss with strong, steady tongue. It's wonderfully frantic, like he can't get enough of me. I can taste myself on his lips, and it excites me further because just the idea of him doing what he did to me makes my nerve endings ignite all over again.

Mac's hands are everywhere—touching me, caressing me, kneading me, teasing me. So I decide to do the same to him. I fist his hair in my hand and kiss him back hard, relishing the feel of our bodies rubbing together, skin on skin. It's quite possibly the most magical thing I've ever felt in my entire life. When I reach down between us and wrap my fingers around his thick heat, he stops kissing me.

"Fuck, Freya," Mac groans, his forehead resting on mine as he pants against my face. "I need to be inside you."

"Then do it already," I pant.

"You have to stop touching me so I can calm down. I don't want to hurt you."

My hand instantly releases him, and as if Mac can sense my uneasiness, he presses his lips to mine, and murmurs, "Your hand on my cock makes me fucking wild with lust."

I smile and bite my lower lip. "That's nice to hear."

He shakes with laughter, and the movement somehow lodges his dick right where my lips part. Our eyes lock. Our breaths hold. My hands reach up to grip his arms like I need to brace myself for what's coming.

"I'm going to kiss you through it."

I nod woodenly. "Kissing would be good."

"Are you ready?" he asks, and I see a small flicker of nerves flit over his eyes. "If you're not ready, we don't have to do this. I want this to be what you want, Freya."

"You're what I want, Mac," I say and reach around to hug him to me and pull him closer. "You're my best friend."

With a tiny, reassuring smile, he leans in and begins kissing me with tender passion as he positions his tip at my opening. When his tongue thrusts into my mouth, his cock mimics the motion down below.

It's a sharp, instant burn that makes me flinch. I break away from his lips and gasp for air. For space. For relief. Everything is tight. Too tight. Mac holds himself over the top of me and looks down at me with so much care and concern in his eyes, my heart nearly implodes from the tenderness on his face.

"Are you all right?" he asks nervously, glancing down at the space between us. He winces slightly, clearly feeling the tight pressure below. "Is it too much for you?"

I sniff and shake my head, willing the burning in my eyes to go away. "I'm okay."

He nods thoughtfully, a worried expression in his eyes as they scan over my entire face. "Are you sure?"

I swallow down the knot in my throat. "I'm sure."

He inhales deeply, lifting his shoulders and hitching himself inside me once again. "I'm going to start moving. It'll probably hurt at first, but then it'll get better."

I nod and look down at where our bodies are connected as he pulls back and slowly pushes back in.

I groan out a noise that's a little less like pain and a little more like pleasure. "Oh my God." I inhale a shuddered breath.

"Relax, my treasure," he says as the tender term of endearment brings a fullness to my chest that takes my mind off the pain below. "You're beautiful like this."

The motion between us begins to creep towards pleasure. Pleasure that I want to enjoy. Relish. Taste. Feel. My hands reach around to cup his arse as he thrusts in and out of me. He grips my leg and holds it to his side, deepening our embrace and adding friction to my clit with the new angle. That tiny bundle of nerves gives me chills all over my body, and I can literally feel my wetness begin to increase.

"God, you feel so good," Mac groans, dropping his forehead to mine in an intimate way. He pulls back and looks down as he thrusts inside of me again. "Too good. Way too fucking good. I wanted this to last longer."

"It's perfect," I whisper, cupping his cheek and looking into his eyes. "I know I don't have anything to compare it to, but this feels perfect."

The corner of his mouth tilts up with the tiniest smirk, and suddenly, he begins driving into me faster, maintaining our eye contact the entire time. His face loses all humour, and he bores into me with such force, I feel trapped. It's intense—looking at someone as they do something so primitive, so animalistic. So feral. It's an exposing moment that lays you bare, and before I know it, I feel that build inside my body again.

As if Mac can feel my orgasm coming, he swivels his hips and hits that special spot inside me. I cry out, gripping his back and failing to hold on to what's left of my sanity.

"Come for me, treasure. Let go for me. Let me feel you all around me." Mac's husky voice opens my eyes, and I find him watching me with a look of awe on his face.

My body locks up around him, and I explode, shattering all over him as he continues rocking inside of me. *Holy fucking shit.* The orgasm I had with his mouth before felt like firecrackers. This one was more like a nuclear bomb.

We continue staring at each other, and it's so…right. Could I look at another man like this and feel so completely at ease? I don't think so. It's then that I realise this was the best way for me to lose my virginity. This is my best friend. He cares about me, and even if this is just a one-time thing, it's special, and I'll always be grateful for this gift he's given me.

Mac's body suddenly goes rock hard as he stills inside of me. He lowers his head, burying his face in my neck while groaning out his release right into my ear. After a few tremors that shake his whole body, he pulls out of me, wraps his arms around my waist, and rolls us so we're both laying on our sides, facing each other.

"Thank you, Mac," I croak without pause, my eyes pricking with tears as I cup his cheek and drag my thumb along his stubble. "Thank you for being my best friend."

Mac's brows furrow, and I stare back at him, trying to discern the shifting nuances behind his intense unreadable expression. Finally, his face lightens, resuming its normally sweet, gentle Macness.

He pulls me into his chest. "Thank you for being mine."

He drops a kiss to my hair, and it's the perfect kiss to seal a perfect moment between two best friends.

CHAPTER 14

Mac

I WAKE THE NEXT MORNING TO A ROUGH TONGUE TOUCHING MY nipple. A smile spreads across my face as I open my eyes and expect to find Freya. My face falls when I see it's her fucking demon of a cat laving at my pec like it's going to produce milk at any moment.

"Fuck off, you wee bastard!" I bellow and shove the animal off my chest.

Hercules takes off down the hallway, and a snort echoes in the room. I turn my gaze to find Freya perched on a chair in the corner of her bedroom. She's dressed in a long nightshirt, her red hair a wild mess of curls, and her makeup smudged like she was properly fucked last night. And she looks positively entertained.

"Did you just sit there and watch your cat violate me?" I croak, sitting up and rubbing my tender nipple.

She giggles and steadies herself so as not to spill the two cups of coffee in her hands. "I came in to bring you a coffee, but Hercules looked like he was warming up to you, so I just sat down here to not interrupt. I had no idea he was going to lick your tit." She bursts out laughing all over again.

"You and I are in a fight then," I reply gruffly, propping myself up on the headboard of her bed. "That was disturbing."

She nods, her face still tormented with poorly concealed laughter. "For us all." Her head shakes as she continues laughing and tiptoes over to hand me my coffee as though it's some sort of peace offering.

I eye her warily as she sits down on the edge of the bed by my feet. "How long have you been awake?" I ask, my eyes reflexively eyeing her legs as she curls them up underneath her.

"Not long," she replies, taking a careful sip out of the kitten mug I bought for her.

I glance down at the mug she gave me and see it's yet another kitten mug. This one says: Cats Make Me Happy. You, Not So Much.

I take a quick sip before asking, "How are you feeling?"

Her eyes are full of sweet innocence. "I feel okay. You?"

"I feel great," I reply with a shrug. "I had sex last night."

Freya rolls her eyes.

"Are you sore?" I ask, leaning forward and glancing down her body, a strong hunger to taste her again overwhelming me.

"Yes," she replies with a small laugh, her eyes drifting from my eyes to my lips. "Does that go away the more you do it?" she asks with the most gorgeous innocence on her face.

My lips twitch with a fondness I've never felt for another burd. "Aye, I believe so. Practice makes perfect and all that."

She nods. "And I bled a little. I suppose that will go away, too?"

"Aye, I don't think it will happen again," I confirm with a frown and grip the back of my neck as guilt overwhelms me. Last night after we finished, Freya nipped off to the loo to clean up while I slung the condom into the bin by her bed. I saw a bit of blood on the condom, but the sheets were okay, so I threw on my boxers and crawled under the covers to wait for her. I didn't even realise I fell asleep until I woke up hours later to find her sound asleep beside me.

"Sorry I passed out on you last night." My voice is remorseful because that's not how I wanted the night to end. I wanted to ask her questions and see how she was feeling. "Was it all...okay for you?"

"The sex?" she asks, her voice hitching up at the end. "God, yes! It was lovely. Everything I hoped it would be. Was it okay for you?"

"Definitely," I reply with a laugh. "Honestly, it was dead brilliant on my end. I was just worried about you because it's been a while since I've had sex, so I wanted to be sure I hadn't lost my touch."

"It's been a while since you had sex?" Freya asks, sipping her coffee and eyeing me curiously.

"Aye, since Cami. Over a year ago."

"Holy shit." Freya chews her lip for a second and adds, "You haven't been with anybody since Cami?"

"I think you would have noticed if I had been, Cookie," I reply, sitting back against the bed to hold my coffee against my chest.

Her brows pinch together. "You travel a lot during the season. Surely, there was some random girl in some random city you went to."

"No," I reply simply. "Just me old hand giving me a crack."

Her nose wrinkles. "That surprises me."

"It's been a proper dry spell, that's for sure," I reply, glancing down at her legs again. "Actually, Roan thought I was shagging you for several months when we first started hanging out."

Freya's eyes widen. "He did?"

I nod and smile. "The thought had crossed my mind."

"It did?" Freya's dropped jaw makes me laugh.

"Aye, are you saying it never crossed your mind?"

Freya flushes and gets an uncomfortable look on her face.

"Okay then, I guess it was one-sided," I reply, my jaw taut as a sense of rejection overwhelms me. My jaw tics as I set my coffee down and move to get off the bed.

"It wasn't one-sided," Freya says in a rush, stopping me by placing a hand on my leg. "I just…never really gave myself the hope, I guess. I was an almost thirty-year-old virgin until last night, so I rarely ever give myself hope with men. I never would have imagined you'd think of me sexually."

I throw my legs off the edge of the bed so I'm sitting beside her, my boxers just barely containing my morning wood. I turn and eye her speculatively. "Do you remember that night we went out in a limo with the Harris family? Vi coupled you and me off for that ridiculous group ballroom dancing lesson, and we ended up at the club downstairs afterwards to test out our moves?"

"The night when my heels trashed my feet so badly you had to carry me out of the club?" she asks, blinking as she recalls that evening.

"Aye, that's the night." I swallow hard as memories of my own flood the forefront of my mind. "I wanted you that night. Badly. Things with Cami and I had just ended, and I was lonely, and you were so cute in your flirty skirt and bare feet."

"Seriously?" Freya barks, a laugh on her face. "You wanted to hook up that night? Was I hot to you before or after I hobbled myself with those ridiculous shoes?"

I fight back a laugh. "I must have a thing for damsels in distress because it was definitely after. I helped you into your flat, and it was the first time I'd been over here, and…I don't know, I thought we had a moment."

Freya's eyes blink in surprise as she clearly tries to recount the night that happened well over a year ago. "I had no idea you even looked at me like that."

I shrug. "Freya, I'm a bloke. I think with my cock ninety percent of the time."

"So why didn't you make a move that night?"

I exhale heavily because it's not the first time I've given that question some thought. God, she was so sexy that night. So unassuming and real. Hilarious without even trying to be. I knew from the moment I met her that she was not one of those women who blends into a crowd, even if she's trying to. She's a standout, and I wanted her naked so badly I could taste it.

But from the moment I met Freya, she'd always felt different than other girls. She made me feel like my true self at a time I wasn't sure who my true self even was. I couldn't risk losing that by shagging her.

"I realised I liked you too much to treat you like all the other women in my life," I reply thoughtfully as I look forward and rub the palms of my hands down my thighs. "Most women I sleep with are such arse kissers, I can hardly stand to be around them for more than five minutes. But you were so interesting and different. You didn't get starry-eyed when Roan and I came into the boutique for that first fitting. In fact, I was quite certain you hated me from day one, which must make me a masochist because I fancied the shite out of you after that. And I knew then I wanted more than five minutes with you, so I resisted my urges."

I turn just in time to see Freya lift a shy hand to hide her pleased smile. "That's actually really sweet, Mac."

I shrug and look forward, trying to lighten the mood. "Then we started Netflix and chilling, and I realised how bloody refreshing it was to just sit on your damn sofa and watch telly like a normal bloke and not think about football for a single moment in my life. I kind of love the fact that you don't give a shite about football. Have I ever told you that?"

Freya's lips curve down with sentiment. "No…but I guess I kind of love the fact that you don't give a shite about my obsession with *Heartland*."

"Fuck, I'm hooked on that daft show," I reply with a laugh and run my hand through my messy hair. "I think I love those bloody ponies just as much as you now."

Freya giggles, clearly pleased with herself. "And look at us now. We've managed to have sex and stay friends anyway. Well done us."

"Well done us, indeed." I grab my coffee to give her a quick cheers.

Freya exhales heavily after taking a sip. "What are we going to do about our friends?"

"What do you mean?"

"Are we going to tell them what we did?"

I flinch. "I'd rather not."

Her lip curls up in agreement. "Me too."

"I don't see the need if it was just a one-time thing, right?" I stare over at her and regret the words as soon as they leave my mouth. "I mean…you wanted to have sex for the first time, and we accomplished that, so there's nothing more to be done, right?"

She chews her lip thoughtfully. "Or."

"Or?"

"Or we keep having The Sex," she says and lifts her brows hopefully as she gauges my reaction.

Her comment scares me a bit, so I deflect with a joke. "I thought after you had The Sex you would stop calling it The Sex."

"Probably not," she says distractedly. "But I was thinking, since you no longer have a friends-with-benefits situation, and I'm so inexperienced with The Sex, it would do both of us some good to continue this new part of our friendship. I imagine I could get better at sex with practice, right?"

I can't even begin to hide my look of complete and utter amusement. "Aye, sure. You get better the more you do it."

"So we keep doing it," she says excitedly as though she's talking about a school project she's eager to work on and not about having regular intercourse with her best mate. "Maybe you can show me how to do some of those things I drank to during that *Never Have I Ever* game."

"Not the fucking dirty Sanchez," I growl, losing all humour. "I'll die before I do anything close to that."

Freya rolls her eyes. "Obviously not the dirty Sanchez. I was just thinking about like, maybe the oral stuff?"

My brows lift. "More than what I did last night?"

She shrugs shyly. "Yeah. I'd like to try it the other way around. Maybe sixty-nine? I googled what that was after the party, and it doesn't look too hard."

I purse my lips together to fight back my smile. "You don't need to ever sixty-nine, Freya. Sixty-nine is something teens do when they're trying to hurry and get everything in before their mum and dad get home."

"Oh," she says, deflating a wee bit.

"But I can show you how to give a proper blow job if that's what you fancy."

"Yes, I think I'd fancy that a lot," she beams happily, her face a picture of innocence that quite truthfully scares me a bit.

It's one thing to have sex just the one time. It's quite another to do a full-blown friends-with-benefits arrangement with someone all over again. Plus, what if Freya wants more than just friendship? I can't risk losing her.

I grip the back of my neck and eye her seriously. "Look Freya, I'm up for more because, hell, I'm a bloke and saying no to regular sex just goes completely against my biology. But I just want to be sure you know what you're asking for. What if you want more than just sex?"

"What do you mean? Like a relationship?" she asks, her lips twitching with barely concealed amusement.

"Aye," I reply, pinning her with a confused look.

She bursts out laughing so hard she nearly spills her coffee with the fit of giggles shaking her entire body.

My face falls as she wipes away the tears in her eyes. "Mac, don't be silly," she says with an amused sigh. "I know you don't see me like that. And believe me, you're not my type."

My brows furrow. "It seemed like I was your type when I gave you two orgasms last night."

She rolls her eyes and gives me a playful shove. "Don't get sensitive. I'm just saying that I know you, and I know myself. We won't fall for each other. We can barely get along for twenty-four hours, let alone be in a real romantic relationship where we have to care about the other person's feelings. You and I are like oil and water. Or like super glue and skin. You and I ending up together would be the equivalent of horse whisperer Amy Fleming falling for a city boy," she adds, referencing her daft *Heartland* show like that reference is supposed to click for me.

Okay, it does click for me. There's no way in hell Amy Fleming could ever give up ranch life for a slick businessman type.

I clear my throat and try to shake away the strange sense of rejection I feel. Of course I shouldn't feel rejected. I should feel overjoyed. Freya is gorgeous, and she's my pal, and she wants to have no strings sex with me. This is a win-win-win situation. Right?

"If we do this, we have to set an end date for this arrangement," I state, running my sweaty palms along my thighs. "That will help make everything neat and tidy."

"That's a good idea," she replies, nodding her head thoughtfully. "How long do you think I'll need to feel experienced enough to go out there and shag someone else?"

The mention of her doing it with someone else sends a strange chill up my spine that makes me feel like a fucking caveman. Of course Freya is going to have sex with someone else someday. She's not just going to be ruined by my cock for the rest of her life…even if that notion makes me positively gleeful.

But it'd be better for her to have more sex with me first than to just rush out there and have sex with anybody. I could show her a few things in the bedroom. Help her figure out what she likes and doesn't like so she knows how to speak up for herself.

However, I'm not going to allow myself to get wrapped up in a long-term Cami situation again. Two years of that shite, only to be left for someone she deemed more worthy, wasn't exactly an ego boost.

If Freya and I do this, I can't let her break me like Cami did. I won't risk my game like that ever again. I'm not a young lad anymore. One distracted game could result in a career-ending injury for me, and I do not want to go through that kind of pain ever a-fucking-gain. No woman is worth that shite.

Freya and I need crystal-clear boundaries.

"We do this for one month." I turn to look my friend in the eyes and show her that I'm not messing around about this.

"A month?" she asks, her brows lifting in surprise. "Why a month?"

Because if we go any longer, I'll become addicted to the taste of you.

I shrug away that thought. "We can cover a lot of ground in a month. Plus, in one month, I'll be leaving for preseason training camp, so I'll need to redirect all my focus back on my job by then."

Her posture straightens, and a cute smile spreads across her face. "Okay…a month then."

"And we don't tell our friends about it. We act normal when we're all together, and then when this is all over, we go straight back to being friends," I state seriously. "Complete with Netflix and arguing." I wink at her as I reference her description of us from before.

"That sounds perfect," she says with a wee smile. "I'm looking forward to this. Now that I've got a taste of what orgasms are like, I rather like the feeling."

My jaw drops as I stare back at her incredulously. "You like the feeling?"

She shrugs like she's talking about her favourite item on a breakfast menu. "Yeah, that orgasm thing you get my body to do is rather nice."

I bite my fist, feeling fit to burst at her adorable innocence. Christ, this is going to be fun.

Freya then chirps, "I guess this means I can forget about finding a date for Allie and Roan's wedding."

I shoot her a cheeky wink. "Aye, you won't need a man by your side when you have your Loch Ness Monster Sex Steed walking you down the aisle."

Freya's nose wrinkles as she moves to stand up. "Nope…can't do it. Deal's off."

"What?" I exclaim, my body tensing at her ominous words that I know she can't mean.

She pins me with a look. "I refuse to shag you ever again if you keep referring to your penis as the Loch Ness monster."

"Just give it a chance," I say with a wry grin because I love winding her up like this. "It grows on you…literally."

I waggle my brows at my sexual innuendo, and Freya wrinkles her nose. "Nope. We're in our second fight of the day already, so the deal's definitely off."

She moves towards the door, and I quickly set my coffee down and jog up behind her in the hallway, my erection growing in my boxers just with the thrill of this wee chase. She squeals in surprise when I wrap my arms around her waist and pull her to me, almost spilling her coffee in the process.

I twist her in my arms and press her against the wall with every inch of my body. "Nothing's off except apparently your bra." I reach up to tweak one of her nipples through the thin cotton. "Now put that bloody coffee down so we can make up."

Freya laughs. "No fucking time! I have to be to work in thirty minutes."

"We can cover a lot of ground in thirty minutes," I growl and dip my head to press my lips to the hollow of her neck. Freya arches into me, and my cock thickens between us. "But no sex," I hum against her collarbone. "I think you need time to recover properly before we try that again."

She shoves me away from her chest and stares up at me with an adorably offended look. "What did you have in mind then?"

I laugh and shake my head. "Oh Cookie, there's so much for me to show you."

CHAPTER 15

Freya

"**S**O GUESS WHAT?" ALLIE SAYS CHEERFULLY AS SHE JOGS UP the stairs to my loft office in Kindred Spirits.

"What?"

"You know how you've been begging me to give you an idea of what I want to do for my bachelorette party?"

"Hen party, Allie," I correct, jutting out my chin. "I know you lived in America for most of your life, but don't ignore your British roots."

Allie rolls her eyes. "Fine, fine, hen party. Anyway, I finally figured out what we are going to do."

"What?" I reply with a bright smile. "Tell me what I need to line up and I'll get it sorted."

"We're going to crash the guys' stag trip in Scotland!" She perches on my cutting table and starts playing with her hair with a big smile.

"What?" My voice is venturing on shrill when I push back from my sewing machine to give Allie my full attention. "We're going to Scotland?"

"Yep!"

"Why?" I ask curiously, my mind flooded with the fear of being in front of all our friends during my new arrangement with Mac. Acting cool during the wedding was one thing. Being around everyone for an entire weekend is another altogether. "Isn't the point of a hen party to be away from your bloke?"

Allie rolls her eyes. "I think a hen party is just an excuse for a party, isn't it? It was actually Mac's idea to make it a group trip. He texted me about it this morning, and Roan is all for it!"

The mention of Mac's name sends a frisson of desire coursing through my veins as flashbacks of last night hit me at full speed. His body, his tattoos, his noises. God, his noises were positively indecent. Even his ridiculous snoring when I came to bed, and he rolled over and started spooning me was oddly nice.

The entire evening could have been a dream. If I didn't have the text exchanges to prove that Mac and I were truly together yesterday, I might be telling myself it was all in my head.

But it wasn't in my head.

It was in my bed.

And it was perfection.

Which is why when I woke up this morning, I wanted more. Mac could very well be the only man I'm ever intimate with. I'm not delusional enough to think that losing my virginity is suddenly going to give me all the confidence in the world to go out there and find another bloke to be with. I know Mac tells me I'm beautiful, and men fancy me, but I didn't grow up feeling that way. And a few sweet words from a man who is my best friend isn't giving me any bright ideas that a romantic happily ever after is in my future. Online dating is a nightmare, and meeting men is just bleddy hard for a girl like me.

But being intimate with Mac was surprisingly easy. And that's why I want to experience as much as I can with him because I've made peace with the fact that I will likely die a lonely old cat lady. At least if I sow my wild oats with Mac, I can feel satisfied in the fact that I've experienced all The Sex has to offer.

And after my morning with Mac, I now know what oral sex has to offer. Talk about a solid first day as an ex-virgin.

Well done, Freya.

I don't think Mac saw that coming from me actually. But the moment I got a clear view of his penis in my loo while we were stepping into the shower together, my curious mind wanted to taste him. To know how the texture of his member would feel against my tongue and lips. A smile lifts my face as I recall Mac's reaction when I dropped down on my knees under the spray of the shower.

"What are you doing?" Mac croaks, his voice hoarse with a sound that I recall from last night.

"I'm going to suck your penis," I reply simply, tipping my head back so my hair gets wet. "Any tips?"

Mac's face goes blank as he watches me on my knees fisting him and waiting with bated breath for direction. He gently combs his fingers through my hair and holds my head in place as he tries to form full sentences. "Just, erm, do whatever your instincts are telling you to do."

So I listen to my gut, and I take him into my mouth as deep as I possibly can. His cock is unlike anything I expected. It's hard and lush, but the skin is soft and delicate. Who knew penis skin was so silky? Certainly not me.

Mac apparently loses all ability to communicate the moment I slick my tongue around his tip and then suck him hard between my lips like a lollypop. I glance up, and the look he's shooting down on me isn't one of a student and a teacher. It's pure, unbridled lust.

God, it's brilliant. What an amazingly powerful feeling to be turning a virile, masculine, sexual man like Mac into putty in my hands.

I didn't know women could enjoy giving oral sex, but apparently they can because I love having this effect on him.

I think I'm a natural at sucking cock!

And when he tells me he's going to come, I pull back, releasing his wet penis from my mouth and fisting him tightly in my grasp. I can feel him grow beneath my fingers, and there's a strong pulsing happening that excites me. I will him to come because I want to see it! I want to watch him explode and lose control even more because of what I've done to him.

His head falls back, and he orgasms, his climax sputtering out in several wild pulses, landing all over my neck and breasts, and even some on my face. It's exhilarating. I look up and see he's now gazing down at the wreckage as I continue to stroke him, milking out every last bit and feeling the texture of his semen on my chest with my other hand. When I bring my finger to my lips to taste his release with my tongue, the wicked, lust-filled look on his face is an image I will remember until the day I die.

"So are you in?" Allie asks, snapping my attention back to the question at hand.

"In?"

"For Scotland! Are you free? I was going to check with Sloan and Leslie and the Harris wives as well. See who's up for a little trip to the Highlands. Mac says there's room for everybody at his grandad's property."

"Erm, yeah, I'm the maid of honour, so of course I'm in," I say, curious about the reasoning behind Mac's sudden invitation and why he didn't talk to me about it first.

"Yay!" Allie squeals and hops off the table to hug me. "I'm going to go see if Sloan and Leslie want a kid-free weekend."

She pulls back from our embrace and pauses, her eyes dancing all over my face. "Something is different about you. Did you colour your hair?"

I feel the colour drain from my face and reach up to touch the wild tendrils of my hair. "Um, no. My hair is colour retardant, which is the reason I've embraced my natural flames. I didn't curl them today like I usually do. I, erm, overslept."

"It's not your hair." She tilts her head and eyes me seriously. "Did you get a facial maybe?"

My brows lift. "No. I use body lotion on my face sometimes." *Maybe semen is like an anti-aging cream no one talks about?*

"Freya! Body lotion is horrible for your pores."

What about semen? I think to myself and then shake my head and shrug. "Freckles are surprisingly resilient."

She rolls her eyes and gives me one last look. "We'll see if I still notice it tomorrow, I guess."

She studies me for a moment longer, and I begin to wonder if she can she tell that I had sex. Is that a thing? Do sexually experienced people have a sixth sense about this? If so, I'm going to be doomed in Scotland!

Allie turns to head down the stairs. "Are you off for the day soon?"

I glance at the clock to see it's nearing on six already. "Oh God, yes. I had no idea it was so late. Hercules is probably wasting away at home."

Allie laughs and gives me one last wave. "All right then, I'll see you tomorrow."

"See you tomorrow," I reply, abandoning my sewing machine for the night.

I head downstairs and wave my goodbyes to Sloan and Leslie before stepping outside to find Mac parked smack dab in front of the shop.

He waves buoyantly from the driver's seat to get my attention, like somehow I could have missed him. I look side to side, still not one hundred percent certain that he's here for me, and not simply dropping off Roan for Allie or something.

He beeps the horn and waves me over like a bleddy maniac.

With a frown, I stride across the street and slip into his car. "Why are you blowing the horn outside my place of work?"

"Well, you were just standing there like you didn't recognise me."

"I wasn't sure you were here for me."

"Who would I be here for? Mr Aged Cheddar around the corner?"

I reach across the console and whack his shoulder as he smirks and takes off down the road.

"What are you doing exactly?" I ask after a few moments of silence.

He shrugs. "I'm picking you up from work."

"Why?"

He shrugs again. "If I'm being completely honest, it's probably because we shagged last night and you sucked my cock like a champion this morning."

I can't help it. I giggle-snort like a fool. "You are such an ox, do you know that?"

"And you're an ungrateful passenger."

The car goes quiet for a minute before I ask, "So are you just dropping me off at home?"

Mac get a salacious grin on his face. "We're going shopping first."

My mood darkens. "I do not want to try on any more clothes for you, Mac. Look, I'm wearing a skirt today!" I state, pointing down at the black pencil skirt that sits just above my knees.

"Oh believe me, Cookie. I noticed. You in that skirt was on my mind all day long." He shoots me a naughty wink. "We're not shopping for clothes. We're shopping for food."

Mac

As Freya and I meander around the supermarket, she starts firing questions at me about Scotland. "Why on earth do you think it's a good idea to bring the ladies on your stag weekend to Scotland? Don't you think it's going to be obvious?"

"Don't I think what is going to be obvious?" I ask as I drop a tray of fresh strawberries and a can of whipping cream into the trolley Freya is pushing along.

"That we've...been *intimate*," she says on a whisper and looks around nervously as though our fellow shoppers can hear her.

"No, I don't," I reply with a shrug. "I can act completely normal around you. Just look at me now, walking around a store and not shouting at the top of my lungs that my cocker has been inside you in the last twenty-four hours."

Freya's eyes go wide as she aggressively shushes me. To my delight, I watch her adorable ears turn as red as the strawberries in the trolley.

"Are you the one we have to worry about?" I ask with a lascivious smirk. "Are you going to have trouble keeping your hands off of me? I'm sure now that you've tasted the Loch Ness monster yourself, it's going to be nearly impossible for you to control your urges."

Freya rams the trolley into my shins.

I bite my fist to stop myself from screaming in agony. "Do I need to remind you that my legs are worth a bit of money?"

"Do I need to remind you that you sound completely ridiculous when you refer to your penis as the Loch Ness monster?"

As those words escape Freya's lips, a flash of movement catches my eye, and we both look over to see a wee blond-haired boy, who can't be more than six years old, staring directly up at us, listening to our entire exchange. His mother stands just behind him, looking outraged. With a scathing look, she drags the wee lad away, no doubt thinking we're a couple of perverts, and I hear his wee voice repeat, "Is my penis called the Loch Ness monster too, Mummy?"

I turn accusing eyes at Freya. "You scarred that wee boy for life. Are you happy?"

"Quite," she replies, jutting out her chin defiantly. "Hopefully, he'll not grow up to be disillusioned into ever thinking his penis is a mythological monster."

I shake my head from side to side, a smile growing on my face. "You're going to have to stop being mean to me, Freya, or I'm going to fall in love with you."

Freya's anger disappears. "What?"

I shoot her a wink. "I get a stiffy for the mean ones."

She blinks at me strangely while I grin and turn to continue our shopping excursion, grabbing all the necessary supplies that we'll need for tonight's festivities, which Freya still knows nothing about.

When we're checking out, Freya says quietly to me, "Do sexually experienced people have a sixth sense about ex-virgins?"

"What?" I ask, looking down at her, and trying—and failing—not to laugh.

"Never mind," Freya says, her cheeks turning red as she glances at the man ringing up our food.

I grasp her arm to turn her attention back to me. "No, no, repeat yourself."

She glances around nervously before leaning up to whisper, "Like, can they sense I had sex in the way police dogs can smell drugs?"

I school my face and try not to laugh too hard at my dear, sweet, innocent friend. "Not to my knowledge, Cookie."

She shakes her head, rejecting my response. "I swear Allie could tell. She said I looked different, and she knows about my lack of experience, so I feel like maybe she knew."

I hand over my credit card and turn to take a good look at my best mate. Tilting my head, I scan her body with great delight. She does seem a bit different now that I'm really looking. Her posture is a bit taller. And her face is always beautiful with those wee freckles, but it's almost like her eyes are constantly smiling even when she's not smiling.

It's hot as fuck.

I need to get her arse home. Now.

"She only knows what you tell her," I state and give her chin a small chuck. "And don't worry about Scotland. It's going to be really fun showing you my favourite kind of sex."

The cashier suddenly drops the can of whipping cream on the floor and frantically bends over to pick it up in a vain attempt to hide the fact he was earwigging.

Freya hits me with an admonishing look but then bites her lip and leans in to ask, "What's your favourite kind of sex?"

I smirk and whisper in her ear. "The secret kind."

Freya snorts out a laugh. "I can't wait to see how that goes."

A while later, we're back in Freya's flat with groceries spread out on the countertop. Hercules has taken cover as usual. *Clearly our intimate moment this morning meant nothing to him.* And Freya has already given me shite about being cheeky enough to pack an overnight bag. I couldn't give a fuck. I owe Freya another sleepover.

One where I don't pass out on her before she comes back to bed. And I intend to follow through this time.

"So what kind of sexual training session do you have in mind with this lot?" she asks, staring at all the food.

"First, we feast," I say, pulling out the sliced chicken breasts and chopped veggies. "Then dessert." I waggle my eyebrows lasciviously and damn near moan when she reaches up to tug on her ears. God, I love how her ears get hot when she's turned on. It's such a quirky tell.

I'm three minutes into making dinner for us when Freya shoves me out of the way to take over, claiming I wasn't doing anything properly, and since it's her flat, she's in charge. With a laugh, I back away and pour her a kitty mug full of wine while grabbing myself a beer.

I put some music on her portable speaker and hoist myself up on the counter to watch Freya work. She's barefoot and still wearing her work clothes as she sets about sautéing the chicken, peppers, and onions for fajitas. Her hips sway slowly to the music as she hums along.

Freya has made dinner for me loads of times before, but now that we've had sex, it just feels different. Not bad different. Not scary different. Just…exciting, I guess? It's freeing to know that I can shamelessly ogle her, and she won't yell at me for it. Well, she might yell at me—but now I'm welcome to enjoy it. I love when she gets all red and snippy at me. She's like a wee pup picking a fight with a giant dog.

There's nothing wee about those hips of hers, so lush in that tight skirt. The curve of her arse is way too tempting as I sit much too far away. I glance up and notice that her pale blue blouse is slightly see-through in her kitchen lighting, and she's wearing a sexy white bra underneath. My innocent treasure is not so innocent anymore.

How did I stay away from her this long? Fucking hell, I deserve a badge of honour because this woman is temptation personified. I've always liked a woman who's not rail thin. I'm a big bloke, and I want my hands full when I reach out to grab something that's mine. And the images of Freya's soft, lush skin laid bare for me last night have been giving me erections intermittently all day long. So much so, that I had to go home and have a crack before picking her up from work.

It's going to be a shame when this arrangement comes to an end.

Freya has just begun plating the food when I press up behind her, my body flush against hers as I skate my hands over her hips to pull her back into my groin.

She gasps when she feels the state of me. "Bleddy hell. Why are you—?"

"Hard as fucking stone?" I ask gruffly against her hair. "Because there's something seriously sexy about watching you cook for me, lass." I lift my hand to move her red hair off of one shoulder to expose her long, elegant neck. "I suppose that makes me an anti-feminist, but fuck it, I'll give you orgasms in exchange for my nourishment this evening if that's what you fancy."

I brush my lips along her shoulder, moving my way up to her ear, which is currently simmering. I wrap my lips around her hot lobe and give it a playful bite. She makes an adorable noise that has my cock thickening even more.

"Orgasms are satisfactory," she states, her voice breathy as she abandons the plates and splays her hands out on the countertop for purchase. "I'm obviously new to them as a concept, but the couple I had yesterday were quite memorable."

I smile against her neck and then frown curiously. "Did you never touch yourself before, Freya?" I glide my hands to her front, the tips of my fingers brushing over her most sensitive area. "Don't you have a favourite vibrator or something that could get you off?"

I trace circles over top of her clit and can feel the heat of her through the thin fabric of her skirt. *God, I bet she's wet for me already.*

"Not really." She lets out a throaty noise, and her head falls back against my chest. "I tried to do it to myself when I was in university but could never get past the fact that it was me doing it and not a man."

Fuck, there go my caveman fantasies again.

"You want a man, my wee treasure?" I ask, unable to hide the proud smirk on my face over the fact that I own her first orgasm too.

"I guess so," she says with a sigh. "Leslie bought me this vibrator, but that thing never sees the light of day."

"And it won't, if I have anything to say about it," I growl, nuzzling into her neck and inhaling her womanly fragrance as if it's my last breath. "Do you think we could skip dinner and go straight to dessert?"

"Skip dinner?" she chirps, her voice deep and breathy and everything my cock loves to hear in a woman.

My hands move from her groin and steal up underneath her blouse. They glide over her ribs and, without any finesse, clutch tightly to her breasts that don't even begin to fit inside my hands.

"Your nipples are hard as stone too," I murmur, pulling her back against my chest and slowly pinching her nipples through the thin white lace. She groans when I roll them between my fingers. "I need to taste them."

I move my hands towards her back to unclasp her bra, then slide them forward again, damn near fucking roaring in victory when I feel the spongy firm nubs of flesh. "Turn around, Freya."

It's a command she follows instantly, and when we're finally face to face, dilated pupils locking with dilated pupils, parted lips level with parted lips, our mouths descend onto each other like starved animals that haven't feasted in days. Freya hums into my mouth, and the kiss turns into one of those sloppy ones that occurs when you're frantically shedding clothes at the same time. Neither of us seems to mind, because we're both hungry for something much more than food.

When we're both naked, I grab her under her arse and hoist her up onto her countertop, dragging kisses down her chest and closing my lips over her perfectly pert nipple while my palms grip her back. "I had plans to use whipped cream and honey. I was going to lick it off every square inch of you."

"Oh, fuck the dessert," Freya cries, grabbing my cock and pulling me towards her centre. "Just fuck me instead."

"Condom," I growl when my bare tip touches her wet centre. Fucking hell, I'd love nothing more than to drive into her completely bare just to feel her on my hard, smooth rod. But I resist, just barely, and grab a condom out of my wallet and put it on as quickly as possible.

I pull her to the very edge of the counter and without warning, impale myself inside her soft, wet heat.

Fuck. Fuck. Fuuuuck.

She's still tight. Still way too fucking tight. I pull back and look at her face, worried that I hurt her. Her eyes are glazed over as she watches where our bodies are connected.

"Are you okay?" I ask, and she answers by wrapping her hands around my arse and pulling me back inside of her.

"Fuck yes. Just fuck me, Mac," she says, nodding eagerly. "I feel as if I'm going to come already."

"Jesus Christ," I mumble and begin rocking inside her. She's soaked and tight and lush, and gripping me so hard it won't be long before I come either.

Her head drops back as her cries grow louder, and out of simple curiosity if she really could come this fucking fast, I reach between us and press my thumb to her tight bundle of nerves. She screams and wraps her legs so tight around me, I can't even move.

That did it, I think to myself as she smacks the countertop with her hand repeatedly. Her sex clenches all around me as her legs begin to quake beneath my hands.

"Ohhh, fuck, fuck, fuck," Freya cries, her breaths coming out fast and ragged as I ride her through her orgasm.

It's only a moment later that I erupt as well, satisfied that she's satisfied and grateful I didn't come before her because after all my Loch Ness Monster talk, that would be a fucking embarrassment.

"I'll call that lesson a quickie," I say with a laugh after I've ditched the condom and we've set about redressing ourselves in our clothes, which are strewn all over the kitchen floor.

"I think I'm a fan of quickies," Freya says with a smile, her hair properly mussed and her cheeks rosy and bright. "The way you tossed me up on the kitchen counter like that? I nearly combusted on the spot! I'd never dreamt of being tossed around like that."

"Well, in case you hadn't noticed, there's a wee bit of a height discrepancy between the two of us," I state, lowering my hand to where her head barely hits the top of my chest. "You must have been always front row at the Christmas concerts."

"Shut it," she replies with an annoyed giggle. "Well, regardless, I appreciate that lesson."

"That wasn't my original plan, woman," I say with a shake of the head. We're only a day into this arrangement and already Freya has surprised me twice, causing me to lose focus on tasks at hand. First in the loo this morning and then tonight. "I had a very different lesson plan all drawn up involving whipped cream and honey… remember?"

"Oh, that's right." Freya's brows lift. "We still have time after dinner, don't we? Or can you not do a round two so soon after?"

I level her with a hard glower. "Freya, I'm Scottish. I was born with a stiffy."

CHAPTER 16

Freya

MAC HAS OFFICIALLY SLEPT OVER THREE NIGHTS IN A ROW. I asked him yesterday where Roan and Allie thought he was all these nights because surely they are noticing Mac's absence. He told me that he told Roan that he and Cami started hooking up again.

I didn't like that very much.

I mean, I know what we're doing is a lie, and we're actively not telling people. But I don't altogether like that his lie about getting back together with Cami is so believable. He mentioned still having lunch with Cami once a week. Will he go see her this week even though we're sleeping together? It's not that I don't think he can have lunch with another woman, but the fact that it's with someone he was intimate with for so long makes my tummy hurt.

I do my best to ignore the pang in my belly as I stand at the counter with Sloan, Allie, and Leslie downstairs in the Kindred Spirits Boutique and await our upcoming fittings. Kindred Spirits is about to be invaded.

As if on cue, the doors open, and I swear the world starts moving in slow motion as Roan and all four of the Harris Brothers stride into the boutique. My ears heat up as I watch their fit bodies make their way towards us.

I don't normally fangirl over footballers. Perhaps there's been a change in me since I've seen one naked every day for the past week? My God, they are physical beauties. Large, thick thighs, big, muscular arses, and wide, swimmer's body shoulders that just seem like they could hug you and take all your troubles away.

Where the hell did that come from, Freya?

"Hi, guys!" Sloan says excitedly as the brood of strong men come waltzing up to the counter. They're all wearing various forms of athleisure wear. I've learnt from being around this crowd for the past couple of years that even though this is their off month, they are still constantly working out. Sloan's husband, Gareth, is the only one kitted out in jeans and a T-shirt. Since he's retired, he's filled out and rocking that "plump and happy" look that my mother always claimed to have. Although, even a plump and happy Gareth Harris is extremely fit by anyone's standards.

The door rings again with the entrance of the Harris Brothers' sister, Vi, her husband, Hayden, and Hayden's brother, Theo, who's Leslie's husband. Quite a convoluted, overly connected bunch if I ever saw one.

"Who's ready to watch our men become highlanders?" Vi squeals excitedly.

"I already have a kilt," Camden says, shoving his twin brother, Tanner. "I wore one when Indie and I eloped, but Mac says I can't compete if I'm not kilted out in Clan Logan, so...here I stand."

Tanner cuts a menacing glare to Camden. "Must you remind us that you decided to selfishly get married without inviting a single member of your family?"

"Not this again," Camden groans, rolling his eyes. "Our wives are best friends. We had our first children within weeks of each other.

Surely you can let one life event slip by without being the absolute centre of attention."

Tanner turns his eyes forward and whispers, "I'll never forgive you."

Vi shakes her head, like she's used to these hysterics from her brothers. "I wish girls could wear kilts because I'm so excited for this trip to Scotland, and I really wish we had a costume."

Leslie walks over to stand by Theo as she says, "Don't worry, Vi. Sloan and I decided we're going to get all the ladies fitted for outfits from the boutique this week. It'll be our gift to everyone for Allie's upcoming nuptials."

Allie's jaw drops as she stands holding Roan's hand. "Are you kidding me? You can't! You guys are already designing my wedding dress and Freya's maid of honour dress. You're fitting these guys for kilts. Gareth booked a freaking private jet for all of us to fly to Glasgow. This is all way too freaking much."

"Stop saying 'freaking' so freaking much!" Sloan says, wrapping her arm around Allie. "You're a Harris, and you're getting married. This is how they are, and if you haven't figured that out by now, they're going to beat it into you with brute force that will involve lots of awkward hugs."

Allie's eyes begin to water, and bleddy hell, my own start to burn as well. Is it too late for the Harris family to adopt me? I've met their dad, Vaughn, and he's still fit. Maybe he'd fancy a young, shapely bride for himself?

Just then the door to the shop opens again, and it's Mac this time. My emotions take another hit as I watch him walk in, his ginger hair wild and unruly as usual, and his scruff shaggier than ever. *You'd think the boy isn't getting much sleep these past few days.*

I smile at that thought, and his eyes find mine instantly. He winks quickly before looking around at everyone else and holding up the huge bolt of green plaid with red and yellow woven through. "The Clan Logan tartan has arrived!"

The group cheers excitedly while Sloan, Leslie, and I get to work measuring all the boys for their matching kilts. It's going to be a lot of work getting them done in a week, but with the three of us working at it, we should be able to get it done before we leave next Friday afternoon.

When I finish measuring Booker, Mac comes striding up to me, holding out his well-worn kilt. He has an adorable sheepish look on his face. "My kilt could use a wee tune-up if at all possible."

I narrow my eyes at him. "And what's wrong with it?"

"The bottom has come undone," he states, and I run my finger along the frayed hemline.

"You're going to have to put this on for me to pin it up properly."

Mac waggles his brows at me. "Why don't you just say you want to see a sneak peek of me in my kilt, woman?"

I roll my eyes and shove it into his chest. "Changing rooms are in the back."

Moments later, Mac comes striding out in his Timberland boots with no socks, his white tee, and his kilt. My eyes drink in the sight of his muscular legs, because bleddy hell, if any man can wear a kilt, it's this one.

His shit-eating grin indicates he knows exactly what he's doing to me, but I do my best to hide it because Sloan and Leslie are just two stands over, measuring Theo and Hayden, while the rest of the Harris family is milling about nearby.

I clear my throat and ignore the burning in my ears. "Stand here please," I state, pointing at the carpeted platform in front of a three-way mirror.

Mac hops up, his kilt swooshing with the movement. "This thing has had a lot of use over the years," he says as I kneel down and begin slipping pins into the frayed hemline.

"This length okay?" I ask as I chance a glance at him in the mirror.

He quirks a brow at me, like he wants me to be doing something very different down there. His voice is huskier than before when he replies, "Aye, sure. That'll do."

I nod woodenly and slip the pins in, running around the side of him as quick as my fingers can handle. I swear I can feel Sloan, Leslie, and Allie all watching our interactions with great interest. I feel like I'm inside one of those aquariums where people are constantly tapping the glass.

"You're going to love Dundonald, Cookie," Mac states grandly. "There's the Dundonald castle, fresh sea air, the smell of mud and filthy man. It's intoxicating."

"Can't wait," I murmur around a pin before pulling it out and slipping it in. "Why is your kilt so well worn? Do you do these Highland Games every year?"

"Every year," Mac says proudly. "Three years ago, I won the entire thing. The Clan Logan tartan is lucky and legendary."

I roll my eyes. "Of course it is."

Mac looks down at me with arched brows. "Are you doubting my grand words, woman?"

I look up at him, and he's got a salacious smile on his face that I can't help but smile back at. "Dundonald is a small town, right?"

"Aye."

"So, can I ask if the people you go against are young, professional athletes from around the world? Or perhaps, grey old geezers who use walkers to meander up to the castle once or twice a year?"

Mac bursts out laughing. "Oh, fuck off with you."

I giggle to myself proudly. "I knew it."

"You know nothing. You should have seen me in the log throwing competition last year. I was facing off against some of the biggest blokes in the county, and I beat them all by miles."

I roll my eyes. "I'm surprised you could compete. I thought your legs are worth a lot of money. Seems like a dangerous sport for you to risk your most prized property."

I glance at him in the mirror, and he pins me with a wicked look. "I'm afraid someone else's legs are my most prized property these days."

I can't help but smile back at him with the biggest, dopiest, happiest smile I've ever felt.

Suddenly, his smile falls. His eyes turn to saucers, and his entire face distorts into a horrifying look of pain.

"My cock!" he booms and buckles over in agony.

I lower my chin and my eyes go wide when I see that my hand is currently up under Mac's kilt and the needle I'm holding is definitely stuck to something. *Shit. Shit. Shit. Shit!*

Without thinking, I yank the needle out of what I'm quite sure was his shaft and quickly lift the kilt to inspect the damage. My gasp draws everyone's attention when I see…

Mac's bare penis.

And balls.

And well, whatever parts of a naked man's crotch might exist down there because the idiot isn't wearing his boxers! Why isn't he wearing boxers? He knew I was going to be eye level with his kilt! Was he trying to get a rise out of me? God, he is a cheeky bugger, and he deserves a severe walloping for this one. Or perhaps a tiny poke to the penis?

No, that's taking it too far, Freya.

"Would you mind lowering my kilt so the entire Harris clan can stop staring at my cocker, woman?"

I drop the kilt and turn to look around at everyone who's blatantly watching the spectacle.

"Why the fuck aren't you wearing boxers?" I screech accusingly while sitting back and replacing the pin into the cushion on my wrist.

Mac's jaw drops in disbelief as he cups his dick over his kilt. "You don't wear bloody boxers with a kilt. Free ballin' is the biggest perk to wearing a kilt!"

"Pardon me for not realising you wanted to rub your balls all over the lucky and legendary Clan Logan tartan," I mimic his voice from earlier, and his eyes go lethal on mine, actually scaring me a bit. "Look, I'm sorry! But if you were wearing boxers, then the damage wouldn't have been so severe!"

"Excuse me for thinking my cock and balls could take in a bit of scenery for a bloody moment. I didn't know you were going to attempt *manhoodslaughter!*" His voice hitches to a high-pitched nerve-wracking tone. "Christ, I think I'm bleeding."

"I'll, erm, go get you a medical plaster."

"You're going to need gauze, woman. And maybe a very big cast. You should well know the state of me by now. A plaster would hardly cover my bloody pee hole."

"Would you stop shouting!" I exclaim, standing up and stomping my feet. "I can't think when you're shouting like this."

Mac's face contorts. "Aye, sure. I'll be sure to address you like a lady when MY BLOODY SHAFT STOPS HEMORRAGING BLOOD!"

I roll my eyes. "Now you're just being dramatic."

And then...the weeping begins.

It's hours later, and Mac is curled up in my bed in the foetal position, holding a bag of peas on his groin. He only cried for an hour after I drove him back to my flat. At first, I thought he was so mad he'd want to go back to his place. But he said he expected me to wait on him hand and foot for this egregious offence, so here I stand, at his bedside... just waiting for him to request a sponge bath at any moment.

Mac moans as he hands me his thawed peas.

I exhale. "Are we still in a fight? Or would you let me finally have a look at it?" I state with exasperation. "If it still hurts this much, I think we should take you to A&E or at least have Indie or Belle come over to look at it. They are doctors after all."

"Enough people have seen my cock and balls today, thank you very much," he harrumphs, draping his inked muscular arm over his face in true Mac dramatic fashion. "And we're still in a fight."

"What can I do to make this up to you?"

He shrugs and lowers his arm. "Just lay here and talk with me until I fall asleep."

My face lightens instantly, and I can't help but smile at the big, goofy idiot. I lower my head and kiss his forehead before taking the peas into the kitchen. I shut off all the lights and slip into bed beside him.

We're lying on our sides facing each other when I say, "What do you want to talk about?"

He sighs heavily. "Remind me what your boobies look like. It's been hours, and I've forgotten already."

I hit him with an unamused stare. "If I show you my boobs, will you stop moping?"

He shrugs sadly.

I sit up and lift my nightgown, giving my breasts a hearty shake before lowering it and snuggling back under the covers.

He smiles like a kid on Christmas morning. "That was very thoughtful of you, Cookie."

"I live to serve," I repeat his words back to him.

His eyes drift down to my kitty cat night shirt. "How many kitty night shirts do you own? It's alarming that I've never seen a repeat performance after this many sleepovers."

I glance up at the ceiling as I attempt to count. "Maybe a dozen? Not sure. But this one has a mini cat-sized one to match."

"You and Hercules have matching pyjamas?" Mac asks, his face lighting up with amusement. "My God, I have to see this. Where is the awful creature?"

I exhale heavily. "It doesn't fit him. Plus-sized fashion clothing for cats isn't really a thing."

"It should be."

"I know," I state, my brows pinching together with that statement. "I've made him a couple of things myself, but whenever I dress Hercules in them, he just goes limp. It's really funny. I actually started an Instagram profile for him, and it's full of videos of him getting dressed up and keeling over."

"Shut it." Mac laughs and stares back at me. "How many followers do you have?"

"Sixty-four thousand!" I giggle. "It went kind of viral after my first post. I've never told anyone I run it, and no one I know ever sees Hercules to identify him."

"That hilarious," Mac states with a pleased smirk. "You should make more plus-sized cat clothes."

"I'd love to," I reply with a smile. "I have a whole notebook full of sketches for the cutest little outfits. I even have dog options drawn up too because, well, people love their chubby dogs. But I never have the time to sew for fun anymore."

"You should make it a job then," Mac says simply.

"What do you mean?"

"If you have the eye to design, then you should be doing more than just altering Sloan's and Leslie's creations."

My giddy mood deflates. "They consult me on their designs a lot. I contribute more than just the alterations."

Mac frowns, and he reaches out to cup my cheek. "I didn't mean anything by that, Freya."

"Then why did you say it?" I ask, pulling my head back.

He reaches out and holds my hand on the bed. "I just think you're extremely talented, and if making pet clothing makes you happy, then nothing should stop you from having the confidence to go out there and do it. Your unique brilliance deserves to be seen."

His words are everything I've tried to tell myself many times before. Even in university, when we did group design projects, I always had ideas but deferred to the more outgoing person in our group. Confidence gets things done. Reticence never gets off the ground.

"I've thought about talking to Sloan and Leslie about bringing a pet line into the boutique," I say softly, looking down at Mac's big hand on my small freckled one. "So many of our clients are obsessed with their pets. You should see how many carry them in their handbags."

"See?" Mac says, giving my arm an encouraging squeeze. "You're full of ideas. You have the confidence to do this, I know you do. And selfishly, I want you to do this so you're never near another man's genitals with a needle ever again."

"Shut it, you," I say and narrow my eyes at him. "You were distracting me with your cuteness."

"You think I'm cute?" Mac asks, his brows tweaking excitedly at me. "I thought you'd only fancy me if I had a cheese hut."

I roll my eyes. "You know you're cute."

He resumes holding my hand, combing his fingers through mine. "And you know you're cute…right?"

I take a deep breath, letting the words sink in because they mean so much more than just physical beauty. Knowing I'm cute is the equivalent to having confidence, and I need the latter more than the former. Hopefully someday, I'll learn how to answer this question without hesitation.

"I know I'm cute," I state finally, hoping eventually I'll believe it one hundred percent. I shake my head, ready to turn the focus back to my patient. "And what about your future? What will you do after football?"

Mac's brows lift. "Hopefully, I have a couple more years left in me, at least. I wouldn't mind being one of those old geezers on the pitch who die of a heart attack right there on the green."

A groan erupts from me. "That's a horrible thought."

Mac shrugs. "I'm just joking mostly. Actually, my dream job after this football life is over would be something in the world of gaming, where I could combine my computer knowledge with my football knowledge."

I blink back my shock. "Pardon me, but did you just say computer knowledge?"

Mac rolls his eyes. "I have my degree in computer science, Cookie. I'm not all brawn."

I sit up, staring down at him with my jaw open. "You what?"

He shrugs and turns onto his back. "My mum would have flogged me if I didn't get a degree in something useful to fall back on. One bad injury and my career could be over in the blink of an eye. Honestly, I'm shocked I've made it this long without anything horrible happening."

My brows lift as I absorb this very new information. "And computers are your thing?"

He shrugs again like everything he's saying is so simple. "Computer stuff was always easy for me. Even as a wee lad, I liked knowing how things worked behind the screen. My dad used to bring old computers home from work whenever they got upgraded, and I was always taking them apart and putting them back together."

"Huh," I say and smile proudly at my best friend. "Maclay Logan, computer science specialist. You'd be the hottest computer nerd at whatever firm you end up with, you do realise."

He laughs and rolls his eyes.

"I'm serious. The Javier lookalikes will think you're the stupid one because you're just too pretty to be smart too, so you're going to have to prove yourself on the first day."

"Okay, boss," Mac says, reaching out and tweaking my side. I giggle and fall down onto his bare chest. My hair spreads out over his pec as I press my ear to his heart.

"I think that's really cool, though," I say softly, allowing the drumming of his heart to soothe me. I spread my hand out on his stomach and slide my finger along his softened abs. "And I'd love to see your caricature as a footballer in a video game."

"Right?" Mac says excitedly. "It's the only reason I got all these tattoos."

I burst out laughing, burying my face in his chest with delight. "You are such an idiot."

His body shakes beneath my head as he laughs, and soon enough, I see the blanket covering his groin begin to rise.

I sit up on my elbow and stare down at it, then back up at him.

He shrugs. "You called me an idiot. I told you mean girls are my thing."

I bite my lip and eye him speculatively. "Well, maybe I'll call you a big faker because my tiny little poke clearly didn't cause any permanent damage."

He waggles his brows suggestively. "You better go down there and inspect it. Our next lesson can involve a bit of naughty nurse role-playing."

My eyes light up. "Oh my God. I can't believe I didn't think of this before!"

I leap out of the bed and dash into my walk-in closet. After a moment of digging through a box in the way back, I slip out of my kitty night shirt and into something that Mac is sure to fancy.

When Freya emerges from her closet, I swear to Christ, I've died and gone to heaven.

"What do you think?" Freya asks, smiling proudly as she does a spin in the most scandalous nurse's outfit ever created.

It's a red fishnet-netted negligee that's much too short to be a dress. Really, it's just a slip that barely covers the tiny matching knickers she has on underneath. It's completely sheer except for the white medical plus signs that are stitched over the tips of her wee nipples. On the top of her head is a matching white and red nurse's hat that I can barely even focus on because her legs are on full display and her breasts are nearly spilling out of that getup.

"Why do you have that?" I ask, sitting up to stare at her properly and trying to keep my tongue in my mouth.

"I bought it for Halloween one year when I was having one of my outbursts, as you like to call them."

"You were going to wear that tiny getup out for Halloween? Are you mad?"

Freya shrugs. "I was at the time. I was sick of seeing all these skinny women at Halloween parties flounce around in their tiny little costumes while bigger girls were dressing up like Shrek. I wanted to feel sexy."

I stand up, my heart rate throbbing inside my chest. "Well, I fucking hope you didn't wear that getup in public."

Freya's jaw drops. "And why is that?"

"Because your bloody knickers are hanging out!" I exclaim, my voice going to a strange, high-pitched, manic place.

"Coming from a man who wears a kilt with no boxers, that's really rich," she snaps. "And this getup is no different than what the thin girls wear on Halloween."

"If you were mine and wearing that, I would shag you all night so you were too weak to go out and show everybody my property."

"Your property?" Freya lets out a peal of laughter. "Well luckily, I'm not your property so you don't need to worry about it."

"You are mine," I state, stepping closer to her and grabbing her by the arms. "You're mine for the next month, and I'd be grateful if you would be willing to accept that."

I breathe heavily down upon her, my cock thickening inside my boxers at the feel of her in my arms when she looks like this. Christ, I want her. I want her so bloody bad I can taste it. But for some strange reason, I need to feel some sort of security in what we are. I know we're just friends, and I know the sex is temporary, but I want it to feel real while we're together.

Freya swallows nervously. "Well, if I'm yours for the next month, then does that mean you're mine?"

"Aye, of course it does," I snap. "Why would you doubt it?"

"Are you still having your weekly lunches with Cami?" she asks and crosses her arms over her chest defensively. She's trying to look tough, but all the change in posture does is push her breasts together and give me the urge to lean down and motor boat my face between them.

Finally, I focus on what she just said. "I called Cami and told her we couldn't meet anymore."

"You did?"

"Aye, Cami and I are just mates, but I'm not going to be shagging you and running off to see her. What's the fucking point in that?"

"Well, why did you need to see her at all if you weren't still sleeping with her?" Freya asks, her brows pinched together in an adorable way as that gerbil spins rapidly inside her mind. "What was the point of you two getting together every single week?"

"I don't know." I exhale heavily and grip the back of my neck. "She was therapy I suppose."

"Therapy for what?" Freya asks pointedly.

I pin her with an unamused look. "I've been wanting to have sex with my best mate for the better part of a year, and I guess I needed someone to talk to about it, all right?"

Freya blinks up at me in shock. "You talked to her about me?"

"Of course I did," I growl, feeling annoyed that all this had to come up. "Who else would I talk to about it? Roan? He's so wrapped up in his own love life he can't tell where his unit ends and hers begins."

Freya looks down, clearly bewildered by what I've just said, but after a split second, she looks up at me again. "Well, good. So we're exclusive for this arrangement then. Fine. Now that that's all sorted," she states, her chest rising and falling with deep, laboured breaths, "can we have sex now?"

"Finally, we agree on something," I growl, and she launches into my arms just as I take a step towards her.

I lift her up, and her legs wrap around my waist as I squeeze her lush arse in my hands. My thick cock angles upwards like it has muscle memory and knows exactly where it wants to burrow in all night long.

My cock is fine, by the way.

Aye, she poked me properly, to be sure.

But considering I got a chubber while she was yelling at me in the shop, I figured there was no long-lasting damage. I've just been milking it for attention until now.

I bring her over to the bed and shed my boxers and her knickers in one swift tug. I move to get on top of her, but she quickly grabs me around the waist and rolls us so she's on top.

"I want to try this way," she says, biting her lip nervously.

"Aye, let's do it," I reply with a smile.

She positions herself over top of me, and I grab her thighs to stop her. "Condom."

She shakes her head. "I want to feel you."

I hit her with a look. "What are you talking about?"

She nods. "I started the pill a few days ago."

"You did?" I exclaim, sitting up on my elbows and staring back at her in shock.

She nods. "But it's not one hundred percent effective yet, so just pull out before you come, okay?"

"Aye, sure. No problem," I state, placing my tip right on her slit. "Christ, I've wanted to feel you like this all bloody week."

"Me too," Freya cries, nodding and looking down as she slowly, deliberately, damn near painfully lowers herself onto my shaft.

"Good fucking God, you feel incredible," I growl, clutching her thighs and biting my lip because I need to get control of myself if I want to make this good for her.

"So do you, you fucking liar," she groans and swivels her hips on

169

top of me. "Your dick was fine, and you made a huge scene just to torment me."

I can't even attempt to fight back my grin. I've never smiled in bed with a woman. I quite like it if I'm being honest. "My cock may have been fine, but the emotional trauma—"

"Shut up," Freya says, giggling so hard I can't help but shake beneath her with my own laughter in return.

My pleased smile falls as she begins to really ride me. She's good at this. She's flexible and taking me in deeper than when I'm on top. Her eyes close, and her head falls back as she grinds down on me with her sweet, perfect pussy.

A pussy that is all mine.

Never been touched by another.

Fuck me, I'm a pig.

I sit up and wrap my arms around her waist, clutching her to me as I bury my face in her red lace-covered breasts. I bite through the fabric and clamp on her nipple aggressively, taking what's mine. She lets out a yelp of a cry that's sexy, but not as sexy as her bare tits. I quickly grab the bottom of this ridiculous nurse's outfit that she actually thought she could wear in public and rip it off of her. It tears in the movement, and a satisfied smile spreads across my face.

"No more naughty nurse, I guess," I murmur against her skin, sucking hard wee spots all over her breasts as they bounce with every thrust she makes. "You're just Freya, and you're mine. All fucking mine."

"Yes," she moans, clearly ramping up to her orgasm already.

I drop back onto my elbows and watch the show, enjoying the sight of my love bites peppered all over her breasts. "Touch yourself, my treasure."

Freya's closed eyes open, and she looks at me with an adorable frown.

I chin nod to her pelvis. "Touch your clit there while you ride me. Give me a show."

She huffs out an aroused sort of laugh but does as I say. She makes a proper show of it as well. Her hand skates slowly from her hair, over her breast, swirling around her navel and making me positively growl with anticipation.

Cookie's a fast learner, I think smugly to myself as her finger dips down to rub over top of her clit. I bite my lip and watch her as she gingerly moves over it.

She can do better.

I put my hand over hers, showing her how to apply pressure and rub it hard and fast. These pressure points make her wild with lust, and she nods eagerly, clearly understanding my direction as she begins speeding up, driving herself higher and higher. Feeling the build grow stronger and stronger.

When I feel her begin to tighten, I lie back, grab her thighs, and thrust up into her hard and fast. Her hand falls, and she collapses over me, crying out her release into my neck as she drenches my entire fucking shaft with her arousal. In a rush, I hug her to me and roll her over, pulling out just in time to finish on her belly and breasts.

It's a good chunk of time that we just lie there. My cock softens while we both fight to catch our breaths and formulate full sentences.

Finally, Freya croaks out, "Fucking hell, I'm starving. You?"

And with that compelling statement, we both laugh our way out of post coitus and right back into friendship.

CHAPTER 17

Freya

"**W**E'RE SERIOUSLY GOING TO NEED A BIGGER CAR. THERE is no way!" I exclaim, glancing into Mac's backseat as we wait in line at the car wash Mac frequents just outside London.

He smiles over at me like I'm an adorable little pet he wants to snuggle. "Cookie, this was one of the *Never Have I Evers*."

I exhale and look back there again. "I just…don't think car sex was intended for people like me."

"People like you," Mac states, his eyes going flat. "Car sex works in a myriad of ways, my wee treasure. Just trust your love coach to guide you. Plus, you drank to this at Tanner and Belle's flat, so it's only right that you turn that lie into a truth."

I stare back at him accusingly. "You're enjoying my discomfort far too much. We're officially in a fight."

"Oh good, something new and different for us," Mac replies with an unamused tone.

Ignoring his snark, I face forward, anxiously rubbing my palms on my skirt. I'm as excited as I am nervous while I stare at the long line of cars going inside the giant building one at a time. I bet none of those people are planning to shag while their car rides the tracks through the wash. This is taking car sex to another level entirely. Damn Mac. Damn him to hell!

Mac and I are well into our second week of this friends-with-benefits arrangement, and if someone would have told me a year ago everything I would be doing for these next few weeks with a famous footballer, I would have told them they were off their rocker.

Yet here I sit, in a car wash line with the man in question.

And it's not just the sex with Mac that's surprising me. We're doing other things that men and women do together all the time. We go out to eat, we go to the cinema, run errands. Just this past weekend, I was sick with a twenty-four-hour flu bug, and I begged Mac to leave me alone. I begged him to go back to his place for a night and get away from my ugliness.

He refused.

He got me soup, ran to the chemist's for some medicine, and waited on me hand and foot. He even slept on the couch when I told him his body heat was making my fever worse.

That was the only night we didn't have sex.

The ample amount of sex we have had has been mind-blowingly brilliant. I was right; it does get better with practice. And there are so many positions that Netflix has never portrayed in the programs I watch. For example, I never laughed so hard as when Mac was trying to show me doggy style and then said, while he thrust balls deep into me, "We're doing it just like the horses on *Heartland*."

The fucking arse.

He had to wait until my fit of giggles stopped so we could continue. Yet somehow, through that entire ridiculous scene, he never lost his hard-on. He really is quite the freak.

AMY DAWS

One of the best perks about having Mac at my place and this arrangement we're doing is the snuggling while watching Netflix. Mac literally spoons me on the sofa and plays with my hair while we're watching the telly. It's marvelous. His heart really is as soft and mushy as his head is thick and obstinate. The cuddling is probably what I'm going to miss most when this all ends.

I take that back. It'll be the sex. Most definitely the sex. And maybe that kiss on my shoulder thing he does when he leaves early in the morning to go for a run. It's just the lightest brush of his lips on my shoulder, but it makes me feel warm and gooey inside like pudding. I'll miss that, too.

"Freya, we're next in line. Tell me we're doing this, for the love of Christ, because my cocker is already standing at full salute just thinking about it."

I glance down at his groin inside his running shorts and bite my lip nervously. "Okay, fine. But no hickeys this time, or I swear—"

"Okay, I hear you, woman." He smirks victoriously. "Now, just wait till the tracks take the car inside, and as soon as the bubbles are on the windshield, we'll jump in the back. We've got eight minutes."

"God, how many women have you done this with?" I groan, looking around nervously for any form of life as Mac slips the car into neutral and the tracks take control.

"None," he states with a shrug. "You're the first one who fell for it."

"What?" I exclaim, and then suddenly, the car is being sprayed with foam.

Mac unbuckles and slips into the back like the agile athlete he is. "Take your knickers off before you come back," he commands, his voice gruff with desire already.

I squint my eyes closed and do as he says because all I can think about is that we have less than eight minutes, so arguing with him like usual really isn't a wise time choice. I toss them into the back seat and turn to make my way over the console. Had anyone been able to see through the rainbow-coloured foam that's currently hitting the car, they would have seen my white, ample rear end filling the entire windshield.

I land with an oomph on Mac's lap, and his eyes twinkle with excitement. He slaps my arse. "Right, now straddle me, Cookie," he commands, his hands spreading out on my thighs as he hikes my skirt up.

I glance down as I centre myself over top of him. "I told you to stop calling me food names when we're shagging."

"I'm sorry, my wee treasure," Mac lifts his face up and pulls me in for a kiss. "Now pull my cock out of my shorts and stop wasting time. We're probably down to six minutes."

My brows lift, and I shift back to do as he says, the hard silky heat of him sending a frisson of desire pulsing between my legs so that I can feel myself dampen with need.

Mac holds a foil packet up for me. "Put the condom on."

I eye him curiously because we haven't used these for several days now.

"Less messy this way," he replies gruffly.

How practical. Biting my lip, I open the packet, take out the condom, and shakily roll it onto his straining erection. "I did it!" I exclaim like an immature idiot.

"Now ride me hard and fast, treasure. Ride me like you mean it."

I can't help the small giggle that escapes my mouth because Mac is being so serious throughout the absurdity of what we're trying to do. You'd think we're solving a difficult math problem instead of trying to shag inside a moving car wash.

But I'm a quick study, so I move to position him between my folds, my body quivering with anticipation for the girth of him that I know will stretch me in the most delicious way. When I have him where I want him, I hold onto his shoulders and sink down over him, my legs spreading out as far as possible.

"Ow, the buckle," I yelp as my knee comes into sharp contact with it. Mac grabs my thighs, scooting over slightly and shifting us to the edge of the back seat.

At this angle, he's even deeper inside me, and my mouth opens in a silent cry.

"Better?" he asks with a lascivious smirk.

I nod and manage to murmur, "My bed would be better."

"Stop complaining and kiss me, woman," he growls with a smile, and I can't help but smile back as our lips and tongues tangle with each other. He pulls away and adds breathlessly, "I need you to start moving on my cock, or I'm going to come just like this without getting you off. You have me way too bloody wound up."

I nod slowly, vaguely aware of the car moving forward, but the action happening in this SUV is far more interesting to me. I start moving on top of him, my hips swooping forwards and backwards as quickly as possible, my clit grinding into him when I roll inward.

My God, this is exhilarating. Like nothing I've ever experienced before. It's hard to believe I've lived my whole life thinking I didn't need this. Now that I've had it, I don't know how I'll ever get over losing it. Would it even be possible to find it again? Could I really be that lucky?

My thoughts and motions are halted when Mac grabs my thighs and thrusts up into me hard and fast, my head bumping the ceiling of the car, as he chases my climax like he knows exactly where it lives inside me.

"Fuck me," Mac growls, grabbing my breasts over top of my blouse. "God, Freya, I need you to come soon."

"Okay," I whine, my breaths coming hard and fast as I groan through a deep throb growing between my legs. "I'm coming, Mac. Oh God!" I cry, my voice loud in the small space of the car.

"Fuuuck," Mac growls, his voice throaty and dry as he squeezes my hips and pushes into me as deep as he can while I arch my back and come all over him.

He releases next with a very vocal growl, his body quivering as he flexes into me with each spasm. My inner core is tingling and oversensitive as I feel every pulse of him against my needy inner core. I drop my head into his neck and sigh with relief before croaking out, "I think I like car wash sex."

He laughs and reaches up to pull my hair away from my face long enough to kiss me. It starts off as a peck, but then he rethinks it and pulls me in for a deep, drugging kiss that is all kinds of intimate as his cock begins to go soft inside me.

God, this feels good.

By the time we tear our lips apart, I notice the car is getting ready to go through its final rinse cycle, and we need to get off each other and get back to the front seat. Mac gingerly rolls me off his lap, his condom-wrapped dick sliding out of me as I move to sit beside him in the back seat. I lazily push my skirt down and button my blouse, which I didn't even realise had come undone, while he ditches the condom in a nearby tissue and pulls his shorts up.

He looks over at me and smiles like the cat who got the cream when suddenly, clear water washes away all of the bubbles revealing several men outside the car with towels in hand. My eyes go wide as they instantly begin wiping down every square inch of his vehicle and I consider ducking below the windows and hoping no one sees me.

However, that plan goes out the window when a man opens my door, his jaw dropping with surprise to find me and Mac sitting in the back. I stare back, unsure what to say, and then my jaw drops in horror as my knickers slide out the door where they had apparently landed and fall to the ground by the man's feet.

"Interior cleaning?" he asks nervously, glancing at his feet and then to my thighs.

Mac voice cuts into the mortification screaming in my mind. "Not today, lad."

And then, without any shame, Mac hops out of the car, jogs

over to my side and picks up my knickers with a wicked smirk before jumping into the driver's seat.

"Where to, Miss?" he asks, adjusting the rear-view mirror.

I cover my face in mortification as he drives us away from the towel guys. "Take me to Hell because that is certainly where I belong."

CHAPTER 18

Freya

I AM CURRENTLY SEATED ON A PRIVATE JET WITH SIX FAMOUS footballers, four London-famous designers of fashion and furniture, two genius female surgeons, two blondes who look like models but are actually really smart and cool working mothers…

And then there's me. Freya. A woman covered in freckles who is seriously thinking this lot would be better off with a partridge in a pear tree.

Honestly.

This is why people like me aren't friends with people like this! Because it fosters insecurities.

Creates complexes.

I need proper friends with social anxieties who look mediocre in bikinis. I need friends who actually finish their plates of food at a restaurant and don't feel bad about it. And hell, since I'm listing out friendship goals, I'd like a friend with some horses. Horses that I could ride someday if I ever learned how. Does a friend with a ranch in Canada where she heals troubled horses sound like too much to ask the universe?

Apparently so, because I'm stuck with this happily-in-love lot.

I bet none of these people have a cat who hates humans.

Sigh.

I really need to calm my mind down. This weekend is supposed to be fun. And I am normally great around this bunch. They're truly lovely people who give me life goals to aspire to, but today their love just seems to mock me. And remind me of all that I will never have in life.

The past two weeks with Mac have been insanely perfect. We're even getting along better than we ever have before, which is messing with my mind completely. I also keep thinking about that conversation we had about Mac talking about me to Cami for over a year. What did that even mean? Was it really just about sex? For a year? It has to mean more, right? Or do I just want it to be more because I'm actually starting to fancy Mac as more than just a shag? A lot more than just a shag.

Crikey, I'm a mess!

Now, instead of relaxing into this friends-with-benefits situation and having fun with our friends, I'm obsessing over the meaning behind everything Mac says and does, and am way too chicken to just ask him about his feelings! And the worst part is, the only person I have to talk to about it all is Hercules, and he seems completely bored by the topic.

I need to get ahold of myself. For the next forty-eight hours, I need to pretend I'm not a daft idiot who is doing exactly what I promised I wouldn't do: falling in love with my best friend.

An hour and a half later, our private plane has landed in Prestwick Glasgow Airport, and our large group of seven couples and two sad singles, who are having sex but not telling anyone they are having sex, files out into the various rented cars waiting for us on the tarmac.

Thankfully, I end up in a vehicle with the ladies and am able to avoid Mac's curious eyes as we drive the twenty minutes towards his grandfather's property. He told us all on the plane that the bed and breakfast has been sitting empty for the past couple of months while minor repairs were being made, but he called ahead to get it fully stocked for our visit. Apparently, Mac's grandad just sold the estate to some wealthy bidder in an auction and has since moved into a flat in Dundonald to be closer to Mac's parents.

The sun is shining as we pull up the gravel driveway to the beautiful Georgian house nestled right on the shore of Prestwick Beach in Ayrshire. A quick glance around shows no neighbours as far as the eyes can see. It's idyllic.

And actually kind of sad when I think about the stories Mac shared about how this bed and breakfast was his grandmother's dream. To watch it all be sold off to some stranger must be hard on the family.

Mac appears relaxed as he walks up to the front door and stands back to let everyone pass through. I'm last through the entrance, and I try to sneak by him, but he grabs my hand and pulls me back into him.

"What's wrong with you?" he asks, crooking his hand under my chin so I'm forced to look up at him. "Are we in a fight?"

I plaster on a smile. "Not at all. I'm fine. This is lovely!"

He's not buying it. "You were quiet on the plane."

"You mean the private jet?" I state with a laugh. "I was just… taking it all in. That was my first time travelling like that."

Mac furrows his brow at me. "You're off."

I shake my head. "Nope. Just excited for the weekend."

He tilts his head. "You'll tell me if something's wrong, right?"

"Of course, pal." I smile brightly and smack his arm.

He looks confused but lets me go inside with the others.

God, Freya. Your poker face needs some serious work!

Mac waltzes in behind me and lets out a quick whistle to get everyone's attention. "So there are exactly eight bedrooms, and it's first come, first serve, except for the bunk bed room on the third floor. I've claimed that one for the two singles of the weekend."

He points at me with a big, goofy smile. "Freya, if the bunk bed is rocking, don't come knocking!"

The guys hoot with laughter at Mac's seriously disturbing joke, which I painfully smile through. "Duly noted." I swing my fist in front of me like a pirate for reasons I'll never truly understand.

Mac shoots me a wink like he's just working on a ruse and then adds, "We're free until seven o'clock, and then we'll be walking to the town centre for a dinner reservation I lined up. Let's meet back down here in about three hours?"

The couples all scamper off up the stairs to claim their rooms while I turn to take in the rest of the house. It's completely divine in all its charming, old-fashioned, grandmother-styled glory. Floral wallpaper, frilly drapes. Marble fireplace. Original crown moulding. Doilies on every end table with tiny little porcelain knickknacks. Even the lace tablecloth in the formal dining area is so quaint, I fall in love with Mac's grandmother without having ever met her.

When I reach the back of the house, I gasp as I step into the conservatory sun lounge and take in the stunning water view.

"That's the Isle of Arran," Mac's voice states as he stands close enough to my back that I can feel the heat of him.

"Quite a view," I murmur, exhaling heavily as I take in the long, lush garden that breaks away into a sandy beach.

"The mountains of Arran are off there in the distance." Mac rests a hand on my hip as he points to the right. "We call them 'the sleeping giant' because it looks like a man laid down in the water from the coastline."

I squint at the sight. "I can see it."

Mac's warmth breath blows into my hair as he huffs. "Aye, on a really clear day, you can see it even better and the sunsets are really something."

I turn to glance up at him. "It's beautiful here."

He tips me a crooked smile. "Of course, I grew up inland with my folks in Dundonald. But I came out here to help out on the weekends whenever I could." Suddenly, he reaches down and grabs my bag. "This way to your chambers, my lady." He waggles his brows at me suggestively. "Allow me to show you to our kiddie room."

I follow him up the two levels to the loft area, where he has to duck to fit through the doorway. There's a small loo attached and the single bunkbeds are perched on a rustic set that looks like it was made out of recycled barn wood.

"I'll take top," Mac says with a wink as he drops my bag on the lower bed. "Most people would look at this room and think it's the worst of the lot. But…"

Mac walks over, grabs my hand, and leads me to the long, narrow window. He stands behind me and holds my waist as he positions me in front of the pane glass. "It has the best view of the house for some people."

I look around blankly for a moment before my jaw drops. "Whose horses are those?" I ask, pressing my hand to the glass and staring out at the big hulking animals grazing in a small paddock off in the distance.

Mac's body shakes with silent laughter. "The barn and the pasture belong to the property here, but my grandad rents it out to a local farmer with horses."

"Oh my God, can we go see them? Please?"

"Aye, I've already called ahead. The owner is expecting us in thirty minutes."

I squeal with delight and turn to drag Mac's face down to mine. The kiss is a reflex at this point. We've spent two weeks together, never going a day without touching.

And regardless of my new, burning feelings, I don't want what we have to end. "Let's call this lesson 'who can orgasm the fastest,'" I state excitedly as I begin to shed my clothes like they're on fire.

Mac laughs and breaks free from me long enough to shut the bedroom door. "Actually, let's call it 'who can be the quietest'. This house is old, and the walls are paper thin."

I bite my lip excitedly, and we set about completing our lesson. I call it a success when Mac only has to cover my mouth twice the entire time.

CHAPTER 19

Mac

WHO KNEW THAT WATCHING FREYA PET HORSES WOULD TURN me on so fucking much? Fuck, at this point, I should know that watching Freya do pretty much anything is going to turn me on.

She only looked slightly disappointed when she learned these were work horses and not meant for riding. When the farmer gave her a brush and asked her if she wanted to comb some of them out, I thought she was going to kiss the old coot.

Luckily, she didn't.

I helped brush them some, but mostly, I just watched Freya positively light up as she put her hands on the beautiful animals. Kittens and horses make this woman bonkers. If Freya were my wife, I'd be a fool not to live on a farm and give her horses.

Not that she'd be my wife someday, of course. She can hardly stand me long enough to shag me for a month, let alone live with me for a lifetime.

Plus, something tells me that as much as Freya enjoys being

with me, she doesn't see me as the type of man she'd ever settle down with. And it was far too easy for her to agree to the end date of this arrangement. Freya Cook's heart is firmly guarded indeed, just as mine is. I'm still focusing on my football career. And I refuse to let another woman mess with my game the way Cami did only a year ago.

I must stick to the thirty day end date. I'll head off to training camp, and that will be the end of that. A clean break.

Freya and I head back to the house to get ready for dinner. I'm ready in ten minutes, so I head downstairs and leave her to do her makeup in peace. When I come striding into the small kitchen with its bright yellow walls and old wooden table, I smile when I see Roan sitting there, reading the paper like an old man.

"Aye, making yourself at home, I see," I say, patting his shoulder as I move by him to the cabinet where my grandad always stores the whisky.

"Allie's getting ready, and I can only watch her curl her hair so many times."

I laugh as I pull down the amber liquid and grab two tumblers to join him at the wee table. "Don't tell me the honeymoon is already over."

I pour us both a finger and hand his over to him. He smells it and winces. "Ag, no. It's not even started." We clink our glasses and down our whiskies in one gulp.

"What about you?" Roan asks as I pour us another. "Haven't seen you at the house in a couple of weeks. Allie is asking all sorts of questions, and I'm curious myself because the last time you and I talked, you were only going to be gone for one night."

The corner of my mouth tilts upward. "Aye, well…things change, I suppose."

"I suppose," Roan repeats. "And this is still just a casual thing? Like how you were with Cami?"

"Different than Cami," I state and sit back in my chair to sip the second whisky slower, savouring the smoky flavour before adding, "Freya and I have a clear, defined end date."

Roan chuckles and shakes his head. "And you think that little detail is going to save you?"

I frown at him. "Aye, of course it will."

Roan purses his lips in judgment. "You say Freya can't stand you, but you've been at her place for two weeks, and you haven't burnt the place to the ground, and she hasn't kicked you out. You don't think she's starting to wish you'd stay there forever?"

I shake my head. "No. Not at all. Freya doesn't look at me like that."

"Are you sure?"

"Positive," I say simply. "I was a means to an end for her, and now she's using me to help build up her confidence. That's all we're doing here."

Roan frowns. "Who are you trying to convince here, Mac?"

"You, because you're the one with all the nosy questions," I reply in agitation, gripping at my neck. "If you have something to say, just say it."

"I think you have feelings for her," Roan states simply.

I eye him harshly. "I am attracted to her."

"And you like her."

"Of course I like her. She's my friend."

"You like her more than Cami."

I jerk away. "I didn't like Cami."

"Cami messed with your head more than you'd care to admit. She messed with your game, and that's the one thing you want to protect at all costs. So the fact that you're risking all of that again for Freya means you care about her, man, so just admit it."

"I care about her as a friend," I growl back, gripping my tumbler in my hand a bit too hard.

"Total bullshit, man," Roan says, sitting back in his chair and downing his second whisky in one gulp. "I saw the way you watched her on the plane today. You were worried."

I scowl and shake my head. "I was worried because she seemed off. She's fine now."

"You were worried because you care about her…as more than a friend. And you don't want to lose her."

"I won't lose her," I snap angrily. "Freya and I are honest with each other. We know what we're doing. We'll finish our one month of whatever it is you call our situation and go right back to being Mac and Freya. Just like always."

And with that, I push up out of my seat and leave my friend in the kitchen to go for a walk and clear my damn head before dinner.

CHAPTER 20

Freya

L AST NIGHT WAS A LOVELY EVENING. THE GIRLS ALL ENDED UP sitting at one table and the guys were at another. I was grateful for the space because my heart needed time to calm down after the wonderful surprise Mac gave me with those horses. Just when I want to pull away from him, he somehow finds a way to reel me back in. He really is a sweet arsehole when he wants to be.

And dinner was such a laugh, as all the ladies gave Allie marriage advice:

1. Have sex at least three times a week because it keeps the poison out and helps the man's disposition.
2. Get drunk together at least once a week because that's when the best deep conversations happen.
3. Shower together at least once a week so you can see all body parts in full lighting and keep an eye on each other's strange moles.
4. Once you have kids, have a nanny on call so you can leave the house whenever you need to scream.

5. Train your man into knowing that his lady is always right. Use sexual threats if necessary.

6. Take the man's last name because it makes their caveman heart thump with pride, and let's face it, guys just need a win sometimes.

7. Never stop giving blow jobs. Your husband looking at you like a hero afterwards is always fantastic.

I have to admit, I could relate to several of those after only being with Mac for a couple of weeks, so I didn't feel as out of touch as I thought I might.

We called it an early night because apparently the Dundonald Highland Games start at dawn, so the men had a car set to pick them up early. The women were to come around noon when the real festivities began.

When I nipped into the loo to change for bed last night, I came out to find that Mac had pulled both of our mattresses down onto the floor and was laid out waiting for me. Shirtless, tattooed, and so perfectly Mac.

I'm going to miss this when it's over, I thought to myself as we made love for the second time that day.

No lesson. No talking. Just two people connecting in the dark with the faint sounds of the sea as our background music.

I wake the next day to the sounds of the girls laughing downstairs. Glancing at the clock, I see it's after ten, and Mac has left already so I tiptoe downstairs in my kitten sleeper to find the ladies all in the formal dining room with mimosas and pastries.

"Morning," I say, and all seven of the ladies turn their wide smiles to me. "I can't believe how late I slept."

"Morning, Freya!" Allie says excitedly and then pats the open seat beside her. "Let me make you a mimosa."

She grabs the bottle of champagne out of the ice bucket and begins pouring me a flute, then takes the orange juice and adds just a splash on top. She hands the glass over to me with a smile.

"Did you sleep well?" Sloan asks from across the table, eyeing me curiously.

"Very," I reply and lift the bubbles to my mouth. "What time did the guys get going?"

"Six A.M.," Poppy says with wide eyes. "Booker was obnoxious as he was stomping around and struggling to get his kilt on this morning."

"I didn't even hear Mac leave," I say with a shrug.

"That's because he was getting dressed in the hallway," Indie says with a laugh. "I came out to go look for Camden's mobile and got an eyeful of Mac's bare arse as he pulled up his kilt right in the hallway. I think he was trying not to wake you."

I roll my eyes. "Shocking. I'm sure he's not wearing boxers today either."

"I was dying laughing watching you and Mac the other day at Kindred Spirits," Vi says, turning her blue eyes to me. "The way you two fight like an old married couple is the cutest thing I have ever seen."

"We're more like mortal enemies," I state with a huff.

Vi shakes her head. "Whatever you are, I love it. When will you two crazy kids just admit you fancy each other?"

The girls all turn expectant eyes to me, and I feel my cheeks begin to heat. "We don't fancy each other," I reply woodenly. "Men and women can be just friends, you know."

"Not men and women who look at each other the way you two do," Belle says, flicking her dark glossy hair over her shoulder and pinning me with a look. "I remember looking at Tanner like that, and it was right before he proposed to me."

The ladies all squeal with excitement, and my lips purse defensively. "Well, you're a great deal different than I am, I'm afraid." I say with an awkward laugh.

"What do you mean?" Belle asks, furrowing her brow.

I exhale heavily. Belle may not be rail thin like the other ladies at this table, but she's curvy like a Kardashian with dark hair and dark eyes. Basically every man's pornographic fantasy. We are not cut from the same plus-sized cloth.

The women are all looking at me with that same blank stare, and it's aggravating. "Look, I don't think it's any secret that I look different than all of you ladies."

"We all look different," Allie argues, with a challenging glint in her eyes.

"There's different," I state with a laugh and then stare down at my champagne like somehow it can save me. "And then there's me. Look, it's not an insecurity thing. I'm just being pragmatic. I have traits that I love about myself. My love of cats and ponies makes me quirky, my ability to quilt and alter clothing is top-notch. I even have some design ideas that I'd love to talk to Sloan and Leslie about down the road. I think I'm quite funny when I want to be, and I know I'm a really good friend. But my appearance is one thing that I can't change, and because of that, I'll probably never get married or procreate, but I'm okay with all of that. Because I'm a realist, and there's a big wide world out there that exists without true love."

I take a fortifying sip of my mimosa, drinking nearly half the contents in one big gulp.

"You're disillusioned is what you are," Allie says with a bark of a laugh. "You are completely blind to your unique beauty, Freya. Seriously, don't you see how you're the type of person who belongs on the cover of magazines?"

"No!" I reply with an awkward laugh. "I honestly don't."

"Fuck magazines actually," Allie replies quickly. "I shouldn't have said that because the magazines are the ones making us feel like there's only one way to be beautiful. You're gorgeous, Freya, and your inner voice is an evil, lying cunt."

"What?" I reply with a laugh.

Allie shrugs her shoulders. "It's true. We all have that bitchy little voice that tells us lies about ourselves. Lies that we think are true.

Like for me…I don't feel like I deserve Roan because of how much I hurt him last year with that stupid video I made. We're getting married in a week, and he still has to remind me that I'm forgiven."

"Allie, that's awful." I reach over to grab her hand. "Roan loves you so much. One mistake doesn't change how deserving of him you are."

"But it's the story she tells herself because of self-preservation," Sloan adds with a wobble to her voice. "She says it to herself because if the worst-case scenario comes to fruition, she thinks it won't break her then. But I can tell you from experience, you'll break regardless."

Everyone's focus turns to Sloan as she continues, "My daughter had cancer, and even though she's been in remission for years now and has a clean bill of health, I still hold my breath every time she complains of pain."

"Oh, Sloan." I inhale deeply at her very vulnerable words, which bring me right back to the year I lived with her and Sophia.

"But your inner voice is a lying cunt!" Allie adds again and pounds her fist on the table.

Sloan smiles at Allie's insistence and nods her agreement.

Leslie stands up, and says, "My father was an abusive asshole to my mom, and anytime Theo gets remotely angry, I tell myself that he could be just like him, when I know in my heart that will never happen."

"Lying cunt!" Allie says again, and this time, Sloan joins in.

Poppy then adds, "Twins are really fucking hard, and I think I might be a horrible mum."

"Lying cunt!" Allie, Sloan, and Leslie bellow.

"I hate my hips," Belle says, propping her elbows on the table. "And they only got bigger after I had Baby Joey. I think my body is revolting."

"Lying cunt!" Allie, Sloan, Leslie, and Poppy chant.

Indie chirps in next. "My pregnancy with Bex gave me angry red stretch marks that make me never want to take my shirt off in front of Camden ever again. He tells me my marks gave him the best gift of all, and he loves them, but I can't help but feel self-conscious all the time."

"Lying cunt!"

Everyone turns their focus to Vi, who's the only one who hasn't said anything through all of this. She shakes her head, tears welling in her eyes as she stares back at all of us. Her voice wobbles when she says, "I'm terrified that I'm not enough to keep Hayden happy and that no matter how hard I try, he could attempt suicide again."

The room goes quiet as everyone stares at Vi, who's just dropped some serious perspective on all of us. I shake my head, shocked and dismayed that all these stunning, strong, successful women have opened their souls to me and revealed dark parts of their inner fears that they believe to be true.

No one is perfect.

And everyone is a liar.

"Lying. Cunt." I reach out and grab Vi's hand.

She nods, tears slipping out down her cheeks as she smiles back at me. "Lying cunt."

Allie lifts her flute of champagne and holds it out to all of us. "Let's drink to all of us shutting up those lies we tell ourselves and going out there and living the lives we deserve!"

"Here, here," I state with a smile.

"Cheers!"

Who knew my outfit for the Dundonald Highland Games would have made me this nervous? I fret to myself as I smooth out my flirty skirt while riding with the girls in a large van to the Royal Dundonald Castle, where the guys are meeting us.

They've been busy all morning with a 10km road race, that

apparently ends with whisky drinking. I can't imagine the state of them if they've been drinking since ten.

Although, if I'm being honest, I'm feeling a little loose myself. The ladies and I polished off several bottles of champagne while we got ready, and it's just barely noon when we pull up in front of the castle, so we're in for a long day ahead.

We make our way out of the car, and Sloan and Leslie smile knowingly at me.

"You look so damn cute," Leslie says, shaking her head. "The pockets are a perfect touch."

She's commenting on the dress I made for the day's festivities. It's a full fifties-style swing dress with a flirty skirt, crew neck top, and three-quarter sleeves. It cinches in tight around my waist and has several large pleats at the hips and down the centre. It's a classic design that isn't necessarily a showstopper on its own, but I made it entirely out of the Clan Logan tartan left over from the bolt of fabric Mac brought into the shop. The gorgeous green plaid makes it a statement piece, to be sure.

I thought it would be a fun joke after Mac made such a big deal out of the kilts being perfect. The girls all ooh'd and ahh'd when they saw what I'd made and began making more assumptions about our relationship. But I assured them my dress was just made for a laugh.

We make our way through the crowd in the parking lot and head across the grass towards the castle. In the distance, I can see all the guys sitting at several picnic tables with plastic cups of what I can only assume is whisky. They're surrounded by other men in kilts, and it's clearly a big booze-fest happening.

Regardless of their varying states of inebriation, they all look seriously handsome in their various colours of kilts with rugged boots and socks on. I note mud splattered up around their legs and flecks of dirt staining their T-shirts, likely from the run this morning.

This look here is what Mac refers to as "casual kilt", which is an apparently very different look from "formal kilt". Having seen photos of formal kilts and now getting a good look at real-live Scots all mussed up and dirty from their day's activities, I can say without a doubt that casual kilt is my preference.

I search the crowd for Mac and puzzle over where he could be when, suddenly, he comes around the corner with a couple of guys who must be local. They all have whiskies in hand and are sipping them while talking.

"Looking good, guys!" Allie shouts as we approach, turning everyone's attention to us.

The men abandon their whisky to greet their ladies with big, proud smiles. Mac and I connect eyes, and I assume he's going to start laughing once he sees my dress.

But he's not laughing.

He's not even smiling.

In fact, he's frowning.

I look behind me to see if there's someone else he could be shooting daggers at, maybe an old local flame that he hates? But there's no one near me. The women have already abandoned me for their men, and now I'm left standing in the grass by myself while Mac gawks at me like I'm the Loch Ness monster.

My belly swirls with nerves as I hustle over to where he stands at the head of the table, passing all the happy couples and ignoring the guys who were talking to him.

I come face to face with him and rush out, "I'm so sorry. I thought you'd think this was funny." I push my hands into the pockets of my dress and look over nervously to our friends watching the scene unfold with sympathy in their eyes.

Christ, what have I done?

I glance back at Mac who's eyes are roving over my dress like it's made of blood and gore. His nostrils are flared, and his entire body is standing ramrod straight as he crushes the plastic cup of whisky in his fist.

"There was fabric left over, and I was feeling crafty," I ramble, my voice high-pitched and uneasy. "I must have blacked out while I was making this, though, because clearly it's too much. And I must have blacked out while I was putting it on today and matching my stupid lipstick to the red tint because clearly, I realise now that I look ridiculous."

Mac's friends begin to back away slowly only furthering my panic.

I step closer. "And the new heels I bought to match the dress pinched my toes, so I'm wearing my wellies instead because I had no idea Scotland would be this muddy. But honestly, I should have taken that pain as a sign that this was a bad, bad idea. I'm probably breaking some sacred Scottish tradition or something. I should have asked you first because clearly, it's not funny, and it's way too much. Way, way too much."

"It's not too much," Mac croaks, his voice deep and gravelly.

"Sorry?" I pant, barely catching my breath from the anxiety shooting through me.

"It's not too much," he says again, his gaze lifting from my dress. His eyes are intense on mine as they swim with an emotion I don't think I've ever seen on Mac's face before. He steps forward, coming within centimetres of me, and a hard, sharp flash of desire overwhelms his expression. "In fact, it might not be enough."

And then, he reaches out, cups the back of my head with both his big hands, and pulls my mouth to his.

When our lips touch, I squeal softly in protest, my hands splaying out against his broad chest because all of our friends are watching. And these guys I don't know. And bleddy hell, maybe half the village of Dundonald.

What is Mac doing? We're not kissing-in-public friends. We're supposed to be keeping our arrangement a secret! We have an end date, and if he's kissing me in front of all of our friends, this is going to get very complicated! *Maybe I want it to get complicated.*

But then Mac catches my lower lip between his teeth, parting my lips before his tongue reaches out to touch mine, and my focus narrows. Suddenly, everything else around us and all my thoughts disappear, and the only thing that exists in this world are his lips and mine.

I don't know how long we stand there in our matching tartans kissing like our lives depend on it. It feels like hours and seconds all at the same time. It's too much and not enough…just like my dress.

Eventually, an obnoxious whistle breaks through our little bubble, and we pull apart to the riotous catcalls of the people around us. Mac's eyes refuse to leave mine as he ignores our friends and tenderly strokes his thumbs along my cheekbones with a smile that makes me weak in the knees.

I don't know if I'm smiling back at him or not. I think my jaw might still be on the ground, but I do know that what I'm feeling inside my chest is utter, sublime happiness.

"I knew it," Allie says, disrupting our embrace and grasping my arm to pull me away. "You've been acting weird, and this is why!"

I roll my eyes as the girls swarm me, and the guys swarm Mac. They clink their cups of whisky to him, and you'd have thought we just got engaged by the way they're all going on and on about how happy they are for us.

Are we an us?

Are we a couple?

I suppose Mac and I should have a talk.

Before I have a chance to pull Mac aside, a gruff voice calls out in the distance. "Is that my wee Macky home at long last?"

Our focus turns to a man walking up the grassy knoll. My jaw drops because if I didn't know better, I'd swear it's the grandfather Jack Bartlett from *Heartland* striding right towards us.

The man is tall and broad and kitted out in the Logan tartan. His hair is white and unruly, and he's sporting a thick caterpillar mustache across his upper lip. Alongside him is an older couple and a young woman who I recognise instantly as Mac's parents and his sister.

"Grandad!" Mac exclaims, leaving the guys and jogging towards them.

His grandfather cups Mac's face and stares at him for a moment before pulling him into his arms for a back slapping hug. He ruffles Mac's hair playfully before Mac turns to embrace his mother, sister, and father. The five of them stand there talking for a moment before Mac turns and leads them up to our group.

"Everybody, this is my grandad, Fergus Logan. My father, James Logan, my mother, Jean, and my wee sister, Tilly."

We all shake hands, and I watch Mac as he stands back and lets everyone make their pleasantries. Fergus makes a big show of all the men wearing the tartan kilts, inspecting the work like he's a tailor himself. Nerves niggle in my belly because with my luck, one wrong stitch could be some sort of Scottish smite.

"Christ, this is good tailoring," Fergus says, grabbing the pleats on Roan's kilt and elbowing his son, James, to have a look. "Look at this wee detail. We need to have ours redone, son." Fergus then turns his inspection to me, eyeing my dress with great interest. "And who is this tartan-wearing lassie?"

"This is my…lady friend…Freya," Mac says, appearing between us with a nervous look on his face. "She made all the kilts and…her dress. She's very talented."

Mac frowns as if he's not sure he said the right thing, but his grandad doesn't seem to notice as I catch a hint of a smile beneath his giant mustache. "Are you Scottish, lass?"

"Cornish, I'm afraid."

Fergus blanches. "How did you get past Hadrian's wall? It's meant to keep folks like you out of our country."

I fight back my smile and school my expression to be serious. "Didn't you hear? Hadrian's wall is actually just a giant dog kennel used to keep the wild Scot's like you inside."

There are a few seconds of awkward silence before Fergus bursts out laughing. "Where on earth did you find this one, Macky?"

Mac smiles proudly at me. "I wish I knew."

Fergus wraps his arm around my shoulders. "Lassie, I'm going to call you Red because you're fiery just like my late wife. Are you sure you don't have any Scottish in your blood somewhere?"

I laugh and shake my head. "No, I'm not sure actually. You Scots are a fertile breed, so it's quite possible a stray dog snuck in somewhere in my lineage."

Fergus laughs again. "Scots are a fertile breed at that."

"I like your handbag there," I state, pointing down to the furry, round waist bag strapped around Fergus's waist.

"Red, this here is called a sporran."

I wink playfully at him. "And here I thought it was just a hairy muff."

"Goodness, she's a cheeky lass!" Fergus states, turning us to face his grandson. "If she can drink whisky, too, we might have to keep this one around, Macky!"

Mac's velvety green eyes flicker back and forth with a mixture of surprise, disbelief, and dare I say, pride? It's the type of look I could spend hours dissecting and a lifetime staring into.

Our attentions are once again disturbed when a horn blows, indicating the beginning of the next event, which apparently is whisky-tasting. Mac directs us all over to the tents that are full of various whisky makers, and everyone spreads out to begin sampling.

I decide that Mac should have some time alone with his family and step away to join Sloan and Leslie when a strong hand grabs onto mine. "Come with us."

I frown up at Mac. "Are you sure?"

"I'm sure I want to continue watching you bewitch my grandad," he says with a smirk. "I've only ever seen him laugh with a woman like that around my gran."

My nose scrunches. "I worried the hairy muff thing was going a bit too far."

Mac's shoulders shake with laughter. "There's no such thing as too far with the Logans."

Suddenly, I whack Mac on the arm. "Why didn't you tell me that your grandfather had a caterpillar mustache and looks like Jack Bartlett from *Heartland*?"

Mac smiles broadly. "Because I wanted to see this look on your face. You look as though you've just wee'd."

"That's because I have." I grab Mac's arm and drag him back towards his family while murmuring out loud, "God, I hope he gives me a life lesson just like Grandpa Jack!"

The group of us make quick work of tasting a lot of whisky in a very short amount of time. There's loads of football chatter going on between Mac, James, and Fergus. They seem very keen to discuss Mac's upcoming contract negotiations and their expectations for Bethnal Green F.C.'s season. It's evident they're all very invested in Mac's career and wanting him to succeed. His grandfather especially.

I watch in fascination because so much of what they are discussing are things I've never heard Mac breathe a word about. And just watching his face as he listens to his grandad makes me feel the amount of pressure he puts on himself to please them. It's…heavy. It's funny how I've become best friends with a footballer, and the one thing we never talk about is football.

By our third tasting, I get the sense that Mac is football-talked out, so I decide to change subjects and share with them the time Mac and I were coupled as dance partners together. I have them all in stitches when I tell them about the number of times Mac stomped on my feet and how he had to carry me out of the dance club in order to take me home.

"I thought it was your heels that murdered your feet!" he exclaims, a look of disbelief written all over his clueless face.

"Heavens, no," I retort with a laugh. "My heels were fine. It was your big mule feet that did all the damage."

Mac scowls at me as though I've just betrayed him, but Fergus nudges him in the arm. "Don't pout, Macky. Not all Logan men are smooth with the ladies like your dad and me. I'll teach Red some moves later."

His reply seems to puzzle Mac as he stares at his grandfather curiously. Just then, a pipe band contest begins in the distance and while the men head over, Mac's sister Tilly asks me if I'd like to walk over to the pet show with her.

"There's a pet show?" I shriek, my jaw dropped. "Where?"

Tilly laughs, her stunning blue eyes a gorgeous contrast to her long strawberry blond hair, which is the same shade as Mac's. "It's just on the other side of the castle."

"Lead the way!" I exclaim and wave goodbye to Mac, who's watching me with a tender look in his eyes that I feel directly on my ears. Maybe a little space is a good idea.

"I take it you like pets?" Tilly asks as we make our way down the winding path.

"I do," I reply a bit too excitedly. I think that whisky is starting to hit me. "I only have a cat right now because I'm in a flat, but I'd love to own some property and have dogs and maybe even horses someday."

"You'll have to get out of London for that, I expect," she says knowingly.

"Yeah," I reply sadly. "It'll probably never happen because God, I love London so much, but it's fun to dream about. You live here in Dundonald, right?"

Tilly nods. "Aye. My flat is just around the corner from my parents."

"Do you like living so close to them?"

She shrugs. "It's fine, I suppose. I just never really expected to end up here. Life is pretty good at forcing you down a path."

Her reply gives me pause. "Where did you want to end up if life hadn't got in your way?" I ask, carefully wording my question so I'm not prying too much.

Tilly smiles. "I love London as well."

I tsk and shake my head. "Then you should get off your current path and make it happen. Your brother is there. Surely, that'd make the transition easy."

"London is not an option for me anymore," Tilly replies with a hard look in her eyes. She then clears her throat and says, "Speaking of my brother, what's going on with you two exactly?"

I press my lips together nervously. "What do you mean?"

She huffs a small laugh. "Unless there was another woman here today wearing a custom-made tartan dress, I'm pretty sure I saw you snogging him at the top of the hill." Tilly pins me with a look. "And this is the first moment he's let you leave his side, so I'll ask again. What's going on with you and my brother?"

I exhale heavily and chew my lip, trying to figure out how to reply to a question I don't know the answer to.

"Relax," Tilly says with a wink. "I'm not the Logan you should be afraid of."

I look over at her. "Which one should I be afraid of?"

"Most would think it's my grandad," Tilly replies, stepping to the side so a woman with a pram can walk by. She rejoins me and adds, "He's the one who acts like women are the devil. But behind closed doors, he's a big old softy."

"I can see that."

Tilly's brows lift. "He's quite taken with you. And he's never taken by women that Mac brings around."

"That's good to hear," I say, and then curiosity niggles in the back of my mind. "So which Logan should I be afraid of then? Your dad?"

Tilly shakes her head. "It's actually Mac."

"Mac?" I ask, my stomach sinking. "We've been friends for over a year. I don't think he's scary at all. Dense sometimes, yes. Maybe a bit inappropriate on more than one occasion. But he's sweet. A really generous friend."

She nods and gets a serious look on her face. "Aye he is, but he's a people pleaser at the expense of his own desires. And he will do absolutely anything to make our grandfather happy. Mac and Grandfather are extremely close."

"I know all that about him," I reply, blinking back my confusion. "Why are you telling me this?"

Tilly exhales heavily and stops walking, turning to face me like she's going to say something big. But the moment she looks into my eyes, she shakes her head and smiles. "Never mind."

"Never mind what?" I ask nervously, reaching out to stop her from walking away.

"It's nothing, Freya. You seem really sweet, and I've never seen Mac behave around a girl the way he is behaving around you. So maybe I'm wrong."

"Wrong about what?" I ask, the anxiety in my belly making me spin.

Tilly looks down for a moment and then looks up. "I just don't want you to get hurt. You're different than the normal WAGs that chase footballers around. You're...real. I hope that means you two can make it."

And with that, she turns and resumes her walk to the pet show that I can't even get excited about anymore.

CHAPTER 21

Mac

THE AFTERNOON IS PACKED WITH ACTIVITIES, AND ENDS WITH me and the guys winning the seven-a-side football. Thank fuck. If we had lost, we'd be an embarrassment to all of our teams to be sure.

The girls watch from the sidelines, drinking merrily, and I even show off a bit for Freya because I just can't help myself. Kissing her in front of everyone like that was unexpected, but I haven't exactly been the most sensible man around her these days. I just knew when I saw her in my family tartan that I had to grab her. Hold her. Claim her as mine and show her physically just how touched I was. The kilts she offered to make were already incredible, but the fact that she made that dress to surprise me meant something to me. It meant that she's more than just a friend. She's...Freya.

Which we clearly need to talk about. But every time we have a moment together, someone interrupts us. Bloody group trip has become a pain in my arse.

My family says their goodbyes after the match, and my

grandpa makes me promise to come to his flat in the morning for breakfast so we can talk. Nerves shoot through my veins at his ominous words because despite how taken he was with Freya, I'm sure he's going to tell me that spending time with her is a bad idea.

And maybe he's right.

If Cami could screw up my game when I wasn't even in a relationship with her, imagine what Freya Cook could do. But could I just walk away from Freya at this point? I honestly don't know. And I don't really want to think about it yet. I just want to enjoy what's left of our trip and dance with my girl.

We clean up after the match, and it's dark out when we go seek out the ladies who have made their way over to the street dance going on down the road. It's a DJ'd dance with a mix of today's music and traditional highland dancing that I'm total crap at.

As we approach, I see Freya sitting with two of my mates that I grew up with, and she's laughing so hard, it makes me ache to be beside her. I'm supposed to be the one to make her laugh. Not Jerry. Fuck that nob. He was always a creepy bugger in school and likely still is.

As we walk through the gates, I see Jerry offer his hand to Freya, and she accepts it willingly. He leads her out onto the dance floor and begins showing her the highland dance that's going on.

The entire scene pisses me the fuck off. Aye, I've had plenty of whisky today, so maybe I'm overreacting a bit, but I'm also not okay with my girl learning a Scottish dance with someone other than me.

I abandon my mates and make my way out onto the dance floor.

"I got it from here, Jerry," I state, giving him a wee shove before taking Freya's hand.

"Easy pal, I was just showing her some steps."

"I know what you were doing." I narrow my eyes at him.

Freya looks up at me with confusion all over her face. "Mac, don't be so rude to your friend."

I scoff and murmur, "Jerry is hardly my friend. And he doesn't need to be showing you how to dance. I do."

Freya laughs. "You're a horrible dancer."

"Aye, but this fucker doesn't need to be the one showing you something in my town." I glance over my shoulder, and a spark of anger ignites inside of me when I see him still lurking behind me. "Jerry, seriously man. What are you still doing here?"

Jerry laughs and holds his hands up defensively before walking away.

I turn back to Freya, who looks positively pissed now. "This is the third time you've barrelled in and ripped me away from someone. Jealousy is not a becoming trait on you, Mac."

My jaw drops. "Jerry doesn't count. He's a bawbag who's just trying to irritate me."

"He's not a bawbag," Freya defends, her brows pinched together in the middle. "He's been telling me stories about you and him growing up, which I've been enjoying."

"Well, by all means, don't let me interrupt you." I gesture back to our group of friends, which Jerry has rejoined. They all seem to be watching us in rapt fascination.

"What's your problem?" Freya asks, grabbing my arm and stepping closer to me.

I exhale heavily and feel an intense pressure building in my chest. "I just thought that maybe you and I could talk finally," I grind out through clenched teeth. "But you seem to be more interested in talking to Jerry—"

"Stop it," she hisses and crosses her arms over her chest. "If you want to talk, then take me somewhere we can talk. Don't pick a fight with me for no bleddy reason."

"Not here with everybody fucking watching," I growl, grabbing her by the hand and dragging her through the crowd.

I glance around in search of a quiet place and see a gazebo across the street with lights hanging from it. A wee bit flowery for my taste, but it's away from all these damn people that have been getting in my way all day. We make our way over and find a bench to sit on.

"What is your problem?" she asks, turning on the bench to face me. "Do you honestly think I'd rather spend time with Jerry instead of you? Why are you trying to pick a fight with me?"

"I don't fucking know," I growl, facing forward and propping my elbows on my knees. I run an agitated hand through my hair. "I'm not exactly a rational man these days when it comes to you, Cookie."

She's quiet for a moment and then asks, "Why is that exactly?"

"Isn't it obvious?" I bark out, turning to face her, mirroring her position on the bench.

She has a soft, tender look on her face as she croaks, "Not to me."

I huff out a laugh as my eyes scan her face. "I fancy the shite out of you, Freya, and it's twisting my guts inside of me."

Her face wars between a smile and a frown, and I hate it. I hate that I can say something like that, and she doesn't know how to respond. I'm crap at this.

"So what does that mean, exactly?" she asks softly.

"I don't know." I stretch my arm out on the bench behind her and lean closer. "I didn't expect for things to feel like this between us."

"Neither did I," she agrees and pulls her lower lip into her mouth to chew on nervously. "So what are we then?"

I shrug and swallow the uncomfortable knot in my throat. "Labels aren't really a thing I'm used to." She looks hurt by that response, so I lean in and cup her freckled cheek in my hand. "I'm not opposed to being together, but I need some time to wrap my head around it before we dive into whatever this is."

She nods and looks down at her hands, clutched tightly together on her lap. "Time."

"Aye, time."

She looks up at me. "And until you're ready...what? We don't see each other?"

"I didn't say anything like that," I snap, a sharp flash of desperation coursing through me at the thought of her even suggesting that. "Can't we just keep things how they are for now, and we'll figure it out as we go?"

She stares at me solemnly for a moment before turning to face forward. I can feel her disappointment and it eats away at a part of my soul. I hate doing this to her, making her feel insecure in what we are. She's my best mate, and I'm not the one who should be sending her mixed signals. But I'm not ready to dive in head first with her either. I need to take this slowly so I don't make any mistakes. She's too important to me to rush into a decision.

"Freya, are you okay with that?" I ask when she still hasn't replied.

She exhales heavily and plasters a smile on her face. "Sure. I'm okay with that."

Relief washes over me as I reach out to turn her to face me. "Good," I state, gliding my thumb along her jaw. "That's good."

I lean in and press my lips to hers. She feels tense at first but then softens, allowing me to tilt her head and kiss her properly.

We'll figure this out together. We have to.

The next morning, the sun has barely begun to rise when I squat down to kiss Freya's bare shoulder peeking out from the blankets.

She moans her discontent. "What are you doing?"

"I'm going to town to see my grandad for a bit."

"It's so early," she moans and snuggles under the covers.

"Grandad is an early riser," I state, kissing her temple. She's so cute like this that I debate blowing off my morning and crawling back under the covers with her. "I'll be back in plenty of time for our ride to the airport, though, okay?"

She nods and turns to look up at me. Her green eyes twinkle in the darkness, and the wee smile she gives me makes my heart melt. "I'll miss you."

Her words pierce through me like my heart is made of butter. I puff out my chest and compose myself before replying, "I'll be back soon." I press a quick kiss to her lips and then head out.

My grandad's flat in Dundonald is small and loads different than the way he and my gran lived when she was alive. It's stark and plain, like a true bachelor pad, all memories of her erased from his life except for a wee photo of her on the mantle. It's not just my grandad's surroundings that have changed, but him as well. He's become thinner since her passing, and for the first time in my life, he actually looks like a grandad.

For a man who says women are nothing more than a distraction, he's definitely taken the loss of my gran to heart. I can't blame the man. As much as my grandpa said that football was the most important thing in the world, I knew he loved my gran fiercely. Maybe the absence of her is what helped him warm to Freya so quickly? Maybe he sees that there's more to life than football.

I'm seated across the kitchen table from him, both of us with cups of tea in hand, and I'm mentally preparing myself for the football talk that I'm certain is about to happen.

Nothing could have prepared me for the three words that eventually do come out of his mouth.

"I'm sick, Macky."

I frown, my body tensing at the severe expression on his face. "Sick with what exactly?"

His eyes focus in on mine as he replies, "The cancer."

"What?" I ask, moving back in my chair and pushing away from the table.

"I have cancer," he repeats as his lips purse together with concern.

My heart plummets with that word again. The C word. I release my cup of tea and ball my hands into fists on my lap. "How bad is it?"

"It's bad," he replies, his expression grave. "They say I've probably had it for years. Your gran was always on me about getting myself checked, and I just ignored her because I'm a damn fool."

"Christ," I reply, my eyes doing their best to blink away the shock. "So what's the plan? Chemo? Radiation? Surgery?"

Grandad shakes his head. "None of that."

I frown back at him. "Why not?"

There's a grim twist to his mouth when he replies, "It's too far gone, laddie."

"What the fuck does that mean?" I growl, denial and confusion overwhelming all my senses.

"Watch your tongue in my house," he admonishes and then re-laxes his face instantly. "I've only got months left, they say. Maybe a year if I'm lucky."

"Months?" I stand up from the table, the sound of the chair scraping the hard wood loud in the quiet heaviness of the kitchen. "You've only got months to live?"

I push a hand through my hair and begin pacing back and forth. This can't be happening. My grandad isn't even that old. Losing Gran was hard enough, now him? There's no way this is happening. He can't be fucking dying. Not yet.

"We should get a second opinion," I say, turning wide eyes on him.

Grandad offers me a sad smile. "We already did, Macky. Your dad and mum and even your wee sister have been shuttling me to all sorts of doctors for the past year."

"The past year?" My voice is guttural as I splay my hands out on the table and eyeing him harshly. "And none of you wanted to tell me about any of this?"

"There was no need," he retorts, staring up at me with pain all over his face. "You didn't need anything else messing with your focus for your first year in the Premier League."

"Fuck football!" I roar, my hands lifting from the table and slicing through my hair as my entire world begins to spin.

Grandad's chair tips over as he stands to meet me toe-to-toe. "Don't say that shite in my house, goddammit!"

I inhale a shaky breath, staring into his angry eyes and feeling so much betrayal that it physically hurts. "You should have told me."

His face softens, his shield of stony Scottishness fading away before my very eyes. "I didn't want to tell you until we knew for certain."

He reaches out and touches my shoulder and it feels like acid on my skin, because all I can think about is the fact that I won't feel this touch again. This man has been my hero my whole life. Everything I've done was to please him. I don't know how to be in a world without him.

"So, what now?" I croak, my voice betraying me as tears sting the backs of my eyes.

Grandad sniffs and turns away from me, his jaw ticking as he fights back his own emotion. He clears his throat harshly and replies, "Nothing. You go back to playing football and making me proud. And I go back to watching you on the telly and cheering you on like the overly chuffed fool that I am."

My stomach twists in pain and my grandad turns to look at me, his expression unlike anything I've ever seen before. He grabs me by the arms and yanks me into his chest, his hands wrapping around me and slapping my back as a sob breaks loose from my throat.

Fuck this. Fuck life. Fuck all of this shite.

"Don't you dare mourn me, Macky," he says into my shoulder, his voice husky as his hand cups the back of my head. "I've lived a good life and I got to watch you live a life I only ever dreamt of. I have no regrets," he says firmly, pulling back and smiling proudly at me through red-rimmed eyes. "Except maybe never seeing you with a Ranger kit on."

He barks out a garbled laugh and I reach out to pull him into my arms again. I know he's joking and I know he's proud of me. But he has no clue how much he's done for me and how much I'd do for him.

CHAPTER 22

Freya

THE NEXT FEW DAYS WITH MAC ARE DIFFERENT THAN I EXPECTED.
He still sleeps over at my flat every night, and we're still having
The Sex every day, but he's not his normal, happy-go-lucky self.
He's contemplative and distracted. And when I tease him, he's barely
able to crack a smile.

At first I assume it's because he's training a lot more than usual
this week so maybe he's just over-tired. But then the other night, we
were watching *Heartland* and Hercules came out of nowhere and
leapt up onto Mac's lap. My jaw dropped with amazement because
ever since the nipple-licking incident, Hercules has been giving Mac
a wide berth. So clearly this is a momentous occasion that would have
deserved some commentary. But Mac seemed completely unaffected
by it. He just mindlessly petted Hercules like it was no bother. The
Mac I know would have made some crack about Hercules watching
where he put his tongue.

Something is off with Mac. Something that I need to address
with him.

The night I plan to talk to him about everything, something incredible happens to me at work.

"Freya! Can you come down here and talk to me and Leslie before you leave for the night?" Sloan calls up the stairs just as I'm shutting off the lights.

"Of course, I'm just coming down now."

I grab my bag and make my way downstairs just as Leslie turns on the closed sign in the window. She turns and gives me a big smile, gesturing to the back where the sofas are by the changing rooms. Sloan is back there looking over the books as Leslie and I sit down to join her.

"What's going on, ladies?" I ask curiously.

Sloan closes her book, looks at Leslie with a grin, then back to me. "We want to hear your pitch."

My brows furrow. "My pitch?"

"Yep," Leslie stares back at me expectantly. "You mentioned in Scotland you had ideas that you wanted to discuss with us at some point. Well...this is some point."

My face falls. "Oh God, I'm not ready. I haven't prepared anything. My ideas are probably shit."

"Lying cunt," Sloan says, waggling her brows knowingly. "We're friends, Freya. We don't need a formal pitch. Just tell us what ideas you have. We're dying to hear them."

My eyes bounce back and forth between Sloan and Leslie as nerves take flight in my belly. That lying cunt of a voice wants to tell me that my ideas aren't good enough and they won't like them. But then I hear Mac's voice say, '*Your unique brilliance deserves to be seen.*'

And Mac's voice sounds a whole lot sexier than that lying cunt.

I reach into my bag and pull out my sketchbook. Here goes nothing.

"Saints preserve me!" I exclaim, bursting into my flat with the biggest, brightest smile on my face ever.

"What is it?" Mac asks from the sofa where he's been waiting for me every single day for the past two weeks and where I want him to remain for the rest of my life.

Woah, where did that come from?

I shake the strange thought out of my head and practically squeal, "Sloan and Leslie love my pet clothing idea!"

"They what?"

I nod excitedly and join him on the sofa. "It was the weirdest thing. They called me downstairs before I left for the day and asked me to give them my pitch. At first I was like...what, you guys are mental...then I was like, nope, not going to listen to that lying, insecure voice in the back of my head anymore."

"That's dead brilliant!" Mac says, the first glimpse of a genuine smile on his face that I've seen since we returned to London. "So what happened?"

"I showed them my sketches and they loved them! And they love my Instagram page and they think Hercules could be the face of the line and they think the line should be called Pleasantly Plump Pets and they're talking about converting my upstairs alteration area into the pet boutique and leasing property elsewhere and hiring another seamstress and bleddy hell, this might actually be happening. I could actually be a proper designer!"

I reach into my bag and pull out the bottle of champagne I picked up on my way home. "We need to celebrate!"

"Absolutely!" Mac says, grabbing the bottle from my hands and taking it into the kitchen.

I follow him in, still rambling on and on about how the meeting went. I think I might be repeating myself but I can't help it. I'm just too excited for original words.

Mac pours us two kitten mugs of bubbly and holds his cup out to me, his tall frame bowing over me as he smiles fondly down on me. "Cheers to you, Cookie. I knew you had it in you."

We clink our mugs and take a sip while I let that comment of his really sink in. Mac did know. I think he's always known and if it weren't for him, I may have never even had the confidence to say I had ideas to share with Sloan and Leslie. This moment, standing here with him in my kitchen, celebrating a success with someone I care so deeply about…it's surreal.

"What's the matter?" Mac asks, reaching out and rubbing his thumb along a wet trail down my cheek that I hadn't realised was there. "This is happy news. Why the tears?"

"I know it's happy news," I state, sniffing loudly and holding his hand to my face. "I just can't help but feel like none of this would have happened if it weren't for you."

"Me?" he asks, gazing back at me with an incredulous stare. "Cookie, this was all you."

His features soften as he continues to tenderly caress my cheek like he's done it his whole life. And the way his eyes crinkle in the corners as he gazes down at me is making it really hard to stop these bleddy tears.

My fingers fist his shirt as I try to figure out how to explain how he makes me feel. "Ever since you and I started spending more time together, you've pushed me in ways I've never been pushed before. And you got me to see my sketches as more than just a hobby that I didn't have time for. Being with you has given me confidence in myself that I've never had before. Mac, I don't know what I'd do without you in my life."

I reach out and grab Mac's mug to set it down on the counter with mine before wrapping my hands around his thick neck. I stare up, relishing in the size and beauty of him as he gazes down at me with a twinkle of pride in his eyes. I want him to look at me like this forever.

That thought propels me into yanking him down onto my lips. This isn't a gentle, ease yourself into the swimming pool inch by inch sort of kiss. It's a cannon ball off a diving board and sinking down to the bottom of oblivion kiss as our tongues thrash against each other and I allow myself to kiss him with wanton abandon as we swallow each other's moans.

Mac's hands wrap around my waist and glide down over my arse, cupping it firmly as he pulls me into his hard groin. The possessive embrace surrounds me with his delicious, manly scent that I want all over my body. My hands greedily mimic his, pulling him tighter against me. It's a claiming of sorts as my hands slide over the delicious strength of him. It's not enough. I need more.

God, I want this man. My best friend, whom I am madly in love with, and whom I think might be in love with me too. That thought causes a shiver to run through my body because is it possible? Could I really have this? This kind of deep, soul-shaking love?

Emotions overwhelm me, and before I know it, we're moving out of the kitchen and down the hall, clumsily stripping off our clothes the entire way. Our mouths are fused together like if we break apart, we won't be able to breathe without the other's lips and yet still, I crave more of him.

We're naked by the time we reach my bed, and when I lay on my back and wait for him to crawl on top of me, it feels like the first time all over again. What different people we both were that night. Me, scared and insecure, him, slow and careful. Now, we move together like one, both of us knowing each other's bodies so acutely, all it takes is a single touch to set our hearts on fire.

Mac holds himself over me as he devours my breasts while my fingers thread wildly through his lush hair. His lips move down over my belly as he drags his silky tongue over my flesh and eventually up my neck like he can't get enough of me, either. The kisses are driving me absolutely insane, and if he doesn't push inside me soon, I'm going to lose my mind.

"I need you, Mac," I pant, pulling him up to my lips and kissing him hard and fast. "I need you inside me. Now."

He looks down as I wrap my fist around his length and position him at my centre. A deep, guttural noise from his mouth vibrates my chest as he watches himself disappear inside of me inch by glorious inch. His thickness makes me feel tight and full as he seats himself deep inside of me, my body a perfect mould for his in every way.

I pump my hips up into him, needing to feel friction, needing to climb this build that's growing rapidly inside of me. Mac's fingers lace with mine as he presses my hands against the bed, preventing me from touching him as he thrusts into me and continues to watch our bodies connect.

It feels good, but it's not enough. I need more. I need him.

"Mac, look at me," I pant, my voice coarse and dripping with desire. I want him to see what he does to me. How he makes me feel.

He ignores me, continuing to drive into me like my pelvis is his only concern.

"Mac," I exclaim, my thighs tightening around his hips to stop his motions.

His head jerks up, his green eyes searching on mine.

"I want you to look at me," I state firmly, my inner voice stretching her muscles.

A pained look flits across his face and is gone in a matter of seconds.

But I saw it.

I saw that doubt, that hesitation. That…regret?

What was that? Where is his head right now? What is he thinking about?

Mac looks down again at our bodies, but that memory of his face chips away at a part of my soul.

"Mac," I whisper his name as I pull my hands free from his grasp. I reach up and cup his face, forcing him to look at me as I croak out, "Why won't you look at me?"

He shakes his head like I'm making this up.

I tighten my hold on his face. "Why?" I ask again, my voice breaking at the end. "What's wrong with me?" *Damn that lying cunt.*

"Nothing, Freya," he says, his gaze bending with emotion as his eyes flick between mine. "There is nothing wrong with you." His mouth tilts up into a crooked smile. "You're my best mate."

His words hit me deep in my soul, and they are confirmation that this is more than just sex between us. This is a building of an unbreakable bond that goes even deeper than love.

Mac stares boldly into my eyes as he moves slowly inside me, careful, appreciative, and searching. Searching for the last part of our souls that still belong to ourselves. I gaze back at him with the same sense of wonder coursing through my entire body.

This is love. This is us. This is happiness.

Suddenly, he begins driving into me harder and faster, his fingers digging into my flesh as his eyes laser focus on mine. He's looking at me, but his face is changed. It's haunted somehow as he reveals a part of him that I didn't know existed. A dark, naked part that is raw and vulnerable, even to me.

It's intense.

It's what I wanted, but it's more than I expected.

"Freya," Mac says my name on a groan that vibrates straight to my core, his forehead lowering to press against mine. "God, Freya. You mean so much to me."

"Mac," I cry out his name because his words push my body over the edge, forcing me to clench down hard on him, and then release into shuddering waves of pleasure.

His face falls into my neck as he prepares to pull out of me.

"Just stay in," I beg, linking my ankles behind his back to hold him inside of me. A painful sense of desperation overwhelms me like if I let him out now, I may never get him back. "I want you to come inside me."

Mac pulls back, his eyes puzzled on mine. "Are you sure? Are we okay to do that?"

I nod. "Yes, we're covered, and I want to feel you. All of you."

Mac's mouth opens, and his lips descend onto mine as his entire body tenses over top of me, and he groans out his release inside me. It's an intimate sensation, one I didn't realise I would enjoy so much as I hold him against my body and relish in the frantic pounding of his heart against mine. I want this. I want this and more, and hopefully, this is just the start.

CHAPTER 23

Mac

MY VOICE IS STIFF AND ALL BUSINESS WHEN I SIT DOWN ACROSS from Santino in his office at Bethnal Green F.C. "I want to officially open up negotiations for me to be transferred to Rangers football club." I swallow the painful sentence that I never imagined I would ever say, and then add, "My agent has spoken with their manager, and they are interested, for the right price."

Santino sits back in his chair, his dark, gelled hair shiny in the overhead lighting. "What the fuck are you talking about?"

I clear my throat and do my best to grind out through clenched teeth, "My decision is final."

Santino gapes at me like I have two heads and then blinks rapidly as he props his elbows on his desk. "Why on earth would you give up Premier League to go to Glasgow? Our club is doing brilliantly. We nearly won the FA Cup this past season, and with the new players we've acquired this year, it's ours to win."

That reminder sends a pang of regret through my stomach, because despite the confidence I have in my decision, walking away from the team that I have come to see as my family just as we're beginning to peak is fucking torture. "It's personal."

Santino levels me with a glare. "How personal could it be? Did you get some lass in the Highlands up the duff? I'm telling you, mate, we can take care of her from London."

Blind rage shoots through my body. "You have a lot of fucking nerve to make that kind of joke to me, of all people."

Santino blanches, losing all humour on his face, like he somehow forgot about everything that happened only three years ago. He swallows slowly and exhales through his nose. "Look, Maclay, I know you hate my guts for events of the past. But for the past three years, I've stayed out of your way, and you've stayed out of mine. Let's not get personal now."

"You didn't stay out of my way when you decided to ask out my best fucking friend," I bark, willing myself not to jump over this table and beat him to a bloody pulp.

We eye each other silently for a moment before Santino replies, "I didn't know how close you and Freya were. None of the team had a clue of your involvement with her, either. Trust me when I tell you, that had I known, I would have stayed as far away from her as humanly possible."

My nostrils flare. "I wish you would have done me the same courtesy with regard to my sister."

Santino's eyes narrow. "You don't know what you're talking about when it comes to Tilly and me."

"I know everything I need to know."

"You don't," Santino growls, his hands clenching into fists on his desk. "What happened between us was a complicated mistake."

"A mistake that you wanted to fucking end," I growl, gripping the arms of the chair like I could turn the wood into dust.

Santino sits back and shakes his head. "You don't know the full story, and I'm not going to tell you. That too is personal, and I don't owe you anything, Maclay. I owe your sister a lot."

"Is that why you sent fucking money to Scotland so she could have an abortion at a private clinic, you bloody bastard?" I growl, standing up and shoving my chair back.

Santino stands as well, his dark eyes slits as he stares back at me. "I did what I thought was right."

"You did what was convenient for you!" I snap, my upper lip curling up in disgust. "Had she not miscarried, what were you going to do then? Force her to end that wee bairn's life? What kind of fucking monster are you?"

Santino inhales a shaky breath. "This is none of your business."

"My sister and my family are one hundred percent my business."

"Then talk to her about it," Santino growls, losing his steely composure for the first time since I arrived.

"She pretends it never happened," I exclaim and shake my head at him in disgust. "Whatever mindfuck shite you did to her changed her, and for that, I will hate you until the day I fucking die."

The two of us stand, eye to eye, breathing heavily while the tension vibrates between us.

"What do you want from me?" Santino asks, his face looking desperate for the first time since I walked in here.

"I need you to make this transfer to Scotland happen with Vaughn."

I can't stomach the idea of facing my manager, Vaughn, and telling him about my decision to leave. In fact, I can't even bring myself to tell Roan yet. As much as I know this is the right decision for me, I know that anybody who cares about me would try to talk me out of it. Hell, even the Harris Brothers would probably band together and do one of their ridiculous Harris Brother Shakedowns.

But the truth is, this is what's best for my family and me. And I'll never regret gifting my grandad his one dying wish.

"Maclay, if I'm going to bring Vaughn on board with this crazy idea, I'm going to need some information."

My jaw clenches, and the muscle in my cheek tics with agitation.

Knowing that I probably can't get away with not sharing something, I reply, "My grandad and I are very close. I just found out he's sick, and it's his dying wish to see me in a Ranger kit."

Santino's brows drop. "Shit."

"Yeah, shit," I reply, clearing my throat and pinning him with a serious glower. "I just need you to do your lawyer thing and make Vaughn believe this transfer is for the best. I know him. He's going to try to act all fatherly with me, but my mind is made up. And after everything you've done to my family, this deal is literally the least you can fucking do."

Santino stares back at me for a long moment like he wants to argue. Like he wants to stop me from doing this, even though I hate him and being farther away from him would be best for both of us. But then he nods and says, "Fine. It's your career, I suppose." He steps back and slides his hands into his pockets. "I'll talk to Vaughn, and we'll get this deal done one way or another. Further negotiations will be made between your agent and us, so you and I need not communicate any further."

"Thank fuck for that," I grind out and turn to walk out of his office. I pause as I hold the doorknob and turn back to look at him. "And it goes without saying that you'll stay the fuck away from Freya after I leave."

Santino shakes his head. "Just go."

"I need to hear you say it." I turn on my heels to eye him again. This is the one thing I'm most terrified about leaving behind in London, and I need to have some form of comfort when it comes to her, or I don't know if I'll be able to go through with all of this. "The Harris Brothers assure me you're a man of your word, so say the fucking words."

Santino exhales heavily and levels me with a glare. "I'll stay away from Freya."

With a sound nod, I turn and walk out of his office and away from Bethnal Green F.C., possibly for good.

CHAPTER 24

Freya

Last night was the first night Mac and I didn't stay together since our arrangement began. Allie and Roan wanted to be separated the night before their wedding, so Allie came to mine, and Mac went back to his. I missed him more than I should admit. It's incredible how, in only a matter of a couple of weeks, I've become so completely dependent on his warmth in my bed. My, how things have changed.

Now, we're hours away from walking down the aisle together, and I feel an overwhelming sense of anxiety niggling away at me over seeing Mac again. It's almost like I'm terrified that spending one night apart is going to break this spell we're under, and he's going to look at me and realise what a mistake he's made in being with me. And the fact that all week we never spoke again about what our relationship is really doesn't give me any comfort.

I shake away those melancholy thoughts and stare at my stunning friend, Allie. She looks beautiful in her tiered tulle wedding dress. The top is a deep V with an intricate lace applique that I helped Leslie stitch by hand. Her golden blond locks are pinned half up, and her makeup is dewy and absolute perfection.

I'm kitted out in a ballet pink chiffon dress also made by Leslie. It's a Grecian-inspired gown with a slit up the front and a soft V neckline with off-the-shoulder frills that wrap around my arms.

It's funny how this was the day that got me in such a fuss over finding a date in the first place. This day right here is the reason Mac started coaching me, the reason Mac kissed me in his bedroom, the reason Mac sabotaged my date with Santino, and the reason I told Mac I was still a virgin and we began sleeping together.

This day was the reason I fell in love with my best friend.

Yet, despite all these new experiences and feelings, I can't help but look at Allie and me in the mirror next to each other, and think, *Always the bridesmaid, never the bride.*

"Okay, ladies. It's almost time!" the wedding planner says, poking her head in through the door of the dressing room where we're waiting inside Temple Church London. "They're ushering the last few people to their seats, and then I'll come back and get you two."

She rushes off, and I turn to Allie, who's fidgeting with her bouquet of pink roses. "Are you nervous?"

"Not nervous," she replies, lifting the flowers to her nose. "Just ready to get this over with."

My lips pull back with a smile. "That's a funny way to look at your wedding day."

Allie rolls her eyes. "I'm just ready to start my life with Roan, you know? This day is exciting, but I'm more interested in the normal days. The days of kissing each other goodbye on our way to work or when I pick him up at the airport after he's been playing abroad for a while. Or hell, even the nights we argue over what to eat for dinner. That's what I'm most looking forward to. Is that weird?"

I smile and shake my head. "Not weird. You're just describing contentment."

Allie nods. "Contentment. Yes. That's what I'm ready for. Dull and painfully ordinary contentment."

My smiles falls when I realise that I felt more content with Mac these past few weeks than I have my entire life. Now I don't know what I feel.

Allie seems to pick up my mood shift. "What's going on with you and Mac?"

"Nothing." I shake my head. "This is your day, and we should be talking about you."

Allie levels me with a stare. "Freya, if it's my day, we can talk about what I want to talk about, and I want to talk about you and Mac."

I roll my eyes and shrug. "I don't know exactly. I thought Scotland was going to be the beginning of something big for us. But ever since we got back to London, he's been distant." I look up at her watching me in the mirror and shrug. "How is it possible to feel someone pulling away when they're literally right beside you?"

Allie's brows pinch together. "Maybe his head just needs time to catch up to his heart?"

I nod and try to accept her words as truth. They are similar to the ones I've been telling myself over and over again.

"Ladies, it's time!" a voice says.

Allie looks to me with a smile. "Let's go get my dull and painfully ordinary contentment, shall we?"

We walk through several hallways until we reach the narthex just outside the sanctuary. It's a bit of chaos because Allie decided to have her cousins' children all be flower girls and ring bearers, and the scene we're walking into is the Harris wives all doing their best to wrangle their adorable children into their proper places.

So first you have Sloan's daughter, Sophia, who's dressed in a pale pink gown like mine. She's holding the handle of a small wagon decorated in tulle that contains Belle and Indie's one-year-olds, Joey and Bex. Then there's Vi's three-year-old, Rocky, who's currently tipping over her basket of flower petals while her mummy tries to scoop them back up. After that, you have Booker and Poppy's twin boys, Teddy and Oliver, who are currently fighting over the ring pillow that thankfully has fake rings on it, because no one would ever dream of trusting those two little hellers with expensive jewelry. And finally, you have Sloan and Gareth's wee one, Milo, who's supposed to be in the wagon, but who is currently running away from Sloan like his pants are on fire.

All of them are adorable little nightmares in white fluffy dresses and tuxedos, and I glance over at Allie, who's laughing at the scene unfolding.

The wedding planner lines me up to walk in. "You go first, and these little terrors will follow, God willing."

The organ swells with a music change and the doors open to a full church. The Harris Brothers are front and centre, poking their heads out from the crowd to see how their wee ones are doing behind me. The wedding planner gives me a shove, and I do my best to make my way down the aisle elegantly.

I see Roan first, his smile large and genuine as he meets my eyes. My gaze slowly drifts past him to find Mac. He's dressed in a smart tuxedo that fits him perfectly because I altered it myself. His strawberry blond hair is freshly cut and styled cleanly, giving him a sophisticated look that's so at odds with the wild Scotsman that I know lives inside of him.

As his eyes drink in my body, I can't help but think about what it'd be like if this were my wedding day. And if I was walking down the aisle as a bride instead of a bridesmaid. The fantasy should give me butterflies, but it actually causes a pit to form in my belly. Before Mac, I didn't have dreams of a happily ever after. I didn't wish for a man to get down on one knee or think about how I'd feel walking down the aisle to marry him. Now that I've fallen for him, all that has changed.

I want more.

And it's terrifying.

When I find my position across from Mac, he eyes me fondly for a moment before mouthing, "Bonnie." And there goes that pit growing in my belly as he smirks at me like he's seen me naked. Well, because he has.

I smile my thanks and turn to look away from him, terrified that he'll see the hopes and dreams written all over my face, and it'll scare him away. He can't even admit to being in a relationship with me, so the last thing I need to do is tell him that I fantasise about our wedding day.

The music changes, drawing the attention towards the Harris children coming down the aisle. It's complete anarchy as Sophia rolls over Teddy's foot with the wagon, and he starts crying. Poppy has to save him while Rocky is attempting to spin her way in circles down the aisle. Joey and Bex seem more interested in licking their tulle dresses than paying attention to the show around them, while Milo is still trying to make the great escape out of the wagon. It's all truly the most adorable mess I've ever seen, and the entire sanctuary is in stitches through the whole thing.

Vi, Sloan, Poppy, Belle, and Indie end up having to walk alongside them while their husbands pop out into the aisle to encourage the little ones' progress. It's sweet really, like herding the most adorable kittens you've ever seen.

Once the children find their seats with their parents, the music changes, and it's Allie's turn to walk down the aisle.

Her father looks stoic as he ushers his daughter towards her fiancé. I chance a glance at Roan, and his face is the picture of happiness as he awaits his bride. Allie and Roan had a whirlwind romance that was almost torn apart at one point, but they found their way back to each other.

The ceremony is beautiful, and tears are shed throughout the church, even by Mac, who looks so happy for his friend, it starts to give me that shred of hope again.

We make our way to the reception, and it's a dark, romantic display of dim yellow lighting and pale pink and white flowers toppling out of tall tapered vases. The room is buzzing with happiness for the bride and groom as we take our seats for dinner.

After standing to watch Allie and Roan have their first dance as a couple, the DJ invites other couples out onto the floor.

Suddenly, Mac's large hands wrap around my waist from behind. "I know you think I'm a crap dancer, but would you do me the honour anyway, Cookie?"

I smile and tip my head back against his chest. "I thought you'd never ask."

He turns me in his arms, and I wrap my hands around his neck while he walks us back into the mix of other couples. My cheek rests on Mac's chest as we dance slowly, letting our bodies reconnect after being apart for only twenty-four hours.

"I missed you last night," I say, pulling back and smiling up at him.

Mac's velvety eyes are fierce on mine as he reaches out to tuck a strand of my hair behind my ear. "Aye, I missed you too."

I nuzzle into his touch. "I've got kind of used to your snoring these past couple of weeks."

He smiles, but it doesn't reach his eyes.

"Are you coming back to my place tonight, then?"

Mac looks away, and his brow is furrowed when he says, "I don't think so."

"I suppose we could go to yours since Allie and Roan won't be returning," I reply, combing my fingers through his hair. I pull him down so I can whisper in his ear. "Now might be a good time to tell you that I'm not wearing any knickers under this dress."

Mac groans and shakes his head, his body going tense under my hands. I smile and look up once more, wanting to see the desire on his face that I've grown used to. My smile fades as I note the hardness in his eyes, which are looking everywhere but at me. "I think maybe it'd be better for us to stay apart tonight."

My lips part in surprise. "Why?"

Mac swallows what looks to be a painful knot in his throat. "I have some news."

I feel my brows pinch. "Okay…What kind of news?"

He looks away from me as if he can't stomach making eye contact with me as he replies, "I'm in the process of getting transferred to Glasgow Rangers."

My body freezes, my feet stopping their movement. "What do you mean, 'transferred'?"

He exhales heavily and turns to look down at me, a coldness in his eyes that I've never seen before. "It means I'll play for them this season. Not Bethnal Green."

"Okaaay," I reply slowly, my eyes swimming as I attempt to process this information. "So, how does that work? Does this mean you're moving to Scotland?"

"Aye. I'm heading to Glasgow on Monday to do a fitness test that will likely check out fine, and afterwards, I'll look at some flats—"

"Wait a second," I interrupt with a laugh and pull my arms down from his neck. "So you're literally moving? To Glasgow?"

He blinks once. "Aye."

"Why?" I ask, beginning to feel faint as my mind whirls with this news, and my heart threatens to beat out of my chest.

His hands turn to fists at his sides. "Because I signed a new contract."

"Why did you sign a new contract?" I ask, crossing my arms over my chest defensively. "You've been doing great for Bethnal Green. Was this Vaughn Harris's idea? I can't imagine he meant to do this. The Harris family loves you. You're an asset to the team! I'm going to have Vi talk to him—"

I move off the dance floor in hot pursuit of any Harris family member, because any one of them will surely have something to say about this.

Mac grabs my arm, spinning me in my tracks to face him again. "It wasn't Vaughn's idea, Freya. It was mine."

"Your idea?" I huff out an incredulous laugh. "Why would you want to go play for Glasgow? Your entire life is in London."

Mac's lips thin, and he looks away before replying, "My grandad is sick."

My stomach drops as the weight of what he's telling me sinks in. "How sick?" I manage to whisper as I grip his forearms in sympathy.

"The dying kind of sick," he snaps, his guttural voice making me jump as his jaw ticks angrily. He pulls away from my touch. "He only has months to live, and you know better than most what my relationship is like with him. So I'm doing this transfer for him. This isn't up for discussion."

"Oh my God, Mac. I am so, so sorry," I reply, my mind reeling with this new information. "So...you're transferring to be close to him. Okay, that makes sense."

He blinks slowly. "Aye, it's what's best for my family."

"Okay, I understand that," I nod as tears begin to burn in my eyes. I reach out for Mac again, the need to comfort him and ground myself like a reflex in my body. But something in his expression stops me. "So then...where do I fit in?"

Mac looks at me carefully for a moment. "As...a mate. You and I were always supposed to go back to being friends after our agreement was over anyhow. I'm just ending it sooner."

"You can't be serious," I croak, my hands dropping as I take a step away from him. "You're moving to play for another team, and now you're just...done with us?"

"I'm not done with us. We'll go back to being friends like before," he replies, his voice flat and unemotive. "My grandad is what's most important now, and I'm not going to feel bad about this."

"I'm not trying to make you feel bad," I whisper, wrapping my arms around myself and trying to come to terms with the idea of that wonderfully cheeky man whom I adored being ill. My heart breaks because I only just met him. And I know how much Fergus means to Mac. They are connected in a deep and personal way. But then, so are Mac and I. Right? Can we really just go back to being friends?

The words that tumble out of my mouth beg to be asked because, despite myself, I still need to hear it one more time. "So even after everything that's happened between us, you just want to be friends?"

Mac's mouth closes before he nods his confirmation. "Aye."

His response makes my face feel like it just had ice-cold water thrown into it, even though I knew what his answer would be. I turn away from him, desperate for some space, desperate for some room to think. Why is this affecting me so much? Why can't I deal with this better?

I make my way through the tables of people, my mind reeling as I think about how stupid I was to think that there could ever be more between Mac and me. All because he kissed me in front of his friends? That meant nothing. Clearly. That was lust. Not love. That was a kiss. Nothing more. Why did I let myself fantasise like it was more?

"Freya," Mac's voice calls out behind me as I make my way out of the reception hall, horrid tears spilling freely from my eyes as I pick up my pace. I have to get out of here.

"Freya, would you just wait?"

I find a side exit and push through it out onto the dark street corner, grateful for the broken streetlight because I can't stand the thought of Mac seeing me like this. It shouldn't be about me right now; it should be about his grandad.

"Freya, stop for a bloody second," Mac says, sounding out of breath.

I don't have any breath either. I'm holding it for fear of breaking apart into a million pieces if I let out one ounce of the feelings inside of me.

He spins me to look at him, his face crumpling when he sees my obvious distress. "You deserve someone that's going to put you first,

Cookie. Not football. And I think now you have the confidence to go out there and find that person."

I bark out a garbled laugh, wiping at the hot tears burning tracks down my cheeks. "That's all I was to you, wasn't I? A charity project."

"No, I didn't say that." He steps into my space, his eyes pained and searching mine for understanding.

But he won't find it. I'm hurt and irrational, and my heart aches.

"You didn't have to say it," I retort with a pained noise, turning away from him and begging my tears to stop falling. "Because if I were more than just a charity project, you'd be asking me to come with you to Scotland. To be with you during this difficult time."

It's a statement peppered with a dark truth I know he will not admit.

Mac exhales heavily. "I'd never ask you to come with me, Freya. You're just starting a new venture with the shop. I won't ask you to choose between me and your career."

"Of course you won't," I snap, a hot flush of anger surging through me. I step back into his space and eye him harshly. "Because to you…career always comes first."

Mac's eyes narrow. "You've known that since the beginning, Freya. Don't act like this is new information. You've also known I don't do relationships for this very reason. Nothing's changed about me. I'm the same man I've been for the past year."

Except now I've fallen in love with you.

I purse my lips together and close my eyes, pleading with my heart to calm down so I can breathe normally again.

Mac's words are all true. I have known how he feels about football. And relationships. And me. I should have seen this coming.

"This is why you've been different with me since we got back from Scotland, isn't it?" My eyes flutter open, a cool, empty calm overtaking me as acceptance replaces hurt. "You knew you were going to leave."

Mac's guilty look is all the response I need.

I nod slowly, rubbing my lips together as I think back to the last night we slept together and how in hindsight, I should have realised he was saying goodbye. It felt so final. The way he looked at me, touched me. Held me afterwards. The way he kissed my shoulder when he left the next morning. I should have known I was in this alone all along.

That lying cunt that tells me I'm not good enough for a happily ever after turned out to be the one voice in my life who I should have been trusting all along. I should have never stopped listening to it because now that I've tasted what I thought was love, I'll always know what I'm missing. And the memory of that feeling will be like a wound that never truly heals.

I inhale a deep breath through my nose and move past Mac to head back inside. "Good luck in Scotland, Mac."

"Don't be like that, Freya!" Mac reaches out and grabs my arm, his grip tight on me as he stares back at me with a wild look in his red-rimmed eyes. "We'll still keep in touch. You're my best mate."

I plaster on a smile because I could so easily mistake that fervent look he's giving me for hope. But I know better now. I know the truth. "Sure, Mac. We can be friends."

He releases my arm, and I walk away, knowing without a shadow of a doubt that I will never be friends with Maclay Logan again. How can you ever be friends with someone who completely shattered your heart?

CHAPTER 25

Mac

Two Weeks Later

"**A**LL RIGHT, THAT'S IT FOR THE DAY, GENTLEMEN. GO HIT THE changing room!" Coach bellows from the sidelines as I finish my last drill and drop down onto the Rangers training centre pitch. We've been pushed to our limit this week as we prepare to play a friendly match against Oxford United in a few days. I often survey my surroundings to remind myself I'm not at Bethnal Green anymore. I'm home. In Scotland.

Everything happened quickly after Roan and Allie's wedding. I went to Glasgow and was checked out by the club's doctors, ran a few drills with the team, and then before I knew it, I was having my photo taken in Ranger gear and signing my name to a new contract that Santino, of all people, helped draft. I barely even looked at the terms, trusting that my agent did me right. It's probably foolish of me. This is how footballers get taken advantage of, but I just don't care at this point. I'm here for one reason and one reason only.

My grandad didn't know any of it was happening until I showed up at his flat in my Ranger kit and turned around to show him the Logan name embroidered on the back. The old man wept in my arms that day, and I knew without a doubt that I made the right decision. Not only will my grandad get to see me play for his team, but I've been able to spend as much time with him as I can between matches and trainings. I lost all of last year with him, so I won't lose what wee bit of time I have left.

My new teammates are good. Several of them look at me like I'm mental because they know what I left behind, and most of them wish they could have just traded places with me instead of play alongside me for this club. But I know in my bones that I'll never regret this extra time I've got to spend with my grandad.

Every night after training, I drop by for tea and talk football with him. He has a hospice nurse that's with him during the day now, but despite his body growing weaker and weaker every day, I can see that twinkle in his eye again. Nothing lights this man up more than football, and for that, I'm glad I came.

But practices could be better for me here. I'm struggling to find a rhythm with the team, and Coach keeps saying that it's just the transition, and it'll come.

After showering, I make my way out to the players' parking lot and do a double take when I see Roan standing next to my car.

"How the hell did you get in here?" I ask, looking at the security gate.

Roan's brows lift. "I told them I was your brother, and they bought it because we clearly look so much alike."

I laugh and shake my head, dropping my bag on the ground to stand in front of my friend, whom I haven't seen since his wedding day—a day that I'm sure he remembers fondly, but one I'd rather forget.

Roan holds his hands up to stop me from hugging him hello. "Can you tell me what day it is? What year? How old are you? What's your last name?"

"What are you going on about?" I ask, cutting him off and propping my hands on my hips.

Roan smiles. "I just wanted to make sure you had your wits about you before I launch into you about how truly fucked up it was for me to get back from my two-week honeymoon to find out that my best fucking friend, roommate, and teammate for the past three years is now playing for another team."

I open my mouth to reply, but Roan lifts his hand to cut me off. "So, of course, I assumed there had been some sort of sabotage. An evil plot against you that's riddled with false information. So I broke down the door to Vaughn's office and screamed at him. 'You get rid of Logan, you get rid of me! I don't care that I just married your niece. I'll quit this fucking sport before I play for someone that could trade our best midfielder.'"

"Fuck," I growl, running a hand through my hair.

"Yeah, fuck," Roan repeats. "Fuck me because then, Vaughn, who can make or break my career had to tell me that my fucking best friend, whom I just offered up my life for, left the team by choice without telling me a damn thing about it!"

I drop my head, unable to look him in the eyes. "I was going to call you when you got back."

"Oh, how kind of you, Mac. Thanks for throwing the dog a bone."

"I didn't want to ruin your honeymoon."

"No, just ruin my football season. Ruin our team's season. The only reason the Harris Brothers aren't up here dragging you home is because they were convinced you were in the middle of a mental breakdown. Because only a fucking idiot would leave a team that's in their prime like we are right now."

"You don't know the full story," I state through clenched teeth.

"Then tell me. Why Mac? Why would you leave now? We've got everything we ever wanted with Bethnal Green. Everything we've ever dreamt of and worked our whole fucking lives for. You've put football first your entire life, so why the hell are you making moves like this that don't make any sense without talking to me about it?"

"My grandad is dying, Roan," I say, my shoulders slumped in defeat. "I found out that weekend we were all in Scotland."

Roan blinks at me in shock.

"I've been visiting him every day between trainings. He's bad, Roan. Worse than when you met him. At this rate—" my voice cracks as emotions overwhelm me. "At this rate, I don't even know if he'll make it to the season opener, which was the whole reason I went through all of this."

"Ag man," Roan says, grabbing me around the arms and pulling me into a hug.

And with that one touch of tender human compassion, I crumple into his arms and weep like a wee fucking babe.

I can't help it. I've been holding it all in these last two weeks… with my grandad, with my parents, my sister. I've been trying to be strong and make them all believe that I'm happy about this decision to come back to Glasgow. That it was an easy choice. But none of this move has been easy. I miss my friends. I miss my teammates, my coaches, my manager.

I miss Freya.

Fuck, I miss her so damned much, my guts are in knots every fucking day. For years I was a football player that bounced from one team to the next without a care in the world. I was the guy that could fit in everywhere. I was the man who knew how to roll with the punches. Losing Freya isn't a punch I've ever experienced. Losing her has knocked me the fuck out.

"I'm truly sorry, Mac," Roan says, holding my shaking body against his like I'm his child, even though I have several inches on him. "I wish I'd known. I wish you would have told me."

"You would have talked me out of it," I say, pulling back and aggressively swiping at my tears. "Everybody would have, and my mind was made up. I didn't want to have to defend myself."

Roan nods thoughtfully. "I respect you for it, and I'm sorry to hear about your grandad. He's a good man."

I nod, and a painful knot forms in my throat. "The world won't be the same without that grumpy old git."

"I'm glad you're getting some time with him. That's important." Roan grips my shoulder, and we share a moment of silence before he asks, "How's your new team?"

I glance back at the training grounds. "They all think I'm mental."

"Well, it sounds like they have a good read on you."

I shake my head and give him a shove. "How are things back at home?"

"The team is good, finished their preseason camp already, and I'm playing catch up. But I'll be joining in on the friendlies in a couple of weeks as a substitute now, and be back as a starter soon, they expect."

I nod, my jaw ticking with anxiety as I add, "And everyone else?"

Roan's brows pinch together. "Are you talking about Freya?"

I nod stiffly. "She won't return any of my calls."

Roan leans back onto my car and crosses his arms over his chest. "I don't know much because Freya won't open up to Allie either. Allie says she's never seen Freya so closed off. You two are maybe more alike than you realise."

My brows lift curiously. "I just wish she'd answer my fucking calls. I thought our friendship was stronger than that." I move to lean on the car next to Roan. "I can't believe she let me moving to Scotland ruin our friendship. It's not like I moved overseas."

Roan turns his head to stare at me like I'm speaking another language. "I told you sleeping with friends when feelings get involved is dangerous."

"Aye, you did," I sigh, wishing for the millionth time that I could just talk to her. "And my game is suffering because of it. You'd think I was a rookie, not a seasoned vet."

Roan crosses his arms and ponders this for a moment. "So is it like when you and Cami split, then?"

I shrug, wishing I had an answer to that question. His memory is right, I played like shite after Cami and I called it off. But that felt more like a me thing than a Cami thing. Once I realised it was for the best and we were better off as friends, my game improved.

Fucking hell, this is why Grandad always said to stay away from women during football.

"I just keep hoping Freya will come around."

"I'm sure she will," Roan replies and pushes himself off the car. "Now, take me somewhere for a pint. I only have a couple of hours before I have to catch a flight back to London, and we need to sit down and figure out what the fuck you're doing wrong on that pitch."

I laugh and shake my head. "Just what I wanted to do this fine afternoon. Talk more football."

CHAPTER 26

Freya

"**S**TOP SNIFFING HIS PILLOW, HERCULES. HE'S NOT COMING back," I snap and then leap up off the bed as if the sheets could burn me. "It's been over two weeks. It's time."

Hercules watches me like I'm deranged as I pull the sheets off the bed and yank the pillowcases free. Ignoring his judgment, I march them straight into the kitchen and throw them in the wash, starting the load without hesitation.

Once the wash is underway, I head into my living room and drop down onto my sofa to pull up the latest episode of *Heartland*. It's time to get back to my life. Who needs a man to watch a wholesome Canadian family drama with, anyway? Certainly not me.

My life's not that bad really. Why bother with real-life romance when you have Netflix? And the fact that I'm turning thirty in a couple of months just means that I have disposable income for the high definition Netflix. And I can watch it in multiple locations. There are people in third world countries who don't get to experience any of the luxuries I get to enjoy. So there. I have a leg up on the underprivileged.

Oh, crap. That sounds terrible. I make a mental note to donate to a soup kitchen in the morning. Also, second mental note…why do even my charitable acts centre around food?

When I can't bring myself to watch an episode of my beloved *Heartland*, I walk back into my bedroom and slowly lift the pillow that was Mac's to my nose.

"God, I can't get rid of him!" I walk over to the window, pull it open, and throw the damn thing out. A familiar voice shouts down below, and my eyes go wide as I rush over to see if I've hurt someone.

Roan DeWalt is standing on the ground, bending over to pick up the pillow I just flung out like a psychopath. He looks up at me and asks, "Did you drop something?"

"It wasn't me," I state stupidly because I'm an embarrassing idiot.

He laughs and then tosses it into the bin beside him. "Can I come up?"

I nod my agreement, wondering what on earth would bring Roan over here by himself. Honestly, I didn't even realise Roan knew where I lived.

I buzz him in and make us both a cup of tea before sitting down on the sofa beside him. It's odd to see another man on my purple velvet couch. Roan's sitting there holding a kitty coffee mug, and I hate the fact that all I can think about is that he doesn't look half as good as Mac did when he sat there.

"Everything okay with Allie?" I ask, breaking the awkward silence.

Roan nods. "Ag, of course. She's great. We had a lovely holiday."

"That's good to hear," I reply and sip my tea nervously.

"I'm here to talk to you about Mac."

I nearly break the kitten mug in my hand. "I'd rather not."

"He's a mess, Freya," Roan states in a rush. "I went up to Glasgow to see him after we got back. We went to a pub before I had to catch a flight home and he's not okay. Says he's struggling with the team, and he's worried if he doesn't perform well at his friendly match tomorrow, they're probably going to bench him."

"Bench him? How could they? Mac is a brilliant player, isn't he?"

"Normally, yes," Roan says, setting his mug down on the coffee table and leaning towards me. "But his mind is not in it right now."

"I understand," I nod knowingly. "He loves his grandfather very much. I'm sure his illness is taking its toll."

Roan gets an uncomfortable look on his face. "I don't think it's just his grandad; that's the problem. I think he misses you."

"Me?" I reply with a laugh. "He's not missing me, Roan. He's missing me no more than he's missing you."

"You're wrong, Freya," Roan says, his brows furrowed in sympathy. "I've never seen him like this. He may have gone through something similar after Cami and he broke it off, but it wasn't this bad. What's happening to him now is intense."

The mention of Cami's name makes my teeth clench so hard that I swear I hear them crack. I don't even want to begin to compare me to Cami. I know Mac was with her for a long time, but I have to believe that what we had was different. And hearing that our split is affecting Mac makes me feel strangely vindicated.

Roan continues, blatantly unaware of the tailspin my emotions are going through. "You know you're more than a friend to him even if that bull-headed Scot won't admit it out loud yet."

My chin trembles at his words because bleddy hell, there goes that voice of hope again, and it's a lying cunt. I shake my head and look out the window. "I don't know what you want from me."

"He needs you, Freya," Roan says in a rush. "You're his voice of reason. His person. And he's yours…Even though you're both too stubborn to admit it."

244

I bark out an incredulous laugh. "So what shall I do? Fly to Glasgow and surprise him so he'll play a good football game at the expense of my own damn heart?"

Roan's eyes soften. "I can't tell you to do that. I can only tell you that your best friend is in a bad place and could use a friend."

Roan stands up to leave, and the tears that I thought had dried up at last return all over again.

CHAPTER 27

Freya

"**M**Y NAME IS FREYA COOK. THERE'S SUPPOSED TO BE A ticket for me?" I say into the round circle of the box office at Ibrox Stadium in Glasgow.

The woman searches in a little box and then comes out with my ticket. My lonely single ticket. "You know it's halftime already, right?"

"I couldn't get here any sooner," I say as I take my ticket and rush through the crowds milling about for their halftime snacks.

This is the second football game I've ever attended, and I'm in a city I don't know, navigating around a stadium I've never been to, and I'm late on top of it. And now I'm looking for people who probably don't even remember what I look like. *Thanks a lot for the suggestion yesterday, Roan.*

"Freya!" a female voice calls out, and I look around to see Tilly's tall model-like body striding towards me.

"Oh good, she remembers me," I cringe and exhale heavily, steeling myself to be friendly.

"You got your ticket, I see," she says with a warm smile.

I nod timidly. "Thanks for securing it for me. It was lucky Roan had your number, or I might have been standing out there holding one of those signs asking for a ticket." I look around nervously. "Sorry, I'm late. Stupid flight delay. I still have no idea what I'm doing here exactly."

She wraps her arm around me and squeezes me into her side. "You're here to cheer on my brother and the best football team in the world."

I nod and let her lead me to the section where her parents and grandfather are. Mac's mother hugs me while his dad gives me a soft smile. At the end of the aisle, my eyes land on Fergus, and my heart sinks at the sight of him. It's only been weeks since I was here last, but he's visibly lost weight and is so pale, it almost hurts to look at him.

"Hiya, Red!" Fergus bellows with a big smile for me. "I saved you a seat right next to me."

I move past Tilly and sit down next to Mac's grandfather, who now only faintly resembles my beloved Jack Bartlett from *Heartland*. "Fergus, you look like you need a whisky."

He barks out a laugh and then begins to cough. When he stops, he turns to me and says, "Thanks for stating the obvious, lass. It's better than what most people do."

I sigh and look back at him. "What do most do?"

His lips purse together beneath his thick white mustache. "Pretend I'm not dying before their very eyes."

My eyes sting with tears because his candor is unexpected. I lean over and kiss his cheek. "In that case, let me be the one to tell you this fucking sucks, Fergus."

His chest shakes with a silent huff of laughter. "Aye, it does." He turns to look out at the pitch just as the players come running back out after the half break. "But this...this doesn't suck, Red. In fact, this moment here is a dream come true for me, even if he had a shite first half of the game."

"He didn't play well?" I ask nervously, Roan's fearful words obviously coming true.

"Played like shite!" Fergus harrumphs. "His head isn't in it. His focus is piss-poor. He doesn't even look comfortable out on that pitch."

I frown nervously at the pitch, searching the players for Mac as I ask, "Doesn't sound much like a dream come true to me."

Fergus turns and looks at me accusingly. "My grandson could ride that bench, and I'd still be just as proud of him as I am when he plays well. We're not fair-weather Ranger fans, and we're not fair-weather Macky fans. Got it, Red?"

I smile and nod. "Got it, Fergus."

I turn to look back at the field, and it's as if our eyes are pulled together like magnets when I see Mac standing on the grass looking right up at me sitting next to his grandad.

He lifts his arms in silent question.

I shrug and thrust my fist up into the air like I'm cheering.

He laughs, and Fergus nudges me with his elbow. "That's the first time I've seen him not look miserable down there. Maybe you'll be his good luck charm. Do you have any luck of the Irish in you?"

I smile and shake my head. "Not that I'm aware of. Are they as fertile as Scots?"

Fergus's nose wrinkles. "Not if they're Celtic fans. Celtic fans aren't bright enough to find the right hole."

I laugh at that filthy joke and turn to stare back at Mac down on the field. The sight of him makes my heart hurt because he's handsome as ever in his kit, looking like a God amongst men. His hair is shaggy and sweaty from the previous half, and I itch to run my fingers through it again.

"Let's go, Macky! Give 'em hell!" Fergus shouts, and I join in like this is a normal Sunday for me, hanging in Glasgow, watching a football match with my unrequited love's family.

The second half begins, and based on the amount of yelling going on in our section, I venture to guess it's not going much better than the first.

Fergus spends most of the game explaining to me why Mac's position is so important on the pitch. "Midfielders run the most and have the ball more than anybody on the pitch, which might surprise most people because they would assume it's the offensive strikers. But nay, midfielders are the true powerhouses of the game. They have to transition from offence to defence in the blink of an eye. It's not easy to receive a pass from a defender, turn the ball up-field, and then pass to a forward. You have to be a big-picture thinker when you're a midfielder and see the whole pitch. Mac is normally great at seeing the big picture, but today, he's off, and it's not a pretty sight."

I cringe at the helpless feeling I have up here in the stands. On the flight over, I had a fantasy that I would show up, and Mac's game would improve. My presence would spur him to victory, and he'd make his grandfather prouder than ever. Afterwards, he'd tell me he loved me, and we'd all live happily ever after.

Some fantasy.

But honestly, I'm not here for reconciliation. I'm here for Mac. It was selfish of me to let my own hurt feelings get in the way of being here for him when he needed me most. When he was grieving the illness of a man who I know means more to him than anything in this world. What's happening to Fergus is real and painful, and I need to see the big picture as well. Mac may not love me, but he's still my best friend.

The final minutes of the match are painful as Rangers give up two goals. I worry Mac's grandfather could hurt himself screaming so loudly down at the refs, but Mac's parents don't seem too worried about him, so I imagine this is the natural Logan volume at football games.

Once the game clock runs out, a staff member for Ibrox Stadium walks over to our section and asks us all to come with her. I try to stand back out of the way, but Tilly grabs my arms and drags me along with them as we make our way down the steps and towards the pitch.

They open a locked gate and usher us down a few steps until we stand right out on the pitch where Mac is waiting, all tall and sweaty, and forcing a smile I can tell he doesn't feel. His eyes jump back and forth from me to Fergus before he finally says, "Sorry about the match, Grandad."

Fergus stands in the grass and turns in a circle, shaking his head as he gazes up at the empty seats all around us. "What the hell are you sorry about, Macky? You could have scored a goal in the wrong net today, and I'd still be fit to die with this happy look on my face."

Everyone laughs, and then Fergus walks over and wraps his arms around Mac for a hug. "I just want to see you happy, lad."

As Mac embraces his grandfather, I can see the tears well in his eyes. "I'm happy, Grandad."

Fergus pulls away and gives Mac a skeptical look but says nothing more and then grabs Tilly around the shoulders. He begins pointing out all the seats he sat in for the matches he got tickets to.

Mac offers a soft smile as he walks towards me with a bewildered look on his face. "What are you doing here?"

I shrug and shoot him a smirk. "Turns out, I'm a big fan of football."

"Are you, now?" Mac asks, the corner of his mouth tilting up into a playful smirk.

"Absolutely. Did you know that midfielders run more than any player on the pitch? I'm so knowledgeable about football now." I smile, plastering on a brave face even though the inside of my body feels like a tight, coiled spring ready to fling me on top of him.

Mac's shoulders shake with laughter as he comes to stand in front of me in all his tatted, ginger-haired, statuesque glory. He smells like sweat and man, and I want to reach out and touch him just for the memory. But I'm here as a friend. That's all Mac wants from me.

Mac eyes me up and down and shakes his head slowly. "It's good to see you again, Cookie."

"It's good to see you again, *Macky*," I retort and waggle my brows playfully at him.

His face loses all humour as he reaches out and cups my cheek. "I'm truly glad you're here."

I inhale and exhale slowly, willing myself not to turn into his embrace because it means nothing, and if I let myself enjoy it, it will hurt more in the end. I pull away from him and smile. "Can you show us around your new club then?"

We get a tour through the grounds, and then I wait outside with Mac's family while he showers and changes. When he comes out, Fergus admits how tired he is, so his parents and Tilly say their goodbyes to Mac and me, leaving the two of us alone for the first time in weeks.

Mac opens the passenger side door for me and asks, "How long are you here?"

"My flight leaves early tomorrow," I reply, hopping up into his car. "Think you could give me a ride to the hotel I booked by the airport?"

Mac frowns as he slams the car door shut and walks around to the driver's side. He folds his large frame in behind the wheel and says, "You're not staying at a hotel, Freya. You'll stay with me."

I rub my sweaty palms over my jean-clad thighs nervously as it begins to sprinkle outside. "I don't think that's a good idea."

"Why?" he asks, his voice low and clipped.

I turn to look at him, his green eyes curious as his hair flops over, partially concealing them beneath the ginger locks. My hand has a mind of its own and reaches out to push the hair off his face. "Because we're just friends."

"Friends can have sleepovers, Cookie. We've done it quite well before if you recall," he says, his voice low as I watch his hand land on my knee and rub slow circles on it. The sensation has an instantaneous effect on me, and I hate myself for it.

I chew my lip nervously and pull my leg away from his touch. "I don't want to be that kind of friend anymore."

Mac's hand suspends in the air, and I feel all the teasing sucked out of the car instantly as he absorbs my response. His face hardens as he pulls his hand back and says, "Understood." He starts the car and pulls out of his parking stall. "Airport it is, then."

We drive in the pouring rain towards the hotel I told him I'm staying at, and I start to wonder if it was a bad idea for me to come. My presence clearly didn't improve his game at all as I'd hoped. And the tension simmering between us makes me wonder if it's even possible for us to just be friends anymore. Maybe we've reached a point of no return. He clearly doesn't want a friendship with boundaries any longer, but I can't survive a friendship without them. I need more or less…I can't survive in the grey area in the middle.

Mac pulls up to the hotel and parks his car, thunder rolling around outside, echoing the stormy mood he's currently vibrating with. "Is this the right hotel?"

"Yes," I murmur and turn to face him as he stares at the building in stony silence. "Mac, look at me."

The muscle in his jaw tics as he grips the wheel so tight his knuckles turn white.

"Mac, look at me," I repeat, my voice loud in the smallness of the car.

He turns to face me, his eyes glowering with anger.

"What is your problem right now?"

He half smiles, but it doesn't reach his eyes. "I could ask you the same thing, Freya. You fly all the way to Glasgow and show up at my match. In the year and a half I've known you, you've only ever gone to one game of mine, and that was before you and I were truly friends. You sit by my grandfather, and you make him laugh with your cuteness the entire time, and now you want to go to a fucking airport hotel instead of spending the night with me. So seriously, you tell me what your problem is because I can't keep up at this point."

My chin wobbles at his scathing tone because he's never directed it at me before. Not like this. "I don't want to go through what I just went through."

"Which is what?"

I shake my head and stare out at the rain hitting the windows so fast that it feels like we're stuck in a grey vortex of hell. "Mac, you left me in London. You gave me no warning that you were planning to leave; you told me after the deal was done. All this happened after you kissed me in front of all of our friends and gave me the impression that we were..."

"We were what?" he snaps.

"More than friends!" I snap. "More than friends with benefits. Just...more!"

"We were more," he bellows back at me. "But my circumstances changed."

"And I'm just supposed to be okay with that?" I ask, my voice cracking at the end. "Mac, I'm not okay with that!"

"What do you want me to do about it, Freya? My grandfather is dying. I signed a new contract. I'm here now, and I can't just leave to be with you!"

I nod, accepting all of this and knowing it has to be this way, but knowing it doesn't take away the ache in my chest over what could have been between us and how easily he left me behind.

"I just can't go to your flat and spend the night and act like..." my voice trails off because I don't know if I should finish this sentence. It's too revealing.

"Like what? Fucking say it," he growls.

"Like we haven't made love to each other," I cry, my voice coming out in a strangled sob. "Like I don't miss your touch and the feel of you lying next to me in my bed. Like I haven't missed the feel of your lips on my shoulder when you kiss me goodbye in the mornings. I miss all of that, Mac. I miss you!"

"So do I!" he booms, and the volume causes me to squint. "I even miss your daft, perverted cat!"

I cover my face with my hands because all of this hurts so much, I just want to cry.

Mac pounds his fist on the steering wheel and adds, "And I miss my best mate taking my fucking calls. I've been here for three weeks going through a lot of shite, Freya. I'm grieving, and all I want is to hear your voice."

The pain in his tone causes tears to well in my eyes, and a sob breaks free from my throat. "Don't you get it? I can't take your calls without hurting, Mac," I whine, sniffing loudly and swiping at the tears on my face. "I'm sorry…but am I supposed to sacrifice my own happiness for yours?"

"So talking to me hurts you," he says it like a statement.

"Yes," I whisper back.

"Why?"

"Because I'm in love with you, you cow!" I shriek, my voice breaking at the end with that honest admission that I never planned to say today. I don't think I ever planned to say it because it's obvious he doesn't feel the same way, so why admit something that only makes you look more pathetic?

But admit it I have.

My voice is hoarse when I add, "And that's why I can't have casual sex with you anymore. I'm in love with you."

Mac's face flashes red as he blinks away his shock. "Why would you say this now?"

I look around the cab of the vehicle in confusion. "What do you mean?"

"You decide to tell me something like that now…when I'm in Scotland, and I've just started with a new club. How the fuck do you see this working out, Freya?"

"I don't, obviously," I exclaim, my chest rising defensively. "Just like you never saw us working out together. The game is certainly up on that."

He shakes his head, his jaw ticking with agitation. "Why did you come today? To make me feel guilty? To fuck with my head?"

"No, Mac. That's not why I came," I argue, hurt and confusion coursing through my veins. "I came because I heard you were struggling, and despite my feelings, I'm still trying to be your friend. I still care about you. Just in a different way."

"Well, clearly you and I can hardly call each other friends anymore. You've made that decision for us." Mac huffs out a laugh and adds, "Christ, I regret this."

"Regret what?" I ask, my chin wobbling because I know what he's going to say before he even says it.

"Adding sex to our friendship. You're not experienced enough to be able to handle it maturely. You're turning thirty soon, but sexually, you're still a child. I should have known better."

Pain.

Deep, soul-shaking, pain shoots through my heart.

"You've always been like this," he growls, facing forward and shaking his head in disgust. "You sit around and wait for life to happen to you instead of grabbing it for yourself. It's why you're going to end up alone."

His words are like a knife that keeps on twisting in my gut. And they confirm everything that the lying cunt in the back of my mind has told me forever.

You're not good enough, Freya.

You're not special enough, Freya.

No one will ever love you, Freya.

I stare forward, my eyes swimming with unshed tears as I realise how wrong I was in coming here. I should have stayed in London. Then, at least the dissolution of our relationship could be because of our locations. Now, the truth is out.

Mac doesn't love me.

And fuck him for betraying everything he tried to make me believe.

My voice is low and calculated when I say, "Well, I'd rather sit around and wait for life to happen than make decisions based on other people's lives."

Mac swerves angry, accusing eyes at me. "Are you seriously going to say that to me?"

I nod, my chin jutting out defensively. "You can't see the hypocrisy here, Mac? You're judging me for not admitting what I want when you're the one in Scotland because you care more about your grandfather's wishes than your own. And the worst part about it all is that you're miserable here and it's showing in your game. Not only your game but in everything you're doing right now. Whoever you have become while being here isn't the man who watched Netflix with me and made love to me. Just admit it."

"It doesn't matter if I'm miserable!" he cries out, his voice low and in pain. "He's fucking dying, Freya!"

"And so are you," I scream, my body nearly lurching across the dash to get into his face. "You're a shell of the man you used to be, and you're a fool if you actually think that's what Fergus wants to see in his grandson before he dies."

"Don't you dare presume to know my grandad better than me. The look on his face today made everything I've done worth it."

I huff out a disbelieving laugh. "Mac, he'd look like that if you quit football tomorrow and told him you wanted to join the circus."

Mac scoffs and turns to look out the window. "You don't know my family, Freya."

I nod knowingly. "You're right, Mac. And I don't think I know you anymore either. Because the Mac I fell in love with would have never said half the things you said to me in this car today." And with that, I slide out of the car and walk out into the pouring rain and away from my ex-best friend for good.

CHAPTER 28

Mac

Six Weeks Later

"**Y**OU LIKED PLAYING FOOTBALL ALL THESE YEARS, DIDN'T you, lad?" Grandad asks, his voice hoarse as his sunken green eyes stare up at me beneath the fluorescent lighting.

A knot forms in my throat at the sight of him lying in the hospice bed. He's been here for the past week, and every day I come to sit in the chair beside him, he seems to look smaller and smaller. Tonight, his skin is as white as the dressing gown they put him in and his salt and pepper mustache is far more salt than pepper.

This is the end. I can feel it.

We were supposed to have more time.

It's been nearly three months since I moved to Scotland and his health only allowed him to attend that one game, which was nearly two months ago. The one that Freya came to.

The thought of Freya sends a pang of regret through my body that I haven't been able to shake since the moment I left London.

What started as an ache back then has now blossomed into a deep, soul-crushing throb that I feel whenever I think back to the moment I let her get out of my car and chose not go after her.

I wanted to go after her.

I wanted to grab her and kiss her and take all the awful, horrid words I said back. I wanted to drop to my knees and beg her to forgive me and plead for her friendship again.

I wanted to feel her soft lips against mine, her body lying next to me. I wanted to hear her laugh again, hear her yell at me, hit me. More than anything, I wanted her to stay with me and hold me as I mourn the impending loss of the man that I have lived my entire life to please. To make proud. I wanted her to look at me like I was the only bloody person that mattered in the world to her.

Anything to erase the memory of the tears streaming down her face when I broke her fucking heart.

Every time that memory floods my thoughts, I find it hard to take a full breath. It's like a two hundred pound weight is sitting on my chest, punishing me for what I've done.

What I said to Freya was unforgivable. I pushed away my best mate because she said she was in love with me, and I hate myself for it. She's important to me, of course, she is. But love? I'm not ready for that. I can't take that kind of admission right now. So I was horrible to her which means, I've lost her for good and must suffer the consequences.

I register Grandad asking me again if I liked playing football, so I clear my throat and do my best to ignore my racing thoughts and the sound of the medical devices beeping softly in the background. "Aye, of course, I loved playing football, Grandad." I sniff and turn to look away. "Why would you ask such a thing?"

He closes his eyes, the wrinkles stacking on top of themselves as he winces at a pain deep inside his body. He opens them to look at me. "I fear I pushed you to do something you didn't want to do. I fear I pushed you to follow my dreams instead of your own."

"Not at all." I reach out and hold his feeble hand, careful not to squeeze too hard. The contrast of his aged, weathered hand over mine is an image I'll remember for the rest of my life. "All I've ever wanted is to play football. You gave me that gift."

"Not this season," he replies sadly, shaking his head. "You've changed this season, Macky."

"What do you mean?" I ask, my heart sinking at the tone of his words. Words that I don't want him to have on his mind during his last days here on earth. Doesn't he know that I've done my best to make him proud? To live up to everything he taught me since I was a wee lad? He must know.

"You don't love playing here in Glasgow. Ever since you transferred, you haven't been yourself. It pains me to see you like this."

My head jerks back. "I'm happy to be here. I mean, aye, I've had a rough go of it this season with the team, but I'll turn things around. You know I will." My words are a half-truth because what I'm not telling him is how this has been the hardest transition I've ever experienced in all my years of playing football, and I'm killing myself to get my focus back.

He swallows slowly, wincing as he attempts to sit up. "I just hate how unhappy you are here when I know you wouldn't have come if it wasn't for me."

"Grandad," I state, releasing his hand so he can sit more comfortably. "I'm here because I want to be. You're important to me. You have to know that," my voice cracks and my eyes begin to burn with unshed tears as I force out the next words. "I would do anything for you. You're my hero."

Grandad's eyes go red around the edges as moisture pools in his eyes. He reaches up and pinches the bridge of his nose before placing his hand on top of mine. "But I'm not what's most important in your life anymore. And neither is football, for that matter. I know I said I had no regrets in my life, Macky, but that was a lie."

The pained look on his face guts me because I know that it's not physical pain he's feeling, but emotional. "What are you talking about?" I ask, feeling my brows furrow in confusion.

He heaves a heavy sigh and stares up at the ceiling, blinking several times slowly before replying, "Ever since your gran died, I haven't stopped thinking about all the things I should have done with her. I should have bought her more flowers. Showered her with wee presents, shown her my love more. Hell, I should have sat my arse on that sofa and watched her favourite programs on the telly instead of watching football all the damn time."

Suddenly, memories of Freya's face when I bought her those carnations flash through my mind. The wee smile she gave me when she opened her kitty coffee mug. The unexpected way she cried when we delivered those rescue kittens. My heart begins to pound in my chest when I recall the hours upon hours we spent on her sofa talking about nothing and watching that ridiculous show, *Heartland*.

I glance down to see my hands are now clenched into fists, my palms slick with sweat as I uncurl my fingers and dry them off on my jeans, my mind reeling over everything I walked away from.

Grandad's shaky exhale pulls my attention to him as he rubs the pads of his fingers along his forehead. "When I look back on my time with your gran, I wish I would have done a lot more of nothing with her. I wish I would have been content to be fat and happy with her." He lowers his hand and looks at me seriously. "It's a very special thing when you can find a lass that you can be fat and happy with."

His colourful words make me smile. "But you made Gran happy. Anyone could see that."

"Aye, I know. But as my time comes to an end, I can tell you with absolute certainty that football is the last thing on my mind." He looks at me, his eyes wide and pleading as tears form in the depths of them. "I've steered you wrong there, Macky. Since you were wee, I've been telling you to stay away from a woman because she could be a distraction. But I never meant for you to stay away from *the* woman."

My mind spins as it tries to play catch up with everything he said. Is he talking about Freya? Shaking my head in disbelief, I swallow, trying to wet my very dry tongue when I ask, "What do you mean *the* woman?"

He tries to turn slightly so he can see me better, and the movement looks like it hurts him. He reaches out to squeeze my wrist as he replies, "The woman who makes you want to give it all up. Like when your dad met your mum."

I sit back in my chair, gripping the back of my neck as I process what he's saying. "You always told me that Dad threw his career away when he met Mum. You said he walked away from a major opportunity."

Grandad blinks slowly, his lips pursed in disappointment. "Aye, he did, but do you think he regrets it for a second?" he asks, his eyes flaring with mischief.

I huff out a small laugh. "I should hope not, considering I'm the reason he quit."

Grandad smiles beneath his mustache. "Exactly. He met his lassie at eighteen. And you've met yours now…in Red."

I blink rapidly at the words that just came out of his mouth and reply, "Grandad, Freya and I aren't together. We're not even speaking anymore. I'm…I'm not in love with her."

"Are you truly this thick-headed?" He shakes his head, his hand closing into a fist as he gently taps the side of the bedrail. "Macky, I love you, boy. God, do I love you. But it amazes me that you are so great at seeing the big picture on the pitch, but you cannot see it when it comes to your own life." He pauses, his eyes taking on a tender look of sympathy before he whispers, "You're heartbroken, lad."

Suddenly, he begins retching, and I stand to help sit him up, propping an extra pillow beneath him before handing him a drink of his water. He takes a small sip and several deep breaths for a moment before grabbing my arm and refusing to let me sit back down. "I saw the way you looked at her at the Highland Games and when she showed up at your match. You're in love with that girl if ever I've seen love."

My face bends at his words. "You can't know that, Grandad. I've never even been in love."

"Of course you're in love with her, you wee idiot!" he fires back, his voice gruff and unapologetic. "You've been playing like shite here in Glasgow, not because you're at a new club or because I'm dying. You're miserable because you don't have that bonnie freckle-faced lass in your life to keep your head on straight. I've seen the loss of her in your eyes these last couple of months, and it guts me to the bones."

He reaches out and presses his cool palm to my hot cheek. "I knew you loved her the moment you introduced me to her, and every moment after, when you would find ways to bring her name up in conversation. I thought you'd been happy your whole life out on that football pitch. But I was wrong. I've never seen you happier than when you're looking at her. I'm mighty grateful I lived long enough to see that."

A painful knot forms in my throat over the tender look in his teary eyes. I've lived my whole life to make my grandad happy, but this is the first time I've realised he's lived his whole life to make me happy. What a pair we make.

And is he right? Could I really be in love with Freya? I know I miss her, but is that love? My voice is resigned when I whisper, "I've hurt her, Grandad. I've hurt her badly. Said things I can't take back."

"I'm not surprised," he says, slapping my cheek with a fond smile before grabbing my shoulder. "You're a stubborn Scot, just like me." His face grows serious again. "But it's not words that matter in the end. It's actions. She's your big picture, Macky. Don't let her out of your sight, or I promise, you'll live to regret it."

CHAPTER 29

Freya

"CAN YOU HELP ME TAKE A FULL-BODY PHOTO OF MYSELF?" I ask Allie the minute she walks upstairs into the loft area of my office at Kindred Spirits. This space once housed men's and women's clothing at various stages in the alteration process and is now chock-full of dog and cat clothing samples.

"The samples are in from China?" Allie squeals, rushing over to the sewing table and picking up a little plus-sized, cat-shaped high-lander kilt. "Shut up! This is the cutest thing I've ever seen."

I bite my lip as I glance at the tartan longingly. I almost didn't pattern that design because it hurt too much. But I had scraps from Mac's fabric, and before I knew it, I was cutting the plaid and dying to see Hercules in it.

Ignoring the ache in my chest, I walk over and sift through the pieces with her. "The factory didn't do too bad with my patterns, did they?" I pick up a green tutu dress sample made for a large dog and add, "There are a few that I couldn't fit on Hercules last night, so I have to go through those few and figure out where we went wrong."

Allie's wide blue eyes turn to me. "Did you get some videos, I hope?"

I smile and nod. "Yes, Hercules just laid there like a corpse. It was darling."

Allie claps her hands excitedly. "Great. Hold onto those until we have purchase links."

"I know, I know," I reply and then drop the dog outfit onto the table. I grab Allie's arm to direct her focus back to me. "As I was saying, I need you to take a full-body shot of me. We can go out back and take it in the alley behind the shop."

"Why do you need a full-body photo of yourself?" Allie asks, her eyes narrowing.

"Because I made the mistake of just doing a headshot the last time I tried Internet dating back in Manchester, and it turned out horribly." I turn and mindlessly play with the tutu fabric on one of the puppy outfits. "I actually had a bloke meet me at a pub, take one look at me and say, 'There's curvy, and there's fat. You, my dear, are fat.' That was before he called me Piggy and stormed out."

Allie gasps, her hand reaching out to touch my arm. "What the hell?"

I cross my arms and turn to face her. "So it's no wonder why it's taken me this long to try it again."

Allie shakes her head and then her brows furrow. "So, why are you suddenly so ready to try online dating again?"

"I don't know exactly," I state, turning and resting my arse on the sewing table. "Maybe because I've lost a few pounds and gained a bit of confidence? Maybe because I'm going to be thirty in three weeks, and I want to get my photos in while I can still say I'm a hot twenty-something?"

Allie mirrors my position and nudges me with her shoulder. "Or maybe it's because you're going through one of the most painful breakups of all time, and you think if you survived that asshole, you can survive another?"

I level her with a glare. "Mac and I would have had to have been a couple for us to break up, Allie. We were never a couple. End of story."

I hold out my phone to her, and she shakes her head. "Don't you think you're rushing into this? It's not even been two months since you went to Mac's game. I still think he'll come around."

I huff out an incredulous laugh. "Allie, I'm done waiting around for things to happen to me. Mac said a lot of horrible things to me in his car that day, but there was a shred of truth to some of them." I replay the scene in my mind for the millionth time, and it still stings because we were clearly on two completely different pages. "I would have probably dropped everything and gone with Mac to Glasgow if only he'd have asked. I would have done long distance with him, or maybe even taken a break and waited to see how the year apart went. I would have made a lot of sacrifices to be with him, but I never said any of that because I was too terrified to ask for what I want."

"And what do you want?"

"I want to be happy!" I exclaim, that familiar ache in my throat returning every time I think of Mac. "When all this with us started, it was supposed to be casual. I just wanted not to be a virgin before my thirtieth birthday. And I just wanted a date for your wedding. But then things changed between us. You all saw it in Scotland. We weren't just friends anymore. We were more. And now that I've had a taste of what true intimacy is, I want it. I want it with someone who knows me and challenges me and desires me. I want it more than just a great job and a great pet. I want it all now; rejection be damned."

Allie smiles affectionately. "You deserve it all, Freya."

I nod, my mind drifting through blips of everything I experienced with Mac and wondering what it would be like to have that with someone else. I can't even imagine it yet. My memories with Mac are still so strong, so bright, so overpowering.

I sigh heavily and add, "I'm also ready to stop being the perfect bridesmaid just because I'm single."

Allie juts out her jaw defensively. "Your singleness had nothing to do with you being in my wedding."

I lift the corner of my mouth into a smile. "I know, but if I had a boyfriend or a husband or a family, you and I might not have had time to become friends."

"Well, if that's true, I'm glad your love life is shit because I can't imagine not having you as a friend," Allie says as she shoves me playfully.

I turn and wink at her. "I'm glad you had a scandalous sex tape released of you and Roan, so you and I had the opportunity to connect on such a *deeply* personal level."

Allie's jaw drops. "Too soon for sex tape burns!"

I lift my hand to cover my mouth. "But you're married now!"

"It doesn't matter!" she shoots back, joining in my laughter. "It will always be too soon for sex tape jokes, okay?"

"Okay," I smile fondly at her and wrap my arm around her shoulders. "Now, will you please get on with taking a full-body photo of me while I'm holding a book for scale so men can really grasp the actual circumference of my arse?"

"With pleasure."

CHAPTER 30

Mac

FUNERALS.

Fuck them.

Fuck the lot of them.

They can go to fucking hell.

Fuck cancer.

Fuck old age.

Fuck sympathetic looks.

And fuck football while I'm at it because on top of the stellar few months I've had, I'm currently nothing but a substitute, riding the bench most games and playing the worst season of my life.

It's yet another rainy day in Scotland as my sister, parents, and I stand beneath black umbrellas alongside the gravesite of my grandad, Fergus Mackenzie Logan. A piper bellows "Amazing Grace" as the coffin is lowered into the ground alongside my gran. The two of them will be resting in eternal peace together now, I expect.

I think that's where my grandad has wanted to be since he lost her over three years ago.

There was a lot I learnt about Fergus Logan at the end. He was in that hospice cottage for two full weeks, and the closer he got to death's door, the more he shared about Gran. He shared stories about their time together at the bed and breakfast. He told me about the holidays they would go on together and the football matches she would let him drag her to. He told me how happy they were to become grandparents and how fond they were of Tilly and me from the moments we were born.

Everything he shared reaffirmed all that he said to me from the hospice bed the week prior. All my life, I've always thought my grandad worshipped football above God and Gran. But sitting with him as he lay in bed, struggling to breathe, and calling out to Gran in his final minutes on earth, made me realise how wrong I was all these years.

He was a man in love with his wife.

We ride in a black car to my parents' house in Dundonald, where the funeral reception is taking place. My sister is weepy the entire ride while I have yet to shed a tear for the man I loved as much as my own father. It's a strange thing because I'm not a lad who holds his tears back. In fact, I like a proper cry when the moment calls for it. Grandad always told me it was better to get that salt out of your eyes than have it festering in your belly.

Grief is a strange, wicked creature.

The house is brimming with locals who all want to talk about football with me. Considering I've been demoted to a non-starting player, I can't stand there and bear it without ample tumblers of whisky.

Eventually, I grab a bottle of whisky and head upstairs to hide out in my childhood bedroom, draping myself over the small twin bed as I look at all the football memorabilia stuck to my walls. Christ, has my life ever been about anything other than football? Freya's words from my car echo in my ear about how I could have joined the circus, and my grandad would have been equally as proud.

At the time, I couldn't believe her.

Now, I know that she was right.

What a surprise, Freya Cook is smarter than me once again.

A knock at my door has me sitting up, throwing my legs off the side of the bed. "Come in."

Tilly appears, her eyes swollen and red-rimmed. "Hiding?"

I nod.

She comes inside, closes the door, and sits down beside me. "If I have to hear one more question about who I'm dating these days, I'm going to scream."

I huff out a small laugh, but don't bother even trying to smile. "If I have to hear one more tip on how I can get my starting position back, I'm going to kick a hole in the wall."

Tilly tilts her head and rests it on my shoulder. "Why do people presume to know what we care about most in life?"

Her question draws my eyebrows together. "Are you telling me your life's dream isn't to have a boyfriend?"

She elbows me in the ribs. "Are you telling me your life's dream isn't to be a football star?"

My voice is flat when I reply, "I thought I already was a football star."

"Yeah, but that's not your dream, Macky."

My brow tightens further, and I look down at her. "What is my dream then, wise wee sister?"

She lifts her head from my shoulder and looks over at me. "You just want to be content and happy."

My brows lift. "Is that so?"

She nods. "You've spent your whole life people-pleasing because you're so worried about making someone unhappy. Now that grandad is gone, it's time to make yourself happy."

I internalize that reply, feeling an ache in my belly because the one person whose happiness I didn't take care of is the one person I care most about in this world. Tilly stands up and walks back over to the door. "Also, Freya is downstairs."

I'm on my feet in less than a second. "Buried the lead there, didn't you?" She smiles a coy smile and shrugs her shoulders while I barrel past her and make my way down.

My eyes first land on Roan and Allie, the two of them dressed in black and standing beside my father as they pay their respects. I stride over, and Roan sees me coming.

He opens his arms for a hug that I accept willingly. God, I've missed him. "Ag, Mac. I'm so sorry about your grandad. He was the shit."

I smile at his choice of phrase and turn to hug Allie next, dropping a kiss to her cheek. "I'm so sorry for your loss." She pulls back, and her eyes are teary. "Are you doing okay?"

I nod and glance around, looking for Freya. "I'm all right. I had some good moments with him before the end."

Allie reaches out and strokes my arm. "I'm glad to hear it. We've missed you in London."

I nod, and my eyes continue to wander. "Is Freya with you?"

Allie's hand falls from my arms, and her expression shifts from sympathetic to guarded. "She was out on the front porch I believe." I step away from them to go find her, and Allie leaps into my path. "Mac…just…be gentle with her."

My stomach sinks as I look down at Allie with shame and regret. I deserve this after everything I said to Freya. I reach out and touch Allie's arm. "I will be, Al. I promise."

When I walk outside, I find Freya sipping a whisky with two old men that I recognise as friends of my grandfather. The men are roaring with laughter, and Freya is positively toppled over in her own fit of adorable snort-filled giggles.

When she rights herself, her eyes fly wide the minute they land on me. "What is it with you charming old Scottish men?" I ask, sliding my hands into my pockets.

"Old?" the man I know named Angus huffs. "We're not old. We're experienced."

Freya turns her shocked expression to amusement as she looks over at him. "Angus, you already shared far more than I ever needed to know about your *experience.*"

My grandfather's car buddy, Alexander, pipes in next. "Aye…and me too, for that matter. I could have lived the rest of my life never knowing the shite you got up to in Prague."

"Me too," Freya says, holding her hand out for a high five to Alexander like it's the most normal thing in the world.

Angus mutters his argument as I step in and hold my hand out to Freya. "Do you mind if I steal her for a moment, gentlemen?"

Freya gazes at my offered hand for a second before standing up on her own. My eyes drink in the sight of her in a fitted knee-length pencil dress that hugs all her curves that I swear have shrunk some since last I saw her. She's lost weight.

I don't like it.

Her heels clunk on the wooden steps as I guide her into the house and up the stairs. "Where are we going?" she asks, frowning as she glances down the hallway.

"To talk," I reply, opening my bedroom door for her.

She hesitates at the threshold. "I don't think this is a good idea, Mac."

"Just talk, Cookie. Come on; I promise I'm not going to bite."

She steps in slowly, her eyes cautiously taking in the small room. "What did you want to talk about?"

I sit down on my bed and pat the area next to me. She chews her lip nervously before coming over and perching on the very edge as though she's ready to sprint away.

"Whisky?" I ask, grabbing the bottle and offering it up to her. "No glasses."

The corner of her mouth twitches with a smile as she takes the open bottle and tips it to her mouth. Her lips are a lush ruddy colour as they wrap around the amber glass and drink. Her eyes squint shut as she swallows the burning liquid before she hands it back over to me.

"How have you been?" I ask, my voice deep and steady.

She nods for a bit too long. "I'm okay." She pulls her lip into her mouth and shakes her head. "I'm so sorry about Fergus, Mac. I know you knew it was coming, but it doesn't make it any easier. He was such a unique man. One of a kind."

I shoot her a wry grin and look down at her hands, nervously clenched on her lap. "He was. And even in the end, he was asking for a shot of whisky."

She smiles fondly. "I'm not surprised."

I lick my lips and eye her face, taking in her wee freckles like I'm seeing them for the first time all over again, when a mere three months ago, I could have drawn them in a portrait of her perfectly. "I've missed you, Freya."

She turns her head to look forward, refusing to meet my eyes. "You've had a rough couple of months."

My brows tweak. "Aye, that's true." I reach out and brush a wisp of her red hair behind her ear, my fingers brushing over her lobes as I do. Her ears are on fire.

She shivers against my touch and pulls away from my embrace. "Mac, don't."

"What?" I state, my voice hoarse. "I can't touch you now?"

She turns her green eyes to me, and instead of seeing uncertainty in their depths, I see fiery passion. "No, you can't." She stands up and moves away from the bed. "No, you can't touch me," she exclaims again, as she begins pacing back and forth in front of me. "There's actually a lot you can't do with me after the last time I saw you. Honestly, being alone with me in a room should be one of those things you can't do with me."

She moves towards the door, and I jump up, splaying my hand out on the wood, my face only a foot away from hers when I rush out, "Freya, I love you."

Her body freezes as her jaw drops. She turns to look up at me with wide, confused eyes. "You what?"

I lick my lips, the words feeling foreign on my tongue because I've never said them to a lass in all my life, but there they are. "I love you."

Her face wrinkles up like she's confused, and she begins shaking her head side to side. "No, Mac. You don't."

She moves to open the door, and I push it closed again. "Yes, Cookie. I do."

She laughs and grabs the handle again. "You don't."

"I do!"

"You don't!"

"Stop telling me I don't love you, woman!" I bellow, my muscles tight with anger. "What's wrong with you?"

She blanches, her face the picture of disillusionment at the scene taking place in front of her. "What's wrong with me? What's wrong with me is that I'm just finally feeling human again after you chewed me up and spit me out in a Glasgow hotel parking lot. You acted like I was only good enough for you if I went home and slept with you that night. And the moment I turned you down, you treated me like I was a waste of your time and confirmed the fact that everything you ever told me was a lie."

"It wasn't a lie," I state, my hands balling into fists at my sides. "Christ Freya, I didn't mean to make you feel like I only wanted to sleep with you. I just wanted to be near you and have you near me again. Nothing I told you when we were together was ever a lie."

She purses her lips and nods, her eyes red around the edges. "So you just lie when you're in a fight with someone. Wow, I feel so much better."

She moves and opens the door a foot before I slam it shut, placing myself like a barricade in front of it so she can't reach it without going through me. "Freya, when you told me you loved me in my car that day, I wasn't ready to hear it then."

"And I'm not ready to hear you say it now, Mac!" Her hands lift helplessly. "You just lost your grandfather. You should be focusing on your grief, not using me as a crutch to get through your pain. You lost that right when you broke my heart two months ago."

Her words pierce through my heart, but what kills me is the finality of her tone. The conviction in her body language. She's changed, and I hate it. She doesn't feel like my Freya anymore. The woman standing before me isn't her.

"I'm leaving." She reaches past my hip, her breasts pressing against my front as she grasps for the doorknob. Her scent is intoxicating. Her hair brushes my chin, and every bone in my body aches to claim her. This can't be over. This can't be it. *Freya is mine.*

In one final act of desperation, I reach down and grab her face in my hands and pull her to my lips. The taste of her, the smell of her, the feel of her against me once again is everything that makes sense in this world. I move my lips against hers, begging and pleading with her to have me. To remember me. To forgive me.

But she's not moving.

Her lips refuse to part.

Her hands won't touch me.

Her heart is in a sealed cage that I cannot access.

I pull away an inch, my breath mingling with hers as I stare into her cold, tear-filled eyes. My voice is a desperate plea when I say, "Please, Freya. I'm sorry. You have to know how sorry I am."

She blinks slowly, and the tears slide down her cheeks like traitors. "It doesn't matter, Mac. There's no going back. You ruined us."

"I didn't!" I roar, my voice hoarse with desperation as I wrap my arms around her and crush her to my body. The softness of her in my arms is complete and utter perfection. It's destiny. It's tragedy. It's love. "I didn't ruin us, Freya. Don't say that."

"I've moved on, Mac," she adds coldly, her voice devoid of any emotion.

"Bullshit," I growl, my lip curling in disgust. "You couldn't have moved on. What we had was too special. You're mine, and I'm yours. I'll never give up on us."

Her chin trembles, and her lips part as she croaks out the words I never expected to hear. "I've slept with someone else."

And with that punishing blow, she pulls out of my embrace and walks away, leaving me shattered.

"I should have never come to Scotland," I groan, my head bowed into my hands as my elbows rest on top of the sticky bar of the pub. I stare down into the tumbler of whisky between my elbows as I add, "The transfer I made was wrong. Even my grandad could see that. If I could get in a time machine, I'd go back right fucking now and never step foot into Santino's slimy office."

I reach down and grab my drink, taking a small sip, and letting the burn sit on my tongue for a moment before swallowing. "And now, Freya is fucking someone else." A chill runs up my spine over the thought of another man's hands on her body. The image makes me physically ill.

Or maybe that's the ninth whisky I'm currently drinking.

Roan sighs heavily beside me and grabs the glass out of my hands. "You didn't expect her to wait for you, did you?"

I turn glazed eyes to him. "Whose side are you on?"

"Yours, man. Always yours." He faces forward and swallows my whisky in one gulp. Thief. "But you can't really blame her after everything that happened."

I do my best to focus on my friend, but there are currently two of him. Roan and I have been drinking at the pub around the corner from my parents' house for the past three hours since Freya ran away from me like I'm a bad habit she's trying to break free of.

"You seriously won't tell me where Freya and Allie are?" I ask him for the eighteenth time.

He shakes his head without even looking at me. "I made a

promise to my wife, and I'm not starting our first year of marriage with broken promises, Mac. No matter how pathetic you look right now."

I groan and rake my fingers through my hair, mussing it and then tossing my fists out in anger. "I must be an idiot to think that saying three words could make things go back to normal."

Roan side-eyes me. "You told her you loved her?" He says the words slowly, as if I might miss the question.

I turn my head to him. "Yeah, pal. I told her, and she couldn't give a shite."

Roan blinks back his surprise. "I didn't know you said you loved her."

"I did, and it didn't fucking matter. She's the first woman I've ever loved, and she looks at me like I'm fucking dirt. Christ, I'm an idiot."

I bury my head into my folded arms on the bar, and Roan jerks me out of my wallowing. "Why did you tell her you loved her?"

I frown over at him, trying to make him into one person. "What do you mean?"

"Why did you say it?"

"Because I love her!" I state again, agitated by his ignorant question. "Christ, get your ears checked, you annoying bawbag."

Roan purses his lips. "You didn't give her any reasons for why you love her?"

My face crumples up as I look over at him. "No…what reasons?"

Roan huffs out an annoyed noise and turns me to face him on my stool, nearly tipping me off of it in the process. "You can't break a girl's heart like you did and expect to just drop an I Love You. Ag, you have to make her believe it, man."

"She doesn't want to believe it!" I argue, my muscles turning to mush with every passing minute. "She's moved on. She's fucking someone else, and she hates my guts."

Roan shakes his head from side to side. "If you can look at that girl's eyes and not see the heartbreak all over her face when she looks at you, then you don't know her at all."

A flash of anger shoots through me, and I sit up and grab him by the collar of his shirt. "Don't tell me I don't know Freya Cook. I fucking know Freya better than anybody in this entire world." I release him with a shove and stare forward broodingly. "I know her favourite Netflix programs and that she prefers Indian takeaway over Chinese, but if I say something sweet to her, she'll always get us Chinese. I know that she'd have more cats in her flat if she wasn't terrified of Hercules getting the shits over it. I know that I can't kill a spider in front of her, but she still wants him dead in the end. I know how she takes her coffee and that she hates shop-bought blankets. I know that she says she hates arguing with me, but deep down, I can tell it makes her feel alive and fuck if it doesn't do the same to me. And I know that her greatest desire in life is just to be seen by some-one, even though she acts like she needs no one."

I turn to face Roan, my hands shaking as realisation dawns on me. "I saw her the moment we stepped into that shop last year, man. I think maybe I've loved her since I first met her."

Roan nods, his mouth tipping into a sad smile. "That's why you have to fight harder to win her back, you idiot." He grabs my arm and shakes me. "Stop feeling sorry for yourself and wallowing over this move to Glasgow and make her see that you don't just love her because you miss her. You love her because she's your entire world, and you're willing to do anything to be with her."

"Fuck me," I grumble, my heart pumping like a maniac. "I'm a damn fool."

Roan laughs and almost slips off his stool. "You've always told me you're a trainable fool, though."

"Aye," I reply, my eyes blinking as I face forward and wonder how hard I have to bash my head into this bar to knock me back in time.

CHAPTER 31

Mac

"**I**'M SURPRISED YOU DIDN'T LOSE MY NUMBER WHEN YOU moved to Scotland," Santino's voice rings into the phone, making my skin crawl. "To what do I owe the pleasure of this call?"

I clear my throat, my head still banging from this shite hangover I have. "Roan told me to call you and ask some questions about my contract."

I hear a huff of breath on the other line. "Did he now?"

I breathe out slowly through my nose, trying to find my patience with this bawbag. "Santino, I have a crippling headache, so if you could lose the slimy guy act, I'd be most appreciative."

Santino chuckles as if he enjoys the thought of me in pain. "Do you want out of your contract with your current club?"

I blink in confusion, the question surprising the piss out of me. "Would Bethnal Green actually consider buying out my current contract for a transfer?"

"No," Santino replies with a laugh, and then I hear the rustling of papers in the background. "But because I knew you were a fuck-ing idiot when you came into my office that day and making rash decisions, the deal your agent and I brokered included a buy-back clause."

"What?" I ask, my face twisting up in confusion. A buy-back clause? Christ, I should have paid closer attention to my contract instead of relying on my agent to handle everything. "So, what does that mean exactly?"

"It means that Bethnal Green can buy you back for a fixed amount when the January transfer window opens up if Rangers agree to it."

"Fucking hell, are you telling me I could be back playing for Bethnal this winter?"

"That's exactly what I'm saying," Santino confirms, his voice crisp and businesslike. "I've already spoken with their team, and they're interested in sending you back since you've been such a shit purchase for them."

"Jesus Christ, will they agree? Would Bethnal Green be willing to buy me back?" I ask, my heart beating out of my chest as I consider the idea that I could be back home in London in only a few months.

There's a pause on the other end of the line. "I'm sure I could get Vaughn to go for it, but I have a personal request that I need to put in front of you before I go and talk him into this."

"Christ, man, what?" I snap, eager to get this show on the road.

"I need to talk to your sister."

My body instantly tenses. "No fucking way."

"Maclay. It's just talking."

"Absolutely not."

"Mac," Santino growls into the phone. "I set up your contract to Scotland with a buy-back clause because I knew you were making an emotional decision that you might later regret. And I knew that Vaughn wouldn't let you go without one. You're too important to this club. So please try to understand that I'm not a bad fucking guy. And there's shit you don't know about me. Shit that maybe I'll tell you someday. But not before I tell your sister, and I don't want to speak to your sister without your blessing."

I exhale heavily at his lofty request, absorbing the serious cadence of his voice. What could he have to talk to my sister about? Haven't they been through enough together? Then I recall how closed off Tilly is about what happened to her, and maybe that's because the two of them have unfinished business they need to discuss. Maybe my sister actually wants to talk to him.

"If my sister doesn't want to talk to you, you don't talk to her... got it?"

"Of course, Maclay. That goes without saying."

I nod, my jaw clenched because I know I'm at a point in my life where I'll do just about anything to get my arse back to London and show Freya what she means to me. And if the Harris family stands by Santino, he might actually have some redeemable qualities.

"Okay," I reply, my tone clipped. "If Tilly agrees to talk to you, I won't get in your way about it."

There's a deep breath on the other end of the line before Santino says, "For the record, Maclay, I would have pushed this buy-back through without your blessing."

"For the record, Santino, I still don't like you."

CHAPTER 32

Mac

"A LLIE, WHERE IS FREYA?" I BARK INTO THE PHONE LINE, pacing back and forth while clutching a pet carrier in my hand. "I'm standing in her flat, and she's not here, and she's not picking up her mobile."

"What the hell are you doing in Freya's flat?" Allie fires back. "How did you get in?"

"I still have my key," I say, fingering the key in my pocket and knowing damn well I shouldn't have used it but not giving a shite.

Allie hisses, "Mac, that is a gross misuse of that key. You and Freya aren't even speaking right now. How do you think it's okay for you to let yourself into her flat?"

"I have a present for her," I reply, my hand gripping the handle nervously. "I need to give it to her right away. It can't wait."

"What kind of present?" Allie asks curiously.

I take a nervous breath before replying. "I bought her a rescue kitten, all right? I got it from this guy Roger who we both know, and I have this wee thing with me now, and I just need to find Freya."

There's silence on the other end of the line. "Mac, you can't just give her a kitten. Not after everything that's happened. It's only been a week since your grandad's funeral. Give her some time."

"I'm not just giving her a kitten, Allie," I growl and flinch when I realise how angry I am. "I'm trying to win her back. I love her, Al."

Allie inhales sharply. "I'm happy to hear you finally say what we've all freaking known for the past year, Mac."

"I get it, Allie. I'm an idiot. I'm trying to make it right, so will you please tell me where she is?" I ask, not even trying to hide my desperation.

There's a pause, and I don't like the sound of it. "You're not going to like what I'm about to tell you."

"What?" I ask, my jaw clenching in preparation.

"She's on a date."

"With who?"

"Some Tinder guy. They're at The Rooftop St James restaurant. I'm on call if she needs a rescue."

"Christ," I growl under my breath, my muscles tensing at the thought of Freya being on a fucking date. Also, what is it with her and rooftop dates? "Has she been on a lot of these dates?" I ask, terrified of her answer.

There's a quiet pause on the other end that I do not like the sound of. I begin murmuring my displeasure, and Allie interrupts. "Mac, what are you going to do?"

I swallow the knot in my throat, and reply, "Whatever it takes."

As soon as I hang up, an orange figure strides out from the darkened hallway. It's Hercules stalking straight towards me with slow, measured steps like he's preparing to pounce.

I drop down on my knees, setting the pet carrier beside me. "Easy, lad. I've just come to bring you a friend."

Hercules turns his blue eyes from me to the pet cage on the floor beside me and approaches it with great caution. The wee kitten releases a high-pitched meow, and Hercules jumps but doesn't run away. Instead, he leans his nose forward and touches his nose to the metal cage and lets out the loudest, most contented purr I've ever heard.

"Do you like him, Hercules? Do you want to meet him?" I ask, reaching out and running my hand down the wee monster's back. He curls into my hand and then lays down in front of the cage, placing the pads of his paw on the door, almost like he's asking me to open it.

With a wry grin, I reach over, and the cage door squeaks as I open it, freeing the small, fluffy grey kitten out of his pen.

He pounces playfully in front of Hercules, who's watching him like a hawk. When the wee kitty steps closer to the big orange, overweight monster, Hercules does something I never expected.

He rolls on his back and opens his paws to the kitten. The kitten pounces, his tiny toothpick-like teeth gnawing into the big cat's ear playfully. Hercules lays there like a corpse, letting the wee thing have his way with him as though this is just a normal Tuesday.

"Are you two going to be pals?" I ask, reaching out and rubbing Hercules's cheek.

He replies with a thunderous purr, and I bite my lip excitedly. This is a sign. A really good sign.

Freya

I'm on a date.

I'm on a date on my birthday.

This must be what thirty-somethings do, right? They swipe right and meet complete strangers in a restaurant to hide the fact that it's their birthday, and they have no one special to spend it with?

To be fair, Allie tried to plan a party for me. Begged, even. I was able to push her off until the weekend when I told her that I had a date lined up for the night. I know I should be spending my birthday with people I'm close to, but I honestly just wanted this date. On this day. It feels like a sense of accomplishment to be back out in the world and dating after everything that happened with Mac.

"So, Freya, I've been doing all the talking since we sat down. Please…tell me about yourself," Jasper says, sitting across from me in a romantic restaurant called The Rooftop St James. It's a posh, outdoor space that overlooks Trafalgar Square. The city lights and people milling about below set the perfect scenery for a new beginning.

Jasper is the complete opposite of Mac. He's an accountant from Southampton who's well over six feet tall with a narrow frame that gives him the Lurch vibe. He's dressed in smart pleated trousers, and I think he's sporting a very nice dad bod beneath that shirt. Just my type.

"I'm a seamstress," I state like a reflex. "Well…a designer now, I guess. I work in a clothing boutique with two very dear friends of mine, and I'm currently working towards expanding their shop into pet wear."

"Pet wear?" Jasper asks, his voice rising in pitch at the end. A nervous look fleets across his face. "Do you…have pets?"

I nod proudly. "I have an orange cat named Hercules. He's completely mental, but he's my baby."

Jasper begins tugging at the collar of his shirt. "That's nice. I, erm, don't have any pets."

I smile and lean forward, narrowing my eyes at him in a playful challenge. "Are you a dog person or a cat person? This is a very serious question, and there's only one acceptable answer."

He smiles awkwardly. "I'll have to get back to you on that one."

I nod and lean back while taking a sip of my wine. This date is off to a very strange start.

Dinner is served, and Jasper begins telling me about the luxury hotel chain he works for and how expensive it is to stay there. He tells me that even with his deep employee discount, he still stays at the cheaper hotel across the street when he has late-night meetings. What a travesty. It takes everything in me not to cringe when he says that he doesn't even buy the coffee at his hotel because even that with a discount is "exorbitant."

I'm so paying for half of this dinner cheque.

By the time dessert is served, I'm exhausted. Jasper has this annoying need to fill in all the silences. There were so many nights Mac and I wouldn't say much to each other at all. We'd just sit on the sofa, watch telly, and enjoy the other's company. Most of the time, there were arguments peppered in there, of course, but on top of all that, there was this ease between us. Contented silence. It was lovely. And I can't help but wonder if I'll ever find that with another man. And will I ever stop comparing all the men I date to Mac? God, I hope so.

"So anyway, I took my shirt back to the dry cleaner, and I said, 'This stain was not here when I brought it in, and I refuse to pay for the service.'"

"So, you still have the shirt then? They didn't offer to replace it?" I ask, taking another big sip of wine.

"Yes," he replies, his lips twitching nervously. "I didn't think they'd go for replacing the shirt. It cost me twenty pounds."

I purse my lips together and turn to look out at the view again— the one saving grace of this evening.

"Freya?" A familiar voice says my name and I think I might be imagining Jasper's voice to sound like Mac's because I'm so bored, I'm just making shit up in my mind. I look to Jasper, who isn't looking at me, he's looking at someone standing beside me.

I turn, and my jaw drops when I see Mac standing over me in all his broad, ridiculously muscled, and sexily inked glory. He's wearing jeans and a white T-shirt, and he's holding a giant batch of pink balloons, and a bouquet of pink carnations are stuffed under his arm.

"Wha—what are you doing here?" I stutter, shocked at the man before me. My eyes quickly fall to the very obvious grey pet carrier in his other hand.

"It's your birthday, Cookie." His shoulders lift with a shrug as he half smiles down at me. His eyes are soft and dancing all over my face like he's committing it to memory all over again.

"What is that?" I ask, pointing to his hand, and as if on cue, a high-pitched meow erupts from the cage.

"Jesus Christ," Jasper bellows, pushing back from the table. "Is that a cat?"

Mac looks over to my date, a stony, intimidating look causing Jasper to shrink into his chair. "Aye."

"I'm...allergic," Jasper stammers, his face turning a beet red shade before my very eyes. "I break out in hives whenever I'm within ten feet of a cat."

Mac's voice is flat when he replies, "You better be on your way then."

My jaw clenches because Mac has a lot of nerve coming in here and scaring my date away. "You don't have to go," I say to Jasper, pressing my hand on the table. "Mac will go."

"Who's Mac?"

"I'm Mac," Mac growls, stepping closer to Jasper, who leaps up out of his seat to back away from the kitten. "I'm her best mate, and this woman loves cats more than breathing, so if you're deathly allergic, then trust me, pal, I'm doing you a favour."

Jasper clumsily moves to stand behind the chair, and I can't fully tell who he's more terrified of at this moment—Mac or the cat. He looks to me, his hands trembling as he says, "Mind picking up the cheque?"

I blink back my shock, and without another look back, Jasper takes off out of the restaurant, probably feeling like he won the lottery because he didn't have to pay for his dinner.

I stand up from my seat, rage tingling all over my body as I level a glare at Mac. "How dare you think you can come in here and sabotage another one of my dates!"

Mac's lips twitch with barely concealed amusement that makes me want to punch him. And hug him. Bleddy hell.

He turns to face me and replies, "Cookie, if the man is deathly allergic to cats, it wasn't going to be a love connection."

"It could have been," I reply, chewing my lip nervously and trying hard to ignore everyone staring at the spectacle we're making. "There are shots people can get for allergies."

"The lad was terrified of this wee thing!" Mac smiles, holding up the pet carrier as proof. "There's no shot he can take for being a big wuss."

"He's not a wuss," I argue half-heartedly as my eyes fall to the tiny kitten. "What are you doing with that poor thing in the first place?" I cross my arms over my chest and try to tell myself not to ask him to hold it because we're in a restaurant full of people and I currently hate the ground Mac walks on.

Mac shoots me a crooked smirk, his eyes twinkling with mirth as he replies, "I'm trying to give you your best birthday ever, Freya."

My face falls as I bend over and look into the cage to see the stunning blue-eyed, long-haired kitten inside. "Did you get this precious darling from Roger?"

"Aye," Mac replies with a smile. "For you."

I stand up and huff incredulously, "Mac, you can't just give me a kitten and expect things to go back to normal with us. You and I are in a massive fight, and teasing me with an adorable kitten that will only terrify poor Hercules means we're in a second fight!"

"You're wrong, Cookie," Mac replies, shaking his head and stepping closer to me. "You think Hercules is too scared to accept another cat into his life, but I think Hercules *needs* this cat to get him to finally come out of the shadows and live a wee bit."

My eyes gloss over at Mac's words because somehow, I don't think he's talking about Hercules. "Hercules is just fine in the shadows away from that kitten. At least there, he won't get hurt."

Mac steps closer again, his tall form bowing over me as he says, "I think a bit of hurt in the beginning just makes it all the more worth it when it works out in the end."

I stare at his chest and hate myself for whispering, "How do you know it will work out?"

His voice is low and deep when he replies, "Because we all have to come out of the shadows eventually."

The sound of the kitten's high-pitched meow breaks the moment of electricity between Mac and I. Mac turns to the man sitting at a table beside us and hands him the bouquet of balloons. He sets the flowers down on the table before squatting down to take the kitten out of the pet carrier.

My heart thunders in my chest when he stands up, holding the tiny ball of fluff in his tattooed arms, and I instantly wish I had my phone out to take a picture because this would be the cutest calendar picture ever printed.

Mac smiles softly as he moves towards me. "By the way, I was at your place earlier looking for you and Hercules came out looking like he was about to pounce this wee bugger."

I look up nervously at Mac as his shoulders shake with silent laughter. "I opened the cage and let them meet, and you should have heard how loud Hercules purred."

"He purred?" I ask, reaching out to pet the soft kitty hair on the adorable darling's head. "Wait, you were in my flat?"

Mac coughs and murmurs, "I still have my key."

"Mac!"

He sighs heavily, "I know I shouldn't have, but I was desperate." Mac hands the kitten over to me and sighs. "And I'm not sorry because I got to see them meet, and it was like Hercules was meeting his best friend for the first time. It was damn adorable."

My chin trembles as I cuddle the little dear to my chest and feel the vibrating of his body as he purrs and nuzzles into my neck, rubbing his sweet face all over me. My eyes tear up. "Two cats is going to be twice as much work."

"I'll be there to help."

I laugh softly. "Yeah, right."

"I'm serious, Cookie," Mac says, stepping towards me and reaching out to pet the kitty. "I'm not just here to give you a birthday gift. I'm here to ask you to move in with me."

"What?" I exclaim, my heart thundering in my chest. "What do you mean? You're in Glasgow, you idiot."

"Aye," Mac says, his hand moving up to tug on my hot ear, the tender affection sending a riot of goosebumps all over my body. He smiles proudly and adds, "But in January I'll be back in London, and I thought then I could move in with you."

"What are you talking about? You're not making any sense."

"The new contract I signed had a buy-back clause. Bethnal Green wants me back, and Rangers have agreed to it. Which means, when the transfer window opens up in January, I'm coming back to London to play for them again."

"What? How? How is that possible? Why did you never tell me that?"

Mac's brows lift. "I didn't know myself until last week. It was Santino, of all people, who set that all up. Apparently, he's not the bawbag I thought he was."

I blink rapidly as I struggle to absorb everything he's saying. "So, you're coming back to London."

"I'm coming back, Cookie." He reaches out and cups my cheek with his large, warm hand, his thumb stroking my lip briefly before he adds, "But I don't want to wait until January to be with you. I want to be with you now. Always. I'm miserable in Glasgow without you. I want you to come out and live with me until I move back. We can spend Christmas in Scotland while you design your plus-sized pet clothes. We can be together and get back to the way we used to be."

"The way we used to be?" I croak, my throat closing up with anxiety because his words are so close, yet so far away from everything I need to hear. I pull away from his embrace. "Mac, I'm done with what we used to be. I have spent far too many hours with you, and now I have these beautiful romantic ideas stuck in my head. Stuff that's even more romantic than a Canadian cowboy on *Heartland*! And I want them for myself. I finally believe I deserve real love with someone who knows how they feel about me. I can't do this with you all over again. I can't survive losing my best friend and the man I love all over again."

Mac exhales heavily, my words clearly knocking him off his feet. But I don't care. I won't be silent anymore. I won't have quiet feelings about what I want out of life anymore. I'm not the same person who just accepts what's in front of me. I need more. I'm worth more.

Mac growls, agitation written all over his face. "Christ, how did I know you'd bring up bloody *Heartland* tonight?"

"Because it's the hallmark of our lives together, Mac!" I snarl, my voice sounding seriously scary.

"I bought you a fucking kitten, Cook! I'd say that's *Heartland*-level romantic. I at least thought it would soften up your disposition towards me as of late."

"Of course, a kitten would soften me up. I love kittens!" I shriek. "I know!" he roars.

The two of us breathe heavily in each other's faces for a long moment, both of our bodies vibrating with anger, lust, attraction, and something else. Something…bigger.

"Excuse me," a man's voice says from beside us, breaking us out of some serious eye-fucking going on. I look over and see it's the person Mac handed the balloons to. "Do I still need to hold these? My food has arrived."

Mac reaches over, yanks the balloons out of his hand and releases them into the air. "Happy fucking Birthday, Cookie. Christ, how am I still screwing this up?" he grumbles, gripping the back of his neck and shaking his head as he appears to search his mind for a moment.

He exhales heavily and pins me with a look. "Freya Cook, I want you to live with me because I'm madly in love with you, and I don't want to wait to start our lives together. I'm trying to show you that I'm all in. I want you in London, Scotland, anywhere you'll have me. I don't want less with you. I want more. *Heartland* more. That's why I want to fucking marry you, you stubborn woman!"

"What?" I shriek, scaring the poor kitty in my hands. "How could you possibly know you want to marry me? Are you an idiot?"

"If that makes me an idiot, then aye, sure. I'm an idiot!" Mac snaps back, his Scottish accent getting thicker with his intensity.

He clenches his teeth and hisses something under his breath before moving into my space and cupping my face in his hands. "My love for you is as real as your love for that daft horse show, Freya. I even love how you sound like Hagrid from Harry Potter when you're feeling poorly. I love that you hate drinking out of anything other than a coffee cup. I love that most designers would sketch beautiful women's dresses or shoes but you sketch cat pyjamas and paw slippers."

"I just think some cats would like sleepwear."

"I know," Mac replies with a laugh, his eyes dropping to my lips in a hungry way. "I love how your crazy mind operates and how you're always doing something unexpected. I love how you hum when you brush your teeth, and have conversations with your food even when I'm standing in the room with you."

"I don't have conversations with my food." A nervous, snort-filled laugh erupts from me as I glance at the people around us.

"You do, and it's so fucking adorable, it's hard for me to keep my hands off you. You also have this uncanny ability of making me happy and at peace. I've never felt more at home than when I'm sitting on your sofa, watching you sniffle during *Heartland*."

"I'm sorry for how I told you I loved you at my parents' house. You were right, I was a mess that day, but I'm not anymore. I'm seeing everything clearly now, Cookie. I think I've loved you since the moment I met you in that damn boutique when you spoiled *Shameless* for me. You blindsided me, Freya. You blindsided me with everything I never knew I wanted."

He leans in and presses a hard, chaste kiss to my lips, his breath coming heavy and fast as he pulls back and adds, "I want to spend the rest of my life with you because you're my wee treasure, and despite how crazy mad you make me and how much we bicker, there's no one else I'd want to fight with in life." He hesitates and gets a serious look on his face before adding. "I wasn't going to do this here, but you've given me no other choice."

He drops down on one knee.

He's dropping down on one bleddy knee!

He reaches into his pocket.

He's reaching into his bleddy pocket!

A blue velvet box appears in his hand. Like he magicked it into existence just by sheer will. He cracks open the box, and there sits a ring. A giant monstrosity of a thing that you would see dangling for dear life on one of those lanky supermodels with bones for fingers. It's the kind of ring that's so enormous it probably tips those tiny model's weight over from ninety-nine pounds to one hundred and two.

I'll take a couple of extra pounds on the scale for a ring like that.

"Freya Cook, it's my turn to blindside you and ask...will you marry me?" God help him, his voice even cracks at the end as his eyes become red with unshed tears. "I know we never talked about this and you're probably wondering what the hell I'm doing with a ring in my pocket but, bloody hell, Freya, I've known you for well over a year, and all I want to do for the rest of my life is argue with you and make love to you and keep you as my best mate...and my wife. You're it for me, Cookie. Partly because I don't think anyone else could stand me but mostly because I don't want to sit and watch telly on the sofa with anybody else. I want to be old, grey, fat, and happy with you. Will you be fat and happy with me?"

An embarrassing sob bubbles up from my throat because I don't think he could have said anything more perfect at this moment. I pull the dear little kitty who has no idea what's going on up to my face and wipe my tear-stained cheeks off on his fur before croaking, "I'd love nothing more than to see you fat, Maclay Logan."

He stands up and kisses me, and for the first time in my entire life, I'm no longer thinking of my flaws or my future or what my ending will be. Because I'm holding my happy ending with a furry little kitty in the middle.

That's a lie. I'm thinking about babies. Lots and lots of ginger-haired, wild, kilt-wearing Scottish babies with this man who I want to have my babies.

Wait...that didn't sound right. Let's try that again.

—the man who I want to have his sperm.

Bleddy hell, that's not right either. Take three!

—the man whose babies I want to rear in my fruitful loins.

Nailed it.

"Just to be clear, that was a yes to you marrying me, right?" Mac asks, pulling away and giving the kitten some space.

"It was a yes," I laugh, and he reaches up to wipe the tears from my eyes.

"Good, because I wanted to wait until I trapped you to tell you the new kitty shat on your rug and left a stain."

"What?" I screech, my eyes wide and accusing on the man that just turned me into a puddle of mush a second ago.

"I cleaned it up, but…it didn't look good when I left."

"Mac!"

"He was having so much fun with Hercules I think the wee bugger just crapped himself with happiness."

"Were you watching him?" *I swear to God if he was digging in my cupboards for food, I'm going to kill him!*

"Aye, sure," he replies with a guilty look on his face.

"If he develops a bad habit because of you, you're cleaning up all the messes."

"Aye, stop nagging me, woman."

"Never," I smile.

He smiles too. And then…we're kissing again.

CHAPTER 33

Mac

FREYA AND I RUSH BACK TO HER FLAT FROM THE ROOFTOP ST James and tear each other's clothes off.

Okay, that's a lie…

We spend our first hour as a newly engaged couple going to a pet shop to pick up supplies for our new wee kitten. The moment we enter Freya's flat, she drops to the floor as Hercules greets us, and she watches with pure joy as her old companion welcomes his new furry friend.

Freya cries.

I cry because she cries.

And then we do the real version of Netflix and chilling. And then of course, a classic Freya and Mac activity called…Netflix and arguing.

"How many dates did you go on with blokes while we were apart?" I ask, my voice low as I lay on Freya's purple sofa with her between my legs. Her red hair is a beautiful mess of post-coital satisfaction draped across my chest, and she's wearing another one of her kitty nightshirts, this one featuring graphic text across the front that says "If Cats Could Talk, They Wouldn't".

She tenses against my shirtless body and turns back to look at me. "What?"

I exhale heavily and run my finger along the freckles on her nose. "I just...I have to know."

She blinks nervously while toying with the hem of her shirt. "Why?"

I frown as my arms tighten around her. "Because I'm a fucking caveman, okay? Can you just get it over with and tell me? I'm not going to be angry...just rip it off like a plaster."

Her lips twitch with barely concealed amusement. "How many women were you with when we were apart?"

I stiffen around her body. "Are you fucking kidding me?"

She turns over, so she's now lying on her belly over my chest and watches me expectantly. "Don't tell me you were celibate for two months."

"Cookie, I've been celibate since the moment I met you, just confirming the fact that I've been hopelessly in love with you from the beginning." I reach out and tug on her adorable pink ear. "After I had you, I couldn't even look at another woman without aching for your body and your smile. Hell, I even missed the way you smack my chest when you're angry at me. So I stayed as far away from women as I could the entire time I was in Glasgow."

She chews her lip nervously and looks down, tracing my nipples with her fingertips. "So you never even dated anyone? Flirted?"

I reach down and crook my finger under her chin, forcing her to look at me. "The closest I got to any women were my mother and Tilly. Now you. Confess your sins." My hands lower, and I squeeze her sides playfully causing her to giggle and squirm on my groin, which in turn causes my cock to demand a second round. But he must be ignored because I want to hear this.

When I notice Freya's cheeks pink up with anxiety, my disposition softens. Maybe I'm putting too much pressure on her. If she slept with several men while we were apart, I can't blame her for that. I was a complete arse, and it would be natural for her to be curious after waiting so long to have sex in the first place.

I lean forward and press a kiss to her forehead. "It's all right, Cookie. I understand if you wanted to explore other options." I kiss her again and add with waggling eyebrows, "Just tell me I'm the best cock you've ever had, and we can move on."

Her face immediately lightens as she pins me with a look and replies, "You're the best cock I've ever had."

I thrust my fist upward, feeling victorious. "God, please put that on my tombstone someday, even if you are lying to me."

Freya goes quiet, looking down at her hands clasped on top of my chest as she adds, "Also you're still the only cock I've ever had."

I watch her for a few seconds, my brows pinched in confusion. "But in my bedroom back in Dundonald, you said…"

She shrugs, glancing up at me, a sad look flitting across her face. "I was just trying to hurt you as much as you hurt me."

I swallow the painful lump in my throat. "It fucking worked."

She reaches out to press her hand against my cheek, whispering, "I'm sorry."

I turn my head and kiss the inside of her palm, letting her know I forgive her as she has forgiven me. "So, who the fuck was that Jasper guy tonight?"

Freya inhales deeply. "He was actually the first and only date I went on since you left for Scotland. I set up my online dating account after that game I attended of yours in Glasgow, but even though I hated you, I could never manage to swipe right on anybody." She scrunches her nose as she continues, "The only reason I went out with Jasper was because I didn't want to spend my actual birthday with Allie and the Harris hoard. Having a date seemed less pathetic, and he looked like the safest choice."

"He did at that," I state glumly as her words hit me square in the gut. I reach out and tuck her hair behind her ear, my finger trailing along her warm earlobes. "I should have been here for you. I should have done better. You should have never doubted who you were going to be spending your birthday with."

Her eyes become glossy as she looks up at me. "I hated not being there for you during your grandad's funeral. Watching you with your parents and sister at the gravesite, it physically hurt me that I couldn't be beside you, holding your hand."

"I didn't even know you were at the burial," I state, a melancholy washing over me at the memory of that day. "I was a mess then, Freya. I was holding on so hard to what I thought was the right way to live based on stuff my grandfather told me as a wee lad. Even at the end, he told me I was being a fool for not going after you. And then you showed up at the funeral, and I thought that was my chance to make it all better.

"I shouldn't have told you I loved you in my room that day. It was the wrong time, and my head was in the wrong place." I reach out and pull her up to me, needing to hug my apology out with my body just as much as my words. I pull back and hold her face when I add, "And I hate myself for what I said to you in my car. The idea that you could ever just be sex to me is utter shite. I was so damn in love with you, but I couldn't put it into proper words yet."

She holds my hand against her cheek and smiles. "You're doing a pretty good job making up for it now."

"I love you, my wee treasure. I love you more than I knew I was capable of loving someone. Nothing about you and me has been expected."

I press my lips to hers in a soft, sensual kiss. She hums a sexy noise when my lips move down her neck and pull her nightgown away to kiss her bare shoulder. Growling in satisfaction, I continue kissing my way across her skin, murmuring against her flesh, "The way you make me crave you…the sex…the way we come together…" My lips part as my hands move from her face and slide down her neck, brushing over her ribs and wrapping around to fondle her sweet, round arse. "…it's like nothing I've ever experienced with another person."

My lips brush across hers as I add, "I know you don't have experience with other men, but you need to know…what you and I have…I'd trade all my past experiences for just one night with you."

Slowly, I pull up the bottom of her shirt and allow my greedy palms to squeeze the flesh of her sweet supple arse. Her breath quickens, thickening my cock between us as she rocks into my grasp over and fucking over again.

God, she feels good.

I kiss her savagely, and she groans into my mouth before I pull back, keyed up and ready to rip this damn shirt off and ravage her for another hour. I pause first and say, "But you should know…I wouldn't have cared if you'd have slept with a dozen men while we were apart… because this body…will always be mine."

She lets out the sexiest whimper, and in a flash, she sits up between my legs and pulls her nightgown off. I move to ditch my shorts, and in a matter of seconds, she's astride me, lowering her sweet, wet pussy over my hard, throbbing cock.

Fuck, she feels good. I'll never get enough of her. I reach out and palm her breasts, relishing in the size and weight of them in my hands, and squeezing as she arches into my touch. Biting my lip, I roll her nipples between my fingers and watch her with rapt fascination as she throws her head back, her moans loud and dead fucking sexy as she rocks herself on top of me, taking my cock deeper with every thrust of her hips.

Desperate to taste her, I sit up, my lips crashing into hers, as I hug her body to mine, feeling her bare chest against mine as my need boils over like water in a pot.

She catches up to my level quickly and runs her hands through my hair, as she gives as good as she gets. I pull back from her lips long enough to croak out, "Christ, I love you."

"I love you too," she cries, her words tipping her over into sweet, complete oblivion as she clamps down around me. I thrust up into her hard and fast, forcing my release so I can be right there with her.

"Forever, my wee treasure." My best mate. My lover. And soon-to-be my wife.

Her eyes open, dazed, satiated, and devastatingly beautiful. "Forever, my brooding Scot."

CHAPTER 34

Mac

"WE HAVE TO BE AT MY BIRTHDAY PARTY IN TWO HOURS," Freya groans, her voice hoarse from all the delicious cries of passion she uttered mere moments ago. "And if you don't let me out of this bed to get ready, you and I will officially be in a fight."

"God, I love fighting with you," I growl, wrapping my arms around Freya's naked waist and pressing my lips to hers as we lay facing each other in her bed, sexually satiated and smiling like a couple of lovesick puppies.

It's been three days since I proposed to Freya, and I actually want her more now than when I first had her. Who knew being able to freely say I love you to a lass when you're balls deep in her would be so fucking...special?

Christ, I'm turning into a sap.

It gutted me to get on a plane back to Glasgow the next morning and leave her for training and a Thursday night match, but I had to go.

However, as soon as we were done with team meetings on Friday afternoon, I was back in London, not giving a shite that I only had twenty-four hours to be with her before I was due back in Scotland.

"Did you talk to Sloan, Leslie, and Allie then?" I ask, desperate to see if a move for Freya is feasible.

She nods slowly. "I did. I think they're confused with the sudden need to move so quickly when we just got back together. But I think it's because they don't know about this old thing." She holds her hand up, her diamond glittering in the soft daylight streaming in through the window.

We've managed to keep our engagement a secret from our friends so we can tell them tonight at the party that Allie is throwing for Freya's thirtieth birthday. We did get around to telling our parents over the phone, at least, when we were finally able to tear ourselves away from each other that night. And despite me not asking Freya's folks for permission beforehand, they seemed chuffed for us, thank fuck.

Telling our friends tonight will be another matter altogether. "Do you think after we tell everybody tonight, the girls will be more supportive of you moving?" I ask, my brows furrowed curiously.

"I think so. It's not that they're not happy for us being together officially. They are totally Team Mac and Freya. I just think they're worried about how to get the pet line launched by Christmas without me here."

I sit up on my elbow and stare down at Freya's worried brow. "Cookie, if you need to stay in London, stay in London. Aye, you in Glasgow sounds dead brilliant to me, but we can make long distance work for a few months."

"You really think so?" The corners of her mouth lift as she reaches up to cup my cheek. "I just...don't want anything to wreck what we have here."

"Aye," I reply, leaning down to press a chaste kiss to her lips. "Nothing is going to wreck this. It's not much more than an hourlong flight, and you can come see me as well. I don't want you to mess up this opportunity just because I'm a needy sod who wants to bed you every single day."

Her lips pull back into a smile. "I'm a needy sod too then because I love that idea."

"We'll have it in January," I state, reaching out and rubbing her cheek affectionately. "And you can still come to Scotland for the holidays. This isn't much different than how my football travel schedule is, so as long as you answer my phone calls every night and send me dirty pictures of your tits, we will be fine. We can look at this as good practice for us until I retire in a year or two."

"Retire?" Freya barks, sitting up on her elbows, her jaw dropped. "I've never heard you talk of retiring."

"I'm not getting any younger," I reply with a shrug and shoot her a crooked grin. "Plus, I never fancied anything more than football until you, so now I'm thinking there are new adventures in life I want to experience."

Her face softens as she drops down onto her pillow and covers her face with her hands. "Crikey, is this ever going to get any easier to handle?"

I chuckle and pull her arms away from her face. "What?"

Her green eyes blink up at me. "Loving you."

"I'm hoping not." I lick my lips and kiss the hand that holds my engagement ring. "Now...let's get back to our fight."

She giggles and turns on her side. "Actually, I was thinking we could make up by doing one of those *Never Have I Ever* things we never got around to."

"Aye, which one did you have in mind next? If we've only got two hours before this party, I want to make them count."

She gets a cheeky look on her face. "What's reverse cowgirl? Because I have to say, I've never heard that term on *Heartland,* and I'm starting to wonder if it's not quite as wholesome as my beloved Canadian program."

A salacious smile spreads across my face. "Oh, this is going to be the best night of my life."

She hits me with a look. "I thought the night we got engaged was the best night of your life?"

I hold my hands up defensively. "It was…but…well, let's get on with it, and I'll let you know which one wins when we're done."

"Cheeky ox."

It's complete chaos when we walk into Allie and Roan's new flat. The last party we went to with this lot was a No Bloody Kids Do that ended up in a dirty game of *Never Have I Ever*.

This one…is not.

Our arrival goes completely unnoticed as we stand in the foyer and watch everyone buzzing around like their heads are cut off. All of the Harris Brothers are in attendance, along with their wives and substantial, wild offspring. Leslie and Theo are here with their daughter Marisa, and of course, Vi Harris and Hayden are here, running around after their wee Rocky.

I haven't been to many parties where children are in attendance, but I have to say, watching all the grown-ups chase after their wee ones looking stressed, but still strangely happy, actually gets me thinking even more about the future.

I'd fancy seeing Freya with a wee bairn on her hip. An image of playing football with my son in our garden while she watches from the sidelines looking bored is a sight I could get used to.

Suddenly, panic overwhelms me, and I grab Freya and yank her back outside before anybody sees us. "I just realised we're engaged, and I never asked you if you want kids."

"What?" she asks, a laugh playing on her lips.

"Do you want children, woman?" I ask again, anxiety gripping at my neck.

She shrugs coyly. "Do you?"

I level her with a glare. "You first."

She narrows her eyes. "How about we both say yes or no on the count of three. One, two—"

"Fuck yes," I growl over top of Freya's own, "Yes."

Relief washes over me, and we smile at each other for a long moment, absorbing the fact that this one part of our lives together didn't result in an argument. I wrap my hands around Freya's waist as she reaches up and clasps my face in her hands. Our lips connect in a slow, cherishing kiss. The kind of kiss that says, *come what may.*

Suddenly, the door opens, and Allie's voice yells, "I thought that was you guys! They're here, everybody!"

Our lips part, and then I hear Allie gasp. "What is that on your finger, Freya?"

With cheeky smiles, we pull away from each other, our eyes still locked for a deliciously private moment before turning to look at the hoard of people that have gathered in the doorway.

"Is that an engagement ring?" Vi squeals, pushing her way to the front of the pack.

"Freya!" Sloan exclaims, moving out onto the doorstep for a closer look. She grabs her hand and yanks her away from me. "Are you and Mac..."

Her voice trails off, and Freya looks to me before replying, "We're engaged."

The entire group cheers with excitement, and a wee bairn begins crying in the background. Everyone laughs and swarms us, offering up their congratulations, and it's the most grown up I've ever felt in my life.

Before we head inside, Freya pulls me back and whisper, "Mac, touch my ears."

I smile and reach out, rubbing both of them in the pads of my fingers.

She presses her forehead to mine. "I'm really happy."

I inhale deeply, breathing in the scent of her. "You know I'm going to buy you a pony when we get married, right?"

"God, don't joke!" Freya cries, throwing her head back dramatically.

My smile grows. God, I love this woman.

EPILOGUE

Freya

A Few Years Later

"**C**HRIST, I'M FAT AND HAPPY," MAC STATES AS HE POKES HIS tiny pouch of a stomach and turns away from the full-length mirror in our walk-in closet. He strides over to where I'm lying on our bed and sticks his belly out. "This right here...Pure dead brilliant happiness."

I snort out a laugh as I prop my hands behind my head to inspect him. The man is hardly fat. He's been retired from football for two years and is working as a developer for a video game company in London. His desk job may have softened his abs just a bit, but he's still clearly a former athlete, even with his little pouch. The lucky bastard.

Although, I can't truly complain. I'm the lightest weight I've been in years. Not skinny by any means, but certainly smaller than I was before. Breastfeeding is apparently a miraculous diet plan.

I sigh heavily. "I've been pondering how many years I can get away with breastfeeding Fergie because being able to eat whatever I want while the weight just keeps falling off is quite a treat." I cross my legs and wiggle my toes, admiring that I can see them again. There was a spell during my pregnancy that I thought they were going to be gone forever. "If I had known breastfeeding worked this well, I would have let you knock me up ages ago. Breastfeeding Fergie through primary is probably not allowed, right?"

Mac's face twists up in disgust. "I think if you like this breast-feeding diet plan so much, you should just decide to breastfeed me and leave the babe out of it."

"You're a disgusting pervert," I snap. "Come to me."

He hits me with a boyish smile and bounds over to the bed, wrapping his ink-stained arms around me, arms that are now peppered with my name and our six-month-old's name, Jacob Fergus. He nuzzles his face in my bosom and murmurs, "Or maybe I'll just keep you barefoot and pregnant until my balls fall off."

I smile and squeeze Mac into me. "Mmm, that sounds nice."

"We could start practicing now." Mac slides his whiskered face across my chest. "I'm tired of Fergie being the only one who ever gets to see your tits."

"God, we really need to discuss boundaries before Fergie is old enough to understand the ridiculous things that come out of your mouth." I groan while still relishing Mac's wonderful weight on top of me.

Mac growls and begins peppering my neck with kisses, his lips wrapping around my earlobe before his teeth bite into the flesh. "Come on and bed me, woman. Your ears are on fire, and the lad is going to wake up from his nap soon."

"I really should work," I groan, wrapping my legs around his hips because my mind and my body are at war. "I need to look at the latest shipment that just came in from China. They finally sent my plus-size pet pyjama line."

"Oh, good. Hercules and Jasper have been so embarrassed sleeping naked on the floor all these years," Mac mocks.

I smile and run my fingers through his hair. We named my thirtieth birthday present Jasper in honour of the man who stepped aside from our date to let me get engaged to my best friend.

We really are sick in the head.

"How about you put off the pyjamas until tomorrow and you play a game with me instead," Mac says, his voice taking on a mischievous tone.

"What kind of game?" I ask cautiously.

Mac waggles his brows. "I was thinking strip poker."

I shake my head, and then an idea comes to mind. "How about *Never Have I Ever*?"

Mac looks around our bedroom. "We don't have any alcohol."

"Obviously," I state, sitting up, so I'm seated like a pretzel on my side of the bed facing him. "That's bad for the breast milk anyway. How about instead of drinking, we kiss if we've done it?"

"Kiss where?" Mac asks, a lewd smirk spreading across his face.

I roll my eyes. "Our lips."

Mac ponders this for a second, then asks, "Upper lips or lower lips?"

"God, you are the worst!" I yell, reaching over to slap him on the chest. "Upper...for now." I giggle excitedly.

Mac groans. "God, I love my wife."

He mirrors my position, sitting across from me and looking highly uncomfortable in the crisscross pose, but bless him for trying.

"Okay, I'll start." I narrow my eyes at him. "Never have I ever kissed a redhead."

Mac smirks and leans over to press his lush lips against mine. *God, I'll never get sick of that.*

He pulls back and eyes me seriously. "Never have I ever given a blowjob on a long road trip and swallowed like a prized pony."

"Crikey!" I exclaim, pulling away from him. "I thought this was going to be a fun, sweet game between husband and wife. You skipped a couple of steps there."

Mac shakes with shameless laughter while bopping me on the nose. "I don't make the rules, my wee treasure. Now kiss me, you saucy minx."

I bite my lip shamelessly as I think back to our road trip to Cornwall shortly after we got engaged. Mac was so nervous that he'd never asked my parents for permission, he was certain my father would give him the third degree. I could only think of one way to calm him down.

I pucker up and give him a big kiss. "Never have I ever climaxed in less than two minutes."

"That was one time, Freya!" Mac yells, his Scottish accent thickening up with his anger. "And it was the first time we'd shagged since having Fergie. Going six weeks without sex is ages! You can't hold that against me for the rest of our lives."

I giggle openly. "I can, and I will."

He glowers at me and adds, "You need a kiss for that one too then because I know damn well I've made you come in under two minutes before."

"No complaints here," I reply and point to my lips, and he kindly obliges me with two kisses.

"Okay. Never have I ever had a threesome."

Neither of us goes for a kiss. I'm very okay with that.

Mac's next. "Never have I ever masturbated in public." I go to open my mouth, but Mac cuts me off. "And yes, that thing you did in my car outside Tower Park counts as public."

I jut out my chin and shake my head, murmuring, "You dared me to do it, and you were watching me the whole time!" I smack a kiss on Mac's lips.

His body shakes with quiet laughter as he points at his temple. "No regrets. It's on constant replay in my highlight reel."

The smile on my face feels permanent at this point when I change course a bit. "Never have I ever wept like a baby during childbirth."

BLINDSIDED

Mac points at his lips. "Lay one on me, Red. I have no shame over my emotions as I watched you bring life into this world."

I grab his face and kiss him proudly, my eyes tearing as I think back to Mac's awed face as he held our son in his hands for the first time. Becoming a mother was an incredible experience, but watching Mac lose it over his son was beyond anything. The photo of him holding Fergie when he was born and the one of him holding Jasper as a kitten are on constant replay in my highlight reel.

Mac eyes me seriously. "Never have I ever wanted another babe."

"Kiss me," I whisper, offering up my lips.

"Finally, something we don't have to argue about," Mac murmurs sexily as he presses his lips to mine and lingers for a while. His hand reaches up and combs through my hair as he deepens the kiss, his tongue slipping in and teasing mine.

Before I know it, I'm on my back, arching into him as he presses himself against me, both of our bodies rolling into each other like a couple of teenagers who can't stop dry humping.

When our lips part, I'm breathless, and happy, and head over heels in love when I say, "Never have I ever fallen in love with my best friend and got everything I ever wanted out of life."

Kiss.

Kiss.

Kiss.

Kiss.

Kiss.

The End

Did you know that Roan and Allie plus all the Harris Brothers have books? Binge all their stories in Kindle Unlimited now!

MORE BOOKS BY
AMY DAWS

The London Lovers Series:
Becoming Us: Finley's Story Part 1
A Broken Us: Finley's Story Part 2
London Bound: Leslie's Story
Not the One: Reyna's Story

A London Lovers/Harris Brothers Crossover Novel:
Strength: Vi Harris & Hayden's Story

The Harris Brothers Series:
Challenge: Camden's Story
Endurance: Tanner's Story
Keeper: Booker's Story
Surrender & Dominate: Gareth's Duet

Payback: A Harris Brother Spin-off Standalone
Blindsided: A Harris Brother Spin-off Standalone

The Wait With Me Series:
Wait With Me: A Tire Shop Rom-Com
Next in Line: A Bait Shop Rom-Com

Pointe of Breaking: A College Dance Standalone by Amy Daws &
Sarah J. Pepper

Chasing Hope: A Mother's *True* Story of Loss, Heartbreak,
and the Miracle of Hope

For all retailer purchase links, visit:
www.amydawsauthor.com

ACKNOWLEDGEMENTS

Book sweet sixteen complete and the crowd goes wild!

It's so amazing that I still get to do this book writing gig, but, as always, I can't release a book without thanking the people who've helped me tremendously along the way.

Jennifer, thank you so much for being my favourite hot, bicycle-riding, book cheerleader. I love when we brainstorm and jinx each other because we both care about my characters so much that we see the same future for them!

Thanks to my PA, Julia, for reading this book bit by painful bit! And thank you for your massive football assistance and helping me with the logistics, even when I do take massive creative freedom.

Thanks to my sister-in-law, Megan, for drinking vodka with me and brainstorming these two characters!

Massive appreciation goes to Jane Ashley Converse, who somehow, someway always gets roped into helping me at the end. Your notes are extremely valued, man, and I look forward to having celebratory drinks with you!

My love to Beth, my Canadian beta who I am constantly striving to impress. Thank you for pushing me and being such a wonderful friend.

And I have to give big props to my Scottish and Britsh friends who helped me get as damn close to authentic as I could for a Scottish hero and a Cornish heroine. Jade, Chanah, Lynsey, and Teresa! You four are aces!

Thanks to my editor, Stephanie, for helping with the voice work in this book and to my second editor, Nancy at Evident Ink for coming in right when you were needed and for Jenny at Editing 4 Indies giving me a fast extra look. Editing is so important and you're all appreciated!

And thanks to Lydia Rella, my proofer and friend who got me giddy and excited about writing this Scottish hero. I loved our late night chats about this book! And thanks to Peggy for another proof job. You can never have too many proofers.

And readers. Dear lovely, awesome, seriously loyal readers… Thank you! Thank you for being patient for my words and for squealing your excitement to me on social media. Thanks for sharing this book with your friends and for being the best part of this job.

And, of course, thank you to my husband, who just deals with it when I get weirdly in the zone and don't communicate with him anymore.

To my kid, Lolo, for being patient with me when I'm on a deadline. I'm so glad we got to celebrate me typing "The End" with you wearing a Harry Potter costume.

Lastly, my six angel babies who are always looking down on me from up above and whose six rings I still wear around my neck. I love you all and I thank you for giving me the courage to tell your true stories so that I could go on and tell these fictional stories. It truly is the gift that keeps on giving.

ABOUT THE AUTHOR

Amy Daws is an Amazon Top 25 bestselling author of sexy, contemporary romance novels. She enjoys writing love stories that take place in America, as well as across the pond in England; especially about those footy-playing Harris Brothers of hers. When Amy is not writing in a tire shop waiting room, she's watching Gilmore Girls, or singing karaoke in the living room with her daughter while Daddy smiles awkwardly from a distance.

For more of Amy's work, visit: www.amydawsauthor.com or check out the links below.

www.facebook.com/amydawsauthor
www.twitter.com/amydawsauthor
instagram.com/amydawsauthor

Made in the USA
Coppell, TX
05 October 2022

84082023R10187